EVA'S SPELL

Eva couldn't contain herself. 'Rubbish! This is just
not so. You have a vast popular following already.
I have the ear of the women of this country. At
the moment anyway. If you got the workforce and
the women behind you there would be no other
party strong enough to go against you.'

Peron looked serious. 'The army wouldn't stand
for it. And I need them to keep order.'

Again Eva disagreed violently. 'Only the way the
government is set up at the present time. Once the
unions have learned their true strength the army
will have to behave.'

She was interrupted by the waiter bringing in their
meal. As they ate Eva stuck to the subject,
shooting down Peron's objections to her argument
that the unions needed him to take a more overt
part in their activities. After the meal he drove
slowly out to a house loaned him by a friend for
the weekend. Before they fell asleep in each other's
arms in the early morning Eva had convinced him
to let her join him in his fight for power.

INGRID PITT
and TONY RUDLIN

EVA'S
SPELL

Thames Methuen

A Thames Methuen Paperback

EVA'S SPELL

First published as *The Perons* in Great Britain 1982
by Methuen London Ltd

Copyright © 1982 Ingrid Pitt and Tony Rudlin
This edition published 1985
by Methuen London Ltd
11 New Fetter Lane, London EC4P 4EE
in association with
Thames Television International Ltd
149 Tottenham Court Road, London W1P 9LL

Printed and bound in Great Britain

British Library Cataloguing in Publication Data

Pitt, Ingrid
    [The Perons]. Eva's spell.
    I. [The Perons]   II. Title   III. Rudlin, Tony
    823'.914[F]   PR6066.I7

ISBN 0-423-01130-8

For Steffanie

JUAN DOMINGO PERÓN

1895 Born in Lobos/Province Buenos Aires, 8 October.
Educated at International College, Olivos/BA and International Polytechnic College.

1911 Enters Military College.

1914 Enters Infantry Regiment with rank of Lieutenant.

1926–9 Argentine Staff College.

1930 Promoted to captain, Perón participates in coup to oust Irigoyen.

1936–8 Appointed military attaché to Chile.

1938 Marries Aurelia Tizón, who dies of cancer at 33.

1940 Sent to Italy on special mission to study mountain warfare. Impressed by Mussolini and fascism.

1942 With GOU (Grupo de Officiales Unidos) ousts Ramon Castillo.

1943 4 June, Argentine military revolution, which paves the way for Perón's political career.

1944 Appointed Vice-President, Minister of War and Secretary of Labour and Welfare.

1945 9 October, is forced to resign all posts in government. Two days later is arrested and imprisoned in island fortress Martin Garcia.
17 October, released after Peronist demonstrations. Addresses the workers from balcony of Casa Rosada.

1946 4 June, elected President of Argentina.

EVA DUARTE DE PERÓN

1919 Born on Los Toldos, 150 miles west of Buenos Aires, 17 May.

1935 Arrives in Buenos Aires.

1939 First comes to notice on Argentine Radio.

1941 Works on radio and in film.

ONE

Colonel Juán Domingo Perón, foils champion of the Argentine Army, turned aside the thrust with a cool negligence born of bravado and egotism. His gliding feet eased his heavy, powerful body back out of range with the practised elegance of a ballroom dancer. His left hand casually rested on his hip and a smile broadened behind the wire grill of his fencing mask.

The kill bordered on insolence.

Perón swept the guarding blade aside, and before his opponent could recover, confidently whipped off his fencing mask and touched the stud of his foil on his opponent's padded chest.

'*Touché*,' he said. A smile tugged the corner of his mouth as the elderly General von Faupel froze into an attitude of rigid attention, head bowed, and acknowledged his defeat. Then, with an effort, he brought his sword to the salute. He responded to Perón's hearty handshake without enthusiasm and then deliberately turned his back to avoid commiseration as his seconds moved in to unstrap his protective padding. Perón winked at the audience and chatted easily while he was stripped and then followed the general across the wide, echoing gymnasium.

'You are coming to our reception tonight, Perón? We have a special guest,' the general barked as victor and vanquished made their way to the changing rooms.

'*Jawohl, Herr General.*' Perón acknowledged the statement genially in German, softened by his warm Spanish accent.

The German military academy in Buenos Aires gave regular receptions, and it was quite normal for visitors to want to meet Perón. His skill with the foils, on horseback and on the tennis court, as well as his reputation as a military theorist, had spread his name widely. Few knew very much more about him.

A Mercedes pulled away from the vine-covered country club. Perón, in the seat next to the driver, took off his hat and laid it with his cane on the back seat.

'What's your name, Corporal?' he asked the somewhat nondescript figure at the wheel.

'José Lopez-Rega, *Coronel.*'

Neither spoke as the chauffeur cautiously picked his way along the pot-holed dirt road to the main highway leading to the centre of Buenos Aires.

The colonel relaxed as the car ran smoothly along the wide road.

'*Cigarillo, Corporal?*' he asked, offering his gold cigarette case, a gift from a grateful admirer.

Lopez-Rega kept his eyes fixed on the road ahead.

'*No gracias, Coronel. No fumo.*'

Perón returned the case to his pocket and lit his cigarette from a heavy gold lighter. He slid down comfortably in his seat until his head was propped on the backrest and closed his eyes. Only the sound of the wind rushing around the car and the occasional punctuation of an authoritative blast on the horn disturbed the embalming midday heat.

'What happened to my usual driver, Corporal?'

Lopez-Rega shot him a guarded look.

'*No sé, Coronel,*' he said evenly.

Perón dismissed the subject with a snort and settled down to think of General von Faupel's sexy granddaughter who had surprised him with a sophistication beyond her years. Lopez-Rega was happy that he didn't pursue the question further. The methods he had used to get his fellow NCO out of the job and himself seconded to the colonel, might not meet with military approval.

The change of pace as the car pulled into the quiet backwater of Calle Posadas woke Perón and he sat up and peered around before reaching into the back for his belt and cap.

'Pick me up at 9.30 tonight. I shall be going to Olivos. I'll need you all evening,' he ordered as he climbed out without waiting for the door to be opened for him.

'*Si, Coronel*,' the driver acknowledged dutifully.

Barging through the heavy street doors Perón gave a terse '*Buenas*' to the porter scuttling across the foyer to open the lift gates and then sagged against the cool wall as the lift whisked him up to his apartment. As he entered he was startled by a smothered giggle.

'Who's there?' he snapped advancing further into the room, his eyes becoming more adjusted to the erratic light.

Renate von Faupel, the sixteen-year-old granddaughter of the general, peeped around the edge of the sofa and grinned at him.

'*Guten Abend, Herr Oberst*. Did you have a good time with Grandpapa?'

Angrily Perón threw his tunic into an armchair. 'How the hell did you get in here?' he demanded.

The girl reached out to him, undeterred by his fierce reaction. 'I told the concierge I was your niece and he let me in.'

Perón lifted her to her feet with more force than was necessary. 'Well now get him to let you out.'

He pushed her towards the door but Renate was not ready to go. Teasingly she looked up into his angry face.

'So, you are afraid of Grandpapa, are you?' She let a hint of disdain creep into her bantering tone. It was enough to provoke Perón's machismo. He let go of her hand and laughed.

'Terrified!' he confirmed.

His good humour was returning. Absentmindedly he unbuttoned his shirt and walked towards the door leading to the bathroom.

'*Bueno*. I'll see you later. I'm going to have a shower.'

Renate quickly undid her dress letting it slip to the floor.

'Good. I feel hot and sticky, too.'

With another giggle she slipped round Perón and beat

3

him to the door. In mock anger he stopped.

'*Dios*, what am I going to do with you?'

Like a puppet Renate's golden head popped around the door jamb.

'Guess!' she breathed provocatively before running off towards the bathroom squealing at the top of her voice with Perón in hot pursuit.

That evening Perón arrived without an escort at the big, square house at the edge of the city. In public he took pains not to become associated with any particular woman. He hoped the evening was not going to be too boring. After his courtesy visit he wanted to get away.

The German butler knew Perón by sight and came to rigid attention with a pistol-crack of heels. 'The general is in the garden, *Herr Oberst*,' he announced.

Perón strolled through the tall, cool rooms with the gold-framed pictures of the former German Royal Family and high-ranking officers in the Imperial Army, shaking hands and cracking jokes with the uniformed men and their prim, bovine ladies. More than one cheek blushed as the colonel bent over to kiss the proffered hand. It amused Perón, as it always did, to see the fawning respect of junior German officers for the Staff ranks.

A white-coated waiter offered him a glass of French champagne but he refused it and asked for whisky. Standing beside a stone urn overflowing with a cascade of brilliantly coloured geraniums and petunias he surveyed the gathered German horde spread out across the flat lawn. Through the trees on the farthest side he could see the flicker of an *asado* fire and smell the mouth-watering aroma of cooking beef. He had expected to see quite a few of his fellow Argentine officers there and was surprised to find only Germans.

Most of them wore the ornate Imperial Prussian Army dress uniform. Here and there an officer of the modern Wehrmacht added a more sombre note in his field-service grey. And over the rim of his whisky glass the colonel appraised the sprinkling of black uniforms with the Death

4

Head badge and the swastika armband. The Schutz Staffel. The SS. Culturally inclined towards the German way of life by his training in the Prussian-inspired academies of the Argentine Army, Perón was interested in the meteoric rise of the SS in the five years since Hitler had seized power.

He spotted von Faupel talking to a much decorated Luftwaffe officer and strolled in his direction. The general saw him coming and turned with military precision to meet him.

'Ah, *Oberst* Perón, pleased you could come.'

He didn't offer to shake hands and his disdainful look at Perón's dinner jacket was an open reprimand. Perón clicked his heels.

'Forgive me, *Herr General,* for not being suitably dressed for the occasion. Unfortunately I have to attend to a personal matter of great importance later this evening and there will not be time to change.'

The general nodded forgiveness stiffly. He turned to the Luftwaffe officer. 'General Lorenz. May I present *Herr Oberstleutnant* Juán Perón of the Academy of War here in Buenos Aires.'

The Luftwaffe general nodded agreeably at Perón and stretched out a welcoming hand. 'Of course, *Herr Oberst.* You are becoming quite famous. I read your treatise on mountain warfare. Very interesting.'

Perón widened his smile. 'I had no idea my little essays were being read in Germany. I must be careful what I write in future!'

Von Faupel indicated the plump, stolid woman at his side. 'My wife you know.'

Perón bent gallantly over the stubby hand extended to him. 'Your servant,' he intoned dutifully with as much warmth as her traditionally braided hair and dark, gauchely cut gown could inspire.

The general passed on to the blonde willowy fourth member of the party.

'I don't think you have met my granddaughter, Renate?'

Again Perón bent to kiss the extended hand. As his lips

5

brushed her soft skin he looked impudently into her pale blue eyes and dropped an eyelid in a conspiratorial wink. Renate suppressed a giggle and fiddled with the belt of her dowdy evening gown.

Her blushes were not lost on Werner Lorenz.

A stentorian voice announced that dinner was served.

Perón gallantly offered Frau von Faupel his arm, regretfully allowing Lorenz the luxury of escorting Renate to the table. With von Faupel leading the way the party crossed the terrace and entered the huge, stuccoed dining room through the french windows.

Perón always felt a sense of wonder when forced to dine with the Germans. The temperature outside was in the eighties but Teutonic society demanded that dinner be held in a depressingly over-furnished room with heavy velvet curtains and dark pictures, that it should consist of a multi-coursed meal more suited to Christmas in the snows of the Black Forest.

The long, white-clothed table was heavy with silver and candelabra. The centre-piece, a boar's head complete with apple, sweated juicily into its silver charger making Perón even more aware of the heat.

The general sat at the head of the table with Werner Lorenz on his right and the wife of the chief of the academy on his left. Perón was about halfway down with Renate on his right and a thin, nervous woman who insisted on talking about horses on his left. Through the torture of the hot, thick soup, the steaming, cooked-out vegetables and the heavily seasoned boiled meat, he nodded politely and spoke the appropriate monosyllables. But he was more interested in the sensual way Renate's leg pressed against his and the nerve-tingling sensation of her fingers brushing along the inside of his thigh.

At last the endless meal and its formalities were over. Perón was about to make his excuses and leave when someone tapped him on the shoulder. It was a young SS captain.

'*Herr Oberstleutnant* Perón. *Oberstleutnant* Bischoff

presents his compliments. He would like to speak to you if you could spare him a few moments.'

Perón mentally cursed but didn't let the irritation show in his face.

'Colonel Bischoff?' The name was new to him.

'*Herr Oberstleutnant* Bischoff says it is very important. He won't take up much of your time.'

Perón shrugged his shoulders resignedly. '*Bueno*. Lead the way,' he said.

The black-clad captain turned smartly and marched away, Perón sauntering casually in his wake. The captain opened the door to the library and stepped inside. '*Oberstleutnant* Juán Domingo Perón of the Argentine Academy of War,' he announced.

Surprised, Perón stepped into the room. He hadn't expected that sort of introduction at a supposedly informal dinner party. He looked about him and at first missed the figure of a man in a blue pin-stripe suit sitting on top of a library ladder, leafing through a book.

'Good evening, *Herr Oberst* Perón,' the reader said as he closed the book and climbed down the ladder.

'*Oberst* Bischoff?' Perón said with a hint of inquiry in his voice. 'We haven't met, have we?'

Bischoff shook hands with Perón in a friendly way.

'No. I'm afraid I haven't had that pleasure. That's why I took this opportunity of speaking to you now. I am only in Argentina until the morning so I ask you to forgive my lack of courtesy in not calling on you at your office.'

Perón turned the apology aside.

The civilian suit worried him. He liked a rank to be tied to a uniform. Bischoff dismissed the SS captain and waved Perón to a high-backed leather armchair and sat on the edge of the desk.

The contrast between the two men could not have been greater. Bischoff was of medium height, with a thin aesthetic face and curved, thin-bridged nose. His piercing blue eyes were set off by hair so blond it was almost white. It made it difficult to judge his age and he was generally credited with more than his twenty-eight years.

Suddenly Perón felt naked and clumsy. He didn't like the dapper man sitting opposite him smiling a cold thin smile.

'Can I help you in any way?' he prompted.

Bischoff pushed himself off the desk and walked around to the swivel chair. 'I think we can help each other.'

He had a dossier in front of him. As he opened it and began to leaf through the contents Perón saw his name in Germanic script printed on the front. It worried him but he forced a smile and leaned back against the over-stuffed leather and crossed his legs.

'Really. How nice for us.'

'We would like you to come to Europe for a while.' Perón smothered an interest he would not allow to show in his eyes.

'We? Who are we, *Oberst*?' he asked politely.

Bischoff shut the folder. 'The *Schutz Staffel*.'

Perón's interest quickened. 'The SS?'

Bischoff nodded but said nothing.

Perón's mind raced. It was totally unexpected. At any other time he would have jumped at the chance but he was just beginning to piece together contacts that had weakened during a recent eighteen month mission in Chile, and another period away might prove disastrous for him.

'I'm flattered, of course, but why me? There must be a dozen colonels more suited than I.'

Bischoff made a point of turning the pages of the thick dossier. 'I think, *Herr Oberst* Perón, you do yourself an injustice. You are a very important man.'

Perón wasn't flattered. He had taken great pains to present himself as nothing more than a fun-loving staff officer. 'Surely you exaggerate, *Herr Oberst*?'

Bischoff shut the file and leaned forward with his chin resting on his hands. 'Possibly,' he said in a tone that admitted no doubt. 'Let me just run through a few details and you tell me where I go wrong.'

He sat for a few seconds gathering his thoughts while Perón forced himself to relax.

8

'You claim a Sicilian senator as a grandfather and an Indian grandmother. Your father was a farmer and your early life was spent in relative poverty in Patagonia. You have one brother, Mario, who runs a small *pulpería* in Chubut and your mother, a half-breed *china*, forced you to learn the basics for a university education. You joined the Army in 1911 as a cadet, and you were promoted a captain in 1924, appointed to the General Staff in 1926 and became Secretary to the Ministry of War. You spent a short spell at the academy as an assistant professor before being sent to Chile in 1936 as a military attaché, with the rank of *teniente coronel*. Three months ago you were expelled from Chile on charges of espionage and since then you have worked in the academy as a full professor of strategic warfare.'

The SS man stopped and looked across at Perón. 'How is that so far?'

Perón nodded towards the file. 'The file is correct. Hardly the sort of career to merit preferment I would have thought.' His relief showed in his voice.

Bischoff rose and picket up a decanter of brandy. 'You sure you won't have one?' he asked. Perón shook his head and the German poured himself a generous measure before returning to his seat.

'I agree with you. A competent but not a distinguished record. But *Herr Oberstleutnant*, I feel that it must have cost you a great deal of money to keep some of the more remarkable aspects of your career out of the records. For instance I see no mention of the group of officers you have been to such great pains to form around you and the amount of pressure you are able to apply, with their support, on the administration of Argentina.'

Bischoff stopped and waited for a comment, but Perón, smoothing back his straight black hair, kept silent. The SS man nodded and continued.

'My informants tell me that you were instrumental in getting your fellow officers to form a committee to guide the destiny of your country and provide a bulwark between the ambitions of high ranking officers and the dictatorship of Argentina.' Again he paused.

'We in the SS understand this. In Germany we have the same problem but we have learned to control it. At the moment you are held together by a common cause. To be really effective you will have to rely on more than good will. Germany is interested in working closely with the government of Argentina. We have many mutual interests. If you come to Europe and study at first hand the workings of National Socialism I am sure that you will be able to apply what you learn to consolidate your position in this country.'

Perón lay back in his chair and relaxed. In Argentina deals were negotiated on the basis of bargaining which always included an element of blackmail. Perón rated himself highly skilled in this field and was more than happy to take on the German.

'If I am already so powerful here, *Herr Oberst*, why should I need to go to Europe? What you are doing is interesting but I doubt it is applicable to the South American way of life. If my support is strong surely it is in my interest to stay here and consolidate what I have?'

Again the SS man opened the file. 'A good point. If it wasn't for the Chilean affair.'

The Perón smile lost a little of its power. 'The Chilean affair?' he queried innocently.

Bischoff nodded brusquely. 'Yes. Some of your fellow officers are not happy. They feel that you are using their association to advance your own ambitions. They would be very happy to get evidence that would discredit you.' The German opened his hands as if dismissing such unsettling speculation.

'But of course you are not to be trifled with. Your handling of the highly respected President Irigoyen showed that. It's not every junior officer that is capable of overthrowing his president and then electing another. But unfortunately your president is worried that what you did once you might decide to do again. If your committee of officers turned against you you could find yourself under arrest and discharged from the Army.'

Perón stood up. 'You have convinced me, *Herr Oberstleutnant,* that I would be very foolish to leave Buenos Aires at this moment. I'm grateful. And now, if you will forgive me, I have more pressing matters to attend to.' He held out his hand but Bischoff ignored it.

'Another rendezvous with General von Faupel's pretty little granddaughter, *Herr Oberst?*'

Perón's smile vanished. 'You have been looking through keyholes, *Herr Oberst?* If you wish to tell von Faupel that his charming granddaughter is spending her afternoons in my apartment I can't stop you. It will be very unpleasant for the old man but in Argentina it will not even raise an eyebrow.'

Again he held out his hand and again the German ignored it. Perón shrugged and turned to leave. He had almost reached the door before the German spoke again.

'And what happened in Chile? Will this raise eyebrows?'

Perón stopped and slowly turned and studied the SS man. '*Bueno.* You have my full attention.'

Bischoff sat down again, and rapped out his demands. 'We want you to go on an exchange course to Europe. At first to Italy. There is a war coming in Europe within the next year or so. It is inevitable. When the war comes we want a base outside Europe where our submarines can refuel and where we can obtain supplies. Argentina has a high proportion of Germans amongst its people and could benefit from the association.' He stopped and waited for a comment from Perón.

'I can see the benefit to Germany,' he said thoughtfully. 'But Argentina can do equally well in a European conflict by siding with Germany's enemies. And I don't see why you are telling this to me.'

Confident, Bischoff smiled. 'Of course, *Herr Oberstleutnant.* I was forgetting the most important aspect. You already have the backing of a strong Army faction. If you decide to take up our offer you will have funds made available to you. How you spend them will be entirely up to you but there will be sufficient money for you to buy the

11

support of all the key officers. The Nazi party is also interested in buying property in Argentina to develop its resources outside Europe. You will be commissioned to do this.'

Perón sat very still. Instead of crudely offering him money for his own use the Germans were delivering into his hands the tools to take over the country. Out of the country – a welcome guest at the table of the strong men in Europe, Mussolini and Hitler – his absence could even work for him. It would give the firebrands time to cool off and it would give President Justo a sense of security to have the flamboyant colonel out of the way. And the benefit he would derive from seeing the workings of the fascist states at first hand would be enormous.

Again Perón rose and held out his hand. '*Herr Oberst*. You have my interest.'

The colonel's smile was not returned.

'Now, if there is nothing else, I have other matters to attend. You know how to get in touch with me.'

Perón turned and without a backward glance left the room.

Colonel Bischoff didn't move for a few minutes. He stood and glared at the closed door. He wasn't happy about the friendly colonel. The man was a libertine and unreliable. But then he was only following orders.

Bischoff picked up Perón's file and was about to put it in the desk drawer when General Lorenz entered. Bischoff snapped to attention and gave the straight-armed Nazi salute. '*Heil Hitler!*'

Lorenz's acknowledgement was more relaxed. 'Everything go according to plan?'

'*Jawohl, Herr General*,' the colonel replied slowly.

Lorenz looked at him, speculatively. 'You are not happy with Perón?'

Bischoff hesitated before answering. He knew that from the dozens of Argentine officers who had been investigated Lorenz had himself picked Perón as the key figure.

'He seems ambitious enough but the man is a playboy. How do we know that he won't take the money and squander it.'

Lorenz shook his head sorrowfully. 'You have read his secret file?' he asked.

'*Jawohl, Herr General.*'

'And you don't see the potential?'

Bischoff didn't commit himself. The general sat at the desk and continued. 'Forget the playboy, Perón recognises that a new order is emerging. He knows that industrialisation is being forced on Argentina and that the landowners will not keep the *peónes* in virtual slavery for ever. He has a natural magnetism for the lower classes and has popular support in the Army.

Bischoff nodded towards the file. 'And that affair in Chile?'

General Lorenz laughed. 'His penchant for children? You don't understand these people. Here children are sexually promiscuous as soon as they are capable. It's a bit sordid and not something he would want to brag about but it will not affect our plans for him. He will understand that what we are offering him is Argentina – and it will prove irresistible. The only thing that worries me is whether we will be able to control him when the time comes.'

TWO

Perón arrived in Italy at the beginning of the greatest war the world had known. The atmosphere – of tension, intrigue and fear – was one in which Perón revelled. His own position – visiting military adviser on Alpine warfare to the Italian Army – gave him an ideal opportunity to study the political and military methods of the fascist regime; and his inexhaustible energy enabled him to combine his studies with more personal pleasures: polo, tennis, and the prostitutes, male and female, available in Rome's *dolce vita*.

Italian society embraced the easy-going Argentinian as he embraced it. But his sponsorship, of course, came from elsewhere, and it was not long before he received the first politely worded invitation to visit Berlin.

A young lieutenant was waiting to meet Perón at Berlin – *Hauptbahnhof* and he was courteously installed in the back of an official Mercedes for the short drive to the SS Headquarters in Prinz Albrecht Strasse, where the Security Office of the *Reichsführer* SS was guarded by black-garbed troopers with automatic rifles.

Without delay the SS lieutenant guided the Argentinian into the imposing building, through a maze of corridors and staircases to the second floor. The lieutenant knocked sharply on a polished oak door and, at the barked word of command, thrust it open and ushered the colonel through.

'*Standartenführer* Bischoff.'

Bischoff had come out from behind his smokescreen of playing soldiers and reverted to his SS title. Since their meeting in Buenos Aires Perón had the measure of the humourless, upper echelon, messenger-boy. Bischoff was under intense pressure from his superiors to bring Perón into the German fold, and Perón did not have to make his task easy for him. Bischoff rose slowly, reluctantly, from behind his desk.

After the normal pleasantries he picked up the telephone. 'Tell the General that *Oberst* Perón has arrived and we will come in immediately.'

Perón raised an enquiring eyebrow but Bischoff didn't respond. He opened the middle drawer of his desk and took out a dossier. Perón concealed a smile. It confirmed his estimate of the man as a file carrier.

Two offices along the corridor the SS officer rapped on the polished panel and waited patiently for the door to be opened by a pretty blonde woman in the black pseudo SS uniform of the Women's *Helferinnen* Corps. Perón eyed her speculatively. He found the uniform off-putting and erotically attractive at the same time. He followed her and Bischoff through to the inner office. Neither the outer nor the inner door bore a name plate.

Ober Gruppenführer Reinhard Heydrich, deputy head of the SS, rose gracefully to meet Perón as Bischoff made the introduction. The Argentinian looked hard at the gaunt, aesthetic face and blond, lank hair of the notorious persecutor of the Jews.

Heydrich clicked his heels and gave the salute. '*Heil Hitler.*'

Perón paused before raising his right hand just high enough to avoid an insult and intoning '*Heil Hitler.*'

The Germans relaxed. Heydrich waved Perón to a comfortable leather chair by his desk and nodded for Bischoff to take the chair behind him by the door.

As the big Argentinian lolled back he made a brief survey of his surroundings. Dark oak panelling lined the room from floor to ceiling. The wall on his left was taken over entirely by a bookcase stacked with heavy leather-bound books with inlaid gold titles. He didn't need to look to know that they would be edifying tomes of deep philosophical significance, matching, no doubt, the records in the heavy highly polished gramophone just behind Heydrich's desk. Prominently displayed was a well used

15

violin that the SS man played when he accompanied the recorded orchestras in his favourite Wagnerian operas. In heavy Germanic style a number of gold framed paintings, extolling the virtues of high endeavour, flanked a painting of Adolf Hitler.

Heydrich opened the conversation with a perfunctory and uninterested enquiry into Perón's health, journey and appreciation of life in Italy. Perón replied smoothly that he was in robust health, had enjoyed the journey and was awaiting the opportunity, with the appropriate eagerness, to study at close quarters what the National Socialist Revolution had to offer to better the lot of the worker in the Federal Republic of Argentina.

For some reason Heydrich was finding it hard to get down to whatever business had prompted him to bring Perón to Berlin. He commented on the Argentinian's reputation with the épée and modestly told him that he, Heydrich, also was renowned as a swordsman of quality. He seemed to be trying to outbid Perón in the manly prowess stakes but his visitor was not willing to be outbid so easily. He smiled encouragingly and listened to tales of Heydrich's skiing proficiency without comment. Coffee was drunk and points of view discussed until Heydrich had to leave for a meeting with his immediate superior, *Reichsführer* Himmler.

'Thank you for coming, *Herr Oberst* Perón. Arrangements have been made for you to see the work we are doing here. You are leaving on Saturday I understand.'

Perón raised his eyebrow and looked at Bischoff. No mention had been made of the duration of his visit but he had no objection to six days in the capital. 'Yes. We have booked *Herr Oberst* on the midnight train on Saturday,' Bischoff confirmed efficiently. Heydrich nodded. 'Good. That will give us time to talk in a more relaxed atmosphere. Perhaps you would be kind enough to join me for dinner at my house on Friday, Perón. My wife would be delighted to meet you. She has always been fascinated by South America.'

Perón shook Heydrich's hand, saying that he would be delighted to come to dinner and was enthralled by the prospect of talking about his homeland to the general's charming wife.

The Heydrich household was situated in Zehlendorf on the outskirts of the city. It was standard suburbia and as Perón stood and surveyed the steep slated roof and white plastered walls set in its garden of green shrubs and trim lawns he tried to assess his host.

The man who held himself accountable only to the top leaders of the country. The man, if rumours were true, who regularly made hundreds of harmless citizens disappear, because – by accident of birth – they belonged to a sect not included in his limited lexicon of desirables.

Yet this same man pushed papers into his briefcase and returned to his little middle-class suburb to worry over his daughter's teeth braces and his wife's extravagances with the electricity.

His knock was answered by Frau Heydrich herself. Narcissism might have made her Heydrich's mate. Her blonde hair, finely boned face and elegant figure were the female reflection of the SS general.

She regarded Perón's casual appearance with evident disdain. He hadn't worn his uniform, a habit he had pursued throughout his week in Germany, preferring the anonymity of a lightweight double-breasted suit, cream shirt and regimental tie, brown and white shoes and his favourite white Panama hat. Perón could tell that Frau Heydrich regarded his clothes as appropriate for a 'Dago'.

He was shown into an aggressively modern sitting room. The highly polished parquet floor was hidden by a square of pseudo Persian carpet on which were set with micrometre precision a four-seater sofa, two armchairs and a coffee table. The chairs were thickly padded and should have been comfortable. Somehow they managed to look cold and uninviting. A smoky fire glowed pessimistically in the fireplace. On the chimney breast hung a small portrait of

17

Hitler. Perón knew instinctively that Heydrich would tell him before the night was through that the painting had been presented to him personally by the Führer. He was not disappointed.

While Frau Heydrich went off to tell her husband of his arrival, the Argentinian took stock of the rest of the room. The highly polished veneered cocktail cabinet, artlessly designed occasional table and escritoire he dismissed as the tasteless affectation of people with no appetite for life.

Perón looked at his gaudy, brown and white shoes and smiled. Now they showed taste!

He was examining the silver-framed picture of Heydrich's two blond-haired children in smart Hitler-Jugend uniforms when he heard a step outside in the hall.

Heydrich entered, predictably dressed in a tight-fitting dinner jacket. His greeting was friendly but formal. He confirmed his obsession with health and travel by asking how Perón had been since their meeting four days before and how he had fared on the strenuous half-hour journey from his hotel. Perón made appropriate noises while Heydrich ran through a plethora of practised conversational anecdotes he kept for such occasions.

Both were relieved when the front door-bell rang. Heydrich carefully placed his glass precisely in the centre of a cork mat on the side table. 'Excuse me. That will be Bischoff,' he said.

When Heydrich followed Bischoff into the room Frau Heydrich rejoined the party and for half an hour stilted conversation formed some sort of bridge between the four. After what seemed an eternity a tall, mousy-looking woman in a severe brown dress came in and announced that dinner was served.

Having seen the sitting room Perón was prepared for the dining room. A nondescript floral wallpaper tried valiantly to impart some colour to the room but was killed by the cubist, light-walnut, veneered furniture. Frau Heydrich prattled on about friends who had gone to Argentina and Perón reassured her that there were flush toilets and some of

18

the natives were quite civilised. Heydrich and Bischoff said little except when called upon to confirm Frau Heydrich's story.

When they had finished eating and had drunk the strong coffee brewed by Frau Heydrich's own hand, Perón decided that enough was enough. Before he could speak Frau Heydrich rose and held out a long, slim hand to him.

'Good night, *Herr Oberst*. It was so nice of you to come to dinner with us.'

For a moment Perón thought his mind had been read and he was being given his chance to escape. Then he realised that Heydrich's wife was going to bed and he was going to be trapped with the two SS men. Mentally he shrugged his shoulders and made the usual sounds of regret that she was leaving them and thanked her for the wonderful evening.

When she had gone Heydrich led the way back into the sitting room and poured three glasses of schnapps. As they sat down, Bischoff on the sofa and Perón and Heydrich in the armchairs, Heydrich spoke.

'How do you see the future development of Argentina?'

Perón thought quickly before he spoke. What he really would like to know was how Heydrich saw Argentina.

'I assume you mean politically speaking, *Herr General*? Argentina is a country of fantastic potential wealth. This wealth is in the hands of a few select families who run vast *estancias* on almost feudal lines. Industrialisation is coming, but slowly. *Peónes* trying to get away are hounded down by the *estancieros* and beaten into returning to the land for starvation wages.'

Perón paused and considered how to proceed.

'The *estancieros* are terrified of communism but all Argentinians are proud, individualistic people who would not readily embrace communism. Equally they would be opposed to any extreme. Ideally I see a third way. A policy that is neither left nor right.'

Again he paused and Heydrich spoke.

'That's been the dream of millions since Plato and a good few before. It's always proved inadequate. People need strong leadership if they are going to follow. Looking for a nonexistent middle way saps determination and support goes to whoever shows himself the strongest.'

Perón shrugged his shoulders, not willing to get drawn into a political argument. 'Leadership is a matter of charisma and personal magnetism. Look at Hitler and Mussolini.'

Heydrich glanced at him shrewdly through hooded eyes. 'Do you see yourself as a South American Hitler or Mussolini?'

Perón gave an amused laugh, aware that he had tacitly admitted more than he had wanted to. 'Me – *Herr General*? No! I know what I want to see happen in my country. I hope that when the time comes I will be called upon to do my part. I'm a soldier and I'm a patriot. What influence I have I use in an effort to find a president capable of moving my country forward into the future it deserves.'

He stopped with another disarming smile.

'But let us say you were asked to form a government, what would you do?' Bischoff had entered the conversation.

Perón looked at him. 'Why do you ask?'

It was Heydrich who answered. 'We have invested a lot of time and money in you so far, *Herr Oberst*. And if it suits us we could do a lot more in the future. But we must know who we are dealing with. If you are interested in the presidency we would like to know now.'

Again Perón considered before he spoke. 'If it was the will of the people,' he started carefully. 'Then I would consider it an honour. But at the present time I am only interested in getting Argentina the government it deserves.'

Heydrich shook his head. 'A country gets the government the strongest want. If it was left to the average man on a bus the country would collapse before he got home for supper.'

Perón agreed with that and nodded. 'In Argentina the strength traditionally comes from the Armed Forces. The trouble is that politics have now become the game of

20

colonels and it is difficult to maintain power for any length of time. Lately I have been studying what is happening in Germany and Italy and I hope to be able to mobilise the power of the workers to set up a stabilising influence on the Military.'

Heydrich gave a stifled snicker of laughter. 'Tell me, *Oberst* Perón, do you see yourself in the role of a twentieth-century Rosas?'

Perón was surprised. Juán Manuel de Rosas was a nineteenth-century leader who, although coming from a wealthy family, sided with the oppressed *gauchos* and held Argentina to ransom while he made himself *Caudillo* – the people's choice. His exploits were mainly remembered for their bloody execution rather than their results.

'Do I see myself as a champion of the poor? Yes! Do I believe the only way to achieve our goal is over the bodies of the people we are fighting for? No!' Perón made the statement with a sincerity which surprised himself.

It was Bischoff's turn to laugh. 'Fine ideals, my friend. But we in the National Socialist German Workers Party have been forced to realise that utter dedication is the only way to bring about a new world. The ideals must be clearly delineated and their pursuit must be swift and undeterred by minor considerations.'

'Like the Jews?'

Perón wished he hadn't said it but Heydrich nodded enthusiastically.

'Exactly. The Jews have sucked the blood of our people for too long. They must go. The State cannot be built without sacrifice. Throughout history it has been proved that the Jews are at the centre of all corruption and tragedy. There is no room in Nazi Germany for the worm gnawing at the core of the apple.'

His hosts were getting excited.

Perón nodded. 'But surely a healthy State would be able to survive even if the Jews were all you say?'

Bischoff jumped in quickly. 'Exactly! A healthy State! But what does a surgeon do when he detects gangrene? To

21

save the man he amputates the leg. Once strength is adulterated to the slightest degree it is corrupt.'

Heydrich took up where Bischoff left off. 'Unity of purpose under an all-powerful leader with a hierarchy of the best brains in the country to carry out his directives is the only way to preserve national integrity. The strongest must and always will survive for the good of the whole. In 1934 the SA, the Brown Shirts, under their revolutionary leader, Röhm, became a danger to the unity of the Reich, the Führer showed his fitness to lead the German people by having these traitors executed. A weak man could not have done that. The Führer was sad to have to order the death of his friend but it was necessary.'

Heydrich paused and took the crisp white handkerchief peeping from his breast pocket and wiped the sweat from his high, pale brow. He looked at Bischoff and smiled. 'The Führer did me the honour of conferring the planning of this painful purge on me. Bischoff actually led the raiding party that did the job.'

The three men sat for a few minutes after this outburst, considering their own thoughts. The conversation then drifted off into more placid areas, but as Perón drove back to the hotel through the dark Berlin streets he thought about Bischoff's simple philosophy of strength through force, and Heydrich's views on leadership. The thoughts attracted him.

Claudia's brown eyes sparkled with happiness as she saw the ball land just outside the tramlines at the side of the court. She gave a little squeal of pleasure and threw her racket in the air and her arms around Perón. He kissed her on the nose and walked with his arm around her to the net to shake hands with their defeated opponents. Appreciating Claudia's excitement he nuzzled his nose into her hair and was stirred by the erotic scent of expensive perfume and fresh sweat. Without taking their arms from each other's waist they walked along the tree-shaded path to the club-house.

Perón was happy with Claudia. She had the social clout to satisfy his ego, she was a minor Italian princess, and had run with the cosmopolitan set long enough to have picked up their mores but not long enough to become hard and cynical. He felt the hot, damp body under the flimsy cotton tennis dress and sighed contentedly.

As they climbed the half dozen steps to the terrace a short, powerful man in white tennis flannels and shirt rose and came to meet them. Perón didn't recognise him but smiled and nodded in a friendly way.

'*Coronel* Perón?' the stranger inquired politely.

'*Si*.' Perón stopped.

'My name is Guido Pedari. I have an export business in Buenos Aires.' Pedari shook Perón's hand.

'May I present Señor Pedari – Contessa Claudia de Bourbon,' Perón said proudly.

Pedari held the contessa's hand briefly to his lips and then turned to Perón. 'I'm sorry, *Coronel*, but if I could see you alone for a few moments?' Pedari suggested.

'*Si, si*. Whenever you like. I will just have a shower and then I am at your disposal.' Perón took Claudia's hand and started to move away but was arrested by Pedari's hand on his arm.

'Now, if you don't mind, *Coronel*. I am in a hurry.' The polite tone had left the Italian's voice.

Perón looked at him sharply, offended by the other's persistence. 'Very well. But be quick.' Perón guided the woman towards a table but again Pedari cut in.

'Alone!'

The smile died on Perón's face. It offended him to be given orders in front of the woman. 'Just who are you, Señor Pedari?' he asked.

'We have mutual friends who asked me to contact you.'

'Mutual friends? Who?'

'Let us say close to the Casa Rosada,' Pedari said enigmatically and sat down at the table.

Switching his smile back on Perón kissed the Contessa on the ear affectionately. 'Will you excuse me, *mi vida*.

Business. I'll see you in the bar in a few minutes.'

She gave a pout of disappointment and walked away, her swaying bottom appreciated by both men.

The colonel took the chair opposite and ordered a drink from the white-coated waiter. 'Now. What can I do for you, Señor Pedari?'

The Italian spread his hands to disclaim involvement. 'I'm only the messenger boy. I was told to contact you and tell you that our mutual friends want a meeting with you to discuss their future.'

They waited while the waiter placed the drink in front of Perón. 'I'm afraid it's impossible unless they can come here,' Perón said, pulling the corners of his mouth down.

Now that he had delivered his message Pedari was anxious to get away. He rose to his feet. 'It has been arranged. You are taking a few days leave.' He picked up a tennis hold-all from beside his chair and took out a large manila envelope and dropped it in front of Perón. 'You will find all the necessary information and instructions in there. *Ciao, Coronel.*'

They shook hands and Perón watched Pedari walk into the clubhouse. He turned the envelope over and over in his hands hardly daring to open it.

THREE

It was still warm, though the blazing heat of Buenos Aires at midday had given way to the relative relief of early evening. Doctor Perina left his four-year-old Auto Union in a small carpark under a block of flats owned by his brother-in-law and walked up the slab concrete ramp to the heavy steel security doors. He tried to think through the possible ramifications of the coming meeting. He had no doubts about the morality of his own position. President Ortiz had been good to him and he liked the sick old man. But the truth was that the president was too ill to continue. Now the pressures of a disintegrating Europe were putting strain on the administration of public affairs, internal and international, that could only be effectively controlled by a strong, authoritative clique. Of all the years of Argentina's presidential vacillations, 1940 was not the year to have an invalid in the Casa Rosada with four years still to run.

Doctor Perina stopped outside the shuttered front of the Restorante La Plata and glanced searchingly around. No one seemed interested in his progress. Quickly he pushed open the door and slid into the dim, cool interior. As his eyes became accustomed to the dark he could see that the restaurant was empty except for a big, fierce-looking man sitting in an unvarnished wooden chair in front of the dusty bar. Perina nodded to him but the man sat motionless, staring straight ahead and seeming not to notice the new arrival. He remembered his instructions on the telephone: 'Go through the restaurant to the back and someone will meet you there.'

A peeling door stood half open behind the seated man. Hesitantly Perina walked forward and sidled past him. The man didn't react so Perina took it as an invitation to go through to the back. There was a short, evil-smelling corridor with a small, even more malodorous kitchen and a door into an outer courtyard leading off from it. Holding his breath and carefully avoiding unnecessary contact Perina rushed to the end door and burst out into the sunlight. Gratefully he sucked in the sweeter air and brushed down his clothes in a fastidious attempt to rid himself of the contamination of the restaurant.

'*Buen día*, Doctor Perina.' A polite voice behind him made him spin around, his heart pounding. He had to admit to himself that espionage wasn't a trade he was psychologically suited to enter.

A young man in his early twenties stepped forward. He was smartly dressed in a blazer and flannels and had the unmistakable military stamp on his bearing. He didn't introduce himself or offer to shake hands. 'If you will follow me, Doctor.'

Outside a laundry van waited. The young man courteously handed Perina through the back door into the interior of the van and indicated that he should sit in one of the comfortable armchairs bolted to the floor. The doors clanged shut. His escort banged on the side of the van and with a jerk it rolled forward along the road. Through one of the grimy windows let into the back door the young man kept a careful watch on the traffic to make sure they weren't being followed.

For a quarter of an hour they ran a tortuous gauntlet through the speeding traffic before turning into a warehouse on the outskirts of the city. Doctor Perina started to rise but his guide waved him back into his seat. With a startling crash the back doors were thrown open and the young man jumped down and stood to attention as a tall, dark figure swung easily up into the back of the van. He waited until the doors were shut and he heard the bolt slide into place before he spoke.

'Doctor Perina. So good of you to meet me.'

A white smile shone in the gloom as the newcomer stretched out a big hand and greeted the quaking lawyer.

'We haven't met before, I think. My name is Perón.' He banged energetically on the wall and smiled when the van surged readily forward.

'I'm sorry about the theatricals but I'm supposed to be on active service in Europe. Absent without leave, I'm afraid. Probably get broken to the ranks if it's discovered I'm skulking about in Buenos Aires.' He laughed hugely at his joke and threw himself into the other armchair.

'Now, I understand you have a problem?' he asked, all trace of levity abandoned. 'If there is anything I can do to help you know I have the best interests of Argentina at heart and I will do all I can.' He looked at the little man encouragingly.

Doctor Perina swallowed and tried to arrange his thoughts. In his office before setting out he had known exactly what he would say and how. Now the unusual meeting and the feeling of nausea brought on by the swaying vehicle had robbed him of his professional poise.

'Well. Er . . . I have been instructed by certain parties – ,' he started but was cut short by Perón.

'Doctor Castillo. The Vice President,' he stated flatly.

Perina nodded, confused by the bluntness. 'Yes. Dr Castillo. There are certain matters that require – '

Again Perón interrupted. 'Dr Perina . . .' he said gently. 'Come to the point. You have asked for this meeting. You have discussed what you want and you have come here to try and enlist my help. Your emissary said that it was of vital importance to the future of our country and I caught the first available flight here. As you are well aware I am in consider-able danger while I am here unofficially. I would not have come if I had not already received, from other sources, information which made our meeting of the utmost urgency and importance. So please, get on with it.'

Perón crossed his legs and relaxed in the armchair. He seemed impervious to the often violent swaying as the van sped aimlessly through the traffic.

Perina pulled himself together with an effort. 'I apolo-gise, *Coronel*. I am unused to doing business in such

27

unorthodox surroundings.' He marshalled his thoughts. 'I will be blunt. President Ortiz' health has become much worse in the last few months and we feel that he is no longer capable of exercising his presidential powers efficiently.'

Perón held up his hand and smilingly halted him again. '*Perdón, Señor Doctor*. But who are "we"?'

Perina made a decision. If Perón was going to help he had to be aware of what was going on. 'Vice President Castillo and his group of advisers of which I am honoured to be the spokesman.'

Perón nodded. 'Go ahead.'

'As you are probably aware, the President has been too incapacitated to perform any of his presidential duties during the last six months. In spite of this he refuses to resign and let Castillo take over the presidency. This is partly due to the fact that Castillo has declared himself in favour of a pact with the Axis powers in Europe. Ortiz is a supporter of the Allied cause. Naturally he has around him mostly people who think as he does. They are not particularly powerful individually but they hold the main positions of power in the government. Doctor Castillo knows your sympathies and is aware of your standing with the Military. He asks your support in putting pressure on the Ortiz administration to force the President's retirement.' Perina stopped and looked hopefully at Perón.

The colonel said nothing for a couple of minutes. He had guessed that this was the sort of proposal that was going to be put to him but he wanted to make sure that what he was about to say was right. Finally he sat upright in the chair and began to talk in a quiet, terse voice.

'*Bueno, Doctor*. Of course I am fully aware of the state of affairs in Argentina but I am not sure that the time is right for the Army to get involved at the moment.'

Perina tried to speak but was cut off by Perón's raised hand.

'All you say is correct except the extent of my power. I am only one of a number of Army officers who feel that Argentina is not being led along the right path. At times I act

28

as their spokesman but I have already been out of the country for nearly two years and it would be foolish for me to speak for the Army at this time.' He paused for dramatic effect.

'What I am prepared to do is speak to a number of my colleagues and suggest that they lend Castillo their passive support. Ortiz will remain as President *de facto* but Castillo will be given the role of acting President during Ortiz' illness.' Perón paused but the Doctor had nothing to say so he continued.

'In the meantime you will see that I am posted back to Buenos Aires. There is no hurry. Take your time and let it go through the normal channels so that no one will become suspicious. Then, when I return, I will be able to use what little influence I may have to get Castillo the full support of the Army. How does that suit you?'

Perina thought quickly. He had hoped to be able to report that Perón had agreed to throw in his military support to back the vice president but he saw the sense in the Colonel's careful appraisal of the situation.

'*Bueno, Coronel*. I shall report your suggestions to Doctor Castillo. When do you intend to return to Europe?'

Perón spread his hands. 'There is a transport plane to Milano tomorrow night. I would like to be back in Italy before questions are asked.'

Perina nodded. 'Very well. I will let you have the Vice President's feelings on your proposal before you leave. How do I get in touch with you?'

Perón nodded towards the young officer now riding in the cab. 'Teniente Cabréra will call on you tomorrow afternoon. You can deliver Doctor Castillo's decision into his hands and he will pass it on to me before the plane leaves.'

When Colonel Perón boarded the airforce plane the next night he had in his pocket a letter from Vice President Castillo thanking him for his co-operation and informing him that he would be happy to go ahead with the plans that Colonel Perón had outlined the previous day. It was a guarded letter that would have meant little to any third person, but to Perón it was another step in the direction he had charted for himself.

'I heard you are going back to Argentina. Have you enjoyed your stay in Europe?'

General Lorenz was making nervous conversation like a village postmistress awaiting the arrival of the vicar for tea.

Perón crossed his legs and made himself comfortable. 'Yes. Very much. It's been a very useful experience but now I feel it's time to be going home,' he admitted with a disarming smile.

Werner Lorenz picked up his coffee cup and took a sip. He seemed to need to make conversation. 'You are satisfied with the way we are making our doctrine work? You will be able to assure your government that it is in their interest to co-operate more fully with us?'

Perón was saved from having to reply by the opening of a small door at the farthest end of the room and a man walking in.

Bormann – Perón recognised him instantly – wore a shapeless brown suit and looked more like a shopkeeper on his way to church than the *Reichsleiter* – one of the Führer's close circle of henchmen.

He walked quickly towards the two men. General Lorenz jumped hurriedly to his feet and gave the Nazi salute. Bormann hardly acknowledged him but held out his hand to Perón. The Argentinian briefly considered following Lorenz' example but thought better of it.

'*Herr Oberst*, I am glad you were able to come before you returned to South America. There are a number of points I wish to discuss with you.' Bormann sat in the third chair and testily dismissed General Lorenz' offer to get coffee.

'We have been putting a lot of money into your country; *Herr Oberst* Perón,' he continued. 'And we would like to broaden our activities. As you know we have considerable holdings in the interior as well as investments in Buenos Aires. Our sources inform us that the United States are

30

likely to be forced into coming into the war before long. It would help us considerably if we were able to use bases in the Argentine more fully. We would therefore like you to speak to your president about this and try to persuade him that we have the best interests of your country at heart.

You will, of course, be furnished with our plans before you leave Europe and facilities to draw on funds we have already deposited in Argentina.'

Bormann had stated his case without pausing. Now he sat and looked enquiringly at Perón.

The colonel thought quickly. He needed the money but he wasn't too keen on appearing to commit Argentina to siding with the Axis power before he was convinced that they were going to win. He wasn't fooled by Bormann's story of bases to take on the North Americans. With the United States in the war the fascist cause was as good as lost. Surely what Bormann was looking for was a reassurance that the Nazis could be certain of a welcome in Argentina if they were forced to flee.

'Of course, *Herr Reichsleiter* Bormann, you know that you have my support. As soon as I reach Buenos Aires I will tell the President of your offer to help us. I am sure he will act according to what he feels is best for our two countries.'

Bormann nodded, apparently satisfied. He stayed for another five minutes chatting about generalities and then, as abruptly as he came, got up and left.

In the car back to the airport Perón smiled to himself. Was it possible that the Nazis who had sought to use him now needed him, desperately, to the extent that he could now use them?

Perón returned to Buenos Aires as if he were a war hero back from the front line. The pro-British President Roberto Ortiz had no option but to welcome him publicly. He had hoped that Perón's support would die away during his absence. After all, General Humberto Sosa Molina, a personal friend of his and a leading member of the Armed Forces, had assured him that Perón was finished.

31

When Perón's boat docked in Buenos Aires a party of loyal supporters met him and they went directly to his apartment in Posadas. Once in the privacy of his rooms Perón did not beat about the bush.

'How are things with the Army? Do I still have its support?'

The officers looked at each other, each waiting for the other to speak. Perón studied them. He was grateful for their loyalty. It was through them that he had been able to reinforce his hold over his fellow officers. In spite of this he knew there would be a lot of opposition. Particularly from the group that had grown up around the President.

Perón relaxed. It was no good making his supporters nervous. He brayed his hearty, good natured laugh.

'Don't look so serious, *amigos*. This is the prodigal son returning – not driving the lepers away from the city gate. Our friends in Europe have promised us even more funds. They are beginning to look for boltholes and figure South America is far enough away. As long as it helps to bring about the New Argentina what does it matter where the money comes from? Now, how about a whisky, and then we can get down to discuss practicalities.'

He took their orders and served the drinks himself. It broke the ice and by the time everybody was settled down with a drink they were ready to talk.

'*Bueno*. Have we got the support of the Army?' Perón asked. Captain Reuteman looked around at the others before speaking. He read in their eyes permission to act as spokesman.

'Generally – yes. President Ortiz has made an attempt to get support but has only been partially successful. He has two things against him. He is hand-in-glove with the British and he doesn't like to spend money.'

Perón laughed boisterously at Reuteman's summing-up of his main antagonist.

Reuteman continued, reassured by his chief's good humour. 'Inflation is rising rapidly and this coupled with the drift of workers from the provinces and Patagonia is beginning to alienate the *estancieros* who have tended to support him so far. There has been a number of ugly incidents with trade unions where Ortiz has sent troops in to break up strikes and he can't expect much support from them.'

Perón nodded and asked a question. 'Which is the strongest union at the present time?'

Reuteman looked at one of the other officers, Captain Picot.

Picot thought before answering. 'Railway workers, I suppose. It is not the biggest but it can wield a lot of muscle now that the British owners are not as popular as they were.'

Perón stored the information away and returned to Reuteman. 'Go on.'

'Your reports from Europe have kept the Army's interest. The young officers will listen to anything you want to suggest as long as they feel that it will be a move in the right direction. Argentina has got to have a radical rethink if it is to make its mark in the twentieth century. Your reports have suggested we model ourselves on Germany, if you talk to the Army about that you will have an audience.'

Reuteman looked at his fellow officers and their enthusiastic nods reassured him of their agreement with his analysis of the situation. Perón went to the window and looked out into the narrow, residential street and smiled to himself with satisfaction.

'*Bueno, muchachos*. Set up a meeting for the morning. I suggest the Academy. Get everyone of importance there. I want to know what our strength is precisely.'

The officers retrieved their belongings and filed past Perón and shook his hand with renewed vows of support and welcome. When Picot shook hands with him Perón suggested in a confidential whisper that he might like to stay behind for a chat. Picot, flattered at the attention, agreed.

Perón came back into the long drawing room and waved the young officer into a seat. He pulled off his tunic and loosened his tie to show the informality of the occasion. Picot relaxed and Perón handed him another whisky.

'*Bueno*. Now, er – Hector, isn't it?'

33

Picot nodded enthusiastically, even more flattered that Perón should remember his name.

'Well, Hector. I understand you are familiar with the unions. I want a man who can organise the labour force for me. He has to know what he is doing and not be too squeamish. Can you think of anybody?'

Picot nodded affirmation. 'Yes. There is one man. He has studied the way the unions are organised in the USA, particularly in Chicago. At the moment he is in hiding in Buenos Aires. He's been making some inflammatory speeches that haven't gone down well with the government and had to go into hiding.'

Perón gave his infectious laugh. 'What's his name? Al Capone?'

The joke passed over the head of the serious young captain. 'No, Cipriano Reyes.'

'Do you know where he is?'

The captain nodded proudly. 'Yes. Some of my men picked him up before the police could get to him. I thought he might be useful so I put him in a safe house in Avellaneda.'

Perón queried, 'Why there?'

'It's where all the meat factory workers live. He has many friends there.'

'And too many people who can recognise him!' Perón suggested.

The captain looked worried. 'What do you suggest?'

'I have an apartment in Belgrano. He's unlikely to be known in a quiet residential area and if he keeps out of sight he won't be noticed.' Perón stood, bringing the interview to a close. 'The address is Calle Rosas 99, flat 7. Get him there, tonight.'

'Si, Coronel.'

Picot left shortly after this; Perón went into the bedroom, stripped off and walked into the adjoining shower. He let the cool water cascade over his body and felt the grime of Europe wash away. His thoughts were cut short by the buzzing of the intercom from the *conciergeria*. He wrapped himself in a towel and padded through his bedroom to answer.

The speaker squawked. '*Coronel* Perón? Espejo – the concierge here.'

'Hello, José. What can I do for you?' Perón asked good-naturedly.

'There is a man here to see you, *mi Coronel*,' Espejo said.

Perón frowned. He wasn't expecting anybody and he tried to keep his Posadas flat as secret as a series of mistresses and various meetings with loyal supporters could keep it.

'Who is it?' he asked.

There was a pause and Espejo answered. '*Sargento* José Lopez Rega, *mi Coronel*.'

Perón clicked through the index cards in his mind. The name was instantly familiar but he hesitated a few seconds before placing it. Of course, it was the corporal who briefly drove his car before he was shipped off to Italy. He remembered the nondescript features and the clever eyes.

'Send him up, José,' Perón said and went into the bedroom to find a dressing gown. A few minutes later the door bell rang and Perón let the sergeant in. He stood a few steps inside the door, stiffly at attention, waiting for permission to state his business.

Perón studied him for a few seconds before speaking. 'Well, Sargento Lopez Rega. We've both come up in the world. You're now a sergeant and I a full colonel. A whisky to celebrate?'

'No thank you, *Coronel*,' Lopez Rega declined politely.

Perón nodded. 'Of course. I forgot. You don't drink, do you?'

'That's right, *Coronel*,' Lopez Rega confirmed his colonel's feat of memory.

'What can I do for you, *Sargento*?' Perón asked.

'I would like to be detailed to look after you again, *Coronel*,' the sergeant blurted out.

Perón smiled. 'That's not up to me, I'm afraid. Why don't you ask the officer in charge of your company. If the job hasn't already gone he may be able to help.'

Perón was disappointed. He had hoped that his unusual visitor might have information of interest to him. He stood up, terminating the interview.

Lopez Rega came to attention but didn't move. '*Mi Coronel*. If you could have a word,' he suggested, pressing the point.

Perón was becoming irritated. He had more important things to do than become involved in getting preferment for a sergeant. Lopez Rega saw the look on his superior's face and knew that he had better make his point quickly.

'*Mi Coronel*. If I may. In the barracks they say that when you return there will be a lot of changes. I have been driving for many of the officers during the last two years. I think I have a lot of information that could be useful to you, *mi Coronel*.'

Perón looked at the sergeant with new respect. He was aware of the courage it had taken for the man to approach him like this. He also knew that mess orderlies and chauffeurs were privy to a lot of careless talk. Senior officers were so contemptuous of the lower ranks that they spoke quite openly in front of them. It said much for Lopez Rega's intelligence and ambition that he was willing to go out on a limb to profit from what he knew.

Perón made up his mind. 'Very well. I will speak to the motor pool tomorrow.'

Lopez Rega looked uncomfortable. '*Mi Coronel, perdón. Pero* – could you call today. The order will be already promulgated by the morning and it will be too late.'

Perón gave a short laugh. 'Very well, *Sargento*. Today! Now have you any other orders for me or can I get ready for dinner?'

'*Perdón mi Coronel – perdón, y gracias.*'

Lopez Rega turned on his heel and went to the door. The colonel stopped him.

'*Sargento*, do you know a man called Cipriano Reyes?'

The sergeant turned. 'Cipriano Reyes, *Coronel*? The name is familiar. Something to do with trouble in the meat trade isn't it?'

Perón nodded. 'I want you to come here early in the morning. There is something important I want you to do for me. Wear civilian clothes.'

FOUR

Lopez Rega parked the unmarked Buick under a tree a couple of blocks from the Belgrano apartment where he was to meet Cipriano Reyes. He didn't know what was behind his visit to the fugitive strike-leader. Perhaps his new boss was trying him out to see if he could be trusted. Lopez Rega didn't mind. He knew that the coming weeks were going to make or break the ambitious colonel but he had heard enough to convince himself that he had to hitch his star to somebody's wagon. Perón suited him.

When he reached the fourth floor he took the service revolver out of the rough shoulder holster he had rigged up earlier and stuck it in his coat pocket. He knocked loudly on the door and stood in full view of the spyhole. There was a flicker of movement. The door opened to the full extent of the safety chain.

'Sorry to bother you, *señor*. I have come for the carpet.'

'Carpet?' the voice queried, puzzled.

'Si, señor. For the cleaner.'

'I'm sorry. It's not convenient today.'

Lopez Rega raised his shoulder and turned as if to walk away. '*Bueno, señor*. But this is the third time I have called and I'll not be able to come again for a month.'

The chain rattled and the door opened. Lopez Rega smiled and walked in. As he heard the door close behind him he swung round and jammed his pistol into the man's stomach.

As the man opened his mouth in surprise Lopez Rega covered it with his hand and pressed the gun in harder. He gestured for the man to walk ahead. The short passageway led off a living room slightly smaller than the one Perón used in Posadas but it was furnished in the same comfortable style. Lopez Rega pushed Reyes down onto a sofa and quickly searched the other rooms.

One was a kitchen, the next a small bathroom and the third a bedroom. Satisfied, Lopez Rega returned to the man on the sofa who had recovered and was watching him alertly. The chauffeur reached into his inside pocket and took out a picture torn from a newspaper and compared it with the man in front of him.

Reyes was in his late twenties, medium built, with the fine black hair and swarthy skin of the Mediterranean people. His eyes were close-set and flickered nervously about the room. His face was strong and intelligent with ruthlessness in his thin-lipped mouth.

Lopez Rega was satisfied he had the right man – but what he had got he wasn't sure. He put away his gun and held out his hand.

'My name is Lopez Rega. You were expecting me, I think!'

Reyes ignored the outstretched hand. 'What do you want?'

'I represent powerful interests in the Army. We want your services to set up machinery to enable my superiors to work with the unions.'

Reyes laughed and took a cigarette out of the pocket of his shirt. 'Is that all? Perhaps you would also ask us to build our own prison cells?'

Lopez Rega stood looking down at the cynical labour leader for a few seconds without speaking then walked towards the door. He turned, and said quietly, 'You have a straight choice. Stay here and watch your support crumble or do a deal with my people and get the protection you need.'

Reyes threw his half-smoked cigarette to the floor and ground it into the carpet. 'Protection? Me? Listen! I can call out fifty union leaders onto the streets at a moment's notice. Each of them can call out two–three hundred workers. They are all the protection I need.'

Lopez Rega's deadpan face didn't flicker as the labour

leader glowered across the room at him. 'And what are you doing hiding out here?' Lopez Rega said softly.

Reyes acknowledged the point with a small shrug. '*Bueno.* What's your offer?' he asked, betraying no concession to the army man.

Lopez Rega moved back into the room and perched on the arm of the sofa. 'My people will guarantee that the police become helpful and the Army neutral. You have to guarantee industrial support whenever it is required,' he said.

Reyes lit another cigarette. 'Okay . . .' he began thoughtfully. 'So we are both scratching each other's back. What about when your people are in power? Military dictators are notorious for their short memories and we won't be in a position to take our grievances to court, will we?'

Lopez Rega nodded. 'True – but you have missed the point, *amigo*. We need your support to prime conditions for a free election. Your supporters will have their power through the ballot box.'

'A free election? That's something new. *Bueno.* So your people get to run the country on the back of my union. You're happy. But we need more than a pat on the head and a promise. We want concrete concessions.'

Lopez Rega agreed. 'Such as?'

'Guaranteed minimum wages, shorter working week, sick pay, fewer – '

The sergeant held up his hand and cut him off. '*Bueno, bueno.* My superiors understand that to get the support of the trade unions they have to look after them. If you give them the solid backing they want – you won't be disappointed.'

Reyes still hesitated. 'Your realise that it is going to be difficult to persuade all my supporters to accept the Army as fairy godmother, don't you. Only a week ago, army rifles killed some workers. If I am to support you, I must get a hundred per cent backing from my people. A few limbs are likely to get broken.'

Lopez Rega shrugged his shoulders. 'All we want is
40

results. What do I report?' He waited.

'Tell them I'm interested and ready to work as soon as I get assurances that my demands will be met. Also tell them that at the first sign of a sell-out I will pull the plug so fast they won't know what hit them!'

Before Lopez Rega reached the elevator Reyes was dialling the number that would stir his henchmen into action.

The meeting in the closely guarded lecture room at the War Academy next morning was noisy but predictable. Perón accepted the handshakes and congratulations until he was sure that everyone was present, some two hundred and fifty officers from subaltern to the most senior ranks, and then he called the meeting to order.

'Thank you, gentlemen. It's a great pleasure to be back in a civilised country and be able to eat some real meat without it wearing a sausage skin or a thatch of spaghetti.'

The officers roared with laughter and Perón waited for them to stop before continuing. 'But the time has come to do something positive to put Argentina into its rightful place in the forefront of the nations of the world. A New Argentina?'

Perón paused and watched their faces for reaction. 'A new Argentina is about to be born and we must be the midwives. It is our sworn duty to right the wrongs that society has brought to the people of Argentina and bring the country – not just in line with the twentieth century – but ready for the twenty-first as a leading nation of the world.' Again he paused as his audience applauded.

'There are those who are in the pay of corrupt politicians. Men who are interested in lining their own pockets to the detriment of the country. They will try to stop us. But we must be more clever. We must be more patient. Our friends in Europe are behind us in this. They need our friendship and commodities now, and in the future they will need them even more. They need a strong government to deal with. A government capable of sitting down at the same table as the masters of Europe and helping them to salvage

41

what they can after the war. Only the new, dynamic and united Argentina can fill that seat. And we must be ready!'

His last sentence he pronounced in the frenzied style of the European dictators and he was gratified when it brought spontaneous applause and cries of 'Bravo'.

'We must use every weapon in our armoury when we are called by the people to rescue them from the chaos brought about by the present administration. Every officer in the Army, in the Air Force, and in the Navy must be persuaded to join us. We must find a man who will lead us, who will be ready to take over the reigns of a provisional government while the process to institute a free and democratic election is undertaken. When the time comes we must not be found wanting. We must be ready to lay down our lives for the good of the new Argentina. My brother officers, we will have only one chance and one chance alone. If we fail – there will not be another.'

He finished on a note of dramatic intensity, his arms raised in supplication like the Pope blessing the crowds in St Peter's Square, as the emotional, patriotic Argentine officers rose amidst a storm of applause. A voice cried 'Perón for leader!' and it was taken up around the hall. Perón waited for the chanting to climax and then held up his hands for silence. When he finally got silence he spoke in a humble voice overcome with emotion.

'Friends. You do me too great an honour. I am but a humble worker, an artisan, pointing the way with the simple heart of a *gaucho*. As a worker I will rise with the sun and work unstintingly until my task is accomplished. But my simple *gaucho* heart has not the capacity for high office.'

He relished the cries of dissent and the renewed chant of 'Perón' but he had no intention of climbing the slippery road to the presidency. At least not at the present time.

Once more he called for attention. 'Gentlemen. We will meet again in the course of the next few days. I suggest you look amongst you for a man of integrity who is willing to take on the heavy burden of responsibility we will give him.'

42

As the renewed applause swept over him, Perón put on his uniform cap and leaped athletically down from the platform. He was immediately surrounded by well-wishers and it took him a full quarter of an hour to get out to his car. Lopez Rega was there, dutifully holding the car door open.

Perón stretched luxuriously in the back of the limousine and laughed out loud. In the mirror he saw Lopez Rega watching him and winked.

'Well, *Sargento*, how did it go?'

'Very well, *Coronel*. He will co-operate.'

Perón reached forward and clapped him on the shoulder. '*Macanudo, che*. We will arrange a meeting soon. Meanwhile try to find some more workers discontented with their lot. We will soon have the bricks to build our New Argentina.'

'*Si, mi Coronel*,' was all that Lopez Rega allowed himself. He knew that it didn't do to get carried away too soon. There were too many pitfalls.

Perón settled comfortably behind his desk in his modest office in the army garrison in Mendoza at the foot of the towering Andes. He was well pleased with himself. In less than a year he had managed to build up a coterie of powerful officers that had even the President looking over his shoulder every time a car backfired in the Plaza de Mayo. Cipriano Reyes had come out of hiding and once more was organising the labour force with promises of better times for the workers and heavy bribes for the union officers.

Those who couldn't be made to see sense were visited by union delegates who soon persuaded them that it was healthier for all concerned to work for a new Argentina. The Nazi-inspired strong-armed gangs of flying pickets were always on hand to make sure that any worker with ideas that didn't concur with their own was given a painful lesson in class solidarity.

Lopez Rega had been busy too. He spent his off duty hours in the *cantinas* and restaurants buying drinks and allegiance amongst the uncommitted working men. President Ortiz, after officially welcoming Perón back with glowing phrases, did his best to get rid of the ambitious colonel. Like all *Porteños*, Ortiz believed that Buenos Aires was Argentina. Within days Perón was posted to the Andean Garrison to instruct the troops in modern mountain warfare.

Nothing could have suited Perón better. As he moved from camp to camp he was able to preach the New Argentina. Of the three and a half thousand officers commissioned in the Armed Forces he now had the support of all but a handful. The change in fortune of the Nazi war machine in Europe had meant more money through his hands and less pressure to account for it. The officers of the SS were daily becoming more convinced that their future did not lie in Germany.

Among them was Colonel Bischoff, whose masters had dispatched him urgently to Argentina. He had telephoned Perón to say that he had urgent business to discuss and would be calling on him at his Mendoza headquarters.

Lopez Rega entered. He carefully closed the door and came to Perón's desk before he spoke. 'Colonel Bischoff has arrived, *Coronel*,' he said quietly.

'Good. Show him in.' Perón got up and stood at the window.

'He has two others with him. I think they are SS men, Coronel.' Lopez Rega sounded concerned.

'Of course they are SS men, *Sargento*. *El Coronel* Bischoff is feeling insecure. He wants to have support. Show him in – alone.'

Lopez Rega opened the door and looked out. '*Coronel* Perón can see you now, *señor*,' he said politely.

Bischoff came through the door with quick nervous strides. His two subordinates were headed off by Lopez Rega stepping behind Bischoff and closing the door in their faces. As Bischoff halted just inside the door Perón turned from his contemplation of the Andes and held out a welcoming hand.

'I am delighted you could come to see me. I get very few visitors here I'm afraid. Can I get you something to drink? A whisky perhaps?' He opened a drawer in his desk and took out a whisky bottle and two glasses, pouring two large measures into the glasses and handing one to Bischoff. 'Now, what can I do for you?'

Bischoff put his briefcase on his knees and took out a sheet of paper, while Perón waited with polite interest.

'My superiors in Berlin are becoming worried about our affairs in Argentina. They feel they are getting very little return for their investment.'

Astonishment spread theatrically across Perón's heavy features. 'I'm afraid I don't understand, *Herr Oberst*. We have done exactly what you asked. What basically is the problem?' He leaned forward with concern.

Bischoff leafed through his papers. In normal circumstances he would have been inclined to take Perón out into the country and let his men beat him to death for daring to misappropriate party funds. But his instructions had been specific. He was to find a way to bring the colonel in line but still retain his co-operation.

'General Lorenz would like to have a full report on all the property bought in Argentina and details of such funds that have been used to secure the services of officers sympathetic to the Reich. He has asked me to express his appreciation of your efforts on our behalf but insists that a detailed accounting for all funds is available for his superiors.'

Perón spread his hands in understanding. 'Of course, *Herr Oberst*. All our records are open for your inspection. It is regretted that the price of land has risen to such a level. It's the war you know.' He said the last sentence without a smile. 'If you could tell me when you wish to examine the accounts it will be arranged.'

Bischoff returned his papers to his case. 'Now! If you don't mind, *Oberst*.'

Perón looked surprised and worried. 'But *Herr Oberst*, the records are in Buenos Aires. I move around too much to risk carrying them with me.' He thought for a few seconds. 'Look. I will be returning to the capital in about two weeks time for a few days. I could probably make arrangements to

45

go into them with you at that time.'

'I'm sorry, *Herr Oberst*. My instructions are to see the accounts before I leave.'

'Of course I will do anything I can to set your mind at rest but I'm afraid that what you ask is impossible. Ten days – probably a week – but now, impossible I'm afraid.' Perón proffered the bottle for a refill but Bischoff declined.

'*Oberst* Perón, do I need to remind you that you were chosen by General Lorenz to help Germany to a situation of mutual benefit with your country? To help you we have put into your hands several million dollars. If you do not satisfy us immediately that this money has been used for the purposes it was intended, your dossier will be laid before President Ortiz.' He paused to emphasise the point. 'I think you know what we have in our dossier? If Ortiz is unwilling to act, copies will be sent to *La Prensa* and *La Nacion*. I am sure that these newspapers will be interested.'

Perón let concern show in his face. He had little doubt that Bischoff intended what he threatened. He also knew that he still held all the cards. If the Nazis got rid of him they would be cutting their own throats. He picked up the telephone. 'There's just one chance,' he said with an anxious smile. 'Rega?' he said into the telephone.

The sergeant knew that he had to be careful what he said. The colonel only called him Rega when he wanted assistance. The sergeant glanced at the two SS men. They were watching him. 'Si, *mi Coronel!*' he answered.

'There is a transport plane due in this evening, isn't there?' That was straightforward enough.

'Si, *mi Coronel*.'

'I need some documents from Buenos Aires. Will you ring and ask them what time the plane will be leaving?'

Lopez Rega couldn't make out whether Perón wanted the information or asked only for the benefit of his visitor. 'I know that, *mi Coronel*,' he ventured.

Perón smiled at Bischoff. 'We may be in luck.' He returned to the phone. 'Well done Rega, does it arrive before dinner?'

Lopez Rega considered the question, but before he could answer Perón continued.

'Good, good! Phone Captain Benito and ask him to come here with all the files on our dealings with our friends in Berlin. Did you get that?'

'Si, *mi Coronel*.'

'Captain Benito' was the codeword to say that nothing was to be done about the order until he had spoken with the Colonel again.

Perón smiled and returned the handset to the cradle. 'There you are, *Herr Oberstleutnant*. By tonight I will be able to satisfy you that you have nothing to worry about.' He thought for a moment. 'The airport is near my house. Perhaps you and your friends would care to come to dinner and then, when Benito arrives, we can go straight to work.'

'Thank you,' Bischoff stood stiffly.

Perón came around the desk with his hand outstretched. 'So nice to see you again, *Herr Oberst*. I'm sure we will soon sort out our differences. And I shall insist you stay the night. I will make up a small party. I'm sure you will enjoy it.' He clapped Bischoff on the shoulder. '*Hasta luego, Coronel*.'

Lopez Rega went back to his quarters and dressed in his civilian clothes. His taste had improved with his fortune.

The cheap, badly cut suit had been replaced with a smart blue blazer and lightweight grey trousers. He no longer wore the dockland trilby but preferred to copy Perón's panama. As he knotted the regimental tie he looked at himself with approval. He knew that as long as he didn't speak he could be mistaken for an officer. His speech was improving with the lessons he was taking surreptitiously with a downtown professor but he knew that whatever he did he would never be able to fool his superiors. It wasn't important. His power had already grown to such an extent that few people cared to lock horns with the ambitious sergeant.

He took the nondescript private car that Perón used to travel unobserved and drove out of town on the road towards San Juán. About five miles along the road he turned off into the drive of a large, double storey house covered with vines. Several cars were parked in front but he drove around the back and parked under a shady tree out of sight.

There was a small door into a dark passage that led through the house and came out beneath a flight of stairs to the upper storeys. Lopez Rega made sure that he was unobserved and then swiftly mounted the steps two at a time. He knocked sharply on the first door on the landing at the top and without waiting walked in.

The room was a boudoir, over-furnished, over-perfumed and coyly feminine. A movement on the ornately decorated, canopied bed attracted his attention. A big, rawboned woman in her mid-forties swung her legs out of the pink satin sheets and rose, wrapping a long, silk dressing gown, fussily trimmed with lace, around her naked body. She was still a handsome woman although at the moment she was angry and flushed.

'What the hell do you mean, *Sargento*. This is a private room. You have no right to – '

Lopez Rega held up his hand in apology. 'I'm sorry, Florentina. I didn't know you were busy. I'm in a hurry. Important business. I need some girls for tonight. They have to be special. Ones that can keep their trap shut and do as they are told.'

Florentina nodded. 'If you are willing to pay there is no problem. How many do you want?'

Lopez Rega spread his hands. 'How many do you have?'

Florentina considered. 'Of the type you are looking for no more than four – five at the most.'

'That's fine. I'll send a car at about nine.'

'The money?' Madame wanted to know.

Lopez Rega looked around the overpowering room. 'Money, madame? I'm considering getting the fire chief in to have a look at the club you run here. It looks a bit of a fire trap to me.'

Florentina's shriek of laughter startled him. 'Cacho? He's my best customer.'

'In that case I'm only joking. If we get the right girls the money will be good.' He turned to leave and then had a thought. 'Have you got a young girl you could send?'

The woman smiled knowingly. 'The *Coronel* wants entertaining, does he?'

Humourlessly Lopez Rega stretched his top lip to expose his white teeth. 'That sort of remark can get you into a lot of trouble, madame.'

FIVE

Lopez Rega stood unseen in the dark beside the hangar. He watched the plane land and half a dozen men in uniform climb out of the cargo hatch and walk across the tarmac to a collection of huts by the main gate. A truck drove across and four men started hauling the cargo onto the back.

Lopez Rega waited until he saw the pilot and his crew leave the plane and then silently walked over. One of the handlers saw him coming and jumped off the back of the truck. The other three ignored the interruption and continued loading.

'All ready, *Sargento*,' the soldier reported.

Lopez Rega nodded and pulled an envelope out of his jacket pocket. 'Good.'

He handed over the envelope and the man banged with his hand on the side of the plane. There was a pause and then two men dropped quietly onto the tarmac. The soldier climbed back onto the lorry and showed no more interest as Lopez Rega led the men across the dark runway and into his waiting car. Nobody spoke as the car skirted the town and drove at a steady speed along the road bordering the house where Perón was entertaining his guests.

The evening was hard going. Bischoff was not a festive man. He sat in the tall-backed wicker chair and cast a gloom over the party that neither the jokes of Perón nor the charms of the girls supplied by Lopez Rega could dispel. The German's two assistants looked as if they would be happy to drop their hard pose for an hour or two but were intimidated by their superior.

Perón gave Bischoff a glass of the heady local wine and signalled the *capataz* to serve the food. The meat was laid out on a grill over glowing wood embers, sending out a
50

mouthwatering aroma of roasting beef. As the *capataz* started to serve the meat on coarse wooden platters the girls squealed with delight and crowded around him pointing out the pieces they wanted. Bischoff's two assistants took advantage of the diversion to get near the girls and chat to them as they ate their meat at the round table beside the fire.

Perón picked up the long silver-handled *asado* knife lying beside Bischoff on the table and handed it to him. The German took it but made no move to go to the fire.

'I thought your captain would be bringing your accounts here tonight?' he said truculently.

Perón shrugged his shoulders and looked at his watch. He was dressed traditionally for the *asado*. Coarse white shirt, the baggy *bombachas* of the *pampa* horsemen and shiny leather boots, concertinaed at the calf. 'He should be here at any moment. Sergeant Lopez Rega has gone to pick him up. He will bring him directly here.'

Bischoff looked sour. 'I hope we will not be disappointed.'

Perón disregarded the hint of threat in his voice. 'I am sure everything will be satisfactory.' He took his knife out of the back of his belt and pointed to the food. 'If we don't get stuck in soon the best cuts will all be gone.'

The German still looked unfriendly but he got up and walked with the colonel to the fire. They were just sitting down again when car lights flickered through the trees on the drive up to the house. Perón put a piece of meat between his teeth and chewed on it as he drew the SS man's attention to it. 'That looks like Benito now.'

The German looked faintly disappointed that the captain should be coming after all. It gave him less excuse to indulge his sarcasm.

But Lopez Rega was alone in the car. He made his way across the lawn to Perón. He saluted smartly and waited for permission to speak.

'What is it, Sergeant?' Perón let an uneasy edge creep into his voice. He looked pointedly behind the sergeant.

'Where is Captain Benito?'

Lopez Rega shifted uncomfortably. 'I beg the *Coronel*'s pardon, but the captain did not arrive on the flight.'

Perón jumped to his feet letting the plate fall to the ground. 'What do you mean, *Sargento*. You told me you had arranged it. What happened?'

Lopez Rega went even stiffer and looked even more frightened. 'He was unable to leave, *mi Coronel*. He will come on the first flight in the morning.'

Bischoff gave a short sardonic laugh. 'And in the morning he will send a message to say that his grandmother is ill and he will arrive in the evening. And so on.' He stood up. 'I think it is time we stopped playing games. I would like to use your telephone to speak to my superiors. We cannot avoid the issue any longer, *Herr Oberst*.'

Perón looked shaken. 'But *Herr Oberst*. It is not my fault. Benito will be here in the morning. Surely you can wait that long?'

Bischoff shook his head. 'It's not possible. The telephone if you please.'

His two aides had followed the argument and detached themselves from the women. Perón looked frantically around and then shrugged his shoulders in surrender. 'Have some food before you leave, *Sargento*,' he said as he led the way to the house and into his office.

He picked up the handset and gave it to Bischoff. He could imagine the scene in the tiny telephone exchange. As soon as his number came up the operator would attract the attention of the *teniente* in charge. And he would come on the line.

'*Si, señor*,' he said in the officious voice of a night operator.

'This is the house of Colonel Perón. I want to be connected with *Obergruppenführer* Werner Lorenz in Berlin immediately. The number is – '

'I'm sorry, *señor*, but all lines between here and Buenos Aires are down and we cannot accept calls out of Mendoza.'

'What! This call is an emergency. It must be put through!' he stormed.

'I'm afraid it's not possible, *señor*. The lines will be restored in the morning. I suggest you try then.' There was a click as the *teniente* hung up leaving Bischoff spluttering into the telephone.

Perón turned from the window and raised his eyebrows inquiringly.

'Your stupid telephones aren't working. It will have to wait until the morning,' Bischoff said viciously in accusation.

Perón permitted himself a smile. 'By that time there will be no point in talking to your superiors,' he promised.

Lopez Rega sat under the trees and watched what was happening. Bischoff's aides had drunk a good deal. They were far from incapable but had put away enough of the rich Mendoza wine to be boisterous.

They were sitting with three of the girls around the table; the fourth girl was sitting beside Bischoff. She was bored and drinking too much. Every time her companions shrieked she looked across wishing she hadn't been selected for the honour of looking after the VIP. Bischoff hadn't addressed more than half a dozen words to her all evening and when she tried to touch him he had knocked her hand away with unnecessary force. She looked across at the tall, handsome man talking and laughing with Popote, little more than a child.

Now there was a man. A pity he liked the young ones.

She glanced back at Bischoff. He was staring at Perón with a look of disdain on his thin features. Bischoff got to his feet.

'I shall go to bed now,' he announced, without preamble.

Perón looked surprised at his abrupt statement but gently shooed Popote off his lap and came across to him. 'Very well, *Herr Oberst*. I will show you to your room.' He hesitated and looked at the girl at Bischoff's side. 'Do you want Nanette to stay?' he asked.

Bischoff shook his head without looking at her. 'That will not be necessary, and my assistants will not require the services of the women either.'

Perón took his three guests off to their rooms while a hundred yards along the road from the house an Army Jeep waited with its lights off at the side of the road. The young soldier kept himself awake by smoking one cigarette after the other as he waited for further instructions. He saw lights of a car approaching and threw his stub away. Lopez Rega got out of the car and came across to the Jeep.

'Take these ladies home, soldier, then go back to the barracks and forget everything.'

The soldier nodded understanding and watched as the five women climbed into the Jeep.

Lopez Rega laughed. 'Look after him girls. He's a good boy.'

The women squealed with laughter and ran their hands provocatively over the blushing soldier.

The sergeant got back in his car, turned it around and disappeared the way he had come. Instead of turning in at the driveway he continued along the road until he was able to pull off under a group of trees. He wound down a window and whistled softly into the dark. Immediately two figures appeared by his side.

'They are going to bed now. Go in at three o'clock. I will wait in the road outside the drive. You will be over the border into Chile in two hours. Any questions?'

'No, *señor*,' one of the men answered softly.

'Good,' Lopez Rega said curtly and swung the car away up the unmade road.

Bischoff was uneasy. He thought of the isolated house and the broken telephone lines. He pulled the mattress onto the floor against the wall by the door. With a blanket he made a mound in the bed that he hoped would look like his sleeping figure and covered it with another blanket. Then he waited. The minutes passed, then suddenly the door burst open and the small room was filled with the deadly hammer of a machine gun. The bed jerked madly as the bullets hit the rolled-up blanket. He heard the chatter of a gun in the next

54

room occupied by his bodyguards and shrank against the wall. Sobbing with fear Bischoff fumbled around on the floor for his boots, tucked his jacket under his arm and silently opened the window and dropped into the flowerbed underneath.

Bent double he ran in the direction of the mountains.

There was a knock on the door.

Perón frowned. This wasn't part of the plan. The gunmen were supposed to be put on the train to Chile by Lopez Rega while he reported the scandalous attack on his house by a gang of terrorists. He drew his pistol and tiptoed to a position out of the line of fire through the door.

'Who is it?' he called quietly.

'*Perdon, señor*. Can we speak to you urgently?'

'The door is open.'

'*Si, señor*. It is regrettable but one of them got away.'

'What?' Perón exploded. 'Where is the sergeant? Get him!'

Lopez Rega rushed in, fear on his face. Perón had suddenly become quite calm.

'A slip-up, *Sargento*?' he said.

'Sorry, *mi Coronel*. Bischoff escaped us. We will capture him before he gets too far.'

'Maybe – maybe not. It doesn't matter.'

'Doesn't matter!'

Perón shook his head. 'No. Bischoff can take my message to Martin Bormann better than the telephone. Next time they want to talk they may be more polite.' He nodded to Lopez Rega and went back to bed.

SIX

Colonel Domingo Mercante was an ambitious man with his own sights set firmly on the presidency of Argentina. As he saw many of his own supporters being seduced by the affable Colonel Perón he gradually began to lose confidence in his own ability to survive if cut off from the all-powerful clique. To go to Perón and openly ask for support was out. His pride forbade that. The sumptuous Jockey Club was a meeting place for high-ranking officers and those whose money gave them a monopoly on the business of the country.

Mercante decided that he would arrange a casual meeting there. The traditional annual polo match between Argentina and Britain would provide the opportunity. Both he and Perón had been avid players in their younger days and it was natural that both of them should be there for the match.

It was one of those heavy, overcast days that brought out the stormflies and reduced linen to a soggy sweat-soaked rag. Perón was there with a large group of friends, entertaining with the warm hospitality he always displayed on these occasions. Mercante joined some of his own friends and watched while the Argentina team scored a narrow victory over the British. He took tea on the sheltered terrace and then moved inside with the rest as the wind rose and rain threatened.

He still hadn't formed a plan for approaching Perón and was almost convinced that he would have to shelve his attempt, when he looked up to see the colonel picking his way through the card tables towards him. Perón shook hands and dropped into the vacant chair beside him.

'Looks like a storm brewing,' he said nodding to the black clouds hanging threateningly over the polo field. Mercante nodded.

'Yes. We came in just in time.' As he spoke there was a brilliant flash of lightning trampled on by a stunning clap of thunder. Without warning the rain sliced down in a grey curtain of exploding droplets. The Wagnerian scene seemed to excite Perón. He watched the rain in silence for a few moments and then turned to the colonel.

'I was hoping I might see you here,' he said artlessly. Mercante felt a pulse of excitement but appeared cool and only politely interested.

'Oh, really. You know I always come to the Internationals if I get a chance. Brings back the old days, I suppose. Do you play now?'

Perón shook his head sadly. 'No. Getting too old for this sort of thing I'm afraid.' He relaxed in the armchair and signalled for a waiter to bring drinks.

Mercante looked at him with mock seriousness. 'Yes. I can see that. Must be about time you were pensioned off. Let's see, *viejo*, you must be all of forty.'

Perón let himself sag and smiled ruefully. 'And the rest . . . And you? How many teeth sleep beside you in a glass these days?'

They both laughed louder than the jokes warranted and then lapsed into silence while the waiter served their drinks. Perón was the first to speak.

'I'm still hoping you will join me on the Army committee. The government is going to fly apart at the seams unless something is done very quickly. Poor old Ortiz can't hold on much longer. Anyway, it's not fair on Castillo. He's running the shop without being the manager. It creates a state of uncertainty that we can do without at the moment.' He looked across at Mercante. 'If you were with us we could act decisively. You would give us the *categoria* with the families. It would mean that we could act knowing that we had the support of the country.'

Mercante was flattered. He had not expected that Perón would be making overtures to him. 'It's nice of you to say so, Perón, but I'm not really a political animal you know,' he said, straight-faced.

Perón looked at him and widened his eyes in mock surprise. 'Of course not, Colonel. Nor am I.'

Their faces held for a moment and then they both hooted with genuine laughter. Perón leaned forward and he spoke with a new intensity. 'What do you say, Domingo, would you consider coming in with us? For myself I'm not interested in the presidency. My committee is looking for a suitable candidate for the future. We want a military government. There is too much vested interest in civilian circles to be able to deal with the country's problems at the present time. Industrialisation is coming to Argentina whether we want it or not. That means a shift of population. Something that the *estancieros* will oppose. We have Rawson, Farrell and Ramirez with us as well as a good percentage of the radicals. The navy and air force are playing hard to get but will come in behind us when the time comes.'

Mercante understood only too well the implied threat that Perón had made connecting his plans for the presidency with the support of the strongest generals in the army. If he acted now he would be on the inside when jobs were being handed out.

'And Vice President Castillo?' he asked.

'We will leave him for the present. President Ortiz is ready to resign. Castillo will take over the presidency. Before long the war will be settled. Assuming that the Allies win we can get rid of Castillo and blame him for not moving against the Axis. If by some unbelievable stroke of luck the Germans should pull the chestnuts out of the fire we remove him for NOT joining them in their struggle. Whichever way it goes it suits us for the moment to back Castillo. When the time comes for a change we will be ready.'

To emphasise his last statement Perón raised his glass in a toast. '*Saludos* to the New Argentina.'

Mercante hesitated for a split second and then held up his glass in acknowledgement. As one they drained their glasses.

Bischoff stared fearfully at the summons he had known would be awaiting his ignominious return to Berlin. The letter had been on his desk when he arrived. It was curt and to the point. 'You will report to *Reichsleiter* Bormann in his office at 10:30 hours.' It was signed 'Heydrich'.

Bischoff was aware, more than most, of the price of failure in the iconoclastic service of the SS. Mesmerised he watched the hands of the small office clock shudder away the time. At 10.15 he stood up and straightened his uniform. He went along to the senior washroom and dashed water onto his face and tried to pinch colour into his ashen cheeks. He ran a nervous finger around his collar, it felt like a garrotte. A short walk took him to the office of the *Reichsleiter*.

The SS colonel stood rigidly to attention a few feet inside the door. Bormann looked up and smiled. That smile made Bischoff feel even more frightened. His hand shot up and he said '*Heil Hitler*' in a desperate bid to appease his master. Bormann nodded, '*Heil Hitler*, Bischoff.' He waved his thick hand invitingly to a low coffee table bearing a silver tray. 'Coffee?'

'Poison!' The thought exploded in Bischoff's head. Without waiting for his reply Bormann poured two cups and held one out to him. Bischoff forced his legs to function and walked across and took the cup with a trembling hand.

'Sit down,' Bormann ordered gently with another reassuring smile, indicating one of the armchairs facing him. The SS man sat bolt upright, confused by his reception. Bormann picked up the other cup and sipped at it before speaking. 'How are you, *Standartenführer*? We haven't met for some time, have we?'

Bischoff fought for control of his paralysed vocal cords. 'No sir,' he quavered.

Bormann took another sip of his coffee and studied him over the rim. 'It seems that you have been very lucky, *Herr Standartenführer*. The Führer has been very magnanimous with you. He has decided to forget your mishandling of the Perón affair and give you another chance.' He paused and waited for Bischoff to react.

The colonel was so shocked by the announcement that he nearly dropped his cup. It was the last thing he had expected. Second chances were almost unheard of in the *Schutz Staffel*.

'You are to be given an opportunity to reinstate yourself. Colonel Perón has not been very co-operative. He is still being financed and does just enough to make it look as if he is looking after our interests. However it is not enough. He is now in a very strong position with the Army and needs only the opportunity to present itself to take over the country completely. If this happens we are afraid that it will become impossible to exercise even the remotest control over his actions.' Again he paused and looked at the man hanging onto his every word.

Bischoff felt called upon to speak. '*Jawohl, Herr Reichsleiter*. What do you want me to do?'

Bormann set his cup down on the tray with controlled emphasis. 'You will return, in secret, to Buenos Aires. The colonel will be quietly eliminated. We have now come to an understanding with the acting President Castillo. He is sympathetic to our cause and is willing to co-operate with us in exchange for a reassurance that we will support him through our people in Argentina. After you have disposed of Perón you will report to the German Embassy in Buenos Aires and they will inform Castillo.'

Bormann stood up and went to his desk. Bischoff got to his feet and watched, still unable to believe his luck, as Bormann took a thick envelope from the drawer and returned to the sofa. He handed the package to Bischoff.

'In here you will find a list of banks holding SS funds. You will be able to draw on those by producing your warrant card. They have been informed. There is also a list of German nationals in positions to be able to give you assistance if you should require it. Perón must disappear completely.' Bormann erased his smile and continued in a hard, unfriendly voice. 'You have *Obergruppenführer* Heydrich to thank for this chance to redeem yourself. For my part I consider that your handling of the situation the last time fits you for little more than traffic control, and that only under supervision. You will report to *Obergruppen-führer* Heydrich through the operative detailed in your instructions. I will not wish you luck because the operation calls for planning and efficiency.' Bormann turned his back in dismissal.

Bischoff gave a fervent salute that was not returned and was ushered out in a daze.

SEVEN

Bischoff's destination was a small club, ostensibly the BA branch of a hunting club in Cordoba, where he was to meet his contact, Otto Jaenisch. The rusty knocker produced a lost, hollow sound and achieved no noticeable result. He tried again.

'You will not get any answer until after ten o'clock, *mein Herr,*' a voice said behind him.

Bischoff spun round, on his guard at having been addressed in German. A small, convertible Fiat had drawn into the kerb behind him. Leaning out of the window was a pretty blonde woman with a smooth golden tan and amused blue eyes.

'Sorry if I startled you,' she apologised with a laugh. 'But you were so determined to break the door down you didn't notice me.' Her smile was infectious. Bischoff allowed himself a small relaxation of the taut muscles around his mouth.

'*Guten Abend, gnädiges Fräulein.* I have an appointment here at this time. Do you belong to the club?'

The girl nodded and swung the passenger door open. 'Get in. Herr Jaenisch apologises for not being here but thinks it would be better if you met somewhere else.'

Bischoff hesitated. He had no taste for taking rides to unknown destinations. Now there seemed no alternative. He got in. Without hesitation the woman drove off at high speed, accelerated across the busy Avenida del Libertador and, blowing her horn, cut a swath through the passengers leaving Retiro Railway Station. She turned a tight left, skidding across the cobbles and fighting the clutch of the steel tramlines. As she reached a narrow road running level with the river front she eased off the throttle and relaxed.

'I'm sorry about that, Herr Gustav, but there was always a chance that you were being followed.'

Bischoff felt better. The girl had used his alias which meant that she must have got her instructions from a friendly source. He looked at her and felt proud. She was a perfect example of the superiority of the Aryan race. Tall, athletic, with a cool beauty that only untainted stock could produce. Looking at her now, her eyes shining with excitement, cheeks flushed and the wind stirring provocatively in her loose hair, he fell in love. Not with the woman but with the concept.

She noticed him staring and gave him an amused glance. 'You must be wondering who I am? My name is Therese von Quast. Otto Jaenisch is my uncle.'

'Thank you for meeting me. Have we far to go?'

She shook her head vigorously and pointed ahead. 'We turn off here. Hold on to your hat. The road is pretty horrific.'

She swung the wheel and the car drifted sideways on the loose earth before straightening up and diving between two trees. The cart track ran straight between high patches of ornamental pampas grass toward a circle of towering trees guarding a bungalow built on stilts. Therese ran the car under a lean-to at the side and led Bischoff around the front of the house. Facing the top of the stairs was a shuttered double door. Therese thrust it open and walked straight through leaving the SS man to follow. Bischoff put his hand in his pocket and felt the reassuring weight of the pistol he was carrying. He followed the woman through the door.

A tall, suntanned man in his early sixties was waiting to greet him, his long, strong chin thrust out as he regarded the new arrival through his schoolmasterish spectacles. He was wearing a khaki shirt and wide, flapping shorts in the same material. His legs and feet bare and brown as a nut. His thinning, once blond hair and intense blue eyes were the only family resemblance to his delicately formed niece.

'Herr Gustav?' the man asked in a soft Austrian accent.

Bischoff brought his heels together and raised his hand in

a limp-wristed imitation of the Führer. '*Heil Hitler.*'

His host ignored the salute and held out his hand. 'I'm Otto Jaenisch. I've been asked to look after you while you are here.'

Therese brought a cup of coffee over to him and handed another to Bischoff who eyed her narrowly.

'*Gnädiges Fräulein*, I wish to speak to your uncle in private. Perhaps you would leave us for a while.'

The woman dropped into one of the creaking bamboo chairs with a low chuckle, and Jaenisch smiled ruefully.

'I'm afraid, Herr Gustav, that although I was required to register as a German subject by the Embassy, I am not interested in doing anything that might be termed as interference in the internal affairs of Argentina.'

Jaenisch revealed his occupation in the didactic way he spoke. For a moment Bischoff didn't know what to do. Therese broke the silence.

'So I suggest you speak to me,' she said, a hard edge to her voice.

Bischoff turned to look at her. She had lit a cigarette in a white ivory holder and was looking at him coolly, all humour gone from her eyes.

Her uncle walked to the door. '*Ja*, I think that would be best. I will wait outside. I do not want to be involved.'

Bischoff listened as the older man walked down the bare wooden steps to the lawn.

Again the woman broke into the silence.

'Herr Gustav. I'm thirty-five. I was born in Argentina. If what you want coincides with what I want I can promise you more assistance than you could reasonably have expected.'

Therese let friendliness show in her face again. 'So, Herr Gustav, do we proceed or must I be rotten and leave you to walk back to the city by yourself?' She threw herself back in her chair and shrieked with laughter at her threat.

Bischoff relaxed. 'You dare to threaten an SS officer with having to walk, Fräulein Therese. All right, I surrender. But please, promise you won't make me walk back.'

64

He was surprised at his own levity. It was a long time since he had indulged in ridiculous exchanges of this sort. He looked at the long, silk clad legs stretched out and crossed delicately at the ankles and felt a pulse of excitement. He cleared his mind of unaccustomed thoughts and gave Therese his cup for a refill.

'What do you think of Castillo?' he asked as a way of opening.

Therese didn't even have to think. 'He's more interested in wearing the sash of president than doing anything constructive.'

'He is interested in forming an alliance with Germany,' he told her.

'But for the wrong reasons. He thinks that with German prestige behind him he will be more secure in the presidency,' the girl said handing him his coffee.

Bischoff looked at her in surprise. 'And won't he?'

Therese shook her head. 'I don't think so. He is trying to saddle two horses at once without putting a bridle on either. Sure he is pro-Nazi but he could just as easily run up the Union Jack.'

Bischoff thought for a moment. 'Do you know Colonel Perón?'

There was silence while the woman thought. 'Colonel Perón?' she said slowly, her forehead creased in thought. 'The name sounds familiar but I can't place it at the moment. Who is he?'

The SS man waved the question aside. 'It doesn't matter who he is. It is important that we convince him not to interfere with the plans we have for Castillo.'

'And can he?' Therese asked in a puzzled voice.

Bischoff gave a deep sigh. 'Who knows? He has some support amongst the army officers and given the right circumstances could probably prove awkward.'

The woman frowned. 'Does that mean he is also a supporter of the Third Reich? Most of the army colonels are.'

Bischoff parried the question. 'It's not important. What is

65

important is that we secure the presidency for Castillo. Once that is done we can complete our plans.'

Therese looked at him sharply. 'What plans?'

Bischoff shook his head. '*Gnädiges Fräulein bitte*, it does not concern you.'

'Very well, *Herr* Gustav. What are your orders?'

'I want to get in touch with someone near Colonel Perón. He has a chauffeur. I don't know his name but if I could talk to him I am sure he could be persuaded to help.'

Therese nodded. 'I expect that could be arranged. When do you want to see him?'

'As soon as possible. Do you think you could find out who he is by tomorrow night?'

'I should think so. Where shall I bring him?'

Bischoff looked around the darkened room. 'What's wrong with here?'

Since the secret meeting with Perón almost two years previously, Dr Perina had changed. He looked tired and frightened and ten years older. Dr Castillo eyed him coldly.

'Have you seen this? Do you know about it?'

Perina picked up the offending cable and regarded it through the pince-nez he used, anchored by a black silk tape to the buttonhole of his black frock coat lapel. It was from Berlin.

OPERATIVE NOW IN B.A. STOP EXPECT EARLY
DEVELOPMENT STOP OPERATIVE WILL CONTACT
YOU WHEN MISSION COMPLETED STOP CODE
NAME FALLEN CONDOR STOP

He looked helplessly at his boss and flapped his hands.

'Why wasn't I informed of his arrival?' Castillo snapped at the distressed man.

Perina swallowed. 'We are checking everyone coming into the country but it is very difficult.'

'Difficult! Difficult! Of course it is difficult. Why do you think we spend so much money on security? You do know why we spend it, don't you Dr Perina?' Castillo asked sarcastically.

Perina jerked his head up and down.

'Good, then perhaps you will point out to one or two of the people you pay that this is the sort of information that we want. That we would be grateful if they earned their keep or they will be joining the ranks of the unemployable.'

Castillo started signing the mountain of papers on his desk effectively dismissing the old man. Perina opened his mouth to say something but thought better of it and turned away dejectedly and left the room. He wished, as he did several times a day, that he had not let himself become embroiled in the court intrigue that surrounded the pretender to the Presidency.

Lopez Rega locked the door of the small secluded house he had recently bought as a headquarters for his burgeoning interests. As he turned from the door he was aware of a movement to his right. Before he could reach for his gun he felt strong arms encircle him pinning his arms at his side. He lashed back with his foot and made contact. He heard a pained grunt but before he could get in a second kick a bag was drawn over his head and he smelt the sickly sweetness of chloroform.

He tried to hold his breath but a vicious blow to the solar plexus made him suck in the suffocating fumes. A blow to the kidneys knocked him to the ground. He tried to reach up with his hands to pull off the sack but before he could get his hands to the level of his neck he slid over the edge of consciousness.

As soon as Lopez Rega stopped moving Therese came out of the shadow of the corner of the house. She was wearing black slacks and sweater and her blond hair was captured under a dark woollen ski-hat.

'Quickly. Get him into the pick-up. And remember – don't mark his face,' she ordered.

The three men who had waylaid the sergeant picked him up and carried him round the side of the house to a small, unmade service road at the back. They laid him in the open back of a pick-up truck and started covering him with sacks filled with straw. Therese pulled the bag off Lopez Rega's face and examined his eyes. He was deeply drugged but would suffer nothing more than sickness and a headache.

No one spoke as they made their way out of the city and jolted along the lanes leading to the house where Bischoff waited.

A stinging blow across the face dragged Lopez Rega back into consciousness. A hand gripped his chin and he was forced to look into a face. A face that filled him with fear.

'Do you remember me, Sergeant?'

'*Perdón, señor*, I think you make a big mistake. I've not seen you before.'

Bischoff looked at the men standing at the side of Lopez Rega's chair and nodded. One of them held him pressed in the chair while the other came around the front and gave him a pile-driving punch in the stomach.

'Now, do you remember San Juán? I came to see Colonel Perón with two of my men.'

Lopez Rega had to think quickly through the pain throbbing in his stomach and the lingering effects of the chloroform. He let dawning recognition show, '*Ah, si si, señor. El Aleman, si* – I remember.'

'Then you know what happened to me.'

Lopez Rega looked puzzled. 'Happened to you, *Señor*?'

Bischoff stood up and stepped back a few paces.

'Yes, Sergeant. Happened to me. Your friendly colonel tried to kill me.'

Incredulously the prisoner repeated the last words.

The SS man looked at Therese von Quast. 'What do you think?'

She raised her shoulders expressively. 'I don't know. You were there. Did he know what was going on?'

Bischoff sat in a chair opposite and gathered his thoughts. 'How much do you earn a month, sergeant?'

Lopez Rega answered promptly but with a hint of grudge in his voice. 'Twenty-five pesos, *señor*.'

'How would you like to earn a thousand pesos now and then receive another hundred a month, every month?' the German offered.

Lopez Rega let his eyes widen at the mention of such untold wealth. It was only a fraction of what he was already earning from his spy system, prostitution and all the perks he got as the right hand of the most powerful man in the country.

'*Señor*. How do I earn all this money? What do you want me to do?'

'Listen to me carefully, Sergeant Lopez Rega. Colonel Perón has made certain arrangements with the German government. Unfortunately he has not kept his word. I have been sent here to speak to the colonel and remind him of his obligations. The last time I tried to talk to him something very unpleasant happened. It is essential that I talk to him in private. Do you understand.'

Lopez Rega slowly nodded. '*Si, señor.* Where do you want me to bring him?'

Bischoff looked inquiringly at Therese. 'Here,' she said.

'It might be difficult, *señor*. What excuse could I give to bring him here?'

'Where do you suggest, sergeant?' the German asked.

Lopez Rega considered before he spoke. 'Well, Colonel Perón sometimes goes to the Fina Food Factory in Avellaneda to meet with some of the people he is interested in. I could tell him that someone wanted to see him. That happens sometimes.'

Again Bischoff looked around at the girl for confirmation. She didn't answer for a while, just stared at Lopez Rega. He appeared not to notice her and watched the SS man's face, eager to please. At last Therese spoke but there was a hint of doubt in her voice.

'It seems reasonable. If you can trust him.'

Bischoff came to a decision. 'In two days' time you will bring the colonel to the factory. Someone will be in touch with you tomorrow to arrange the details. You will check that the colonel has no other appointments that might

69

interfere and tell him that he has a meeting with whoever you think might convince him to go.'

Bischoff nodded to the two men still standing behind him. 'They will take you back to the city and drop you off wherever you want.' His face went hard. 'Don't try to be clever, sergeant.'

The two men took Lopez Rega by the arms and hustled him to the door. He looked back over his shoulder with an ingratiating smile. 'And the money, *señor*? When do I get the money?'

Bischoff gave a short, ugly laugh and threw the girl a look of smug assurance. 'The money. Yes – of course.' He reached inside his coat, took out his wallet and extracted ten one-hundred-peso notes. 'Here,' he held the notes out, a look of disdain on his face. They watched him in silence while Lopez Rega excitedly counted the notes, naked avarice flushing his face.

Lopez Rega walked ahead of Perón to the packing side of the huge complex that was serviced by the slaughterhouses that bordered a sluggish, evil smelling tributary of the Rio Riachelo. They reached the bottom of a greasy flight of metal stairs and Lopez Rega stood on one side to let Perón go first into a glass-fronted office. Sitting at a desk with his back to them was the dark figure of a man. 'You wanted to see me, *señor*?' Perón asked politely. Slowly the figure turned and leaned forward into a better light.

'Yes, Colonel. That is right. I did want to see you.'

'Bischoff!' Perón reached for his gun but stopped as he felt a hard object dig into his spine.

'Please, Colonel. Do not reach for your gun. Colonel Bischoff only wants to talk to you.'

Perón let his hand drop and Lopez Rega reached around his wide body and took the Luger from its holster and threw it down on the table in front of Bischoff. The German picked it up automatically and checked that it was loaded. He pointed the gun at Perón's stomach.

'Thank you, sergant, you may go now.'

Lopez Rega looked at him sharply. '*Perdón, Coronel*. But I will stay if you don't mind.'

Bischoff rose to his feet. 'You will do as you are told, sergeant, this is an affair between officers. I will see that Colonel Perón is delivered home safely.'

Still Lopez Rega hesitated.

Bischoff shifted the Luger. 'If you do not obey my order you will be shot.'

Lopez Rega raised his shoulders in resignation. '*Si, Coronel*. I go.' He put his gun back in the holster and with an apologetic look at Perón, left.

There was silence for about twenty seconds and then the sharp bark of a shot. Perón half rose to his feet but was motioned back by the SS man.

'That takes care of the sergeant!' he said with a snigger. 'I'm glad we have been able to arrange this meeting, *Herr Oberst*. It's so nice to meet old friends. We were interrupted last time we met. I was forced to leave in a hurry. Perhaps you remember?'

'I'm sorry. It was an unfortunate incident. A terrorist raid. They were looking for me but unfortunately they found you first. I tried to find you afterwards. I am so happy that you were able to escape.'

Bischoff accepted the story gracefully. 'Of course, *Herr Oberst*. I understand. Most unfortunate.' Again he paused, enjoying his cat and mouse game. 'Unfortunate for you as well, *Herr Oberst*. My superiors didn't understand. They felt that you may have had something to do with what happened.'

Perón started to protest but Bischoff cut him short. 'We will forget all that now. Circumstances have changed. We have made arrangements with other factions in Buenos Aires who we feel are in a better position to fulfil their promises.'

Perón leaned forward. 'Who?'

'No less a person than the President,' he said, and watched Perón's reactions.

The Argentinian looked desperately around. 'Castillo.

But I put him in office.'

'He knows that but he feels that what you have done before you can do again – with another candidate.'

Perón drummed with his fingers agitatedly on the desk top. 'But General Lorenz –'

Bischoff cut in with ruthless self-confidence. 'General Lorenz has nothing to do with it. *Reichsleiter* Bormann has put the matter entirely in the hands of *Obergruppenführer* Heydrich now and he has sent me to clear it up once and for all.'

He stood up and raised his hand. 'Now if you would just come downstairs. I have some friends I would like you to meet.'

Perón walked out of the office like a man in a trance. Bischoff followed, the Luger levelled at Perón's back. The Argentinian colonel stopped at the top of the stairs and looked down at four dark figures waiting at the bottom. Bischoff pushed him forward, his face an expressionless mask. Slowly Perón walked down the steps to the waiting men. They closed around him and led him across the factory to the huge conveyor belts that brought the dismembered carcasses into the vats for processing.

'This will do,' Bischoff stopped them. They turned to face him.

He stood in front of Perón and slowly raised his pistol, relishing his moment of triumph. 'Goodbye, *Herr Oberst* Perón.'

Perón straightened himself up to his full height and regarded his executioner evenly. He saw the German's finger tighten on the trigger, saw the flame in the barrel and flinched as the burnt cordite stung his face. The smoke drifted up from the gun. Bischoff's mouth dropped open as Perón stood unhurt, smiling at him.

He fired again and again. Suddenly he realised it was Perón's gun he was using and it was filled with blanks. His hand darted for his own gun in the side pocket of the overcoat he was wearing. Before his hand touched the butt the Argentinian moved with the swiftness of a striking

72

snake. The German felt the bone in his nose break as the iron-hard fist exploded in his face. He slumped to the floor and before he could recover Perón knelt heavily on his chest and removed the pistol from his pocket.

Bischoff screamed at the four men standing, unmoved, to shoot Perón. Instead they swung their guns to cover him. Cowering on the slime covered concrete he felt defeat ebb over him like a corroding tide. Perón waved two of the men forward to help the SS colonel to his feet and then stood back and surveyed him slowly from head to foot. '*Herr Standartenführer* Bischoff, you disappoint me. I rated the SS higher.'

Bischoff heard someone approach from the side. It was Lopez Rega.

'And now, I am afraid, the sergeant wants you to atone for your insults. If I could I would spare you this – as an affair amongst officers . . . But I can't, I'm afraid.' He looked at Lopez Rega. '*Sargento!*'

Lopez Rega came forward drawing a long, silver-handled *facon*, the knife of the *pampa gaucho*, from the back of his belt. '*Mi Coronel!*' he said.

The two men looked in each other's eyes, then Perón laughed and pointed to the huge vat supplied by the conveyor belts.

'Do you know what that is, *Herr Standartenführer*?'

Bischoff's terrified eyes followed the pointing finger.

'It is where the less appetising meat is cooked and turned into corned beef. You will be going home shortly, *Herr Standartenführer*. In little square tins!'

Perón turned and walked from the building without another word. As he climbed into the back of the car he heard Bischoff's terrified scream as Lopez Rega drew his sharp knife across his throat in a ritual *gaucho* execution.

Hidden behind one of the vats Therese watched the bright blood spurt from the German's throat and was quietly sick on the floor.

EIGHT

Colonel Juán Domingo Perón stood, dressed only in his underpants, examining his face in the bathroom mirror. He turned his head to see it in a better light and cursed for the tenth time. His face, neck and chest were lividly decorated with an ugly pattern of red rash and yellow pustules. He poured more mineral water onto the piece of cotton wool he was holding and dabbed at the irritation. Recent events had strained even his iron constitution. He completed his dressing as the doorbell rang.

Mercante was also dressed in uniform. Perón greeted him with a friendly *abrazo* and the two men stood side by side looking out of the long, balconied window at the tops of the stately houses along Avenida Alvear which backed onto the building in Posadas. Perón began the conversation.

'It's time to get rid of Castillo. He spends more of the day preening himself in front of the mirror he's had installed behind a curtain in his office than he does trying to run the country.' He started to finger the swellings on his face and then realised what he was doing and snatched his hand away. 'It's time we had a man from the army in the Casa Rosada. What do you think?' Perón willed himself not to touch his face while he waited for a reply.

'Why the change of plans?'

The big man shrugged. 'It's not a change of plan. Just bringing it forward a few months. You know as well as I do that we have a certain commitment to the Germans, whatever the outcome. I think that if the war does go against them they will try, before long, to establish themselves much more strongly throughout South America. Especially here, in Uruguay and Paraguay where they have a sympathetic public and vast commercial investments. All I am suggesting is that we must protect ourselves so that when the time comes we can do what is best for the *patria*.'

Mercante nodded. '*Bueno*. I have no objections. What do you want me to do?'

Perón paced the room as he spoke. 'First I want you to help me convince the others that we need to move. Next we have to get Castillo to leave without creating too much fuss. Heydrich's assassination shook him and Martin Bormann has been on to me privately. It seems he didn't share Heydrich's preference for the President and wants to renegotiate with us. That's his story anyway. He has agreed to let the past be buried and wants urgent, secret talks about Argentine–German co-operation.' Perón dropped his oratorical style and lowered his voice confidentially. 'This is where you can be a big help. This has got to go through without a hitch. You are the only one I can trust. I want you to take a few of the other officers to see Castillo and convince him that unless he makes himself scarce he will find himself under arrest and charged with misappropriation of public funds and corruption of civic officials. We know enough about his administration to make a charge stick.'

The two colonels sat in silence for a few seconds while Mercante considered. '*Bueno, che*. I'll do it.' He hesitated. 'And who is to replace him?'

Perón raised an eyebrow and looked at his co-conspirator. 'Do you want me to offer you the job?' he asked.

Hastily Mercante shook his head. Perón walked back to the window before answering. 'Ramirez! Have you any objections?'

Mercante slowly shook his head. 'No objections. It just seems that we are going to a lot of trouble to exchange one self-opinionated pro-Nazi for another.'

'But an army man. It makes a difference.'

Mercante nodded acceptance.

Perón's acne-fevered face split into a wide, satisfied grin. He grabbed his friend's hand and pumped it enthusiastically. '*Macanudo! Macanduo!* A drink to celebrate?' He turned to the sideboard and poured a whisky for Mercante and red wine for himself. He held his glass up in the toast. 'To the new President!' he proposed.

'To the New Argentina!' Mercante suggested, softly. Perón nodded tolerantly.

'That goes without saying, *ché*!'

'When do you want me to see Castillo?'

'Give it about a fortnight. I'll organise the *junta* that will do the actual takeover.'

Lopez Rega had made her an unlikely conquest.

Therese, weak and ill, had been discovered crouched behind one of the giant pieces of equipment in the abattoir. His first inclination was to kill her and feed her into the vat with the German, but her pale, Saxon beauty had saved her. Not for the sergeant. He was well aware that emotional attachments could be dangerous and had rigidly schooled himself to avoid the pitfalls of romance. But he knew the sexual proclivities of his fellow Argentinians. Especially the upper-class men who believed that women were made for their gratification.

Therese von Quast could do a lot of gratifying and, if she could be handled correctly, provide an interesting and valuable addition to his spreading net of spies. She had obviously seen what had happened to Bischoff. Her immediate instinct would be to report it, either to the police or to Berlin. It was her connections with Berlin that had convinced him a little application might be worthwhile. If he couldn't get her co-operation he could still get rid of her later. If her indoctrination went well it might mean a secret pipeline for him into SS Headquarters.

It took him time to complete her subjugation. With beatings and threats of torture, and even death if she refused to co-operate, he made her write to her uncle telling him that she had gone away to the *estancia* of a friend and would not be back for a while. Then she had telephoned her uncle and told him that Señor Gustav had finished his business and left for Montevideo. She also told him that the SS colonel had asked her to forward Lopez Rega's name to Berlin as a possible contact close to the coming man, Colonel Perón. Gradually he began to make her feel less threatened. He brought her flowers and arranged for special food to be sent in. Before long Therese was coming under his spell. As soon as he saw the signs he reverted to the bully, beating her for the smallest offence, fancied or real. With a mixture of kindness and cruelty he made her his creature. After two months he was ready to try her out.

He arrived at the house one afternoon looking worried. Without explanation he told the guards, who constantly watched over her, to leave. Therese was surprised but had learned that it was safer to keep quiet. If her captor wanted to tell her something he would get to it in his own time.

Lopez Rega let a shudder run through his body. He looked up at the attentive woman and said in a subdued, defeated voice, 'Okay *chica*. You can leave.'

She looked at him suspiciously and then at the half open door. She didn't know what to think. It might be a trap.

Slowly she walked to the door and looked out. There was no-one about. She looked back at Lopez Rega slumped in the chair. Every cell in her body wanted to break into a wild rush and get out of the house that had been her prison for so long. But the sergeant had done his job well. Long practice with other women whom he had introduced into the sleazy world of prostitution had stood him in good stead.

Therese took the fatal step back into the room and was lost. 'What is wrong, "Daniel"?' she asked, using the occult name he preferred to the more mundane José.

He looked up startled. As if surprised that she was still there. 'Nothing to worry you *linda*,' he answered in a soft voice. 'I have a problem. That is all.'

Therese ventured to sit by his feet and put her head on his knee. 'Poor "Daniel". Can I help?' she asked.

Lopez Rega stroked her hair. '*Gracias, chica*, but I'm afraid not.'

There was silence for a minute then Lopez Rega said softly, 'Maybe. There is something you could do.' He slid his hand down the front of the open neck blouse she was wearing and fondled her breasts.

She sighed and pressed against him. 'Tell me what I can do to help,' she breathed.

Lopez Rega, with suitable reluctance, told her that he had reason to believe that a certain officer had found out his part in Bischoff's death. He had proof and intended to present it to his commanding officer in the morning. Although he himself enjoyed high-level protection, Lopez Rega said, there was nothing to be done if the case was put into official records. It meant arrest and imprisonment. Unless he could get his hands on the evidence.

Therese agreed to entertain the officer while the sergeant searched his flat. Lopez Rega made the introduction by the simple expedient of giving her an envelope which she was to deliver to the officer, a willing accomplice in the experiment.

Two men followed her when she left the house. They had orders to kill her, preferably by arranging an accident, if she tried to contact anyone else. At the officer's flat, Lopez Rega installed himself in a spare room and waited.

He heard Therese arrive and sat patiently while the eager seducer did his work and then left by the back entrance when sounds from the bedroom indicated that his work on the young woman had not been wasted.

Shortly after this he had arranged for her to meet a young member of the ubiquitous de Benedetti family, one of the richest and most influential in Argentina. The connection quickly came alive. Her fair complexion, blond hair and German ancestry soon made her a firm favourite and before long she was spending weekends at the family's far flung *estancias*. She was able to report back to Lopez Rega which people were sympathetic to the government and who was for the coming confrontation with the armed forces. He in turn reported faithfully to Perón.

Dr Perina sat in the small office on the second floor of the Casa Rosada. His stomach contracted as the telephone gave

out a flat, low burr. He took a deep breath, pulled tog\
the tattered remains of dignity and went to attend
President.

As soon as he entered the room he realised that the day
that they had both feared had arrived. Castillo was slumped
in the engulfingly ornate chair behind the wide presidential
desk, a sombre speck of deflated humanity in a rich setting
that embalmed him.

'It seems that Colonel Mercante's predictions are about to
become true. I have been asked to submit my resignation by
four o'clock this afternoon.' His voice sounded near to
tears. 'It's Perón of course,' Castillo continued in a calmer
voice. Perina didn't feel called on to reply.

'It's an impossible task. The Army want me to declare
war on the Allies and the *estancieros* want me to side with
them. They can't understand that neutrality is the best way
for Argentina. So what should I do?' He stopped in front of
Perina and glared. 'What can I do?'

Perina tried to think of something to say but couldn't.

Castillo was talking to himself. 'Perhaps if I go to Perón
and make an agreement. He promised me the presidency. If
I agree to go along with him perhaps we can work something out.' Talking seemed to calm him. He sat back behind
his desk and pulled a pad of paper towards him.

'Perina. I want you to take this note to Colonel Perón
yourself. Make whatever arrangements you can for a meeting. Get him to call off the ultimatum while we discuss our
mutual interests.'

Castillo's voice had become firmer now. He was writing
rapidly when the door opened and Captain Juarez came in,
red with excitement.

'*Señor Presidente*. There is a man here with an urgent
message from *Coronel* Mercante.'

Perina looked back at the President. He was on his feet
staring. He tried to speak but could not persuade his vocal
cords to co-operate. He knew now that his defiant act of
writing a letter to Perón was nothing more than a hollow
gesture. For a few seconds he had fooled himself into

believing that he could outsmart the strong forces closing in on him.

A tall figure in a dark grey suit appeared behind Juarez. He didn't wait to be introduced but quickly rushed across to the President and came to attention.

'*Perdón, mi Presidente, Capitán* Carrusso. *Coronel* Mercante presents his compliments and most urgently urges you to leave while there is still time. Arrangements have been made for your safe conduct to Uruguay. *Coronel* Mercante has taken the liberty of placing a boat at your disposal with a loyal crew to take you to a place of safety. *Coronel* Mercante will contact you there.'

President Castillo tried to summon up some dignity but failed. He picked up a briefcase that he had already packed by the side of his desk and prepared to leave.

'Where do I go, *Capitán*?' he asked, misery thickening his voice.

'I have been instructed to escort you, *Presidente*. There is a car outside the rear entrance with half a dozen soldiers to see you are not molested.' Without waiting further, Castillo headed for the door. Perina watched him go with relief. He had been afraid that he might have been included in the invitation to exile. Now he could retire to his little *quinta* in the country and forget his precarious venture into politics.

He carefully placed the file he carried on the President's desk and quietly left the Casa Rosada for good.

Perón remembered the overthrow of Hippolito Irigoyen in 1930. At one time it had been touch and go. The President had refused to budge from his office. The once great old man's stand had produced a waver in the resolution of some of the more conservative officers that could have grown and frustrated the aims of the revolution.

Perón remembered, with a faint smile, how he had convinced the geriatric President to leave for gentler pastures. While the others talked in hushed whispers, trying to make up their minds on the course to take, the young Captain Perón had picked up the head of a statue of Irigoyen that had been knocked off in the attack, and heaved it through the window.

There had been no more resistance.

Perón brought his thoughts back to the present, 4 June 1943. He was disturbed by reports coming in of the resistance at the naval college and sporadic fighting elsewhere. He had been assured by Admiral Lima that the navy would not interfere with the overthrow of Castillo. He would not commit his service to active participation, preferring to stay a spectator for the present time. That had been all that Perón had wanted. He regretted the fighting. It was a foolish waste of life that would be a hook for anyone looking for a cause on which to hang their spurs.

He pushed the unpleasant thought to one side. The outcome was inevitable.

A lieutenant brought in a radio and plugged it into the socket. 'General Rawson is making a speech from the Casa Rosada, *Coronel*, would you like to hear it?' he asked politely. Perón smilingly nodded. He liked Rawson. A bluff hearty soldier who could be relied upon to do as he was told.

The set warmed up and Rawson's distorted voice filled the room. He was in a state of near-hysteria. Never before had he been exposed to the heady drug of crowd adulation. Perón's smile froze as he heard the general's closing remarks.

'Also – *Argentinos*, I pledge myself to bring about the glorious future I have promised. The army is the servant of the people. It will jealously guard the hopes and aspirations of all our comrades in the fight for Utopia which we have begun today. The task will be long and arduous. But we must not flinch or let our ideals be tarnished by adversity. As guardian of these ideals I humbly accept the enormous task as Chief Executive of the nation.'

At his announcement the crowd lifted its compound voice in wild adulation. Tears sprung unchecked from the general's eyes and ran down his leathered cheeks unashamed. He raised his arms above his head once more and stepped back into the office he had just claimed as his own. He was still in a bemused state of detachment when the telephone on the desk rang. One of his officers smartly stepped forward and answered it. He had to speak three times to the general before claiming his attention. 'General. *Coronel* Perón would like to speak to you.'

General Rawson looked at the proffered telephone uncomprehendingly. Then it sank in. His eyes widened and he looked, almost fearfully, at the balcony. He took the telephone and sat for a few seconds staring blankly at it trying to think of something to say.

At last he overcome his reluctance.

'*Si*, General Rawson here.'

Perón's voice came on the line, cold and distant.

'Good afternoon, General. I have to congratulate you, I understand. According to what I heard on the radio you have just become the twenty-sixth President of Argentina.'

Rawson looked at the other men in the room but got no comfort from that quarter. 'Yes, well. I . . . er . . . I didn't mean . . . I'm afraid I got carried away . . .' he stuttered. 'Would you like me to go and make another announcement?'

Perón was relieved that he wasn't going to have trouble with Rawson. He had thought for a moment that the general had made an ill-conceived bid to out-trump him. If he had wanted to hang on to the presidency it would have taken some time to unseat him.

'No. Not now. We will leave it overnight. Then tomorrow you can make the announcement that you are resigning in favour of Ramirez. It might not be a bad thing at that.'

Rawson agreed eagerly. He wasn't cut out for president but had enjoyed his brief hour on the balcony. Now he wanted to submerge himself in the ordered army life that suited him.

'Very well, *Coronel*. I'm sorry if this has in any way upset the aims of our society.'

Perón laughed pleasantly. 'Not at all, General. We are all very pleased with your handling of the situation. I will call in to see you later this evening and we will talk about how we shall handle the announcement. *Hasta luego, Presidente.*'

'*Hasta luego, Coronel,*' Rawson responded gravely.

As soon as Perón put the telephone down he pushed back his chair and roared with laughter. Mercante arrived with a report from the *fracas* of the naval college. He had heard about Rawson's *faux pas* and was surprised to find Perón so amused.

Perón slapped him on the back. '*Chè*! It just goes to prove that every *Argentino* can be president. Rawson today, Ramirez tomorrow, you the day after and my Aunt Clarida the day after that.'

The next day Rawson stood on the balcony that had proved his undoing the day before and formally handed over the presidency to his brother-in-arms, General Ramirez. Perón was to wish in the future that he had let the arrangement stand as it was.

NINE

Eva Duarte was bored.

She rested her elbows on the table and let her eyes drift aimlessly about the restaurant. She ignored the assured grins and winks of unaccompanied men at other tables. The restaurant was one of the middle-class eating houses catering for the German community scattered throughout the city. It was patronised in the late evening almost entirely by businessmen and army officers feeding their girlfriends and mistresses.

Although Eva's attention wandered, it was not apparent to her companion. With a skill learned at a long succession of late dinners, she nodded and smiled on cue, automatically gauging the reaction required. She was dressed fashionably in a dark blue, tight satin dress with squared shoulders and a gathered neckline. The skirt fitted skin-tight over her slightly plump thighs and was a fraction shorter than good taste demanded.

Her blond hair was piled in heavy sweeps onto the top of her head in a slavish imitation of Lana Turner. Scarlet lipstick made a feature of her well-shaped mouth and the paleness of her hollow cheeks was covered by a layer of dark powder and rouge.

Eva's companion was typical of many of the men in the smoky restaurant. Over sixty, suntanned, wearing a well cut suit, he talked volubly to his young guest. Don Attilio Vernet was a leading cosmetic manufacturer. Reaching the age of retirement now he found it daily harder to impose his will on his three sons who now managed the day to day running of his business.

Eva was suddenly aware that Don Attilio had stopped talking and was looking at her expectantly. She hadn't a clue what he had been talking about but correctly guessed it was another woeful tale of his sons' lack of respect. She smiled sympathetically and stroked his face gently.

'*Pobre cito*,' she cooed.

Gratefully the old man took her hand and held it to his lips. He liked her and treated her like a friend. When they had first met he had felt impelled to put on a show designed to impress the young girl. Eva had soon put him straight.

He was relieved that she was willing to bolster his ego in public without demanding satisfaction in the bedroom. The arrangement protracted his hard-earned reputation as a ladies' man and gave him a pleasant listener to dispel the mounting feeling of inadequacy that old age and three thoughtless sons engendered.

Eva had also welcomed the undemanding union. Since arriving in Buenos Aires, seven years before, her constant search for work in theatre and radio had exposed her to every tinpot impresario and director along the glamorous Calle Corrientes. It didn't bother her morally. She found it amusing, in a sad way, that men could be so infantile that they demanded five sweaty minutes on the studio couch as the tax on a part in one of their productions. But it didn't endear them to her.

Lately things had been better. The radio work helped. Jaime Yankelevich, the emigré Russian who ran Radio Belgrano, was giving her more work and he wasn't demanding body-tax. The money wasn't good but at least it was constant and gave her a basic income. She still had a little money left from the bit-part she had in one of the interminable love sagas spewing out of the cutting rooms of Sona Films. But it wasn't stardom.

Attilio touched her hand. 'Shall we go my dear?'

She nodded and picked up her crocodile handbag.

'*Momentito, corazón.* I have to see to my hair.'

Politely the old man half rose as she left and then called the waiter for the bill. When Eva returned Don Attilio was speaking to a short, aggressive man in an off-white linen suit. She recognised him vaguely.

Eva turned on her warmest smile as she approached the table and hoped that the ladder in her nylons didn't show. Attilio said something to the other man and they half turned as Eva arrived.

'Eva, *querida*, I would like to present an old friend of mine, Colonel Imbert. You may have heard of him. He works in the Ministry of Communications.'

Eva took the proffered hand and put the full force of her personality into the blazing smile she turned on the tubby army officer. Of course she had heard of him. He was one of the band of officers close to President Ramirez who had been rewarded for his part in the recent revolution by his present ministerial position. She felt her pulse race. It was the sort of introduction she had been angling for since she had come to the city.

Vernet took her hand possessively to show his prior claim on her favours. Irritated, Eva snatched it away and concentrated on the Colonel.

'Of course, *Coronel*. I have seen you at the radio station,' she said, carefully enunciating her words to hide the provincial accent she had paid dearly to eliminate.

The colonel looked mildly interested. 'Radio station, *Señorita*? Which one is that?'

Eva had hoped that he might have heard of her. 'Radio Belgrano,' she prompted.

'Ah!' Imbert said. 'You work there?'

She nodded brightly. 'Yes. I'm an actress.'

Again Imbert smiled politely and then turned back to Attilio Vernet. 'Well, nice to see you again.' He shook the old man's hand and bowed formally to Eva then made his way through the tables to a group of friends.

Eva watched him go, her mind seething in an effort to find an excuse for prolonging the meeting. Don Attilio took her arm and gently guided her out onto the pavement. As they walked through the tables surrounding the outside of the restaurant Eva questioned her escort about his friend Colonel Imbert. They had known each other for years. Imbert was the son of an old school friend and had been briefly attracted to his oldest daughter. Now he was married but had no children. Lately he had become heavily committed to the new Officers' Corps that was running Argentina.

Eva made up her mind. There had been many occasions when she had met someone who appeared to have the necessary standing to help her. Usually they were either not as powerful as they claimed or were unwilling, once they had got what they wanted, to give her the push she needed.

She thought she could do something with the introverted colonel. In the car driving along the broad, elegant avenues she slid closer to Don Attilio and rested her head on his shoulder.

'Attilio, *mi vida*, I want to meet Colonel Imbert again. He could be very useful to me at the radio station. You know what a pig Yankelevich is. If he knew Imbert was a friend of mine he would have to give me more work.'

Attilio protested 'He is giving you more work now. I told him when I let him have the contract for the soap commercial that I wanted you to star in the show.'

Eva patted his hand. 'I know, *mi vida*, it was terribly sweet of you. But you know Yankelevich. As soon as he has got your money he will think up all sorts of reasons for not honouring his word. If he knew Imbert was interested in my career it would be a different matter.'

Vernet felt jealousy burrow into his stomach. It was an emotion he hadn't felt for a long time and made him realise how much he had come to depend on his sessions with the little actress.

'I suppose you have got all you want out of me now,' he said, self-pity shaping his words.

Again Eva squeezed his hand. 'Don't be silly, Don Attilio. You know I am really grateful for everything you have done for me. But this is business. My profession. You wouldn't want me to give that up, would you?'

'Why not?' Vernet jumped in. 'I could look after you. Set you up in a house somewhere nice. Then we would be able to spend more time together.'

The suggestion sent a cold shiver through Eva's body. It

was the past all over again. She had seen her mother turned out with her four children when her 'protector' had died. Eva was one of the children of that liaison and was determined not to follow in her mother's shuffling footsteps.

'And your wife?' she said coldly.

Vernet looked at her, amazed that she should mention his wife. He thought it bad taste that his little *casa chica* should bring up the subject of his wife at all.

'My wife?' he asked incredulously.

'Yes,' Eva snapped. 'Do you intend to run a *ménage-à-trois?*'

Vernet hastily changed the subject. 'How can I introduce you to Imbert? I haven't seen him for months. Probably won't see him again for months either.'

'Telephone him, suggesting a meeting.'

She thought for a while. 'Better still. Tell him that I have a project to discuss with him. A radio programme. Something to do with the army. Anything you can think of. Give him my number at Radio Belgrano.' Her companion reluctantly agreed.

President Ramirez sat in the ornate office that had been the temporary bastion of power for the long line of presidents who had flitted erratically through Argentine political life for nearly a century.

So far he had not had any trouble from Perón. When Ramirez handed out the favours after the Coup he had been surprised that the enterprising colonel who had organised it wanted only the comparatively minor position of Secretary to the War Ministry. General Farrell, another leading member of the GOU, moved into the seat, vacated by Ramirez himself, of Minister of War.

Cut off from the day-to-day working of the army, Ramirez had only been vaguely aware of what was going on behind the scene. His own informers told him of the mounting labour unrest, the general hardening against the Axis cause, the discontent about the rising prices, but

88

nothing about Perón. Nothing of any significance, anyway. Ramirez picked up the foolscap sheet in front of him and read it through carefully for the fourth time. He was sure that there was a hidden significance that obstinately evaded his scrutiny. Why would Perón, an army officer with power far in excess of his rank, want to take on a rubber-stamp job with no political standing? He would soon know what it was all about. Perón was due for an audience. As he thought about it there was a sharp rap on the door and his ADC came in.

'Colonel Perón has arrived, *Presidente*.'

Ramirez waved his hand to show in the visitor and walked to the door to meet him. Perón saluted smartly before removing his hat and shaking the President's hand. 'So good of you to see me, *Presidente*.'

Ramirez waved his thanks aside and asked his ADC Major Moráez to pour some drinks. When the major had left Ramirez came straight to the point. 'My dear Perón. I have seen your request to be offered the post in the Secretariat of Labour and Welfare and frankly I am puzzled. It seems hardly an ample reward for your strenuous work on behalf of the army and the country. Surely there is something more suited to your talents that you could take on?'

Perón appeared to consider the President's words for a few moments. He gave his superior officer the benefit of his white, filmstar smile. 'Truth is, my work appears to be about finished. My job at the War Ministry hardly takes any of my time now that General Farrell has taken over. I did think of going back to the Academy. Maybe I'll do that later. Right now I want a job that's not going to give me too many headaches. Had a touch of ulcer problem lately.' He smiled ruefully. 'I seem to be falling apart. Need a good rest.'

President Ramirez pursed his lips and nodded sympathetically. He wanted to believe the story Perón was giving him.

'Well, if that is what you want, Juán, of course it is yours.

89

It isn't a full ministry but it could do some useful work at the moment. Is there anything else I can do?'

Perón graciously took the enquiry as a dismissal and rose. 'Thank you, *Presidente*, that is all I came for – unless you can suggest an alternative I will move my office into the Secretariat of Labour.'

Ramirez agreed. 'Of course, my dear Perón. *Che* – I am sure there is ample accommodation there.' The two clasped hands like old friends and Perón let the major show him out.

His limousine was waiting at the side entrance. The driver opened the door and gave him a smart salute as he approached. Lopez Rega only drove him on special occasions now. He was much too valuable in other, more delicate, matters, to waste his time as a chauffeur. 'The Secretariat of Labour in Las Heras,' Perón ordered.

The Secretariat was housed in a low, ugly building faced with dirty concrete in square, unattractive blocks. The side street it skulked in came from nowhere and went nowhere. Inside the building was even more depressing. Low wattage, sparsely placed bulbs did little to combat the gathering dusk. There was a short, smelly lobby covered with graffiti that opened into a large dusty room without the relief of one spot of colour. It was bisected by a heavy, wooden counter guarded by a three-foot grill.

On the other side of the desk were half a dozen or so tables and about the same number of scratched filing cabinets. In spite of the people waiting to be attended at the counter, the pace behind was lethargic and the manner abrupt. Perón took off his hat so that he would not be too noticeable in the dim light and sat on one of the rickety folding chairs along the walls.

The workers around the hall noticed his uniform and gradually the word spread. Perón took out a cigarette and puffed contentedly at it as he examined the crowd of labourers waiting for attention. Most were obviously newly arrived in the city. Probably straight off the *pampa* looking for the crock of gold that was whispered on the wind to be waiting in Buenos Aires. They didn't look much but, if he had read the mood of the country right, they were ripe for picking. He winked at a big, unshaven man who pushed his way to the front of the gathering crowd and was standing over him belligerently.

Perón took out his gold cigarette case and offered it to the man standing in front of him. The workman looked at it suspiciously but then overcame his misgivings and helped himself. The colonel took another himself and then offered the case to those nearest him. Within seconds the gold case was empty. Perón took out his lighter and applied the flame to the dark, savage faces pushing forward. He gave them one of his sunniest smiles.

'*Buenos tardes, Señores.* I hope you haven't had to wait long. If you would just give me a few moments I'll see what can be done. I'm afraid I'm a new boy here so it might take me a minute or two to grasp what has to be done but bear with me.'

He smiled his friendly smile at the big man still barring his way. 'What is your name, *che*?' Perón used the familiarity without a hint of condescension.

'Gordia!' the man answered truculently.

'Well, Señor Gordia. If you would ask these other gentlemen to line up in four queues at the desk I will see that you are all attended to as quickly as possible.'

As he finished speaking a handbell began to ring. The destitute workers seemed to sag as the bell rang on their hopes for finding employment for another day. Perón looked enquiringly at Gordia. 'Closing time,' he said viciously. 'Now we all go and try to find somewhere to sleep.'

'Stop anyone leaving,' Perón snapped and pushed through the crowd to the counter and leaped onto it. The crowd had sensed something unusual happening. The grumbling that had followed the bell quieted and Perón saw the faces turn towards him.

'*Señores. Por favor.* If you would just wait for a few moments, I am sure we will be able to sort something out for you.'

He felt a hand tug at his trouser leg and looked down.

An elderly man in a civil-service rig peered anxiously over his glasses at him. The noise in the room rose as men started shouting at Perón, trying to attract his attention. He couldn't hear what the man behind the counter was saying. That he was annoyed was obvious. Perón glanced behind him. All the clerks were on their feet staring with fright-filled eyes at the growling mass on the other side of the counter and at the tall, handsome officer straddling the protective grill.

Exhilaration throbbed like a tangible force in Perón's body. Suddenly he felt invincible. One-handed, he reached down and grasped the complaining manager by the back of his coat collar and heaved him up beside him. A howl of laughter that rapidly turned to something deadlier went up when the hungry men saw their enemy manhandled. There was a surge forward. The office manager was terrified. Perón's strong wrist held him in place. Over the top of the shouting heads he could see Gordia still guarding the door.

The colonel gave him an urgent wave and, as the big man pushed through the crowd, held up his hands for silence. Gordia sprang onto the counter beside Perón and also held up his hands. Seeing one of their own backing the colonel the crowd gradually quietened until only the occasional, yelled question broke the silence as the roused labourers waited for the next act in the totally unexpected drama to commence.

Perón looked them over. If these men were typical of the millions of workers throughout the country it only needed the right incentive to weld them into a force that no opposition could break.

'Señores. If you will just give me a few moments with the manager I am sure we will be able to look after your problems in a satisfactory manner. Señor Gordia here –' He indicated the man beside him. 'Will look after you. Just do as he says and then everything will be got through as quickly as possible.' He handed the manager down off the counter and then repeated his instructions to Gordia to organise the waiting men into lines so that they could be dealt with as expediously as possible.

He vaulted down from the counter. 'Where is your office?' he demanded of the terrified manager who pointed, speechless, to a glass-sided cubicle at the back of the general office. Perón nodded towards it and then turned to the clerks huddled around staring at him in a state of shock.

'All right. Don't worry. Get everything out on the desk tops that will help us sort out these people's problems. I will just have a brief word with the manager and then we will get down to work.'

He embraced the clerks with a confident smile and strode after the manager. The poor man was slumped, shaking like an aspen, in his chair. In his whole life the most exciting thing he had ever done was buy a ticket in the lottery.

'Snap out of it, man. What's your name?'

The manager looked at him, his eyes brimming with tears. 'Who are you?' he whispered.

Perón slapped his hand down hard on the desk. 'It doesn't matter who I am. You have a mob out there who will tear this place apart unless you do something about it. Now, what's your name?'

'Costen, Emanuel Costen, *Señor Coronel*. What can I do – it's not my fault.'

Perón pressed the point. 'Come on now, Señor Costen. I'm sure we can soon sort this out together. What is the main trouble?'

Costen spread his hands. 'There is no work, *Señor Coronel*. Every day there are more workers coming here looking for work. There is no organisation. We send them to other parts of the city and then they tell them to come back to us. But it is not our job to find them work. We are here to co-ordinate the employment service throughout all of Argentina.'

Perón nodded understanding. 'Right, now we can start.'

Costen looked up in surprise. It was not usual for military personnel to get mixed up in labour problems, especially high-ranking officers who walked in off the street. The

93

colonel saw the look of surprise and laughed.

'Don't worry, Señor Costen. We are all in this together, I'm the new boss. Now, let's talk to a few people.' He walked out of the glass box leaving the flabbergasted manager to follow in his wake.

Without preamble Perón jumped back on the counter. It wasn't Mussolini's balcony and he didn't need built-up heels to impress the small crowd but he sensed that this was only a small rehearsal for what was to come. He held up his hands to silence the buzz of conversation that had risen on his reappearance.

'*Señores*. Your attention please. I have just been appointed to look after you by the President. He is aware of the hard time you have been having and has decided to do something about it.' He stopped and looked down at his smart uniform. 'Don't be put off by the gear I'm wearing. Underneath I'm just a workman.' Again he stopped and looked around. 'Any of you from Patagonia?'

There were shouts from two or three people in the crowd. Perón looked towards one of the men holding his hand above his head.

'Welcome to Buenos Aires, *Che*! You won't find the streets paved with gold but there is plenty of work to be done although you might not believe it at the moment. But we're not frightened of work are we?' He looked around at the rest of them. 'I can vouch for my *compadres* from Patagonia but what about the rest of you? Do you want to work for the *Patria* or are you here because you have heard that there are easy pickings to be had in the city?'

There were cries from the hall denying that they were there for any other reason than to work.

Perón laughed and held up his hands again for silence. '*Bueno, Muchachos*. Remember that I only want men who are prepared to work hard for a fair wage. If that's too much for you – now is the time to go back where you came from and tell the *estancieros* you are prepared to be good boys.'

There was a roar of laughter.

'You are still here? Well, you had your chance. If it's work you want it's work you are going to get.'

Just as he was about to leap down there was a commotion at the back of the hall. The double doors burst open and a detachment of blue-uniformed policemen, led by a police lieutenant, burst in and quickly lined the walls, covering the excited workers with their riot guns. They had been summoned by the manager of one of the other offices who had been frightened by the unaccustomed noise coming from the labour office.

Perón again held up his hand. 'Quiet everybody. I called for the police. They are here to help you. *Teniente*. Come here please. I want to talk to you.'

Perón held out his hand. The lieutenant regarded it without moving for a minute, completely at a loss, then tentatively reached out to shake hands. The colonel gripped it and almost picked him up bodily on to the counter. A cheer went up from the men and Perón saw the policemen relax slightly.

'What's your name, *Teniente*?' Perón growled at him as the policeman stood beside him.

'Gauna, *Coronel*,' he answered.

Once more Perón called for silence. '*Teniente* Gauna has been asked to give us what help he can to find you suitable lodgings for the night and get you to work as soon as you are fixed up.'

There was a hum of conversation as the amazed men commented to each other on the totally unexpected turn of events. Perón took advantage of the noise to whisper urgently in Gauna's ear. 'Tell your men to put up their arms and relax. Get some of them back behind the counter to help and tell the rest to leave.'

He once more got down from the counter. The steel grill was a psychological barrier more than a practical one.

'*Teniente*. Get a couple of your men to dismantle this grill. It gets in the way.'

Perón turned and walked back towards the glass cubicle at the back. The policeman shrugged his shoulders and did what he was told. By tomorrow he guessed he would be a hero or back on the beat. As Perón passed a youngster he clapped him on the shoulder. There was too much noise to speak. He pointed to the little office and indicated that he should follow.

'What's your name?' he asked the boy.

'Delgado, *Señor Coronel*. Pablo Delgado.'

'*Bueno*, Pablo. There are a few things I want you to do for me.'

Delgado nodded eagerly.

'First I want you to ring this number,' he turned to the desk and jotted down a telephone number on a piece of paper. 'Ask for *Sargento* Lopez Rega. Tell the operator that it is vitally urgent that he is contacted immediately. Tell him that Colonel Perón says he must come here immediately. Immediately, you understand? It doesn't matter what else he is doing. Next tell that man out front, Gordia, that I want to see him. Then go to the nearest café and tell them to send sandwiches and coffee and whatever else you can get. Take one of the policemen with you. Don't take any argument. If you haven't got enough supplies insist they send out for whatever they need.'

Delgado was looking at the colonel, puzzled by the order.

'What's the matter?' Perón asked.

'*Perdón, mi Coronel, pero* . . . who is the food for? How much must I get?'

Perón laughed and held his arms out to embrace the whole room. '*Todos, muchacho*. Everyone.'

Delgado's eyes widened as he looked at the crowded office. 'The workmen as well, *Coronel*?' he asked unbelievingly.

'*TODOS!* Pablo. *Todos!*'

Delgado ducked his head in acknowledgement of the order. Then Perón swung round to the manager cowering behind a desk that had suddenly become too big for him.

'And now, Señor Costen. What are we going to do?'

Costen stared at him fearfully, tears in his eyes. It was just as he had expected. Now that the big man had turned his secure world on its head he expected him to sort it out.

'Do, *Coronel*? What can we do? There is no work for them. I can't manufacture jobs.' His words were drowned by a cheer from the outer office as the sweating policemen finally managed to tear down the metal barrier.

Perón looked pointedly at the excited men crowding the counter. 'Tell them that,' he said flatly and turned and walked out of the office.

Costen watched fearfully to see what the maniac in an officer's uniform would do next. He saw the colonel approach the group of clerks and start talking to them, emphasising his points with short punchlike movements of his heavy hands. Perón was enjoying himself.

'Right, have we got full files on all these men?' One or two of the clerks overcame their fear and shook their heads. 'Well, that's the first thing to do. You four.' He pointed to four of the least mesmerised clerks. 'Start taking down the details. Age, address, where they are from, what sort of work they are used to, dependants, you know the form. A complete dossier on each man.' He frowned.

'And remember – they are workers just like the rest of us. They want the chance to contribute, to do their bit for the country. So treat them with respect. Show them you care. Smile at them. I don't want to see any officiousness. If you can't do it you can give me your notice immediately.'

He let a friendly smile chase away the frown. 'Okay, gentlemen. Any questions?' Nobody said anything so he clapped his hands and waved them to the counter. He looked the others over.

'The rest of you make sure that they get all the help they want. I've sent out for some refreshments. See that the customers get what they want first and then, if there is any left over, divide it up amongst yourselves.'

When Lopez Rega arrived an hour later Colonel Perón was in his shirt sleeves serving sandwiches and hot *empanadas* to the crowd of men waiting their turn to give their details to the clerks.

The sergeant was in uniform and had been surprised by the warm reception the crowd had given him when he turned up in the staff car with the corporal. The crowd had somehow got the news that something exciting was happening inside and it was swelling by the moment.

As soon as Perón saw him he handed the tray to one of the policemen and drew Lopez Rega into the glass cubicle. 'What's happening, Colonel?' the sergeant asked in amazement.

Perón threw himself in the chair grinning like a schoolboy. 'Happening, *Sargento*?' he said with mock innocence. 'I'm just getting jobs for a few friends.'

Lopez Rega understood. He had wondered when his boss was going to take advantage of the huge labour support he had been busily fostering while the colonel consolidated his position with the army. 'I want work for all the men out there. Starting tomorrow.'

Lopez Rega was startled. 'By tomorrow, *Coronel*? But where?'

'Get Cipriano Reyes on it. Tell him he has to absorb that lot right away. Tomorrow there will be four times as many as the news gets out. I want all the union chiefs here to see me tomorrow. Not all at once. Spread them out through the day. They have been sitting on their fat arses long enough. Then I want a few specially chosen men to go around the factories and shops and explain our need for more job vacancies. No violence. No threats. Just explain the situation to everyone and ask for their co-operation. Keep records on each place you visit. Who's co-operative. Who's being unhelpful and so on. Explain that the government are meeting with all the unions and want their support. You probably won't get a lot of co-operation but at least we will have given them a chance. I also want to have a meeting with the chief of police. Don't take no as an answer from anyone. You have backing right up to the President.' He grinned again.

'He just doesn't know it yet.'

TEN

Therese von Quast opened her eyes and rolled over on her back. In the dim light of the stabbing slats of sunlight lacing the room her naked body made a dark surrealist pattern against the white sheets.

She wanted to get back to Buenos Aires. When Armando de Benedetti had asked her to come along on a business trip she had jumped at the chance. The prospect of ten days or so in the hot Brazilian sun had excited her. She felt that if she could just lie in the sand for a while she could straighten out her head.

Lopez Rega still dominated her thoughts. She didn't love him, that was for sure. What drove her mad was the degradation she felt at not being able to break the spell. Her emotions were in such a turmoil that the planned holiday with Armando had been a disaster.

Even before the plane landed in Sao Paolo ice had formed on their relationship. Therese knew it had been her fault. Packing the evening before they left she had been deliriously happy. Too happy?

The mood couldn't survive the restless night. Determined once again to make a break with Lopez Rega she had rigidly schooled her mind to avoid all thoughts that might bridge a connection. While her hands had plenty to do she was able to force her mind to obey. But lying in bed was a different matter. Every time her mind slid into the comforting morass at the edge of sleep Lopez Rega was there waiting for her.

She fought the feeling that she couldn't get away, the erosion of her will. But it was all a losing battle. When she did finally drop off her dreams produced so much tension that when her maid called her at six o'clock to go to the airport she felt physically ill. A cold shower revived her body somewhat but it did nothing for her spirit. A dozen times she resisted the urge to phone Lopez Rega and tell him where she was going.

The hire car came and loaded her bags. She gave last instructions to her maid and had almost made it to the front door when she turned back and picked up the telephone.

'Daniel' had been sweet. She had taken a lot of trouble to convey the right attitude. Armando de Benedetti was crazy about her. Probably wanted to marry her. She was considering it. She thought it would be for the best if she didn't see Lopez Rega again.

The relief she felt when Lopez Rega soothingly told her that she must do what she thought best and wished her good luck was replaced by a panic of rejection. She heard herself asking her tormentor if he really loved her. Saying that she could still call the jaunt off if he needed her.

Offhandedly Lopez Rega had excused himself saying he had a lot to do. He wished her luck and hung up leaving her staring in misery at the dead telephone. Fury flooded through her and she picked up the heavy instrument and hurled it to the floor. Without a word she rushed past the maid and into the waiting car.

Her righteous indignation at the way she had been treated buoyed her through the customs and onto the plane. Only as she fastened her safety belt and saw the big engine gout smoke and whirl into life did the panic that she might never see Lopez Rega again return. By the time the plane touched down in Brazil the holiday was in ruins.

Armando had been sweet to her. He couldn't guess the cause of her depression but he had been around long enough to guess that a man was at the root of it. Therese had always been detached. It was her aloofness, coupled with her blonde Saxon beauty, that attracted him. Marriage was a possibility. She was well liked by his family and was handsome enough to match the other de Benedetti ladies.

The trip to Brazil had been with the intention of breaking through her reserve and suggesting a more lasting union.

By the time they had cleared customs at Delestra airport he knew that whatever had been attracting him to her was dead. She had hardly spoken at all on the plane, just sat staring out of the window, her face drawn and forbidding.

Armando picked up the hire car that had been ordered at the airport and fetched her from the telephone where she had been making a desperate but unsuccessful attempt to contact 'Daniel'. He held his temper in check with difficulty on the sixty-mile drive to Guarujá. The last chance came as they turned onto the beach road and ran along the shore in the final stretch to the large beach house his family owned.

The scene was so beautiful it was unreal. The lush green forest bordered the silver sanded beach that gave the clear water a metallic sheen. From the green fronds nodding in the heat haze, birds called and fluttered technicolour wings. Armando waited in vain for Therese to be enraptured by the view.

She said nothing. Even prompting was answered with an absent-minded nod. The only time she spoke was as they turned off the beach road and drove between the high formal privet hedges that flanked the drive. Then it was to ask if there was a telephone. Armando had seen her safely installed and then excused himself saying that he had to go to Sao Paolo for a business engagement. Therese had accepted the lie without comment. Happy that he was leaving and she would get another chance to phone Buenos Aires.

Later Armando rang from Sao Paolo and said he would have to stay overnight. She hadn't seen him since then. Next morning he had telephoned again to say that he had to return to Buenos Aires. He told her to use the house as her own and when she had had enough to get the taxi from the village to take her to the airport.

That had been three days ago. Three days of wrestling with her feelings. Being passionately in love with Lopez Rega and hating him with the same savage intensity. Three days of listening to the echo of the telephone bell ringing unattended in his flat. Three days of hell.

She stood and looked at herself in the long mirror on the end wall. Her face looked ugly and distorted with insufficient sleep. She ran her hands over her body. The sudden craving for Daniel made her feel sick. She had to get away. Without waiting to dress she burst open the french windows and ran at breakneck speed across the sand and dived into the cool water. At full stretch she drove her body through the water until her exhausted arms no longer responded. Breathing heavily she turned on her back and floated, her eyes closed against the blinding white of the sky. She didn't try to control her thoughts as they stuttered across her mind. She was going back to Argentina. She was going to see Lopez Rega and have it out with him. If he didn't want to see her again that was all right with her.

The four hundred yards back seemed to take for ever. As she got nearer she could make out the figure of a man sitting on the beach watching her. Then she realised her mistake. The man sat directly in her path back to the house. He lolled back on one elbow, a cigarette between his lips, his jacket folded neatly on the sand beside him. It was obvious that he had no intention of moving. Therese put him down as a chance passer-by who had decided not to miss the opportunity of indulging in a little harmless voyeurism.

It didn't worry her but she swam a few yards down the beach before wading out of the water and running swiftly across the sand. As she climbed the half dozen stairs which marked the boundary of the house she glanced back. The man had picked up his coat and was now sauntering up the beach after her.

She dismissed him with a shrug and ran through to her bedroom and rang for the maid. Not bothering to dress she began emptying the drawers and closets. There was a tap on the door and the maid came in.

'Fetch my bags, please, I'm leaving,' she said, not pausing in her haste to empty the drawers in case her freshly blossoming resolve faded.

The maid left the room and Therese quickly selected the clothes she should wear for the journey. Again there was a tap on the door.

'Come in,' Therese called from the bathroom where she was putting on her make-up. She heard the door open and close. 'Put everything in the cases. I'll be there in a minute.' She quickly finished and went back into the bedroom. At the door she stopped.

The man from the beach was sitting on her bed. He had his coat on now but the cigarette still billowed acrid smoke.

'What are you doing here?' Therese demanded, more startled than frightened. 'Who are you?'

The man made a lazy placating motion with his hand and stood up. He was tall and well built with the easy grace of an athlete. The sun had turned the bridge of his nose and cheekbones crimson but he looked as if he were used to living in the tropical heat in spite of light blue eyes and brown hair.

'*Morgen, Gnädiges Fräulein.* I'm sorry if I startled you. SS *Sturmführer* Hans Brüler.' He threw her a towelling beach-wrap to cover her nudity. 'Your uncle suggested we might find you here. Berlin has been trying to contact you for days. It seems your uncle's patriotism for the Fatherland extends only to passing on messages. You, we understand, take your obligations more seriously.'

Before Therese could speak, the door behind Brüler opened and she heard the maid's startled exclamation as she saw a man in the room. Like an uncoiled spring the SS man pulled the maid into the room and threw her onto the bed. Therese stepped quickly in front of her to protect her from further violence.

'What do you think you are doing?' she snapped at him.

He smiled and gave a mock bow towards the girl cringing on the bed. 'I beg your pardon, *señorita*. I'm afraid I do not like people creeping up behind me.' He turned his attention back to Therese. 'Is my assessment right, Fräulein?' he said, dismissing the maid from his thoughts.

Therese touched the girl on the shoulder. 'Go and telephone for a car to take me to the airport. I'll be all right. The señor is a friend of the family.' The maid didn't seem convinced but she got up to do her bidding. Brüler stopped her.

'That will not be necessary. I have a car here and will be happy to take you to the airport.'

The maid looked to Therese for instructions.

She nodded. 'Very well. We will have some coffee on the terrace. You can pack my bags then. I will leave as soon as everything is ready.'

Without waiting for Brüler's agreement Therese led the way through the french windows onto the terrace and selected a chair in the shade. Captain Brüler sat opposite. He admired the view for a few seconds before returning to the subject of Therese's loyalty.

'*Gnädiges Fräulein*. You haven't answered my question. Can I count on your assistance in a matter of vital importance to Germany?' he demanded.

She nodded slowly. If it would shut him up she would agree to anything. All she wanted to do was be alone with her thoughts so that she could rehearse her reunion with Daniel.

'How well do you know Sergeant José Lopez Rega? I understand you are the one that acts as a contact with him?'

She blanked out all expression on her face as she looked at him. Sudden fear gripped her. Why did they want to know about Daniel? Did they suspect he was responsible for the disappearance of their agent? Again the scene in the slaughterhouse flashed across her mind. The gurgling scream, the sickening stench.

'I don't know much about him. He is the chauffeur of one of the colonels who is now pretty powerful in the government. He passes on any bits of news he picks up and I pay him a hundred pesos a month.' She made it sound as matter of fact as she could.

'Can you trust him?'

Therese's face expressed uncertainty. She wanted to know more before making any sort of commitment. 'I suppose so. Why? What do you want him to do?'

'We need a closer contact with the Argentine government. We feel that Perón is playing a double game. Since the new President took over, Perón's activities have stepped up considerably. Once he had secured his place at the Ministry of War he took over the running of the Secretariat of Labour and Welfare. Reports say that he spends hours every day talking to the trade-union leaders working out a strategy to consolidate the power of labour. He has already put his man Cipriano Reyes in complete control of all union activity in Argentina. We feel he is about to make his move to take over the country. It is vitally important that we know exactly what is going on so that we can be prepared.'

He paused and watched as the maid brought out the coffee and placed it on the low wicker table in front of him. As she left he continued. 'We are willing to pay Lopez Rega a lot of money for detailed information of Perón's activities.'

'Of course, *Herr Sturmführer*. I will do my best to see that he does as you want. What sort of money can I offer him?'

Captain Brüler shrugged. 'I leave that to you. Results are all that matter. The interest is at the very top level in Berlin. Failure would not be taken lightly.'

Therese stood up. 'Very well, *Herr Sturmführer* Brüler, you don't need to threaten me. I have said I will help and I intend to keep my word. Now, if you will drive me to the airport please, I can catch the afternoon flight and probably get you your answer from Lopez Rega by tomorrow.'

The journey back to Buenos Aires seemed interminable. Therese ached with the need to see the man who dominated her. Thrusting a handful of change at the taxi driver she quickly ran up the steps.

At first the house appeared to be in darkness but then she noticed a flickering light coming from one of the windows on the side. The front door was open. She went inside and carefully picked her way in the dark to the door at the back. A low murmuring claimed her attention. It came from behind the door. She listened.

There was the sound of chanting, low but intense and

eerie in the still night.

Carefully she turned the handle and pushed the door open a fraction. At first the flickering light from the candles, placed around the room at intervals, confused her. The scene was so unexpected it refused to register on her brain. Slowly the picture formed.

Around the large room, in the form of a horseshoe, stood a number of men and women. They were all completely naked except for a face mask in the shape of an animal. They were all watching with intense concentration, a man in a flowing robe standing on a dais. In front of him, apparently unconscious, was the figure of a young, dark-skinned girl, her long black hair spilling over the side of the altar.

As Therese watched, stunned by the unexpected spectacle, the priest picked up a long knife. He held it above his head as the long, hypnotic chanting rose in volume. Suddenly Therese realised that the priest, standing over the naked body of the little Indian girl, was Lopez Rega. The shock was so great that she recoiled as if physically pushed. The door slammed shut with a bang and the chanting stopped abruptly.

There was a pause and then she heard Lopez Rega's voice rap out an order. Too horrified to run she backed away slowly from the door. She watched it jerk open.

Lopez Rega rushed at her, his face a mask of fury. Too late, she tried to run but his fist lashed out and thudded heavily into her face, and she felt the bone break in her nose.

Before she could protect herself another blow struck her hard on the temple. She hit the wall and slid down as she sank into unconsciousness . . .

She was aware of the naked figures with the grotesque masks crowding around her. Her head, too heavy to hold up, crashed onto the flagstoned floor. The last thing she was aware of was blood spreading across the floor from her mutilated nose. For no reason she muttered the one word which offered any comfort: 'Daniel . . .'

ELEVEN

'Forty–fifteen.' The umpire gave the point against Perón. Perón hitched up the knees of his white flannels and prepared to return the serve of the muscular lieutenant at the other end.

He made sure that his smile was fixed in place. The first set had been easily taken. At forty-eight he still retained enough bounce in his legs to back up the court-craft he had learned over many years of competitive tennis. Six games to two had looked good. Then tiredness weakened his concentration as the lieutenant equalised by taking the second set by seven games to five.

The five minute rest before starting the final had allowed Perón to recuperate and think out his tactics. He dearly wanted to win the match.

It was supposed to be a friendly match between two companies of infantry that he was formally attached to as colonel. It was an annual event that he had won many times in the past. Never had he felt the need to win as much as now. But now he faced defeat. The score stood at five games to four in the lieutenant's favour and he was serving at forty–fifteen. Perón watched carefully as the younger man prepared to serve at match point.

As he threw the ball into the air Perón jumped back lashing at the air with his racket as if attacked by a bee. The server caught the motion out of the corner of his eye and let the ball fall to the ground. Perón looked suitably chastened and lifted his hand in apology.

'Sorry.'

He settled down again, occasionally waving the racket across his face as if troubled by a plague of flies but gallantly carrying on. The serve ball thudded into the net. Perón straightened and made sure that his opponent noticed him take three paces forward. The lieutenant eyed him calculatingly. Perón was standing only a couple of feet behind the service line. It was a gambler's ploy. If the second service was fast and deep he wouldn't stand a chance.

It made the lieutenant reconsider. Maybe it was better to play the ball in safety and then rely on his greater speed around the court to win the match. He shook himself. No – dammit! That wasn't the way to win. It was the big serve. But there was just enough indecision in his swing to put the ball out of court.

'Forty–thirty,' intoned the umpire.

Perón walked slowly across to pick up the ball from its resting place under the edge of the spectators' stands. He moved slowly knowing that he was stretching the nerves of the younger man. As he picked up the ball he heard a pleasant voice say just loudly enough for him to hear: 'Bravo, *Coronel*. You've got him now.'

Surprised he looked up into a pair of shining brown eyes. He smiled and nodded to the man sitting next to his pretty supporter. Still taking his time he waited until he got back to his base line before knocking the ball to the other end – making sure that it bounced about in the court a good deal before coming to rest. He again smiled his readiness to the server and then swayed from side to side on the balls of his feet waiting for the ball.

The lieutenant tried to concentrate. The first service touched the net and fell just outside the line. Perón threw up his hands in sympathy and then crowded into the service area again. This time the lieutenant decided on safety for his second serve and lobbed the ball deep at the centre line hoping to restrict the angles open to the return. He raced into the net only to see Perón float a courageous return over his head to drop just inside the base line.

'Deuce.'

Through the applause Perón again heard the encouraging voice urging him on to victory. He turned and gave the woman a smile like a matador dedicating a bull and then settled down to await the next serve.

The lieutenant's game was totally destroyed now. He double-faulted and then gave Perón the game with an indecisive volley into the net.

Nobody clapped louder than Eva Duarte. Colonel Imbert, sitting beside her, cursed the folly that had induced him into letting her talk him into bringing her. Not that she didn't look a picture. Her quadrupled salary, since she had been escorted by the fat little Colonel who was responsible for the radio stations, had been well spent. In fact she was too pretty. It drew unwanted attention. Now she was cheering Perón on with more enthusiasm than was necessary and drawing even more eyes. It wasn't unusual to bring a young mistress to the tournament. It was one of the few acceptable places where a man could be seen with anyone other than his wife. But a certain decorum was expected. You introduced her as your niece or the daughter of a friend. Nobody was fooled but it satisfied convention as long as the woman wasn't too brassy or made herself too noticeable. Perón held his service game and went into the lead. Eva leapt to her feet and clapped enthusiastically. Again Perón smiled at her and nodded. It gave him added confidence as he faced the service of the now thoroughly dispirited lieutenant. The last game was a farce after the tenacious play in the earlier games. The younger man double-faulted twice and let the colonel kill a weak return to win the match.

As Perón shook the lieutenant by the hand he looked over at Eva. She was on her feet again, clapping twice as hard as everyone else. Perón saw Imbert's red face as he tried to pull her back into her seat. She shrugged him off without interrupting her applause. The winner winked and waved his racket at her and then followed the lieutenant off court and into the changing room. As he stood under the streaming cold shower he felt unbeatable.

Tables shaded by wide umbrellas clustered closely together under the vine-covered wall of the sheltering gymnasium. The late afternoon wind swirled and buffeted the tablecloths but was refreshingly cool after the earlier heat.

Colonel Imbert would have preferred to follow the example of most of the other members and take tea inside. In fact, had the choice been left to him, he would have quit the club altogether and taken Eva to one of the more discreet establishments that bordered Palermo Park. But it was not up to him.

At twenty-four Eva felt that time was passing her by without the courtesy of opening a door for her. Wasting time was a luxury she could no longer afford. Her determination to push the Colonel Imbert connection had been taken quite calculatingly a week before.

Like thousands of other aspiring actresses throughout the world, Eva had turned her eyes to Hollywood. The half dozen or so films she had managed to get into in Argentina hadn't brought the big break that every fan magazine said was necessary. It wasn't that she hadn't tried. Ceaselessly she patrolled the offices of the impresarios without success. Eva didn't claim a great acting talent but thought she was at least as good as some of the names that smiled through comedy and melodrama from the flickering screen.

Several photographers had indicated a wish to have her as a model for the usual payment for far less conventional shots to peddle in the cafés. She couldn't afford to pay money for them so she agreed to the terms. With glossy blow-ups to impress the producers she felt sure that her work would soon be recognised. Two months earlier she had carefully packed the pictures in stiff envelopes and sent them, with a highly sensationalised account of her work to date, to a number of Hollywood Studios. Only one had bothered to answer. When she read the kind but firm letter telling her to forget acting as a career she had broken down and cried.

Her tears didn't last long. She had been disappointed too many times in her short life to believe that tears would wash away the cause of it. Besides the letter confirmed what she had always known. The only way to succeed was by knowing the right people. An example wasn't hard to find. Since she had bulldozed Colonel Imbert, the powerful head of the Ministry of Communications, into taking her out a few times the doors at Radio Belgrano had opened wide for her. Yankelevich considered the extra pay she had demanded and her new programme on topical events a small price for a preferred place with the military.

The trouble was that Imbert wasn't dependable. He was easy to handle at the moment but when the pressure was on he would run for cover and she would be back where she started. She needed more insurance. Another protector. Colonel Perón attracted her.

He was everything the pulp magazines had promised. Tall, handsome, athletic, seemingly rich, with a sense of humour and – powerful. She had used her contacts at the radio station to get some background details and was surprised at the current flowing beneath the affable, placid surface. That's why she insisted that Imbert sat out in the blustering wind rather than in the crowded clubhouse. The men's changing rooms were on the other side of the gymnasium and it was necessary for them to walk around the building and across the terrace to enter the club lounge. Her perseverance was rewarded.

Eva was sitting with her back to the clubhouse and was able to see Perón approaching around the side wall. Her timing was perfect. She stood up and smiled at Imbert.

'Come on then, *querido*, if you insist we will go inside.'

Surprised, Imbert quickly stood up and gathered his walking cane and straw hat from the chair beside him. Perón had set a course that would pass within ten yards of where she stood and Eva appeared to see him for the first time.

He had changed into a blue and white striped blazer and white flannel ducks, a regimental scarf billowed in the neck of the open white shirt he was wearing. He was Eva's ideal of a gentleman.

She spoke to Imbert in a slightly louder voice than was necessary. Perón looked across. She smiled at him and he changed direction and came over.

'Imbert – you old rogue. What are you doing keeping this

beautiful creature to yourself. I demand to be introduced at once.'

Imbert was grateful for the distraction. He would be happy to pass Eva on to Perón, perhaps that would still the tongues he was sure were already wagging about his indiscreet outing.

Eva judged her performance well. It helped that she was attracted to the big man. As Perón bent to kiss her hand she blushed.

'Thank you for your support, *señorita*. I am sure I couldn't have won without you to cheer me on. I'm just about to buy the champagne. Perhaps you can persuade this old reprobate you are with to let you join me in a celebratory cup?'

Imbert nodded happily, an escape route opening up easily in front of him.

Dawn had broken above the small mountain town of San Juán. In one of the many simple, mud-plastered houses, a woman awoke. Immaculata's eyes opened in sudden fear and her hands flew to her swollen belly. She could feel the frightening vibration that wakened her. Fear seared her mind. A little animal whine of terror struggled between her clenched teeth.

She reached to shake the recumbent figure sleeping on the straw mattress next to her but stopped, puzzled. Her first reaction had naturally been to ascribe the violent shaking to the advanced stage of her pregnancy. But that didn't account for the rattle of bottles and the dust drifting from the walls in the shafts of morning sunlight penetrating the crude linen curtains. Fearfully she laid the palm of her hand flat on the hard packed earth floor.

The ground vibrated like an unsprung, fully laden wagon on one of the rough roads hewn crudely out of the mountain rock. The water jug seemed to leap from the window ledge and shattered as it struck one of the low, home-made wooden stools. Immaculata felt Manuel's hands on her, urging her to get up and quit the tiny, familiar room that had become terrifyingly alien. She heaved her heavy body up and clasped her hands protectively around her unborn child.

The trembling was greater now. It disturbed her balance and she would have fallen if her husband hadn't been there with his strong, supporting arms. In disbelief she watched a crack run down the wall of the mud-plastered room. Pieces fell to the floor. Light shone through the crack and in slow motion a segment of the wall fell outward dragging some of the roof rafters with it. As the roof started to cave in Immaculata screamed, a high pitched, soul-piercing sound above the growl of the tortured earth.

Manuel threw her bodily through the door and fell protectively across her body. A steadying thought flickered through his scrambled senses.

'*Terremoto! Terremoto! Terremoto!*'

Others were running into the streets screaming as their houses angrily shook themselves.

The church had been specially constructed to withstand earthquakes. If they could reach that they would be safe. He hauled his dazed wife to her feet and pushed her in the direction of the low sturdily built place of worship. The bell, as if of its own volition, began to ring.

Manuel could see the church now. Hundreds of crazed survivors fought to get within the safety of its walls. Sobbing, Manuel again tried to urge Immaculata into movement. She didn't respond. He dropped on his knees beside her, screaming at her to get up. It was useless. She had fainted. He put his arms under the child-heavy body and forced himself once more on to his feet.

He looked up again at the church and stopped open-mouthed. The shock running through the bedrock was now continuous. The tortured bowels of the earth growled a menacing, low pitched warning of the catastrophe still to come. The sound seemed to hang in the dust. The church was directly in the path of one of the cracks opening up in all directions. Without warning the strongly built building simply split in two and collapsed into the crevasse.

Terrified figures fled in all directions, but few managed to escape as the earth reared upwards and they slid, screaming into the black maw of death.

Suddenly the ground under Manuel's feet surged upwards. He tried to brace himself, driving his fingers deep into the hard sand, feeling his nails torn from the roots. Immaculata's unconscious body began to roll down the slope as the angle steepened. Head down, with nothing to grip, Manuel watched in helpless agony as she slipped silently over the edge and disappeared in the obscene black mouth.

'Immaculata . . .'

He felt his precarious grip weaken as the tilting table of earth gave a final shudder and pitched him head-first down the slope.

As unexpectedly as the catastrophe started – it was over. There was a final crescendo of sound and a settling convulsion and the dust began to drift down on the remains of what had been, less than a minute before, San Juán. The bodies of Manuel and Immaculata, and hundreds of others, were crushed by the last act of the restless giant and became a statistic.

A statistic that President Ramirez, holidaying at his estate in the seaside town of Mar del Plata with his domineering wife, read and passed back to his Aide without comment. He was more worried about the outcome of the war in Europe and his own security of tenure of the Casa Rosada to get involved in the destruction of a small town on the edge of the Andes.

TWELVE

'. . . and you can then give your children a really beautiful present without it costing you a peso.'

Eva sat in the small, overpoweringly hot room. She felt depressed. The sweat welded her tight-fitting suit to her and made the heat more unbearable. Droplets of perspiration joined and cascaded down her cheeks and nose. She dabbed ineffectually with a sodden linen handkerchief.

It was a price one had to pay for silence. The sound of ventilation fans could be picked up by the microphone, so she accepted it. The last couple of days had been hell. Now that her daily stint, giving housewives hints on how to cope, had become routine, she was bored.

Giving herself a mental shrug she carefully laid a sheet of paper to one side and was about to launch into the next projection of trivia when she was aware of a disturbance in the control room.

Through the glass she saw Pedro Bateman rushing around shouting orders, a long sheet of telex paper in his hand. Pedro saw she was looking at him and ran his finger across his throat to indicate that he was cancelling her broadcast. As the green light winked on, putting her off the air, she gathered her script together and rushed out of the cubicle and barged through into the control room. Before she could speak Pedro waved her to silence and pointed to the monitor that claimed the attention of every one in the room.

The announcer's voice was grave and he used his words ponderously as fitted the occasion.

'. . . remain standing in the town. Reports are still coming in but from our first communication we can state that this is a major national tragedy. Deaths, so far, have been estimated by the police to be somewhere in the region of 10,000. There are many more injured and Major Velasco of the San Juán police said that it will not be possible to give a final figure for some time.

The President has been informed of the tragedy at his home in Mar del Plata and he is expected to return to the capital to take charge of the rescue operations. The earthquake in San Juán is the first . . .'

Pedro lowered the volume of the speaker and turned to Eva. 'Sorry to cut you off but the news couldn't wait.'

'Why didn't you let me do it?' she asked.

Pedro shrugged and jerked his thumb upwards. 'The boss wanted Blasco to do it. I suggested you, as you were on the air at the time, but he wouldn't have it.' It touched Eva that Bateman had tried to help her. He was one of the few who seemed genuinely to want to help without attaching strings.

Impulsively she gripped his arm and smiled. '*Gracias*, Pedro,' she said and turned and hurried out of the control room. She was determined to get put onto the earthquake story whatever opposition she had to flatten to do it.

She considered ringing Colonel Imbert and trying to get him to intervene. A few weeks ago there would have been no problem but the colonel had been practically unobtainable since the day at the tennis match. She had managed to convince everyone at the radio station that the affair was still on but she felt Yankelevich was beginning to get suspicious.

Eva was playing a risky game. Every day she made sure that someone heard her ring Imbert on one of the office telephones and have long, intimate, though entirely imaginary, conversations with her protector.

As she ran up the stairs she thought of Perón. If only she could get him interested. He had been great fun at the party after the match and she felt strongly attracted to him. That was unimportant. What she wanted was his support. She hurried along the dimly lit corridor and rapped on the Director's door. Without waiting to be invited she pushed open the door and walked in.

Yankelevich was sprawled in his chair with his feet

propped up on one of the open drawers of his desk. He picked idly at his bulbous nose while he evaluated the latest telex report on the San Juán disaster. Eva's abrupt entrance startled him.

'Don't you ever knock?' he demanded.

Eva smiled confidently. 'Sorry but I had to see you urgently.'

Yankelevich waved the telex copy at her. 'I'm busy. Come back tomorrow.'

Eva stuck to her guns. 'It will be too late tomorrow. I want to cover the earthquake.'

The owner of Radio Belgrano carefully lowered his feet to the ground and stood up. 'You want to cover the earthquake, do you?' he repeated unpleasantly. 'Well – you can't. It's a big news story and will be handled by my top man.'

'It's a big human interest story as well and that can be handled better by a woman,' Eva insisted.

Yankelevich thumped his hand down on the desk top. '*Vaschu nji panjumaetje? Boscho moi*! I told you, I don't want you on this story. Keep within your limited capabilities. *Dawai*! Go.' He spoke with a thick Russian accent that became almost incoherent when he got excited.

Eva braced herself and sighted her big guns. 'I'll see if Colonel Imbert can change your mind.'

Yankelevich laughed. 'Why not tell the President?'

'I won't need to go to the President. The colonel will be enough,' she shouted.

Yankelevich considered. He had a feeling that the affair between his pretty announcer and the Communications Minister had gone cold. He regretted his generosity in quadrupling her salary. Although he would never have admitted it he admired the plucky little girl from the provinces.

He knew that it hadn't been easy for her. When she had first come to see him he had laughed at her affected voice with the underlying coarseness of the *pueblo*. Eva had stood up and stormed out of the office. Three months later she was back. She had spent every penny she could on taking speech and drama lessons and now spoke a passable version of society Spanish. He was impressed, although he didn't show it, and had found her an uninteresting job in the station at a pittance wage. Eva had stuck and fought her way up to being one of the more recognisable voices on Belgrano.

He looked at her, standing provocatively, sweat staining and moulding her clothes to her nubile figure and wished he was twenty years younger or had the over-confident Argentine chauvinism that would support him in a bid to start an affair with her. Then he pushed the thought aside. He was too old and he enjoyed their stormy relationship too much to jeopardise it by making an embarrassing pass. He lowered his buttocks gently onto the rubber ring on the seat of his chair. Increasingly he was troubled by the curse of ageing metabolism, piles, and the irritation made him more irascible than usual.

'I don't care who you run to. You are not doing the earthquake story – *konjetzu* – that's that!' he snapped.

Eva stood and looked at him, anger suffusing her face. 'Right! We will see about that. If you think you can push me around you had better think again. I want that story and you are not going to stop me.'

Yankelevich leaned across the table, his eyes bulging behind his rimless spectacles. 'Get out! *Dawai* – get out! I've had enough of your threats. One more word out of you and I'll see you never get another day's work here again in your life. Do you understand me? *Dawai* – *dawai!*'

Eva glared back at him. '*Bueno.* You asked for it.' She turned and marched out of the room slamming the door behind her.

Jaime Yankelevich leaned back in his chair exhausted. He shook his head, half in frustration, half in admiration. Troubled by a restricting accent himself he was able to appreciate that, in spite of the emotion of the moment, Eva had held on to her newly acquired elocution. Picking up the telex again he finished reading through the salient points

118

before ringing down for the sub-editor to discuss how they should handle the developing story. He briefly wondered who Eva would rally to her aid.

Eva was excited. The adrenalin pumping through her veins after the stormy encounter with her employer had produced an idea. An idea that she had now worked up into a full-scale plan of action.

First she had to get to a telephone where she could have some privacy. The call she had to make wasn't for effect. At least not on the Radio Belgrano employers.

In the outer office there was only a receptionist and a boy that made the tea and ran errands. She called him over and sent him out to get some cigarettes. Eva didn't smoke but on the spur of the moment it was all she could think of as an excuse.

The receptionist Isabel Ernest was the nearest Eva had to a girlfriend at the station. She had made an effort to cultivate her because through her hands passed all the corespondence and most of the telephone calls of the station. Eva gave her a captivating smile and took her into her confidence.

'Quick. I must make a telephone call before the boy gets back. I didn't want him to hear. Is it all right if I use the booth?'

The booth was a small, panelled cubicle that had originally been the domain of the chief clerk. Extensive staff reductions by the parsimonious new owner had reduced the staff to a level that bordered on the non-existent. Somehow the work still got done and, in spite of regular protests, no additional staff were taken on. The booth represented the only privacy any of the employees could get in the building and they guarded it strenuously.

Isabel nodded. Her glamorous friend overwhelmed her. 'Shall I get the call for you?' she asked, happy that she should be included in the secret.

'Not this one,' Eva laughed and gave Isabel a big sugges-tive wink. The receptionist went red and bit her bottom lip, thrilled and slightly shocked by her own imagination. 'I'll put a line through,' she said and went back to entering addresses in the post book.

Eva sat in the little cubicle and drew a deep breath to calm her nerves. She didn't need to rehearse what she was going to say, it was all there, clearly and concisely written in her mind. She dialled the number she had written on a piece of paper but had not found an excuse to ring before. The distant telephone rang three times and then there was a click and the voice she remembered so clearly answered.

'*Hóla.*'

'Colonel Perón?' Eva enquired politely.

'*Si, señora*' he answered with equal politeness.

'Hello. Eva Duarte speaking.' She pitched her voice low and friendly.

'*Señorita Duarte. Pero que placer. Que tal, guapa?*' Perón answered without hesitation.

Eva smiled to herself, relieved that it hadn't been necessary to jog his memory. An embarrassment that might have set up a barrier between them. She wasn't aware that Perón had made enquiries about his pretty fan and had been intrigued to find that she worked for a radio station. He had intended to follow up the introduction but had been too busy organising the unions to spare the time. Even now he was about to go to yet another meeting but he was willing to spare the time to chat to the charming radio announcer.

'Ah, *Coronel.* Tell me. Do you intend to go to San Juán?'

'San Juán?' Perón repeated slowly, puzzled by the question. He had already seen some of the reports coming in but like most of his colleagues had attached little importance to the disaster.

'Yes. I wondered if, by any chance, you were thinking of taking the situation in hand.'

Perón thought rapidly. It was the first time he had even considered such a thing. 'Well, of course, if the President should want me to do . . .' he began.

Eva cut in. 'I thought the President was on holiday, *Coronel?*'

'Yes . . . but –'

Again Eva stopped him in mid-sentence. 'This is such a

big international story I was sure that the government would put one of the top officers onto the job.' She paused but before Perón could say anything rushed on. 'Well I'm sorry to disturb you, Colonel Perón. Perhaps you could tell me who is likely to take on the job. Señor Yankelevich has put me in charge of making all the necessary link-ups with all the radio stations throughout the world and I must be able to talk to someone in authority.'

She knew she was laying everything on the line and if it backfired she would be lucky if she could get a job on an *empanada* stand but she sensed that this could be her big break.

Perón nibbled at the bait. 'You really think it's that big, hey?' he said slowly.

Eva's pulse raced. '*Si, Coronel*. Already we have had enquiries for coverage from the States, Germany, England, and all over the world. It is a change from the usual news about the war. And of course internally it will be of colossal interest. There are so many people with relatives in San Juán. It will need strong decisive handling. I hope the government appoint the right man for the job.'

Perón thought quickly. His standing with the army was good although a little delicate. The officers were suspicious of his new-found interest in organised labour. The unions were playing a waiting game. They had heard his promises and now what they wanted was some action. The time was coming when he would have to get rid of Ramirez and put someone in his place who was one hundred per cent under control.

It wouldn't hurt if he took a hand in the tragic situation in San Juán. By implication it would lose the President support. It would look bad that he continued his holiday while thousands of his voters were starving and homeless after the biggest disaster Argentina had known.

He made a snap decision. 'Thank you for bringing this to my attention, *señorita*. You are quite right. The situation does call for aid on a national basis. I will talk to the President and, if he is willing, go to see what is happening in

121

San Juán immediately.'

That was what Eva wanted to hear. She had no doubt that the inventive colonel would get his way. An opportunist herself, she had been impressed with Perón's immediate grasp of the possibilities inherent in the dramatic situation when they were called to his attention. Now she had to forge the link that would give her the edge she needed.

'I'm glad we have been able to help. Radio Belgrano will, of course, be at your service and happy to help in any way it can. Will you be able to put in reports yourself or would you prefer to have a reporter covering the situation from the government's viewpoint?'

Perón thought carefully. 'What do you suggest?'

Eva breathed deeply before answering. 'Well, of course, we could send you a reporter but then the story would be third-hand by the time it's broadcast. Perhaps it would be better if I contacted you at certain pre-arranged times and you let me know how the situation develops.' She heard Perón grunt interest and pushed on. 'It might save you a lot of time if you cleared all your stories through Radio Belgrano instead of being pestered by every radio station in the country – as well as some outside.' She held her breath and waited.

Perón gave a short, barking laugh. 'That sounds very reasonable. In that way you get exclusive material and I get sympathetic coverage. It's a deal. If the President agrees I will go to San Juán immediately and you will get all the inside information you want. I don't have to say how grateful I will be if you happen to project me in the right way.'

Eva was so overwhelmed by the way she had pulled off her coup that tears of gratitude formed in her eyes. But she kept her voice steady. '*Gracias, Coronel*. I don't think you will have any complaints. Perhaps you could telephone me here at Belgrano with the details as soon as possible so that we can make the necessary alterations in our programme schedule.'

'I will do that, Señorita Duarte. Thanks once again for ringing.'

'Goodbye for the moment, Colonel Perón,' Eva said formally.

'Ciao, Señorita Duarte. *Hasta luego*,' Perón responded with a laugh and hung up.

Eva sat and stared at the telephone. She felt like pinching herself to make sure she was awake. Isabel said something to her as she walked through the office. She didn't hear her. The office boy thrust the cigarettes in her hand and she thanked him with an absent-minded smile. Excitement flooded back as she sped up the stairs to Yankelevich's office. Without knocking she burst in.

Before the annoyed man could speak, she grasped him by the lapels and shouted in his face. 'We have got exclusive coverage of the earthquake. Colonel Perón is going there himself and will report directly to me on what is going on.'

Yankelevich disentangled her fingers roughly. 'So you say. But you will still not be doing the broadcast.'

'Then you don't get your exclusive news,' Eva snarled. She walked to the door. '*Coronel* Perón will be calling me shortly. What do I tell him? If you're not interested I'm sure I could do a deal with Radio Rivadavia.'

She opened the door but before she could leave she heard Yankelevich snarl bad-temperedly. 'Come back here.'

She controlled her grin of triumph before turning towards him.

THIRTEEN

The small town that had been San Juán lay in piles of rubble in the shimmering heat of the afternoon sun. Crude canvas canopies had been strung up on poles to shelter the bewildered, grief-stricken survivors. Working in the debris soldiers unearthed shattered, already putrifying bodies, and others sewed them into canvas shrouds that were to be their only privacy in the huge common graves that excavators were tearing in the earth close to where the church had once stood. Children, more resilient than their parents, had already shaken off the nightmare and scrambled over the heaps of clay bricks and played hide and seek around the few still standing walls. Personal possessions, unclaimed, were loaded into army trucks and guarded by armed policemen until ownership could be decided.

Perón picked his way along walkways, stopping here and there for a word with soldiers and people made homeless by the catastrophe. Following him, comforting and blessing the hopeless men and women, came Cardinal Copello. He had heard that Perón was taking a party to San Juán and had asked to be allowed to come along. Perón had been happy to oblige the churchman. The church was one of the areas that he, so far, had not been able to penetrate and he saw the cardinal as a possible ally in getting ecclesiastic support.

Perón was still not sure about the wisdom of leaving the capital to take on the onerous task of trying to bring order to the chaos which nature had brought to the people of San Juán. Instructions had been given to an air force plane to stand by at Mendoza airport to take him back to the city that evening if he decided that nothing was to be gained by staying in the disaster area.

He made his way to a number of caravans brought in by

the police as a makeshift headquarters. As he approached a door opened and a figure in police uniform leaped to the ground and hurried towards him. He recognised the handsome, powerfully built chief of police, newly elevated to the rank of major on Perón's recommendation, Velasco.

They shook hands like old friends. Velasco's head was bandaged under his cap, the result of a piece of falling timber from the ceiling of his house on the outskirts of the town.

'*Buenas, Coronel*. It's good to see you,' he said and meant it.

So far all his requests for assistance had fallen on deaf ears and he hoped that the influential visitor might be able to get things moving. Perón knew of the Major's frantic requests but had deliberately held up any action on them until he had arrived on the scene. He was aware of the publicity value of appearing to be the man on the spot. Perón introduced Velasco to Cardinal Copello and the other officers he had brought with him. He looked solemnly over the nightmare landscape.

'*Bueno*, Velasco. Bring me up to date. We must get something done about all those poor people out there.'

Velasco led the party into one of the mobile blocks and ordered everyone out. On the wall was a large scale map of the surrounding area. He waited for his visitors to sit down and then picked up a cane and pointed to the map.

'The worst devastation is along the north of the town here and then east towards the Andes. Estimates of the dead run into several thousand. It is hard to be accurate, you understand, but a figure as high as seven thousand has been given with many more injured.

'Water is the most pressing need. The movement of the water table has drained water from most of the wells and a crack in the reservoir here,' he pointed to a spot on the mountain edge, 'has drained out sixty per cent of the water reserve and the rest is badly contaminated by silt. Our experts say it will be several days before we can get supplies from there as the filter beds have also been put out of action.

'We have been trying to get water brought in by trucks

but so far there is no organised supply. Just a few thousand gallons that I have been able to get on the old boys' network. So far we haven't had a big run on food. Appetites are still depressed by the disaster but soon there will be a problem.

'With rationing we can last maybe two days. The shelters we have rigged up are okay as long as the weather doesn't break. If "la Zonda" arrives there will be problems.' He saw raised eyebrows and explained. 'La Zonda is a storm that comes down from the mountains every two or three weeks or so in the summer. The wind will tear anything down that hasn't got a firm foundation and the torrential rain that always follows will turn that lot out there into a quagmire – and that means disease.' He finished his briefing and looked hopefully at Perón. Like Perón he recognised the potential for his own aspirations if he handled the job efficiently. The colonel had always favoured him and this could be his big chance. Before he had left home that morning he had stood by the pale blue swimming pool and realised for the first time that his tenure of the post of police chief in the normally sleepy town was at an end. The crack that had drained the water from the pool was an omen.

Perón spoke first. 'What about the telephones. Are they still functioning?'

Velasco pulled down the corners of his mouth in an expressive gesture. 'We have commandeered the few lines that still work and we have a couple of shortwave transmitters.'

That suited Perón. He wanted control of information going out of the stricken town. '*Bueno*, Major Velasco. You have done an excellent job so far. Now we must kick a few arses and get supplies brought in.'

He turned to the cardinal. 'Sorry, *Eminencia*, but I find the lack of co-operation from the government unbelievable.'

Copello waved the profanity aside with a smile. 'Please, Coronel Perón. Take no notice of me. It is essential that these poor people are brought relief as soon as possible. If you will give me a telephone I will get in touch with my office in Buenos Aires and mobilise the clergy. When the people hear of what it is like here I am sure they will respond generously.'

Perón agreed and told Velasco to see that the cardinal got the line he wanted. 'Now I want a full report on the situation. Number of homeless, orphaned, badly injured. I'm not so interested in the dead. They are beyond our help.' He looked at Copello. 'Perhaps you would care to have a special service for the dead, *Eminencia*? I'm sure it would comfort the bereaved.'

Copello solemnly bowed his head in acknowledgement. Perón felt he had scored his first point with the clergy.

'See to it, McKinloch,' he said to one of the captains he had brought with him. 'I want the dead to be buried with full military honours. *Bueno*, Velasco. Now show me the telephones and I'll get some action or resign.'

Velasco led him into an adjoining radio truck that housed the transmitter and the last tenuous remains of the telephone service. Perón asked the operator to open the line to Buenos Aires for him and then told him to leave. Major Velasco sensed that he wanted to be alone and excused himself. Colonel Perón took out a small leather bound book that contained the telephone numbers of his most important contacts and dialled Radio Belgrano.

FOURTEEN

The huge classic tableau of sportsmen cut in bas relief and floodlit by a dozen spotlights seemed to float above the crowd, suspended by nothing more substantial than the pinpoints of reflected light in the puddles of water left by the torrential rainstorm an hour earlier.

The downpour, and the threat of more to come, hadn't deterred the thousands of sightseers, jostling good-humouredly behind the wooden barriers erected by the police. All attention focused on the succession of limousines that drew up to the wide entrance of the modern sports arena that was to be the venue for the latest and most ambitious drive to raise money for the San Juán Earthquake Disaster Appeal.

Luna Park had been chosen ultimately for the insurance it offered of a completely closed in stadium. The football stadium of 'River' was bigger but the late summer nights in Buenos Aires are notorious for wild unexpected storms and finally the vote was to sell less tickets and be certain of a success.

Eva would have preferred to take the gamble and hold the rally in the open air but as the black ministerial car edged its way forward to the entrance she was glad that she had been overruled. Nothing must go wrong tonight. She smiled happily at the faces craning and thrusting to see into the car.

Colonel Imbert, sitting stiff and formal in his dress uniform stared stolidly ahead, choosing to ignore the shouts and whistles of the enthusiastic fans.

Eva looked at the roly-poly figure hanging on desperately to his dignity and wanted to laugh. She didn't. In fact she felt quite warm towards the little colonel.

After Perón had started to ring her with his reports and

128

Yankelevich had reluctantly agreed to let her have extra air time, she had hit on the idea of launching an appeal for funds to alleviate the hardship of the survivors of the earthquake. She wasn't prepared for the overwhelming response she got from all walks of life.

Within a week the thousands of *pesos* pouring into Radio Belgrano needed a separate bank account. Even Doña Maria Unzue de Alveár, the autocratic head of the Sociedad de Beneficiencia, had got her secretary to offer assistance with the appeal.

Eva had never had any experience of administration. She had never had enough money at one time to make it necessary to keep accounts. At first she had dutifully written each contribution, with the name of its donor, in an exercise book. Soon the time taken in clerical work was cutting into the more important aspects of her work preparing the material Perón was sending her to go on her regular Earthquake Appeal spot. The old Russian had steadfastly refused to risk more money by taking on extra staff so Eva stopped accounting for the cheques and notes flowing into the fund and just put the money in her special bank account.

Every day she extolled the virtues of the gallant Colonel Perón fighting a lone battle against bureaucracy to bring comfort and aid to the homeless and starving of San Juán. Perón had been as good as his word. After listening to a couple of her stirring broadcasts he realised that he couldn't do better than leave his promotion in the capable hands of the talented and exciting radio announcer. From then on all enquiries were passed straight to Eva. It gave her importance and she had risen to the occasion. Each morning before her midday appeal she gave a brief press conference filling in the less privileged with the latest bulletin. Some of the press rebelled against what they saw as press censorship but Eva shut them up by the simple expedient of not inviting them to her press briefings.

She was indefatigable. At seven o'clock she arrived at Belgrano often calling Perón while he was still sleeping for the latest reports on what was going on. Her twice-daily contact was not really necessary as far as material for her broadcasts was concerned. These were confined to almost totally emotional appeals and propaganda rhetoric. But she didn't want Colonel Perón to forget who was behind his rapidly blossoming popularity.

Their conversations were mainly about policy. San Juán had been the object of an unprecedented deluge of aid from all over the world. Even strife-torn Europe had sent clothing and various commodities that could be spared from the war effort. Britain had even sent a consignment of tents, a surplus from the desert campaign, that had been well received in San Juán. The official response had been so good that there was little need for charity. But that didn't suit Eva's books. It was the biggest thing she had been involved with and she was determined to milk it for all it was worth.

A number of times she had talked Perón into giving up plans to return to Buenos Aires. He didn't mind particularly: it was just that he was bored. Even Cardinal Copello had returned to the city and Eva convinced him, with the harrowing stories she poured out daily, that he had more to gain by staying – and he stayed. To help her he had given her Lopez Rega's number and told her to use him for any errands she might not be able to do herself. She loved it!

Every morning the Sergeant or a corporal picked her up and drove her to the radio station and then was available in the evening to take her to wherever she had to be. Her frantic fear was that it would all fade away and she would be reduced to fighting Yankelevich for the odd job that he hadn't already earmarked for someone else. She couldn't have that. She thought she would rather die than lose the impetus that the earthquake had given her. Once Imbert had been talked into the idea of presenting a grand appeal she had set to work to make it a success.

With the help of ministry personnel she had canvassed the commercial and industrial interests throughout the country to sponsor parts of the show. Then she contacted the top names in entertainment and sport to give their services free for the charity gala. She hadn't forgotten the military. It was her big chance to get in with the men of power and show them what she could do.

Imbert had basked in the reflected glory of staging the huge entertainment and working in the glamorous world of show business. His wife and children were still in their country *estancia* and he was free to spend most of his time organising the coming event. Eva hadn't forgotten him in her broadcasts, and his efforts, spurred on by her public admiration, had gone a long way to building the solid foundation for success that her more emotional efforts had overlooked.

When Eva had suggested that he accompany her to the gala he agreed without hesitation. She could have had the pick of almost anyone for that night but she had chosen Imbert because of his obvious lack of appeal. When the time came she was prepared to dump her escort and she didn't want the extra problem of appearing to be romantically attached.

As the car stopped at the double line of soldiers forming a spectacular guard of honour in their ceremonial uniforms, Eva took Imbert's arm and squeezed it affectionately. She was aware that without his practical sense and organisational ability the night could not have been arranged. The colonel smiled his cold, strained smile and patted her hand before getting out of the car and escorting her along the red carpet to be welcomed by the Governor of Buenos Aires who had agreed to be patron of the appeal.

The Governor thanked Eva for all she had done and Eva modestly waived responsibility. She gave the credit to Colonel Perón and Colonel Imbert and said that without Perón's selfless dedication to the poor people of San Juán and Imbert's unceasing drive to provide even more resources for his gallant comrade, the plans that at that moment were being finalised to rebuild the earthquake town could not have been undertaken.

The Governor introduced her to several other notables

including the redoubtable Señora Unzué de Alveár. In her heavy satin evening dress and sparkling tiara the dowager looked out of place in the barnlike sports arena. Eva was glad that she had blown her bank account on an expensive dress for the occasion. It made her feel secure in her looks but she couldn't quench the slow burn of resentment that clawed in her breast to see the socialite welcoming guests to the glittering function that she had nothing to do with organising. Eva felt slighted.

She shook hands with such evident bad grace that Imbert felt called upon to smile an apology as he greeted the old woman. Behind the makeshift stage, which had been set up off-centre to accommodate a larger audience, there was a reception lounge where artistes, organisers, friends and hangers-on could have drinks and gather between acts. When Eva walked in on the arm of Colonel Imbert she had the satisfaction of seeing all eyes turn curiously towards her. She had become almost as much a celebrity as Juán Domingo Perón. But unlike the colonel practically nothing was known about her. Some of the numerous gossip magazines that crowded the little pavement kiosks about the city had run potted biographies and a few pictures but in the more elevated circles her name was only just becoming known.

She saw Perón as soon as she entered the room. He was talking to Libertad Lamarque, one of the top movie actresses who had starred in *La Cabalgata del Circo*, a run-of-the-mill film in which Eva had a minor role.

Imbert was talking to a group of acquaintances interested in his tales of the trials and tribulations of being an impresario. The fat colonel was enjoying his hour in the limelight and giving a blow-by-blow account of how he had set about the mammoth task of getting all the elements together to produce the show.

Eva had heard it all before. She had let him tell her in detail what he had done as the production progressed, partly because it gave him pleasure but also because she wanted to know exactly what was going on. But that was all in the past now. The bank account of the San Juán Disaster Appeal mounted steadily. Everything that could be done had been done.

She looked around at the dozens of celebrities drinking free champagne and talking animatedly to their eager entourage. Without warning a fit of depression settled on her. The rally in Luna Park was the end of the road as far as the earthquake was concerned. She would soon be expected to turn the funds over to the government or a recognised charity. They would thank her for her efforts and then set about dividing the spoils that her hard work had garnered.

One thing was certain. By the time the money had passed through the hands of lawyers, accountants, wholesalers, shippers, advertising agents and all the other predators eager to do their bit in rebuilding San Juán, there would be very little left for the destitute people it had originally been intended to help. Unless she could, somehow, hang onto the reins. Push her participation onto a new level. She needed a strong sponsor. One who had the necessary hunger to succeed and didn't mind taking a few unorthodox opportunities to get what he wanted. She needed Colonel Perón.

She excused herself from Imbert's admiring band and walked slowly through the crowd in the direction of Perón. Occasionally she stopped for a few words with actors or directors she knew. There was a new respect in the way they addressed her that was music to her ears. It made her even more determined to hold on to her developing status whatever the cost.

Perón had his back to her as she approached and was listening politely to his actress companion. Libertad Lamarque was riding on the wave of success that the steady stream of Latin American pictures over the last decade had brought her. When she had been told that the heroine of the hour had worked on one of her films she had been hard-pressed to equate the skinny, mousy-haired extra with the confident blonde who now seemed to be well in with the military junta running the government.

Colonel Perón swung around with a warm welcoming smile as Eva stopped at his elbow. 'Señorita Duarte. I've looked forward to meeting you again. Do you know Señorita Larmaque?'

The two beautiful women looked at each other coldly.

'I believe we have worked together,' Libertad said with enough hesitation to suggest that if they had she hadn't been aware of it.

Eva was equal to the put-down. She let a puzzled smile flit across her face. 'Have we?' she said slowly. Perón concealed a grin. Over the past weeks, talking twice a day to the competent Eva, he had developed an appreciation of her cool, controlled approach. It was a change from the simpering, thoughtless conversation of the marriage fodder he was used to escorting, the serious compilation of trivia that expensive finishing schools had taught was the mark of a gentlewoman.

Libertad took the rebuff well. She didn't want to get into a slanging match with the little nobody enjoying a brief moment in the sun before sinking once more into obscurity. She excused herself to Perón, nodded imperceptibly to Eva and joined a party of entertainers being marshalled into the order in which they were to make their appearance on the stage.

Perón offered Eva his arm. 'Shall we get some champagne?' Happily Eva tucked her arm in his and they walked slowly across the room to where white-jacketed waiters poured an endless stream of the sparkling product of Mendoza vineyards into the ever extended glasses.

'That was a bit cruel – Señorita Duarte,' Perón said with another of his wide smiles.

Eva was enjoying her moment of triumph too much to understand her escort's allusions instantly. Then she laughed.

'Libertad needs cutting down to size. Her films aren't as popular as they were but the way she acts you would never believe it. The only reason she gets so much work is she has so much dirt on the producers they are afraid to drop her in case she decides to write her memoirs.'

Perón handed her a glass of champagne and indicated a small table situated out of the way in the corner. 'Let's sit over there,' he suggested.

Eva looked around at the sparkling company. She was loath to hide away in the corner. She wanted everybody to see her with the dashing colonel. 'I want to talk to you,' he prompted.

Eva led the way to the corner and sat down facing the room. Perón pulled his chair around so that he was sitting beside her. She liked that. Now everyone could see her and the colonel sitting quietly out of the way having a serious conversation.

Perón held up his glass in a toast.

'To Eva Duarte and the San Juán Earthquake,' he proposed.

Glass raised, Eva added, 'And the Saviour of San Juán, *Coronel* Juán Domingo Perón.'

Solemnly they drank and then looked into each other's eyes and burst into loud laughter. Heads turned inquisitively. Eva leaned forward intimately. 'Were you happy with the way I covered your work?' she asked. Perón screwed his bent index finger into his cheek and winked the Latin gesture of appreciation. '*Macanudo, señorita. Fantastico*! The people of San Juán owe you a great debt.'

Again Eva denied any part in the operation. 'Without you and *Coronel* Imbert nothing would have been done,' she said modestly.

Perón shook his head emphatically. 'Nonsense. It's your show and you did a magnificent job.' He paused and then continued more diffidently, '*Coronel* Imbert. Er . . . is he . . .? Do you . . .'

Eva gave an embarrassed laugh. '*Coronel* Imbert? Of course not. He just comes into the radio station a lot and I got to know him. He has been very helpful but there is absolutely nothing between us.'

Perón nodded acceptance of her denial. He didn't really care but he didn't want to move in on a fellow officer's preserves.

A sergeant came to the table and saluted Perón. '*Coronel* Perón, His Excellency the Governor of Buenos Aires presents his compliments and requests that you are ready to be introduced on the stage in five minutes.'

Perón excused himself and rose from the table. A sudden panic hit Eva. There were so many things she wanted to say. If the colonel left now it might not be possible to get him alone again for weeks. By that time it would be all too late. The fund would be taken out of her hands and she would be back to giving home hints for the thrifty. Her fears were groundless.

Perón bent down towards her. 'If you are doing nothing after the show perhaps we could have dinner together?' he requested.

She had promised Imbert that pleasure but she didn't intend to let that stand in the way of her plans. 'That would be nice,' she accepted.

'*Bueno*. We will leave as soon as I've done my bit on the stage.' He winked and followed the sergeant to his appointed position at the side of the stage to wait for his introduction. Eva finished her drink and went to find Imbert. She hoped he wasn't going to be too upset. She couldn't stand a row, her nerves were stretched too tautly for it to be anything less than a frontal attack with all guns blazing and she wanted to avoid that.

Imbert was still talking. It was a different set of people but they reacted and looked the same as the others. Eva tapped him on the shoulder. She had discarded the subterfuge of a headache and decided to tell him the truth.

'*Querido* Anibal, *Coronel* Perón wants to discuss a few points about my broadcast in the morning. Would you be terribly annoyed if I went to dinner with him?'

Imbert was riding high and he had already drunk several glasses of champagne. He was in an ebullient mood. 'Mind! I would be heartbroken. But . . . how can I hope to compete with the gallant Juán Domingo Perón. You have my blessing.' He lurched forward and kissed Eva wetly on the nose.

She ran her hand down his perspiring cheek. '*Gracias*. I'll telephone you in the morning after the transmission.'

Imbert waved expansively to her. 'Always at your service, *mi amor*. Have a good time.' He turned back to his friends and she heard him pick up his story where he had left off.

As she crossed to the bar she saw Yankelevich skulking in a corner looking uncomfortable in a tight, old-fashioned dinner jacket. She went over to talk to him. 'Well, Señor Yankelevich, are you satisfied now? I told you I could pull it off, didn't I?'

The old Russian looked slowly around the room. 'And what good does it do me? You going to arrange another earthquake?'

'You're impossible,' Eva snapped, annoyed that he wouldn't give her credit for a good job.

He raised his glass in a mock toast. 'And you too, *tovarisha*.'

Angrily she stamped away to wait for Perón at the foot of the stairs leading to the stage.

Yankelevich watched her go with self-pitying tears in his weak eyes. He wished he could have congratulated Eva on her success but the tone of their relationship had been settled long ago and he could no more act in a friendly manner towards her than go back to Russia.

Standing below the stage Eva could hear Perón addressing the crowd. She heard him mention her name a couple of times and felt better. She knew she had a problem to solve. Custom dictated that Perón, having fed her, would expect to bed her. That didn't bother her. In fact the thought of spending the night with the tall colonel excited her more than she could remember for a long time. The problem was that she didn't want it to be on the basis that he was servicing the little lady as a reward for her help. Payment rendered in kind in a strange bedroom.

If she let him push her off to bed it was inevitable that he was going to feel that he had done his duty and had no longer obligations to her. On the other hand, if she refused to play along he might feel that his manhood had been insulted and not bother to prolong the relationship. She pushed the problem behind her as Perón came down the stairs.

Eva kept out of the way while he circled the room shaking hands and chatting to the rest of the guests. Her heart wasn't in it but she thanked a few of the people who she knew had actively supported the campaign and made vague remarks when they asked her what she was going to do next.

At last the time came to leave. Perón caught her eye and with a slight movement of his head he indicated they should go. She acknowledged with a smile and made her way to the exit. He took her hand and led her out into the foyer. The crowd outside were even more vociferous than earlier and as Perón and Eva came out to get in his car a friendly cheer greeted them.

Without hesitation Perón walked out to the spectators jostling against the barrier and reached past the close-ordered line of police guards to shake the outstretched hands. He looked back at Eva and nodded encouragement. Diffidently she joined him and followed his example. Some of the younger ones thrust pieces of paper at her for an autograph. She had never had such a reception and would have stood there all evening signing old programmes and scraps of paper if Perón hadn't taken her arm and led her back to the car.

Lopez Rega was standing holding the door open for them. Eva smiled happily at him and he bowed politely in reply. As Perón followed her into the car she heard him tell the sergeant to take them to the *Caverna del viejo Conde*, an exclusive restaurant in the residential area of Vicente Lopez.

When they arrived Perón told Lopez Rega to take a cab home and leave the car. The sergeant gave the keys to the doorman and said goodnight. The head waiter ushered them into a small bar and fussed over them while they ordered drinks. Perón told him he wanted one of the small curtained-off alcoves that were a speciality of the establishment and then turned his attention to Eva while the head waiter went off to arrange it.

Perón was a witty companion and Eva felt herself drawn under his spell. Eva brought the conversation around to the success of the Earthquake Appeal. Perón was unstinting in his admiration for the way she had handled the publicity. She looked sad.

'It's a pity it has all got to end,' she said quietly.

Perón agreed. 'I suppose so. What are you going to do now?'

She shrugged. 'I suppose it's back to the soap commercials,' she said with a forced laugh. 'Unless there is some way that I can get onto the next phase of the operation. I hate to let go now. Once all that money gets out of my control I doubt much of it will get to San Juán.'

Perón gave a cynical laugh. 'I doubt if ANY of it will get to San Juán. But I suppose that's the way it goes.'

Eva shook her head slowly. 'It needn't be.'

Her companion gave her a sharp look. 'What do you suggest?' Interest edged his voice.

'Well,' Eva spread her hands on the table and selected her words carefully, 'you are the man who is identified most closely with the appeal. If you were to express interest in the projects being considered for rebuilding the town it would carry a lot of weight. It would mean that the appeal would go on and that would generate a lot more publicity.' She looked at Perón shrewdly. 'It would identify you more than ever with the people who are trying to rebuild Argentina.'

'Yes,' Perón said slowly. 'Trouble is I'm fully committed with the unions at the moment. There's a big confrontation coming shortly. The factory owners still haven't got the idea that they are fighting a losing battle. Any time I had to spend on the San Juán project would mean less time with the unions. I couldn't risk that.'

'But I could help you with the unions,' Eva burst out.

Perón raised a quizzical eyebrow. 'And just how could you help with the unions?' he asked with gentle sarcasm.

Eva considered carefully before she spoke. 'If we keep on the appeal that means I will keep the radio programmes

139

going. It's not too hard to link your fight for the homeless in San Juán with the plight of the workers in industry. In fact one will help the other. We can point out how you organised everything at the scene of the disaster and how that has given you the drive to help others not sharing in the prosperity of the richest country on earth.' She took a quick look at the Colonel to see how he was taking her suggestions.

'I could be interested. Give me an idea of how you would handle it.'

Thirty seconds passed before Eva spoke. When she did it was in a low intense voice that startled the listener. 'I'm told that you are not interested in becoming President. I'll leave that aside for the moment. What you are interested in is power. You have it at the moment but you are not sure that you can keep it. It's touch and go whether the military can stick together long enough to form a strong administration. There are too many generals and not enough balconies.'

Perón smiled but didn't say anything.

'There are two areas that nobody seems to want to know. One is labour, which you have already made a start with, and the other is women's suffrage. Argentina claims to be a sophisticated nation and yet it still regards women as a chattel. In the polling booth they could represent a block of votes that could decide an election.'

Perón stopped her. 'Señorita Duarte. Eva. Women have been campaigning for the vote for years but they haven't found a serious supporter. If I went out on a limb for them I would have the Forces and the Senate against me. Maybe it's something to think about for the future but I have too much on my plate to risk it at the moment.'

Eva couldn't contain herself. 'Rubbish! If you will excuse me. This is just not so. You have a vast popular following already. I have the ear of the women of this country. At the moment anyway. If you got the workforce and the women behind you there would be no other party strong enough to go against you.'

Perón looked serious. 'The army wouldn't stand for it.

And I need them to keep order.'

Again Eva disagreed violently. 'Only the way the government is set up at the present time. Once the unions have learned their true strength the army will have to behave.'

She was interrupted by the waiter bringing in their meal. As they ate Eva stuck to the subject, shooting down Perón's objections to her argument that the unions needed him to take a more overt part in their activities. After the meal he drove slowly out to a house loaned him by a friend for the weekend. Before they fell asleep in each other's arms in the early morning Eva had convinced him to let her join him in his fight for power.

FIFTEEN

Cipriano Reyes sat out of sight on a canvas cover on the back of one of the box cars. Through the open door he could see the factory hands from the slaughterhouses gathering on the piece of open land between the long sheds and the railway siding. They were nervous and excited. In defiance of the owners they had walked out of the factory and said that they refused to return until their demands for higher wages and better conditions had been met.

Reyes could make out the massive figure of Gordia standing on a packing case talking to the agitated crowd. He hadn't needed much prompting to organise the demonstration. Reyes had found him a job in the slaughterhouse at Perón's request. Several others had joined him and Reyes had put them to work consolidating the workers into a union. It hadn't been done without breaking a few heads but now all the workers were solidly behind Gordia and his henchmen.

A movement on the road leading up to the stockyard caught Reyes' eye. Three dark blue trucks swept into the yard and before they had stopped blue uniformed police jumped from the back, brandishing riot carbines. Their sudden appearance had frozen the agitators in a silent tableau. They watched nervously as the police encircled them. Another car drove through the gate and stopped in the protective shadow of the police vans.

Reyes watched as Señor Guba, the managing director of the slaughterhouse, climbed down from the back and went to talk to the captain in charge of the police. His arrival had signalled a murmur of anger from the crowd of workmen.

Guba stepped up onto a packing case and raised his arms above his head. 'Now you men. I want you all to give up this foolishness and go back to your benches. You are being led astray by a few communists who are trying to ruin the country. No action will be taken against you if you go back to work immediately. The police have orders to arrest anyone unwilling to do what they are told. Return to your work!'

A voice in the crowd shouted, 'What about our wages?' It was taken up by the others.

A stone thrown with unerring accuracy came out of the back of the crowd and struck Guba a glancing blow on the temple making him stagger and fall off the box. Instantly the police carbines came up and covered the crowd. Reyes had seen enough. He climbed down from his hiding place and trotted across to a place where the fence was down and squeezed through. In a small garage opposite he telephoned to Perón and told him what had happened.

The colonel sounded delighted. 'Fantastic! There has been a change in plans though. I don't know how you are going to like this but instead of sending in the troops I think it will be more effective if just you and I go in. It will be more impressive if we are seen to be *compadres*.'

The switch had been suggested by Eva. She had also persuaded him to take her with him but promised to sit in the car. Reyes heard the new plan and swallowed hard. He hoped the colonel could be relied upon.

Lopez Rega darted through the traffic. In the back Eva and Perón sat in silence holding hands. Lopez Rega wasn't too happy about what they were doing. It was too dramatic. It worried him that Perón had let his latest girlfriend talk him into something so risky.

He could smell the factories before he could see them. Glancing in the rear-view mirror he saw Perón wrinkle his nose as the smell penetrated the closed windows. Eva didn't react. She had lived with the smell and squalor of the slums too long to be affected.

Lopez Rega braked sharply to come to a halt beside Cipriano Reyes. So far the noise of the fighting in the stockyard had not attracted too much attention. A few onlookers stared curiously as Perón stepped out of the car and smoothed the creases out of his uniform. The only sign of strain was a livid boil that swelled beneath the skin of his cheek. He was followed by Eva. Startled, Lopez Rega glanced at Perón. Eva had dressed with care. White, stylishly cut costume, expensively coiffeured hair and skilfully applied make-up emphasising the eyes and mouth were designed to attract attention amongst the unskilled workers battling with the police.

'Where are you going?' Perón demanded, nervous agitation sharpening his voice.

Eva patted her head to check that every hair was where it should be. She looked cool and unconcerned. She had watched this scene played out in many films and it needed steely nonchalance to carry it off successfully.

'Get back in the car!' Perón ordered abruptly.

A shot rang out from the scene of the battle. Eva quickly stepped past the two men and started walking along the narrow lane.

'You bloody fool,' Perón growled and lumbered after her.

Behind them Lopez Rega and Reyes exchanged exasperated looks. The whole movement was being endangered by his infatuation with a woman. Reyes came up on the other side of Eva. Only the brightness of his eyes betrayed his uneasiness. At the entrance to the yard they stopped and studied the situation. The police had confined a hundred or so men in one corner and had them covered with their guns. Several bodies stretched out on the dusty cobbles.

At the end, where the siding holding the empty boxcars backed onto the warehouse, a number of men defiantly hurled rocks and pieces of timber at the police as they tried to move in.

Eva gripped the arms of her escorts tightly. '*Bueno, amigos*. Smile and walk slowly.'

Without hesitation she stepped forward, a wide smile on

her heavily painted lips. The two men had to follow her example. Arm in arm they walked into the stockyard and, undeterred by the violence about them, sauntered like friends out for a Sunday afternoon stroll, through the arena of battle. They came up behind the police barring the way at the gate.

The strikers, who were facing the gate, stopped in amazement at the apparition in white flanked by the tall military man and the worker, in a loose blue suit, whom they recognised instantly as one of the union leaders. The violence died down as Eva, Perón and Reyes walked steadily towards them, selecting individuals for the full force of their friendly smiles. The mass of bodies parted and they walked through.

The sudden quietness attracted the attention of the captain of police. He ordered his men to stand fast and then ran across the yard to intercept the unarmed trio. He slid to a halt in front of them and gave a hasty salute to Perón. '*Perdón, Coronel*. But I must ask you to leave. You are in grave danger here. We are trying to put down a riot.'

Colonel Perón gently disentangled his arm from Eva's and stepped forward as coolly as at an Academy party. 'Thank you for your concern, *Capitán*. I am Coronel Perón.' He turned to Eva. 'This is Señorita Duarte from Radio Belgrano and this gentleman is Cipriano Reyes of the CGT.'

Perón directed his attention to the suddenly quiet yard. 'I think Señor Reyes should speak to them now, don't you?' Unbelievingly the captain nodded. Reyes vaulted up on to the packing cases. Eva darted off to a young workman sitting futilely trying to stop the blood from a wound in his head. Eva dropped on her knees beside him and unwound the silk scarf from her neck and held it to his temple. Blood dripped down the front of her white suit. The captain was still standing where they had left him, undecided what he should do. Eva called him over.

'*Capitán*. Perhaps you could get an ambulance here to pick up the injured men.'

Pleased to have something to do, he nodded and trotted across to one of the trucks and ordered a man to carry out the order. Reyes stood on the boxes and waited while the men from the other end of the yard made their way over to join the men clustering around him.

'Brothers,' Reyes began conventionally. 'Violence is not the answer.' He paused as hecklers shouted him down. 'I know your problems. For weeks now we have been talking to the government. Explaining our demands in moderate terms.' Again he was overwhelmed with a roar of sound. He knew what he was doing.

'The President has kindly offered to see a delegation of union leaders to discuss the possibility of making some concessions.' He paused dramatically. 'After Easter.'

He quieted the shouts with his upraised arms. 'Brothers. I agree! We want some answers NOW. Some of you may know that there is a new man in control at the Secretariat of Labour and Welfare. You may also know that he is a man of action. This man knows hardship. As a boy he worked as a *gaucho* in Patagonia. He has made the Argentine workers' cause his own. Brothers. With me today is that man. Listen to him. You all know me. I am one of you. I swear to you that he means everything he says. Brothers – *Coronel* Juán Domingo Perón!'

Perón stepped forward to join the union man and raised his arms above his head. '*Amigos*. We heard about the trouble you were having here, Señor Reyes, Señorita Duarte from Radio Belgrano . . .' he gestured to where Eva knelt beside another of the fallen men, her white suit now dramatically stained with blood. Heads turned and men whispered to each other.

Perón continued. 'And I. I came here to give you my personal assurance that your demands will be met. But I want you to help me to show the managements that I have your co-operation. When I leave here I intend, with Cipriano Reyes and any other delegates you care to elect, to see the management. I will demand that they increase your wages by a minimum of forty per cent.' He waited for the

146

cheering to subside and then rushed on. 'I consider myself, first and foremost, an Argentinian. I have the honour to wear the uniform of an officer in the great Argentine army. But my heart is the heart of an Argentine worker. Without the men who toil with their hands, use their strong backs for the good of all, there can be no Argentina.'

Again the thunder of applause forced him to stop. 'I pledge you my honour as a *gaucho* that these promises I have made will be fulfilled. You *will* get the rise I have promised. Within twenty-four hours – or I will join you at the barricades. I will put myself in the forefront of your battle. *Amigos*. Do I have your support?'

Theatrically he lowered his head as the hundreds of striking workers cheered and clapped their unlikely supporter. Reyes stood beside Perón and the colonel draped his arm around the smaller man's shoulder.

'Right, Brothers, do as the *Coronel* says. Go back to work. I will inform you of events as soon as we have finished our meeting with the management.'

The two speakers jumped down from the packing cases and waited for Gordia to join them. Eva moved amongst the slowly dispersing crowd, joking and countering ribald remarks with scathing retorts. She loved it. She saw the police captain walking over to Perón accompanied by the dishevelled managing director, Señor Guba, and quickly joined the party. *Capitán* Mendez, the battered Guba and the colonel shook hands. 'I don't know what you think you are up to, *Coronel*,' Guba said angrily, 'but you are making promises you cannot keep.'

'Really, *señor*?' He indicated the mob making its way through the gates. 'Perhaps you would like me to call them back so that you can tell them?' he suggested.

'It is impossible to meet their demands. A forty per cent increase in pay would cut our profits so much that the share holders would not stand for it.'

Perón put his foot on the case beside the angry director and leaned his forearm comfortably on his knee. '*Amigo*. I suggest your stockholders would be a lot more upset if work came to a complete standstill and the factory was torn down around your ears!'

Guba looked at him sharply. 'Are you threatening me, *Coronel*?'

Perón looked astonished. 'Threatening you, *Señor*?' He looked around at the still bodies being loaded into the ambulances that had arrived in answer to the captain's call. 'I thought I just rescued you from a riot. Or perhaps you thought it was just a game? The players would all file docilely back to work when the final whistle blew?' He pointed to the police Captain. 'Ask Captain Mendez. I think he will confirm that the strikers weren't playing games. He has seen a lot of unrest amongst the workers.

'Wake up *señor*! The days when you could pay starvation wages and expect unqualified obedience are over.' He straightened up and adjusted his cap. '*Bueno, Señor*. Do we go and convince your board of directors that shareholders in Washington are less important than workers in Avellaneda or do I withdraw the police and let the men speak for themselves?'

'Very well, *Coronel*. If you insist. But I will report this directly to the President. He is a friend of mine.'

Perón gave a mocking bow. 'Of course, *señor*. If you can find him I would do exactly that. In the meantime – let's talk about wages.'

Ramirez had come to a decision. Unsure of the army, disturbed by labour unrest, he had given them orders. Commodore Vasca wondered what he would do if Perón refused to go. He got no comfort from the squad of naval marines escorting him. In the narrow road outside the Secretariat building he gave the lieutenant in charge of his escort instructions to guard the doors and not let anyone either in or out. He braced himself for the task ahead and marched into the hall that had been the scene of Perón's triumph the day he had taken his new office. For a moment his courage failed him as the dozen or so workmen waiting for interviews turned to stare at the totally unexpected sight

148

of a naval officer in the labour hall.

'Looking for a job?' a wag shouted and a ripple of laughter swept the room.

Vasca gave a weak grin and asked one of the men behind the counter for the colonel's office. Perón had moved upstairs to a bigger more private office since the first few days spent in the greenhouse in the corner of the general office. As Vasca turned to go out of the door to take the stairs he saw one of the clerks lift the telephone and guessed his arrival was being signalled to the colonel.

It made no difference, he had his duty. Perón answered his knock on the door promptly and the commodore entered. The office was unpretentious. About five metres square with only a wooden desk, a small sideboard and a number of chairs as furnishings. A pretty, young stenographer sat opposite Perón taking notes. As the naval man entered Perón dismissed her with a smile and turned with his hand extended.

'Colonel Perón . . .' Vasca began officiously. Perón looked at him sharply. 'The President has directed me to inform you that he commands you to prepare your official resignation from your commission in the army of the Federal Republic of Argentina.'

Perón's reaction was totally unexpected. He dropped back in his chair and burst into loud, mocking laughter. He clapped his hands in mocking applause. '*Bravo*, Commodore. Beautifully put.'

He stood up again and walked around the table to the confused naval officer. 'Now go back to the idiots who sent you and tell them that I do not intend to resign. If they want to get me out they will have to kill me first and I don't think you have got the guts for that, *amigo*.'

Perón's laughter followed Vasca back across the city to report the debacle to the President. But the laughter had disguised the colonel's feelings of fear. Just the fact that Ramirez was willing to make the gesture spoke volumes. It could only mean that he had done a deal with the Navy.

He had to move fast. First he had to get away from where

he could easily be picked up. The apartment was the best place for him to go. From there he could telephone around and see what support he could count on. He didn't bother to wait for his staff car but flagged down a taxi and directed the driver to Posadas.

José pressed the button for the lift when he saw him coming. 'If anyone comes looking for me – I'm out!' Perón instructed him. Espejo nodded understanding.

The lift arrived.

'Ring Lopez Rega and tell him I need him urgently. Tell him to alert Reyes. I may need him tonight.'

Perón pressed the button for the seventh floor. As he entered the flat the telephone rang. It was the faithful concierge, Espejo. '*Perdón, mi Coronel*, but it is Señorita Duarte. She insists on speaking to you.'

'Put her on,' he said, pleased that she had phoned. He had begun to rely on her unerring sense of occasion in the last four weeks.

Before he could speak Eva burst her bombshell. 'Have you heard the news? Ramirez intends to declare war on Germany!'

'What?' Perón asked, stunned.

'It's true. A copy of the statement has been sent to Radio Belgrano.'

Perón thought quickly. 'Has it been announced yet?'

'No. The announcement will not be made until the morning because of the time difference,' Eva informed him.

Perón burst into wild, self-satisfied laughter.

'What is it, *mi vida*?' he heard Eva's tiny voice in the earphone ask.

He controlled his laughter and quickly told her what had happened.

'What has that got to do with Ramirez declaring war on Germany?'

'Don't you see? Ramirez has strung himself up to the highest branch he can find. The GOU will take great delight in swinging on his legs. They still want to do a deal with the Germans in the belief that the Nazis will come out ahead.

They are not going to stand for the President declaring war on Germany without their permission.'

'What are you going to do?'

'Do? I'm going to kick that pompous idiot out. That's what I'm going to do.'

Eva caught her breath. She still hadn't the experience to understand the politics of power. Getting rid of a president was something out of her sphere of knowledge. 'Do you want me to come over?' she asked.

'No. You hang around the radio station. I will let you know how the operation progresses. I might need your support on the air.'

Organising the army was Perón's forte. She could do more good at Radio Belgrano.

'Well, good luck. Phone me when you get a chance.'

Perón promised and hung up. Then he got out his little book of telephone numbers and started rallying support.

SIXTEEN

The crunch of wheels woke President Ramirez. Instinctively he knew what was coming. Terrified he reached for the telephone. A strange voice answered. Without speaking he got quietly out of bed, slipped into his silk dressing-gown and ran nervous fingers through his hair. As he reached the door he heard his wife stir and her querulous voice ask what he was doing. 'Just going to get a breath of fresh air, dear . . .' he told her soothingly.

If he had to go he wanted it to be with as much dignity as possible. Not being berated by his wife. As he reached the foot of the stairs he heard footsteps. A party of six officers came through the archway from the reception hall and stopped when they saw him. He looked them over coldly, determined to gain their respect in defeat.

'What is the meaning of this, gentlemen?' he demanded firmly. One of the officers stepped forward and Ramirez' heart sank as he recognised the big shoulders and smiling, sunburnt face of Colonel Perón. With an extravagant bow Perón stopped in front of the beleaguered President.

'General Ramirez. I have come to repay your spokesman's call of yesterday afternoon in person. You may remember that you asked for my resignation?' His voice hardened but was still edged with mockery. 'Too soon, *Señor Presidente*, too soon.'

He indicated the others standing self-consciously behind him. 'We are here to demand *your* resignation as President of the Federal Republic of Argentina. We have to inform you that the city is in our hands and the provinces will be by tomorrow morning. The Residency is completely surrounded.'

Ramirez drew himself up to his full height. 'This is

preposterous. You have no constitutional right for this act. I demand a meeting of the Senate to decide the validity of your action.'

'If you wish to take that course, you may. In the meanwhile General Edelmiro Farrell – the Minister of War – will be acting President of Argentina.' Perón was ready to let Ramirez' indignant demand – to go before the Senate – rest. They both knew that once a coup had taken place it was virtually impossible to retract.

The ex-President gave a little bow. 'Gentlemen, you force me to accept the situation for the time being. I shall remain in my quarters. In the morning I shall consider what steps to take.'

His dignified exit was spoiled by the strident voice of his wife calling from the bedroom. 'What are you doing, Pepe, come up at once or I'll have you in bed with a cold before you know where you are.' In confusion Ramirez turned and ran up the stairs leaving his ex-colleagues to splutter in ill-concealed derision.

'Be a patriot – kill a Jew!'

The crude letters ran streakily down the shuttered windows giving the sentiment an added malevolence.

'Pacho' Dieter stood back, swaying a little from drink, and admired his handiwork. It made him feel important to be actually doing something for the revolution. He could imagine the shop-owner's fear when he saw the words as he counted his money in the squalid, evil-smelling pigsty he lived in. His hand would tremble knowing that he could no longer expect to live off the backs of the Argentine workers he had exploited for so long. Pacho wished he could stay to see the sight but he wasn't sure that he wouldn't get into trouble. The police were unpredictable. Generally they ignored the growing anti-Semitism but you could never be sure.

He wished he could go back to his grandfather's Germany where they really knew what was going on. The Nazi Party recognised that seventeen years was old enough to know what was what. It was up to the German Jungvolk to push through the dreams that the older generation, with its prissy, outgrown ethics, were too chicken livered to grasp.

Since he had been a child, living on the pittance his father earned as a packer in one of the Jewish owned clothes manufacturing companies, Pacho had heard the stories of exploitation. He had no doubt that the child-stealing and white slavery existed in Buenos Aires just the same as it did in Germany. You only had to look at a Jew and you could tell. The pale skin with the straggling filthy hair that bred a deadly form of lice that, once it got into the hair of anyone without Jewish blood, caused baldness and made you deaf. And the hooked nose dividing the crafty close-set eyes.

Pacho often boasted that he was extra sensitive to Jews. He claimed that his pure Aryan blood prickled in his veins whenever a Jew was near. In a city with a high percentage of Italians in the population this was a brave claim. But then, until now, other than passing the odd derogatory remark or telling highly dramatised stories of his anti-Jewish crusade when he was out by himself, he had never made an actual attempt to implement the solution that Himmler visualised.

Today he had broken through the barrier that had separated him from his blood brothers in the Nazi Party. His first problem had been finding a Jew. In spite of his boasting he had no idea what a real Jew looked like. Then he remembered that the firm his father worked for had several retail outlets. When he had been younger his father had taken him when he delivered stock to the shops. The next problem was what to do.

He thought of setting fire to the place but the prospect frightened him. Maybe break a few windows? No. That was childish – anyway most of the shops had put up shutters since the unions had become militant and taken to marching through the streets. Pacho remembered the mottoes he had seen scrawled on walls throughout the city. That seemed a way to strike for his ideals and run the least risk of ending up in a cell.

He had only just finished his message of hate when he was

154

aware of someone close by. Before he could move, a hand struck him a heavy blow across the bridge of his nose. Automatically he swung up his arm to ward off a second blow. The heavy paint tin thudded into the head of his assailant, splashing paint in all directions. He saw the dark figure fall to the ground.

The pain in his nose had brought tears to his eyes. Without thinking he kicked the stunned body on the floor. Suddenly he noticed that his assailant was a woman. The discovery excited him. Whenever he talked about women he pretended that he was an experienced and much sought after lover. In fact, beyond a few frightened scuffles in back alleys and playgrounds, his sexual experience was confined to his imagination and his right hand. Fear, pain and intoxication exploded into an overpowering sexuality.

He dropped on his knees beside the girl. For a moment he thought he had killed her but then she moaned softly and her eyes fluttered open. Panicking he punched her in the face and stood, ready to run off. The girl had fallen on her back, her white legs splayed open revealing the dark tops of her stockings and suspender belt fasteners. He giggled to himself and nodded his head sagely. Cautiously, like a novice tightrope walker, he bent down and eased her skirt up further to reveal a wide-legged, lace trimmed pair of silk knickers. Pacho forgot everything as his wine blanched brain, heated by virgin sexuality, pushed all consideration aside. Like an animal he grabbed the girl's legs and dragged her unconscious body into the darkness of a narrow alley running between two of the buildings.

Isabel Ernest was aware that she was crying. She couldn't think why. It took concentration and for some reason her mind refused to act responsibly. She brought her hand to her face and noticed with surprise that it felt cold and sticky. She turned her head to the side and frowned. Something was wrong. There seemed to be earth on her bed. Pain and memory crowded back together so sharply that she gave a shriek. Slowly she pushed herself into a sitting position and looked around. Vaguely she could see the outline of buildings. As she tried to get to her feet she realised for the first time that her clothes were missing. The shock made her slump back to the ground. She had been raped!

Pain and fear were forgotten for the moment, thrown aside by the enervating thought that she had been violated. A noise in the darkness brought back the fear. Sobbing she scrambled around on the dark ground looking for her clothes. Her skirt still hung in tatters from her waist. She found her blouse but her shoes, panties and brassiere eluded her.

Desperately she ran for the nearby buildings. Cowering in the dark she tried to organise her thoughts. Embarrassment stopped her from stepping out onto the street and running to the shop. Her father had never liked her coming home after dark by herself. This would only confirm his often repeated argument that good Jewish girls should stay at home and look after the household. Isabel sunk to her knees and pressed her forehead against the rough plaster wall. If only her mother were alive she could go home. Tears ran uncontrollably down her face, mingling with the blood and paint.

She didn't know how long she stayed crouched, sick and aching, in the little space between the houses when a name came into her mind.

Eva Duarte.

Eva had always been friendly to her and even now, when she practically ran the radio station and was going out with one of the most powerful men in the country, she always stopped for a little chat or to ask how she was. Eva's friendship was all that kept Isabel behind the reception desk at Radio Belgrano, in spite of her family's pressure to come into their business.

Whenever she walked past the tall apartment building on the corner, where her street joined Rivadavia, she got a little thrill by looking at the name opposite one of the push buttons and reminding herself that her friend lived in the exotic elegance of her own apartment. As soon as Isabel thought of Eva she began to calm down. She thought how she could get to the corner of the street without being seen.

Shakily she got to her feet and started picking her way along the path that ran behind the shops. It was used as a garbage tip by most of the shopkeepers and several times she stumbled and fell on unseen obstacles. Through a gap in the buildings in front of her she could see the headlights of cars as they swept swiftly along the main road. Without knowing how she got there she found herself staring at the little oblong of cardboard under the glass nameplate. 'Srta. Duarte.'

She focused her eyes on the black button beside it and willed her trembling, filthy hand to reach out and press it. A tinny, distant voice queried, '*Quien es?*'

She put her mouth next to the grill circle and whispered: 'Isabel Ernest.'

There was a pause and then the voice came again. '*Quien?*'

'Isabel Ernest. Please, Eva, let me in. Let me in,' she shouted wildly.

There was a buzz. Isabel turned the handle and collapsed into the small hall.

Perón was about to leave when his telephone rang. He was taking Eva to the Colón Theatre to see a programme of excerpts from operas put on by the resident operatic company. It wasn't really his type of show but Eva had insisted. The theatre had been doing good business and Eva wanted to go so that she could discuss it on her radio programme the next day.

Eva's voice was short and angry. 'Are you coming?'

Perón was surprised. 'Of course, *querida*. There's plenty of time.'

'Forget the opera,' Eva said shortly. 'Get here as quickly as possible.'

'*Si, mi General!*' Perón answered, irritated by her tone of voice.

The phone clicked as Eva hung up, leaving Perón holding the phone. He shrugged his shoulders, slammed the phone on the hook and went down to his car.

Eva swung her flat door open before he could knock. She avoided Perón's attempt at a clumsy embrace and walked into the bedroom. He followed slowly, wondering what he had done to deserve Eva's disapproval. He was never sure with her. It was one of her traits that annoyed him but at the same time attracted him to her.

The figure, lying deathly white in Eva's fussy feminine bed, surprised him. He looked at Eva for an explanation.

'Do you know who that is?' she asked.

Perón looked closer. He noticed for the first time bruises and cuts on the woman's face and what seemed to be paint plastered in her hair and drying on her face. Mystified he shook his head.

'No, should I? What's happened to her?'

Instead of answering, Eva caught hold of the blanket and pulled it off the unconscious figure. Perón looked at the naked woman. Paint streaked her body and it was a mass of contusions. Eva had tied some of the worst cuts up with bandages that leaked red globules onto the sheets. Eva covered the battered body of her friend.

'She's been raped. That's what happened to her,' Eva stated baldly.

Perón pulled the corners of his mouth down and raised his shoulders expressively. 'So? I'm sorry for your friend but what has it got to do with me?'

'Do you know why she was raped?' Eva continued in a flat, unfriendly voice.

Again Perón shook his head. 'No. And I don't particularly want to know. Get the police if it concerns you that much.' He took a cigarette from his gold case and walked back into the sitting room. Eva rushed after him and swung him around to face her.

'Well – you should be interested. She was raped because she's a Jew!'

'So! She's a Jew. Women get raped all the time. Why should her being a Jew make her case different.'

Eva clenched her fists in frustration. '*Dios mio*! Don't you

158

ever think? Okay. So the Jews aren't popular. They never have been popular. Until now? Last week you were complaining that Roosevelt and Churchill had compared Argentina with Nazi Germany. You told me that you weren't interested in going down the road that the Fascists in Europe had taken. So why do you condone anti-Semitism?'

Perón held up his hand in a placatory manner. 'That's not true. I believe what Mussolini and Hitler tried to do in Europe was right. It's just that they got diverted. I know where they went wrong and I'm not likely to make the same mistake.'

Eva jumped in. 'Then why allow your enemies to point to what's happening all over the city. It's Berlin all over again. Tonight it was just a few boys out on the streets. Tomorrow they will be heroes and others will join in. There's hardly a street in Buenos Aires that doesn't have walls plastered with anti-Jewish graffiti. And remember this. A lot of our business abroad is done with Jewish companies. If they hear what is going on here they are going to hit back. At the moment they have Ramirez and Farrell to blame. Let them. Put the word out to the police that anti-Jewish activities are to be discouraged. It will win you more friends than you imagine.'

Eva sat on the arm of a chair, exhausted by her outburst. She watched Perón take out another cigarette and walk slowly up and down the room, deep in thought.

He stopped in front of her.

'*Bueno* – you are right, of course. I'll pass the word along to lay off the Jews.' He laughed. 'After all – we do have the imperialistic British and the capitalistic Americans to throw stones at.'

SEVENTEEN

SS *Sturmführer* Hans Brüler studied the face of the blonde girl opposite him. He could hardly recognise her as the golden girl he had seen run naked through the surf at Guarujá a few months earlier. Then she had been angry and withdrawn but there had been a spark of life in her pale blue eyes. Now she sat, a well-dressed doll, automatically answering questions when asked but switching off and not adding anything voluntarily.

Physically she had changed too. Her hair was still blonde and well cared for, her clothes chic and well-tailored but they hung on her awkwardly as if they had been made with the measurements not quite accurate. But the biggest change was in her face. It wasn't just the thickening across the bridge of her nose. Brüler had broken enough bones in his time to recognise the cause. Or the skilfully concealed scar on the side of her cheek. Her face had become more gaunt and deep lines made her look older.

They were sitting under the plastic marquee of one of the bistros lining the wide pavement opposite the tall, obelisk landmark soaring up from the ornamental gardens running down the centre of the Avenida Neuve de Julio.

Therese von Quast had been as good as her word. A few days after her return to Buenos Aires she had contacted Berlin to say that José Lopez Rega, sergeant in the Argentine Infantry, was willing to become more active on the part of the Nazi Party.

For information on the movements of his boss, Colonel Perón, and such other titbits he might be able to pass on he wanted two thousand pesos a month, paid in cash, plus whatever expenses he might incur. Berlin had automatically endorsed the deal without expecting to get much out of it at the time. They were buying for the future.

From the start the connection had come alive. As Perón's grip on the country tightened Lopez Rega had passed on more and more inside information that had led Berlin to believe that Perón would be happy to get the continued support of the Nazi Party in spite of the inevitability of the defeat of the German Army in Europe.

It was a simple equation. Perón's support depended on the backing of the officers in the GOU. Without the financial aid that Germany could give him he was just another Colonel with ideas. Lopez Rega had told them about Perón's part in the overthrow of Ramirez when the ex-President had wanted to declare war on Germany. The need for a friendly harbour had become desperate as the Allied Forces got a toehold in France and then began to sweep across Europe.

With the puppet President Farrell in the Casa Rosada Perón had wasted no time in consolidating his own position. He had added the Ministry of War to his bag; the Secretariat of Labour Welfare now had the status of a ministry and now he held the position of vice president as well. The vice presidency wasn't a job for an ambitious man. The constitution specifically excluded the vice president from running for the top job. It suited Perón. It backed up his claim to have no ambition to become President.

He had prompted Farrell into offering it to him because it at least eliminated others having easy access to the Casa Rosada and using it to their own advantage. The unions had been organised into a tightly unified bloc that had been purged of dissenting voices and filled with leaders who could be relied upon to back the Perón line. Newspapers were expected to print only what was compatible with the administration. Reporters or editors stepping out of line were quietly taken into an alley and beaten up by the increasing number of gaberdine-clad secret police patrolling the capital.

Berlin had mulled over Perón long and hard. They were

161

aware that they had been very clumsy in their handling of the astute and ruthless colonel. When they had been conquering nations overnight, the admiring Argentinian had seemed an easy manikin to wind up and point in the right direction. Too late they had realised that, safe in the fortress of his own country, the lessons he had learned in Europe could be used effectively against them.

The money that had been poured directly into his pocket to secure the Argentine army as a quisling force for Hitler had been used to consolidate Perón's own position. Now, when the crunch was coming, the Nazi Party had to come on their knees to beg the Argentine *Caudillo* to let a few pesos slip through his fingers to give the disintegrating Master-race somewhere to hide from the wrath of the world. This was why Brüler was now sitting across from Therese von Quast in the centre of Buenos Aires waiting to meet Lopez Rega.

Therese sat up straight. Brüler looked at her inquiringly but her attention was fixed across the avenue. Brüler followed her gaze but there were so many people milling about he failed to notice the nondescript man in the well-cut suit picking his way across the road towards them.

Now that 'Daniel' was near Therese experienced the feeling of sexual arousal and longing mixed with the cold fear that she always felt in his presence. She had long ago stopped hating herself for her unhealthy attachment to the demanding sergeant. Little by little her mind had collapsed in on itself. There was no longer the smallest objection to any of the unsavoury tasks Lopez Rega forced her to undertake. She entertained politicians in the luxury flat she now lived in, organised exotic parties in isolated *estancias* for officers, secured the services of any young girl who might catch the eye of her master and had begun to act as a principal in his consuming interest in the art of Black Magic.

Away from the influence of Lopez Rega, unless operating on instructions, she withdrew into the remnants of her mind, neither hearing nor seeing what went on about her. Her uncle had seen the change and tried to break the

162

indecent influence the sergeant had over her. A painful visit from a couple of big men in gabardine raincoats convinced him that he should mind his own business.

Now, fascinated, Brüler watched the transformation in the woman sitting opposite him. Colour flooded her cheeks, she seemed to grow into her clothes and dullness in her eyes melted into an intense, adoring glint of utter devotion.

Brüler looked up and tried to evaluate the new arrival. Medium height, a plain, closed face, expensive but unassuming clothes. Nothing that could account for the change in the cool, fashionably dressed woman of a respectable family into a devoted, fawning slave. Then Lopez Rega looked at him. Brüler had seen the look before. The power that blazed from the brown, hooded eyes made the German uneasy. He waved a hand towards Therese to distract the comfortless eyes.

'Señorita von Quast suggested we meet here. I hope that was all right.'

Lopez Rega nodded and patted the woman on the head like a favoured puppy. 'Captain Brüler. I'm glad we have been able to meet at last. What can I do for you?'

The SS man looked quickly around to see if he was being overheard. 'My superiors in Berlin want your opinion on the present situation in Argentina. Of course we know the political line-up and the strength and weaknesses of the various factions. What we want is an assessment of Colonel Perón's ability to push through all the promises he has made and still retain a command of the army and the goodwill of the *estancieros*.'

Expressionless, Lopez Rega looked the German over. 'What do you expect me to say?' he asked. 'If I knew the answers to that I wouldn't need to do underhand deals with you for a few *pesos*.'

'Hardly a few *pesos*, Herr Lopez Rega.'

Lopez Rega shrugged. 'You are talking about your investment of thousands of millions of *pesos*. You are asking me to guarantee it for you and you pay me no more than you spend on a night out in Hamburg.'

Brüler's face went hard. 'Perhaps you forget, Sergeant, that you have been selling information about your superior officers to a foreign power. That would not look good if it got back to them.'

Lopez Rega leaned across the table and his eyes bored into Brüler's soul.

'Captain. Don't be foolish,' he said simply.

Brüler's mind supplied the material for the deadly threat the Sergeant implied and he covered up hastily. 'I'm sorry sergeant. But I have to have something to report back to Berlin. Tell me your opinion. That's all we want.'

'My opinion?' Lopez Rega looked around. 'You don't need my opinion. You can ask anyone here or on the streets. In a year Colonel Perón has done more for the people of Argentina than anyone has ever attempted before. Wages have gone up by fifty per cent. Every man is entitled to two weeks' holiday with pay a year. The unions really mean something now so a working man has protection.

'Of course it hasn't been done without upsetting a few people. The oligarchy, which traditionally controls the country, hate him. Generally they own the press and the radio. Perón has had to control these. They ignored the basic fact that the *Coronel* was the first man in the history of this country to do anything for the working class. The unions are aware of this and support him unquestioningly.' Lopez Rega paused.

'And the army?' Brüler asked.

Lopez Rega gave a short dry laugh. 'The army are so stuffed with ideals they can't shit. They feel that Perón is an adventurer. Not quite the gentleman. Unfortunately all his detractors owe him money. They don't want to be forced into paying it back. So these honourable gentlemen mutter amòngst themselves and hope that the *Coronel* will make a mistake so that they can dance all over him. In the mean- while they will do what he says. If it came to a show of strength I would back the unions against the army any day.'

Brüler accepted that. 'And will Colonel Perón honour his

164

agreements with us?'

Lopez Rega gave a grimace of indifference. 'Why not? It's a big country. If your bosses want somewhere to run and are prepared to pay for it Perón will do a deal. He has big plans for Argentina and needs money. Tell your people to make a bid and I'm sure they will be accommodated.'

Brüler spluttered in amazement. 'But – but . . . Perón has already been paid.'

Absentmindedly Daniel put his hand on Therese's neck and gently massaged it. She closed her eyes in ecstasy.

'That was before. That was when victorious Germany had something to offer us. The deal was that you would take Europe and then together we could unite the world under our combined influence. You've fallen down on your end of the deal. It's time to re-negotiate.'

Suddenly Brüler realised that he was not talking to a paid spy. The man spoke with too much authority.

'What do you want?' he said simply, dropping the pretence of having a strong hand.

'It's not what I want, *Capitán*. I'm only Perón's chauffeur. He confides in me. I overhear things. You wanted my opinion. If you are prepared to negotiate I am sure *mi Coronel* will listen. More than that I cannot say.'

Lopez Rega stood up. 'If you want to talk to the *Coronel* tell Señorita von Quast and I will arrange it. In the meantime she will look after you while you are here. Have a good time.' He turned to Therese. 'You are to make sure that the captain has a good time in Argentina. I will contact you shortly.' Without another word he turned on his heel and disappeared into the crowd.

Therese watched him go and then turned to Brüler. 'What shall we do? I've booked a room at the Plaza, I hope that's all right. Is there anything you particularly want to see?'

Brüler looked at the friendly face with the warm inviting lips and dead eyes and felt sad.

EIGHTEEN

The blue Jacaranda trees lining the Avenida del Libertador heralded the spring. Everywhere thrusting buds were shaking off their dowdy husks as the hot sun raised the temperature above the winter sixties. As the black limousine with the Ministry of War identity plate swung into Calle Posadas, nannies sitting watching their charges in the shade of the giant *cohigues* trees nudged each other and with prim nods told each other of the arrival of the painted lady who was seducing the country.

If it hadn't been beneath their dignity to gossip, they would have repeated the tales whispered in the servants' hall of how the notorious Señorita Duarte spent her nights carousing with groups of officers in her sumptuously furnished apartment. The walls were said to be draped with silk to hide erotic paintings. And, above the huge, circular bed covered in black silk sheets was a gigantic, pink tinted mirror. But the nannies couldn't tell each other all the hundreds of colourful stories that were currently being circulated about the little actress from Radio Belgrano.

Not that Eva had time to worry about them. As her influence with the government had grown her interests now extended beyond Radio Belgrano. An intimate friend of her mother, Nicolini, had been given the post of Minister of Communications, enabling Eva to exercise a tight control over all broadcasting. The newspapers continued to snipe at the Farrell administration, making ill-advised comments on the growing power of Perón and charging him with nepotism and corruption. They had to be brought to heel, and Eva didn't think it would be hard to convince Perón. Newspapers depended on the supply of newsprint. It would be an easy job to hold up import permits for any of the papers that continued to try and sabotage Perón's efforts. But first she had a larger ambition to pursue – to push Perón into taking over the running of the country as President. If he wanted to come out from the shadows it would be a simple operation. Farrell would do whatever he was told. It was foolish of Perón to play second fiddle, having to negotiate through his power with the unions and the GOU.

The car pulled up outside the Posadas apartments and Eva took the lift up to the seventh floor. She now had her own apartment in the building next door to Perón. Apartment A.

As she stretched out in the bath she heard the outer door open and close. Perón came through and sat on the end of the bath. He looked worried.

'Nicolini's appointment is causing problems. It might be as well if we gave Communications to someone else. For the moment at least,' he said without preamble.

Eva sat up abruptly. 'What do you mean?' she demanded.

Perón gave his expressive shrug. 'General Avalos is being awkward. He says that Nicolini has no qualifications for the job. Perhaps he has a point. Nobody has come out with it yet but there is a lot of muttering about what they see as your interfering in government issues.'

'Do you think that?'

Perón went to the mirror and peered at the spots marring his cheeks. He looked at her in the mirror. 'It's not what I think. It's the problems that are being caused by giving critics a handle to hang on to. Perhaps it might be an idea if you went away for a while. Go to Europe for a holiday. By the time you come back it will have blown over and we can get down to planning ahead.'

'Like Hell!' Eva shouted violently. She pushed herself to her feet, water slopping onto the marble floor. 'Oscar Nicolini is doing a good job. We are getting a good crew around us. Avalos is kicking because he sees himself in the presidential sash and he knows that without breaking you first he doesn't stand a chance.'

Perón dabbed at his face with a piece of cotton wool. 'We

are moving too fast. Too many people are complaining. If we are not careful we can throw everything away that we have gained. It's not just Nicolini. People want to know what happened to the money from the Earthquake Appeal. They want to know what happened to all the plans for rebuilding San Juán.'

Eva snatched a fluffy pink towel from the rail at the end of the bath. 'You know what happened to that as well as I do. If you didn't feel this compulsion to buy everybody there wouldn't be any problems. When are you going to realise that your only safety is in taking the plunge and running for President?'

Perón swung round angrily. 'And when are you going to realise that it is better to work from behind the scenes?'

'Bullshit!' Eva shouted explosively. She hurled the damp towel into the corner and stamped through to the bedroom.

Perón followed. 'It's not bullshit. I control everything. But Farrell is up there taking all the stick if anything goes wrong.'

Eva took a pair of silk pyjamas and held them in front of her, turning side to side to get the best effect from the long mirror. 'Double bullshit,' she said quietly.

Perón grabbed the pyjamas and threw them on to the bed.

Eva stood in front of him, naked, and smiling. 'Why are you in such a state about Avalos wanting poor Nicolini out then? If you're so powerful tell him to go jump in the Rio de la Plata.' She retrieved her pyjamas and put them on.

Perón sat heavily on the end of the bed. Deliberately Eva turned to face him. 'I'll tell you this and then you do what you like. You can't stay in your present position. You have made too many enemies who want to stick a knife in your guts and drink the blood. You haven't got any choice. You must run for the presidency.'

'You know that's impossible. As vice-president I can't stand,' Perón said testily.

Eva came and sat beside him on the bed. 'How strongly do you believe in your New Argentina?'

Perón answered without hesitation. 'There is no alterna-

168

tive. Whether I do it or someone else, the order has got to be changed.'

'Well then, *mi amor*, if you think like that why don't you put your trust in the unions. Force a confrontation with the army before they force one on you.'

'What if I fail? Everything will have been for nothing.' Indecision made his voice weak.

Taking his hand Eva tried to soothe away his misgivings. 'You won't fail, Pappi. You know you won't!' She jumped up and pulled him to his feet. 'Now what time is Avalos and his band of old ladies due?'

Perón glanced at his watch. 'About a quarter of an hour.'

'Good. Go and change. Put on something casual. Tell them that you don't intend to do anything about Nicolini and they will have to go and see the President. Farrell won't do anything without you and they know it. If they cut up rough we will get Reyes on the streets with his men and that should convince them that they are backing a loser.' She pulled his head down and kissed him on the ear. 'I'll be in shortly.'

Perón stopped. 'Don't you think you should keep out of the way while I talk to them?'

'Not likely. I want to see their faces,' Eva laughed.

Perón tried to smile but it wasn't very effective. 'I hope you're right,' he muttered as he left.

As the door closed Eva heard the bell ring, and then a murmur of male voices.

In the next room Perón, with a mighty effort, slipped on his mask of relaxed urbanity. General Avalos was the one who showed symptoms of uneasiness. He perched awkwardly on the most uncomfortable chair in the room, tapping his foot. The three other officers held themselves to rigid attention as they studiously avoided looking at Perón and sipped their whiskies.

The colonel himself looked a picture of unconcerned friendliness. '*Bueno, Amigos*. Now we can talk. You have some problems you wish to discuss? As always I am at your service. It is something to do with the army?' He saw Avalos stiffen.

'It is about the appointment of Señor Oscar Nicolini to the post of Minister of Communications. We feel, *Coronel* Perón, that this appointment is totally unjustified. The Ministry is a vitally important department. It needs a man with a wealth of experience to run it. Someone who knows more about radio and telephones than Señor Nicolini, who was only a minor official in the post office a month ago.'

Perón studied the liquid in his glass before speaking. He smiled apologetically at the four men. 'I don't understand. Why do you come to me about this? Nicolini's appointment was surely made by the President? It's nothing to do with me.'

General Avalos interrupted him. 'You recommended him for the job.'

Perón nodded. 'True. The members of his union petitioned me to honour Nicolini in this way for his long and excellent work in the post office. I told them that it was not in my power to authorise such a promotion and passed it on.' He looked innocently at Avalos.

'But the man is totally unsuitable for the position,' the general said loudly.

Perón pursed his lips reflectively. 'You have met him, General?'

'I have no wish to meet him,' he said.

Perón uncoiled his long legs and went to refill his glass. 'A pity. I have met him and he seems to me to be exactly right for the job. He has worked all his life in the post office. He is a self-educated man of charm and wit. There are few areas of the postal service that he hasn't worked in or has some first-hand knowledge of its operation. To me, I must admit, he seems eminently qualified.'

Avalos spluttered. 'But he has no experience at government level.'

Before Perón could reply the door behind the general opened and Eva stepped into the room. She was still wearing her silk pyjamas and had made her face and hair a copy of the sensual photographs in the film magazines.

Perón walked around the general and drew her to the centre of the room.

'I would like you to meet my neighbour, General. Señorita Duarte. You may have heard of her. She does a lot of work on Radio Belgrano.'

Avalos got to his feet. The *señorita* had been the second subject that he wished to discuss with Perón.

Eva turned her blazing smile on the other three. She accepted a glass of orange juice from Perón, and then sat on the floor to sip it. She looked at the men staring down at her, nonplussed by her behaviour. She waved the glass at them.

'Don't mind me. You just carry on.'

Perón smiled at the other men reassuringly. 'Gentlemen, please sit down.'

The three who had insisted on standing earlier felt uncomfortable towering over the diminutive Eva so they sat down.

Perón smiled encouragement at the general. 'Now, General, what were you saying?'

The general pulled himself together. 'I said that Señor Nicolini had no experience to take on such an important job.' Avalos' voice wavered as he finished and stared in amazement at Eva.

Perón controlled the impulse to turn. 'Surely that's not true, General. He must have been more suitable than Colonel Imbert who had the job before. His only experience of the telephone service was dialling a number.'

He heard the rustle of silk and saw all four pairs of eyes staring behind him. He shifted his position slightly so that he could see what Eva was doing. It was so unexpected that Perón had difficulty in not bursting out laughing.

Eva had taken a cushion from one of the chairs and was now standing on her head in the corner. The wide, silk legs of her pyjamas had ridden up to reveal practically the whole length of her shapely legs. She saw him looking and her scarlet mouth split in a cocky grin. Quickly he turned back so that he could not see her and continued as if nothing untoward was happening.

'The job is one needing common sense and a good working knowledge of post office routine throughout the country. I believe in the principal of promoting a man to high office if he has proved that he is worthy of promotion. His background should cause no objection.' He stopped, realising that he had lost his visitors' attention once more. He could hear Eva's rasping breath as she continued her callisthenics. He eased around again until he could see her. She was now rhythmically bending down and touching alternate toes. He shook his head. Whatever she might not be doing for Perón she was certainly upsetting Avalos' equilibrium.

Perón called attention back to himself. 'Was that all, General?'

The general shut out the unbelievable sight of the beautiful blonde woman standing in the corner doing physical jerks while he discussed serious business concerning the government.

'No, Perón, I'm afraid not. It has been decided that Señor Oscar Nicolini is totally unsuited for high office. We therefore intend to ask for his dismissal. We understand that you proposed his appointment and we therefore extend to you the courtesy of informing the President of his unsuitability. We are quite prepared for Nicolini to be given a less senior position.'

To Perón it seemed a storm in a teacup. Eva had suggested Nicolini to secure the control of all communications. If he hadn't been the lover of Eva's mother nobody would have objected. He was about to make some conciliatory gesture when he became aware that Eva's breathing had become harsher. He looked around. She was lying on her back, feet above her head, her legs peddling furiously. She gave him a fierce look.

Perón attracted the general's attention again.

'I'm sorry that I can't oblige you, General Avalos, but I'm afraid there is a matter of principle involved,' he began slowly. 'While I have no interest, basically, in who is appointed to government posts outside my sphere of

172

influence, I feel that you are objecting to Nicolini's appointment for reasons other than those that can be termed pertinent to the case. If Nicolini is forced to go I will resign immediately.'

As he finished talking Eva got to her feet. She was satisfied with the way Perón had handled the situation. She smiled brightly around the room. 'Coffee anybody?'

The men shook their heads.

Eva sat down in a chair by the window and beamed healthily. Avalos' nerves failed him. He couldn't bring himself to mention the subject of Eva's increasing interference in areas that didn't concern her. He stood up and his three silent aides hastily followed suit.

'I'm sorry that you have taken this attitude, *Coronel* Perón.'

He led his coterie of officers from the apartment. Perón shut the door and leaned against the frame, hooting with laughter. Eva watched him, an occasional tic puckering her cheek. With an effort Perón controlled his hilarity to rush across the room and scoop Eva up and collapsed with her in his arms onto the sofa.

'You little cow, what was all that about?' He started to tickle her sending Eva into wild convulsions. 'Tell me,' Perón insisted. 'Tell me or I won't stop. Why the hell did you put on that performance? Avalos can't wait to get back to the Campo de Mayo and tell them all our sinful secrets.'

Eva at last managed to roll off the sofa. She quickly put a chair between herself and Perón. 'Leave me alone. You know very well why I had to stick my oar in, you would have won him over by selling Nicolini to them.'

Perón became serious. 'So? I'm not that enamoured of your mother's lover that I fancy risking everything to keep him in a sinecure,' he said.

'It's nothing to do with Oscar. If he threatened your position I would see that he went myself. You yourself keep telling me that the GOU don't like your association with the unions. While they continue to look on the unions as a rabble they are going to continue cracking the whip every so

173

often. Show them you are stronger than they are. Force a show of hands and then take the presidency. If you don't – I will guarantee that you are slung out before the end of the year.'

There was no hint of a smile on Eva's face as she uttered her warning in a flat hard voice.

NINETEEN

In the plush office that nobody had used long enough to have had any effect upon for thirty years, the present incumbent, General Edelmiro Farrell, sat daydreaming of the sexy little torch-singer, Toca Tampa, he had been seeing late at night after her stint at El Gato Loco was over.

In front of him were three large leather covers in different colours, each containing letters or orders that needed his signature.

The presidency bored him. Several times he had tried to get Perón to let him go. Retire so that he could flirt with women and play his guitar without having to consider his august position. Miserably he pulled one of the books towards him and took up a pen. How different it could have been if he had studied music instead of being forced into the army by his ambitious but impecunious father.

As so many presidents had done before him he looked at the gilt clock on the mantelpiece and groaned inwardly. Farrell had agreed to see Avalos. He knew what the general wanted but felt unequal to the task of making a decision. General Avalos arrived and launched without preamble into the reason for his visit. He told the President of Perón's intention to resign unless Señor Nicolini was confirmed in his new post as Minister of Communications and the determination of the officers stationed at the Campo de Mayo to force the issue. His call on the President, he explained, was a courtesy visit so that he would be aware of the situation.

Farrell nodded miserably. It was what he expected. Having delivered his message Avalos excused himself and officiously bustled off. Farrell tried to bring himself to sign some more letters, but was suddenly interrupted by the unexpected arrival of Perón himself. The colonel had been in the building for some time although his arrival hadn't been signalled to Farrell. He had guessed that Avalos would visit the President and wanted the general to say his piece first.

Perón now walked into the President's office unannounced. The two friends clasped hands warmly and Perón accepted a drink before sitting comfortably in the chair facing Farrell across the wide desk top.

'I've come to give you my resignation, *Che*. I've had enough. Besides I've not been feeling too good recently. A change of pace will do me good.'

Farrell protested. 'Surely it's not that bad? If it's this Nicolini affair I'm sure we can straighten that out. I'll get rid of him myself. That should satisfy Avalos. He can hardly push for something that doesn't exist.'

Slowly Perón shook his head, letting Farrell see the pained gratitude in his eyes. '*Gracias, amigo*. If you insist I will stay. But I do not intend to let you interfere on my behalf. If Nicolini goes – I go.'

'And if I can get Avalos to withdraw his ultimatum?' Farrell asked.

Perón bowed his head. 'My fate is in your hands, *Presidente*. If Avalos will stand down I will be pleased to continue as Vice President.'

Farrell stood up quickly. 'Very well. I will go myself to the Campo de Mayo and talk to the chiefs of staff. I will convey my decision to you as soon as possible.'

Perón stood and solemnly shook hands with his President. '*Gracias, mi Presidente*. I count myself fortunate to have such a good friend.'

The President's chances of persuading General Avalos to back down were nil but Perón wanted it to go on record that he had acted responsibly in the unfortunate matter. After Perón had left to go back to the War Office Farrell called his car and went on his futile errand to see General Avalos at the garrison of the Campo de Mayo.

Perón was beginning to enjoy himself. Carefully studying all the variations and computations of Eva's master strategy he had realised that it was workable. It was involved and depended on a great deal of theatrical device but the outcome would give him undisputed command of the instruments of power. Already he had warmed to the idea of being President. He had what no president had been able to count on before. Mass support of the workers. And it was going to turn the history of Argentina on its head.

Like a child playing with toys he had leaked the coming confrontation to a few loyal supporters in the army. He had the Third Division, stationed at Paraná, standing by. Brigadier de la Colina was ready to swing into action with twenty-four Glen Martin bombardment guns as well as ten naval guns on the alert. More than enough to subdue any move General Avalos' troops might make. But he didn't intend to use the force available to him. It was there so that he could point to the restraint he had shown in not pitching the capital into a state of bloody civil war to save himself.

That devious move had been suggested by Eva. She was well aware of the need for Perón to appear to be the powerful but humane leader who was besieged by unscrupulous and treacherous colleagues motivated purely by self interest.

But as the showdown came closer Perón could not altogether control a nervousness that manufactured surplus acid to gnaw at the walls of his intestines. It was late afternoon when his secretary came in to say that General Carlos von der Becke and General Pistarini were in the outer office and wanted to see him urgently. Both were old friends from their cadet days.

He swept out into the outer office himself and held his arms wide in welcome. The guilty look the two men exchanged amused him. 'Von der Becke, Pistarini. How nice to see you. Come in! Come in!' He shepherded them into his office.

As soon as the door closed von der Becke said in a low serious voice: 'We come from the President.'

Perón let his face freeze into seriousness as if for the first time he associated the visit of his friends with Avalos' demand for his head. 'What has the President decided?' he asked coldly. He addressed the question to von der Becke who was obviously the more distressed of the two.

The general swallowed. 'Pistarini will inform you of that,' he blurted out and turned and hurried from Perón's office.

Perón looked at Pistarini. 'Von der Becke appears to be somewhat emotional about the President's decision. Perhaps you will be good enough to let me know what it is?'

'The President feels that, in the circumstances, it would be advisable if you resign.' The general spoke quickly to get the moment over.

It was exactly what Perón had expected. What he had planned for. But unreasonably he felt the blood drain from his face and his stomach give a painful lurch. He slid his hand inside his coat and gently massaged the pain. It was one thing to plan and another to execute such an audacious plan.

He said nothing to Pistarini and called his ADC. In a quiet controlled voice he gave his orders. 'I want you to give the order that all troops movements are to cease and they will return to their barracks without provoking incidents. I do not wish to have the blood of one soldier on my hands when my resignation is announced.'

The ADC looked up, startled by Perón's order. 'But – *mi Coronel* –' he started to protest.

The order had been for Pistarini's sake. Perón wanted the general to know that even in apparent defeat he operated from a position of power. 'Bring me a piece of paper so that I can write my resignation immediately.'

The ADC went to get the paper, leaving Pistarini and the colonel to await his return in an uncomfortable silence. Perón took the paper from his ADC and dismissed him.

Without a word he sat down and wrote: 'His Excellency the President of the Nation. I hereby resign my position as Vice-President, Minister of War and Secretary of Labour

178

and Welfare with all of which your Excellency has deigned to honour me.' He signed it 'Juán Domingo Perón', without rank or status, and handed it to Pistarini.

'Please, be kind enough to convey this to President Farrell,' he said evenly.

General Pistarini read it through quickly. 'Do you want me to have it typed for you?' he asked.

Perón opened the top drawer of his desk and started clearing out his personal effects, lining them up on the blotter on the desk top.

'I have written it by hand so that the President can see that my hand did not tremble as I wrote it,' he stated pompously.

Pistarini, humbled, bowed, and backed out of the room. When the door shut Perón got out his calming milk of magnesia and took a long draught straight from the bottle.

TWENTY

Eva kissed Perón goodbye at the door and then waited by the window until she saw his car drive out onto the avenue before sitting down at the polished walnut escritoire and taking out her address book.

What she was about to do excited her. It frightened her too. That was why she hadn't said anything to Perón about it. Since she had convinced him to manoeuvre for the presidency his grasp of the tactics had been surer and more organised than she could have managed.

He had got himself dismissed from the Vice Presidency without losing sympathy. Now she had to make sure that his powerful enemies didn't stamp him out of existence while he was down. Already she had been given one example of how easy it was to fall out of bed.

When she turned up at Radio Belgrano there was a message waiting for her to go to see Yankelevich. Avalos had not wasted a second. He knew how powerful Eva could be on the radio and he had told the Russian that if he didn't get rid of her immediately the transmitter licence might not be so easy to come by in the future. Without Perón's protection Yankelevich had to comply.

As Eva walked in the door Yankelevich covered up his sense of treachery with bluster. 'Get out! You're finished here. Your lover Perón can no longer prop you up. Get out!'

Eva had been too surprised to utter anything more forceful than a stream of dockside invective as a protest. But she had gone. She was realistic enough to appreciate her ex-employer's situation but was not forgiving enough to forget his rejection. She hadn't told Perón what had happened. She didn't want him getting cold feet now.

The first number she rang was that of Oscar Nicolini in

Calle Paraguay. Avalos, in the excitement of his unexpected ousting of Perón, had forgotten the original cause of the confrontation and Eva's friend still occupied his position in Communications. She was quickly put through.

'Oscar? Eva here. How are things going?' she asked in a calm, friendly voice.

Nicolini was happy to hear from her. Few people dared to ring him at the moment and he was already aware that acquaintances hurried off pretending not to see him when he approached. '*No hay problemas, linda,*' he said gratefully.

'*Bueno.* Then I want you to do something. It's important if you want to keep your job,' Eva told him bluntly. 'Perón has just gone down to the Ministry of War to clear up a few things and say goodbye. Later he is going to the Secretariat of Labour and Welfare. I'm arranging for a bit of demonstration. Quiet and dignified. Perón will say a few words. I want you to get onto all the radio stations and let them know what's happening. I want his speech to go out live. The newspapers have been having a field-day with his resignation. I want Perón's side of the story to go out unedited. You understand?'

'*Si* – I understand,' he whispered, fearfully.

Eva laughed. 'Don't be so pessimistic, Oscar. It's not over yet. Not by a long way!'

Her dynamism lifted Nicolini. 'Right. I'll get on to it straight away.'

'Give my love to Mama,' Eva told him before hanging up.

Her next call was to the police force. Eva had always been careful to cultivate the police. So far there had been no new chief appointed so she asked for the captain in charge of the watch.

It was Captain Mendez. She remembered him. It was the same man who had been at the confrontation in the railway yard behind the slaughterhouse. His support for Perón at the time had stood him in good stead so far but now his known affiliation with the discredited colonel could work against him.

'*Capitàn* Mendez?' she trilled brightly.

'*Si, Señora?*' Mendez answered discouragingly.

'Eva Duarte here.' She gave him a second to adjust.

'Ah – *si, señorita. Como esta?*' he said in a more friendly voice.

'*Estoy bien, Capitán, gracias.*' She paused dramatically. 'That is . . .' She let her voice trail away.

'Something wrong, *señorita?*' He guessed it was to do with Perón but didn't know what to say. For months he had been building up his hopes on the colonel successfully taking full control and his downfall had come as a blow.

'You've heard?' Eva said enigmatically.

'*Si!*' he answered shortly.

'Can I depend on your help?' she asked softly.

Excitement welled in his chest.

'Of course, *señorita.* But isn't it too late?' he asked.

'Not if we act quickly,' Eva assured him. 'Did you see the newspapers today?'

'*Si, señorita.*' The papers had crowed over Perón's downfall making much of his pro-Nazi leanings.

'And did you see the bit about the troops being put on the alert and moved into strategic parts of the city?' she asked.

Mystified Mendez could only repeat, '*Si, señorita.*'

Eva's voice became brisker: 'The state of emergency still exists, doesn't it?'

Light dawned for Mendez. '*Si, si, señorita.* Of course it does.'

'Then . . .' Eva said measuring each word carefully. 'What are the newspapers doing reporting troop movements. Aren't they forbidden to do this on pain of closure during an emergency?'

Mendez was already reaching for the inter-office telephone. '*Si, señorita.* You are right. Under emergency powers we can act when an obvious breach of security exists. This is a flagrant breach of security. An injunction will be slapped on all the newspapers straight away.'

By the time Eva had dialled the next number squads of police were being briefed about closing the newspapers, which had danced too soon on Perón's grave.

Lopez Rega was with Perón at the Ministry but slipped away unnoticed when he was called to the telephone. His fate was still bound with that of Perón and he knew that the power he exerted through his own hand-picked bunch of operatives would be hard to maintain if he no longer had the colonel's backing.

'*Hóla!*' he said into the mouthpiece.

'*Sargento* Lopez Rega?' Eva carefully affirmed before saying anything more.

'*Si, señorita.*' Lopez Rega recognised her voice. He always felt uneasy talking to Eva.

'What's the *Coronel* doing now?' she asked.

Lopez Rega looked automatically towards Perón's office. 'He is talking to some of the staff,' he reported.

That suited Eva. '*Bueno.* Now listen, Daniel. Keep him there as long as you can then get him over to the Secretariat of Labour. I've got the radio people arriving there in an hour or two and I want you to get onto Reyes, and whoever else you can think of, to arrange a spontaneous demonstration of support. At least a thousand I want on the streets. Two if you can manage it. Can you do that?'

This was something Lopez Rega could understand. 'Right away, *señorita.* Don't worry – I'll have more than that outside the Secretariat.'

Eva gave a low, conspiratorial chuckle. '*Gracias, che.*' She hung up and consulted her book again. As she telephoned she kept one ear tuned to the radio. At last she heard what she was waiting for. The commentator told of the huge spontaneous demonstration going on outside the Secretariat of Labour. In an emotional voice he told of women holding babies up for Perón to touch, and grizzled workmen in their sweat-stained clothes begging the colonel, with tears in their eyes, not to desert them. She waited impatiently. At last Colonel Perón was announced and after the crowd had been quietened he spoke in a deeply sincere voice. A calm man of destiny, saddened by the hold up in his altruistic plans for a better future but prepared to stand aside rather

183

than plunge his country into bloody civil war.

'*Amigos! Compatriotas*! Thank you for your support, for coming to say goodbye as I lay down the burden of public office. I do this so that I can continue to fight for the poor and the oppressed. So that I can, in my small way, take up the cause of those whose poverty is a stain on this great nation of ours. I am happy to do this if it will make the workers of Argentina walk into a newer and brighter future where there is no poverty, no oppression. There are those who say it is not proper for an Argentine army officer to fight for the rights of the working classes.' He paused dramatically. 'Who then must I fight for?' he asked, his voice rising passionately. He waited until the applause died away. 'Yesterday I gave my resignation to President Farrell. He did not want to accept it but was forced to do so by the threat of armed intervention. I told him that rather than have one soldier or one worker hurt I would lay down my sword and stand before you as one of you. A civilian – a worker!'

He held up his hands to silence the listeners. 'Before I finally quit my office at the Secretariat of Labour and Welfare I signed a decree. A decree that I have worked to bring in to being since I first took up the cause of the workers. All workers in Argentina will receive salary increases of thirty per cent. They will also receive a share of the profits created by their toil.'

Applause crashed out at this announcement. López Rega's promise to get more than the two thousand supporters asked for by Eva had been handsomely kept. Jamming the streets for blocks around, workers, hastily summoned from the factories, shops and docks began to chant what was to become their rallying cry: 'PE-RÓN, PE-RÓN! PE-RÓN POR PRESIDENTE!! PE-RÓN, PE-RÓN!'

At last the colonel got their attention again. '*Gracias – Amigos*. Thank you once again for your support. But remember! I am no longer able to fight for your rights from within the government. If you wish to secure your conquest, I will give my life to defend you against the oligarchy

184

and the capitalist interests.'

He threw open his arms and embraced his listeners. 'Give me your support and victory can still be ours!' Eva smiled as the thunderous applause vibrated the wireless speaker. Perón had lived up to her highest expectations. Across the town, at the Campo de Mayo, General Avalos was less happy.

'Open up, please. This is the police.'

The bedroom door opened a fraction and a male voice spoke. 'Light the lamp so that I can see you. The matches are on the table by the door.'

Lieutenant Santos looked at Colonel Mittelbach, who nodded. As the Calor gas hissed into life driving the stark shadows of Santos' torch away, the door opened and Perón stepped into the room. In his hand was his service revolver. He was wearing a pair of purple pyjamas that were badly creased but his hair lay black and slick close to his skull and he was mentally alert. He recognised the new chief of police and lowered his gun.

'Mittelbach. What's the meaning of this?' he asked, his voice relaxed and friendly.

'I'm sorry, but I've had instructions to arrest you,' Mittelbach blurted out.

Perón's eyes narrowed. 'On whose authority?' 'The President's,' Mittelbach replied apologetically. 'I'm obliged to take you to the gunboat "*Independencia*" and keep you there until such time as the President can decide what should be done.'

Perón walked past Mittelbach and took a cigarette from a box on the table. The police chief eyed the bottle of whisky standing in a silver tray surrounded with glasses but decided it wouldn't be proper to help himself without invitation.

'And the charge?' Perón demanded.

Mittelbach looked vague. 'The President will inform you of the charge in the morning. My instructions are to escort you to the boat.'

'And if I refuse?' Perón suggested softly.

185

Before Mittelbach could speak the bedroom door opened and Eva came into the room. She had taken the time to brush out her hair and make up her face. She had put on a long, satin housecoat cut low in the front and hugging the contours of her body. The two policemen bowed politely. Eva ignored them.

'*Que pasa, Juán?*' she asked Perón.

Perón laid his gun on the table and put on the silk dressing-gown she handed him. 'President Farrell has sent these men to arrest me.'

Santos spoke for the first time since Perón entered the room. '*Perdón, Coronel.* But we also have orders to arrest Señorita Duarte.'

Eva looked at him sharply. 'On what charge?' she demanded. Santos didn't answer. She looked at Mittelbach.

'I'm sorry, *señorita.* No charge has yet been laid. You will be informed of this in the morning.'

'Well – come back in the morning, you bloody pigs. Tell your *canalla de Presidente* that if he wants to arrest us he can come here and do it himself. Now get out before I throw you out.'

Perón pulled the fuming woman away from Mittelbach. 'Colonel Mittelbach,' Perón began formally, his fingers digging into Eva's biceps to keep her quiet. 'May I suggest you convey my compliments to the President and inform him that I am completely at his disposal but wish to know the reason for my arrest.' He looked at the lieutenant. 'Perhaps, the *Teniente* could go back to the capital for instructions while you stay here – *Coronel*,' Perón suggested.

Mittelbach nodded. He ordered the lieutenant to go to the President and tell him what Colonel Perón had said and then return with new orders.

Santos left and was heard giving orders to the police surrounding the house before getting into the launch and returning down river to where they had left their cars. Without a word Eva walked into the bedroom and slammed the door.

186

Perón smiled apologetically. 'I'll go and change. Help yourself to a drink.' He picked up the cigarette box and held it out to Mittelbach but he refused. Perón lit a cigarette and made for the bedroom.

As he went through the door he heard the colonel's trembling hand pour a glass of whisky. He could sympathise with the old man's nervousness. In spite of his nonchalant front his own nerves were stretched like drying catgut.

Eva was waiting for him in the room. She was standing in front of the dressing table glaring at her image in the mirror. As Perón entered she swung around to face him.

'Why didn't you warn me this might happen?' she demanded angrily. Perón held his finger to his lips and jerked his head towards the door, warning her to keep her voice down. She took no notice. 'What will happen?' she asked.

Perón looked at his face in the mirror and started applying zinc ointment from a pot on the dressing table. 'We gain a little time but there is nothing we can do. If the President says we go to jail we go to jail. A handy prerogative when you are on the right side of the cell door but a nuisance when you're not.' He forced himself to speak lightly.

'What the hell – that *mierda* is not going to lay his hands on me! I'll scream and kick so bloody hard I'll knock the bottom out of their sodding boat!'

Perón stripped off his pyjama jacket and got out his uniform from the wardrobe and laid it on the bed.

Eva watched him curiously. 'What's that for, to show you're a good little soldier?' she asked sarcastically.

Perón ignored her. He knew the value of a uniform in the army-conscious government. In civilian clothes he could be ignored. As a colonel he got respect.

Eva waited until he had put on his shirt. 'What are we going to do?' she asked in a small voice.

Perón eyed her nervously. It worried him when his mistress appeared to be soft and vulnerable. It usually meant she was storing up her batteries for an onslaught.

'Do?' he repeated. 'There's not a lot we can do at the moment. We will have to go to the "*Independencia*". What happens after that is anyone's guess.'

'What about Reyes? He must be able to do something.'

Perón shook his head. 'Not soon enough. Maybe by the beginning of next week they could lay something on but really he wasn't expecting to have to do anything as quickly. And by that time, if this goes along the usual lines, you and I will be lying in the sand on the beach in Punta del Este with all the other refugees.'

Eva jumped to her feet. 'What the hell are you talking about? Why are you taking it all so calmly. Don't you realise this could ruin us?'

Perón stopped in the middle of putting his tie on. 'Don't you realise that we are ruined? I told you not to push but you thought you knew better. I was mad to listen to you. I had everything sewn up until you came along with your big ideas. I told you it was dangerous going out on a limb. We'll be lucky if we get out of this with just being slung out. You don't think they aren't going to have an investigation, do you? They'll want to know what happened to the money we have been using to pay off all your union friends.'

'*Mierda*! Is that all you can say? You were happy enough to go ahead with it when you thought it was plain sailing. Now it looked as if there is some trouble you want to crawl out by blaming me. Well Perón, you can forget that! We have no other course but to go ahead. You do what you bloody well like but I'm not lying down and letting that *boludo* Avalos have the last laugh!'

In the next room Mittelbach heard the angry voices and poured himself another drink.

Perón continued to dress in sulky silence. Eva paced the room thinking fast. In a calmer mood she went over the cogent points, more to herself than to her lover.

'*Bueno*! We thought that if we kept out of the way for a few days while the unions organised support we would be able to go back to the capital and calm everything down. Now you are no longer Vice President there would be no

188

problem in bowing to the workers' demand for you to run for President.' She paused and looked at the floor. 'So – what has changed?' she asked and then answered her own question.

'Someone had convinced Avalos of our intentions. Once we are gone there will be no rallying point for the unions. Even if they demonstrate, without you the Army will have a free hand to break up any attempt they make at rousing the people.'

She helped Perón on with his uniform tunic. 'We have to stop Avalos sending us out of the country. Demand to see the President, say you are ill – anything. But don't let them get rid of you.'

Perón looked at her curiously. Already he was feeling less hopeless. Eva always had that effect on him. 'But what about you? They are going to arrest you as well.'

Eva gave a strident laugh. 'Are they? Can you see that old ponce out there allowing a lady to be manhandled? I'll take care of that. All you have to do is see you don't get shuffled off somewhere inaccessible.'

In spite of himself Perón was beginning to believe that the situation was not as hopeless as it appeared. He pulled her to him and ran his hands over her satin-clad body. '*Bueno – mi vida*. We will see. Meanwhile let's go and convince the "old ponce" that you are a lady.'

Eva kissed him on the lips and gave a low, seductive laugh. With an exaggerated wiggle she walked to the door. Looking back over her shoulder she fluttered her lashes. 'And if the guy don't fancy the groceries – I'll scramble his eggs,' she said in a passable imitation of Mae West.

Colonel Perón, correctly dressed, sitting upright with formal dignity and Eva Duarte, in clinging dressing gown exposing more leg than was proper in polite company, sat opposite Colonel Mittelbach in the small sitting room and waited for the return of the lieutenant.

Dawn was breaking before the sound of the launch chugging up-river was heard. Mittelbach jerked awake from the fitful doze he was having in the uncomfortable upright chair and looked apologetically across the room. Perón, still spruce and upright, smiled sympathetically and Eva scowled belligerently.

Mittelbach rose as the door opened. Instead of the lieutenant it was a lieutenant colonel who entered the room. He saluted the two officers and then stood in front of Perón.

'I come from President Farrell. He regrets the circumstances that make it necessary but he orders you to accompany me to the Martin Garcia prison. The President gives his word that within twenty-four hours you will be transferred to quarters more suitable to your rank.'

The lieutenant colonel was a different man from Mittelbach. He was short, energetic and believed that everything should be done strictly by the book. He turned to Mittelbach. 'With your permission, *Coronel*, I will now conduct *Coronel* Perón and Señorita Duarte to the boat.'

The colonel's permission was still-born.

'I'm not going with you, you little creep,' Eva snapped. 'You have no right to come in here and arrest us. If you want to get me out you will have to carry me!' She sat down with a firm defiance.

Mittelbach was at a loss. 'But *señorita*. It is the order of the President.'

'Then crawl back to him, you arse licker, and tell him that I refuse to be bundled out of my own house in the middle of the night like some whore who's forgotten to pay your stinking police captain his protection money.'

The lieutenant colonel bustled forward officiously. 'You will come –' Before he could finish his sentence Eva swung her hand, stiff-armed and caught him a stinging blow on the face. His cap flew across the room and landed in a corner as he staggered back holding his cheek.

Before he could take reprisal, Mittelbach stepped quickly forward to defend the lady. 'Please, please. This is all so unseemly. *Coronel* Perón – I appeal to you. Tell the lady that she must obey the President's order.' The old man's voice broke and he seemed close to tears as he begged Perón to intervene.

Perón shrugged away responsibility. 'I'm sorry, *Coronel*. Señorita Duarte is a civilian, I have no authority over her. You represent the police. It is something you must deal with.'

The little lieutenant colonel had recovered his hat and now stood, a livid mark decorating the side of his face, waiting for orders. Mittelbach quivered undecided in the middle.

Eva broke the tension. She walked to the bedroom door. 'If you want to take me you will have to drag me out!' she warned them flatly before slamming the door.

Out of sight she collapsed on the bed and sat fighting back the tears until she heard the front door close and a few minutes later the motor of the launch start up and push off downstream taking Perón into captivity.

Then she threw herself back on the bed and let the tears flood. In the cold light beginning to outline the trees outside the bedroom window she felt small and deserted. Her grand schemes suddenly appeared flimsy and insane. How could she possibly prevail against the officers, the lawyers, the politicians? And Perón? She wasn't even sure of his affection. She amused him. Made him feel secure. He appreciated her undemanding sexuality. But was it enough to hold them together now that they stood on the brink of disaster? She let the tears and the negative thoughts run their course.

By the time the launch she had summoned, that plied a trade to the weekenders, pulled in at the rickety jetty by the side of the house she was dressed and ready to go. Sentimentally she stood in the doorway and looked back at the pretty sitting room where she had talked with Juán the night after the charity performance in the Luna Parque. A lot had passed between them since that time.

As the boat worked its way slowly downstream the boatman told Eva of the troubles in the capital. Word had already drifted along the river that Perón had been taken away so he felt free to air his opinions to the quiet, forsaken mistress who had basked in the reflected glory and must now pay the price.

'Been a lot of trouble in Buenos Aires according to the Radio. Had a crowd outside the *Circulo Militar* for the last couple of days it seems. They're not too happy about the way the Army are running things. Seems your friend's not too popular either.'

He gave a covert glance at Eva to see how she was taking it. Encouraged by her lack of response he carried on his garrulous monologue. 'Got so bad yesterday afternoon the mounted police had to charge the crowd. That's going to cause a stink. The police can get away with that sort of thing when it's the manual workers but it's different when it's people from the professions. They're too well connected.' He sat nodding to himself for a while then took up his story again. 'They say that they were demonstrating because the Army are ruining the country with all the high wages they are allowing to be claimed by the workers' unions. The government's in a right state. Everybody's either walked out or been sacked. All that's left is the President, the new Minister of War, General – er – Avalos and that admiral.'

At the mention of the admiral Eva looked startled.

'Lima?' she asked.

The boatman nodded. 'Yes – that's the one. In the end he had to promise that *Coronel* Perón would be arrested and the government taken over by the Supreme Court before the fighting would stop. But I expect you know all this?' he asked curiously.

Eva shook her head. 'Where did you hear it?' she asked.

The boatman smiled mysteriously. 'I have my sources. You and the *Coronel* weren't the only ones who thought of hiding out on the river.'

As the ungainly boat covered the last kilometres of the journey, Eva had time to assimilate the latest information. She had no reason to doubt that the man's account, as far as it went, was accurate. It explained a lot. The oligarchy had taken advantage of Perón's absence to force the government to declare itself against his policy of a new deal for the workers. That wasn't what worried her particularly.

Admiral Lima's sudden appearance did. She remembered now that the island prison of Martin Garcia was a naval establishment.

Without waiting for the boat to be tied up she leaped ashore and hurried to the railway station. She had to wait an hour but it was time well spent. She was aware that her chances of really getting anybody moving before Monday were remote. What she had to do was figure out the best way to use the forces she intended to raise. Back in her flat in Posadas she quickly phoned Mercante and told him what had happened. He was of the same opinion as Perón. It was better to keep quiet and try to get out of the mess with the most grace possible. Eva soon cut that sort of talk.

'Don't be silly, Domingo. The plan goes ahead as before. All I want you to do is try to get Juán brought back into Buenos Aires. It's not easy to get a crowd on the dockside to do anything effective when they are separated from their goal by water. Get word to him to say he is ill or something and get him transferred to a hospital. What do you think?' Eva was careful how she handled Mercante. Although he had proved a staunch supporter she never forgot that he had his own ambitions. She wanted him inextricably tied in with Perón so that his only course was to try and save his incarcerated comrade.

'Do you really think you can get the unions onto the street?' he asked before committing himself.

'Of course, I've spent all morning talking to the union leaders and they have promised a million workers in the city by Thursday,' Eva lied confidently.

Mercante sounded less apprehensive. 'A million! Well – I hope you are right. I'll do what I can about Juán. It won't be easy. The Navy feel that they are gaining control at last. It depends on Farrell. He spent all yesterday trying to stop them making the arrest. Maybe I can convince him that now that Perón's in custody he should be in the hands of the Army.'

'Better still in a civilian establishment like a hospital,' Eva insisted quietly.

'Maybe you're right. I'll see what I can do.' The colonel capitulated.

'Is there anything else you want me to do?'

'Not really. Not at the moment, *querido*. I might need some introductions to military personnel at a later time but I'm sure you are talking to them anyway. *Hasta luego*, Domingo.' She hung up and put a call through to Lopez Rega's house. The sergeant had lain low for the last couple of days waiting to see what would happen. He had tried to make sense out of Perón's astrological chart but it was all very indecisive. Lopez Rega answered the phone cautiously, ready to deny his own existence if the caller posed a danger. With relief he heard Eva's voice on the line. Earlier there had been a radio broadcast reporting Perón's detention and hinting that Señorita Duarte was also being held.

'Daniel?' Eva also acted with caution, calling him by his assumed name in case anyone might be monitoring his calls.

'*Si, señorita!*' Lopez Rega's normally respectful tone had the added warmth of relief.

'I'm at the flat. Can you come straight away?'

Lopez Rega was already on his feet and buttoning his shirt. '*En seguida, señorita*. Give me ten minutes.'

He was almost as good as his word. In just over ten minutes he was ringing the bell on Apartment A and being greeted excitedly by the colonel's young mistress. Eva didn't beat about the bush.

'You know what happened?' she queried.

'*Si, señorita*. I heard it on the radio,' he told her.

'*Bueno*. Then let's not waste time. I want you to take me to see everybody you can think of who is likely to help. I need at least a million in the streets by Thursday. Colonel Mercante has promised to get Perón into the hospital in Buenos Aires. We have to make such a noise that all Argentina will hear it.'

Lopez Rega agreed.

'*Bueno*. How are the police force now?' she asked him.

He raised his shoulders and slowly shook his head from side to side. 'Confused! But they will probably get into line.'

'*Bueno*, and the Army?'

The sergeant took in a noisy breath and let it out through pursed lips. 'Hard to say, *señorita*. General Avalos has picked up a lot of support in the last few days. It depends on whether he allows Admiral Lima to get too much say. If he does then he will lose a lot of muscle. The Army aren't going to let a naval officer take over the running of the government. I think they would fall in behind *Coronel* Perón if the cards were down.'

'*Bueno, che*. There is just one other thing I want you to do for me. I want you to go to the home of Isabel Ernest. She lives just off Rivadavia. Tell her I must see her tonight urgently. Tell her she can stay until Monday and then go straight to work from here.'

She scribbled Isabel's address on a piece of paper and gave it to Lopez Rega. 'When you have made arrangements for me to talk to your contacts let me know. I don't want them coming here. It will be more forceful if I visit them. Try to make the appointments in a café or restaurant where we can be seen by the rest of the workers. If there are any problems with the employers use whatever means you need to make them see sense. We can't afford to fail. Not Perón! Not you! Not me! We either win everything or lose everything!' She linked her arm through his and drew him with a friendly smile to the door. 'You are all I have to count on, Daniel. Don't let me down.'

As the door shut behind him the sergeant allowed himself the nearest he ever came to a smile. He appreciated Eva's parting remark. Of all the people he knew, Eva, with all her hang-ups, insecurity and complexes was the most well-equipped to survive. When the door bell rang a couple of hours later and Isabel Ernest arrived Eva had already compiled a list of supporters that she hoped would stand by her in the present emergency.

Isabel had fully recovered from her ordeal but the memory of the way her friend Eva had looked after her still was a shining point of wonder in her mind. The result of her suffering had brought positive results. Eva had promised her that Colonel Perón would discourage the mounting attacks on Jewish property and person. The problem hadn't vanished but it had certainly abated and it was just another favour that Isabel owed her glamorous friend.

The two women hugged each other affectionately and then Eva got briskly down to business.

Tears welled in Isabel's eyes as she nodded affirmation.

'*Bueno, querida.* I need your help,' Eva stated without preamble.

'Of course, Eva. You know I will do anything you ask,' Isabel said, eagerly sitting forward on the edge of the chair.

Eva touched her friend's face caressingly. '*Gracias*, Isabelita. I promise you won't be sorry. First I want to get on the air for half an hour on Monday.'

Isabel's face fell. 'But Señor Yankelevich has cancelled all your broadcasts. He's a horrible man. I hate him.'

The outburst brought a brief smile to Eva's lips. 'He has no choice. Now, he doesn't usually get into the office until three o'clock in the afternoon unless he is called in specially. I want the schedule to go up late on Monday. Instead of doing it at nine hold it up until 10.45. I'll arrive about that time. What I want you to do is put me down for "*Argentina Hoy*" at eleven o'clock. I'll see you won't get into trouble.'

Isabel waved her hands excitedly in front of her face. 'It doesn't matter. I'll do it.'

'Now, I want you to sit down here and get all these names copied out in alphabetical order while I telephone a few people who might be able to help.'

Before she could dial the first number the phone rang. It was Lopez Rega. He had been able to get in touch with Cipriano Reyes, and the union boss had promised to round up some more supporters by midday.

'*Gracias*, Daniel!' Eva thanked him warmly. 'Will you pick me up?' she asked.

'*Si, señorita*,' Lopez Rega told her solemnly, as if he had a choice.

'One other thing, Daniel. Do I have to arrange transportation for the demonstrators or do you arrange it?'

It was something that he hadn't considered. 'Well, I suppose the best way would be for me to talk to some of the companies that run buses and trucks when they open on Monday. If Reyes puts the word out to the drivers we should have no trouble. But what about payment?' 'Get all the bills sent to me. If there are any waverers get Reyes' shop-stewards to pay them a visit.'

'*Si, señorita*. There's no problem. It will all be done in time.'

Eva hung up and spent the rest of the evening and next morning telephoning would-be-supporters. Lopez Rega called next morning and took her to the café where they were to meet Reyes and some of the other union bosses. Isabel was left in the flat to take any messages that might come through while Eva was away.

The actress had chosen her wardrobe carefully. A simple, blue figure-hugging dress with short white cuffs and a white Peter Pan collar. On her blonde hair she wore a wide-brimmed, picture hat in pale blue with a darker band matching her dress. With elbow length white gloves and leg-flattering high-heel shoes completing her outfit she was not likely to be overlooked in the slum area that was their destination.

They were about twenty minutes late, punctual by Argentine standards, and the half dozen men sitting around the stained wooden table in their smart Sunday suits, rose as a man as she entered.

TWENTY-ONE

Colonel Juán Domingo Perón sat, fully dressed in his uniform of the Infantry Regiment, and listened to the reports of the massive march on the capital by workers from all over the country.

When he had been marched off to prison and found that it was the Navy who had been given the responsibility of keeping him out of the way, he had fully expected to be killed. An unfortunate accident, maybe, or a heart attack. He knew, better than most, how easily these things could be arranged when the reins of power were in your hands. Without warning the attitude of his warders had subtly changed. He was still kept in a cell but a batman had been detailed to look after him. He was allowed to write to Avalos reminding him of the President's pledge that he would be taken from the jail within twenty-four hours.

Sitting in his cell, cut off from all communications with the outside world, he was easy prey to depression. Soon he was convinced that all his carefully laid schemes of the last fifteen years had been brought to nothing by his weakness in letting Eva take control. With a pang of jealousy he wondered where she was. He let his imagination run away with itself and saw her in the arms of General Avalos, urging him on to the ultimate coup that she had wanted Perón to undertake.

He remembered the way they had parted. She hadn't even said goodbye or given him an encouraging smile. Blood throbbed in the huge swellings that had characteristically probed through the surface tissue of his face to plague him. Cramps in his stomach were so bad that at times he feared a ruptured intestine.

The batman brought his midday food and set it on the
198

bare table in the centre of the small room. A naval guard stood behind him making sure that he did not speak unnecessarily to the colonel. As the batman finished he turned to Perón and said politely: 'Will that be all?'

'*Gracias*,' he grunted.

The batman hesitated. '*Mi, Coronel* . . .' he said and paused.

Surprised, Perón looked up. The guard stepped quickly forward but before he could do anything the servant asked innocently, 'Is there anything special you would like for supper?' As he spoke he grimaced and darted his eye at the food laid out on the table. Before Perón had a chance to reply the guard pushed the man towards the door.

'No talking. You know the rules.'

The colonel sat and listened to the batman's complaining voice disappearing along the corridor outside and then quickly looked under the covers. He found a scrap of food-stained paper stuck to the inside of one of the lids. His hands shook as he smoothed it out on the table. It was unsigned and to the point.

'ARRANGEMENTS MADE TO TRANSFER YOU TO HOSPITAL! BE SICK!'

Hope flooded back. If Eva could get a message into prison it must mean that she could still command some respect on the outside. He grinned. Being sick was going to be easy. He had so many symptoms he didn't have to put on an act. Within an hour of seeing the army doctor, brought in specially to examine him, he was on his way to the Central Military Hospital in Buenos Aires.

Although he was still kept in isolation and wasn't allowed visitors he felt he was no longer a prisoner. More in quarantine. If the rash of failure reoccurred he would quickly find himself in an intensive-care ward.

All through Tuesday he had listened to the growing reports of incidents happening throughout the capital. Already a number of workers had marched through the city demanding Perón's release. The police appeared to be standing by but so far had made no attempt to step in and break up the marchers.

Perón gathered that Eva had somehow managed to make a radio broadcast the previous day. She had brought Perón's incarceration to the attention of the people and blamed it on the oligarchy and the capitalists. She begged the workers not to desert their champion in his hour of trial. Since then nothing had been heard of the dynamic Señorita Duarte but as the factory workers, field hands and labourers continued to flood into the city it was obvious that she had by no means deserted the cause.

Early on Thursday morning he had been woken up by a message from President Farrell who begged him to be ready to come to the Casa Rosada later in the day. He regretted the fact that he had been forced to acquiesce to the Army's pressure to arrest him and wanted him to return to the government.

Perón dismissed the courier and then lay back on his bed and let the tears of relief course, unheeded, down his cheeks. Later, after coffee and some fruit, he dressed with fastidious care and waited for a car to come and fetch him. Shortly after midday there was a knock on the door and, smiling broadly, Colonel Mercante walked in. He gave Perón a good-humoured salute and then the two friends clutched each other in a long, elated *abrazo*.

Driving through the wide city streets in a nondescript, un-insigniaed car, the freed colonel looked in amazement at the crowds. Although he had listened to the commentator describing the scene endlessly he had been unable to imagine the extent of the popular uprising. That it had been organised was obvious. Too many banners blazoned the same message above the heads of the endless press of people, some stripped bare to the waist, to be random expressions of support. 'PERÓN CUMPLE!' 'PERÓN POR PRESIDENTE!' 'PERÓN Y PATRIA!' were the recurring themes.

The colonel, sitting in the dim obscurity of his car, only half-listened to Mercante telling him of the way Eva had bludgeoned his supporters into coming out into the open. It

200

wasn't lack of interest, it was just that he was overwhelmed by his change of fortune.

Perón and Mercante strode rapidly through the long, tall corridors and up the sweeping stairs to the presidential reception rooms. At the door to the day-salon, next to the President's office, Major Quiroga saluted and grasped Perón's hand, genuinely pleased to see him once more in command of his fate. As Major Quiroga closed the door behind him Perón surveyed the officers crowded into the room and gave Mercante a wry smile. The conversation died away.

Perón wasn't willing to make the first move. Major Quiroga had told the President of Perón's arrival and further embarrassment was avoided by Farrell, followed by General Avalos and Admiral Lima entering through the President's private door. Farrell threw protocol aside. Smiling eagerly he rushed across the room, arms open wide.

'Perón!' He made the name sound like a hymn of welcome as he embraced his friend. Avalos shook Perón's hand briefly and said how glad he was to see him back in circulation. Admiral Lima couldn't even get that much out. He merely touched Perón's hand then turned away. The colonel didn't mind. He had seen the crowds on the streets and he felt his power was invincible.

Encouraged by the example of the President, the other officers in the room filed passed the reinstated colonel and shook his hand with varying degrees of enthusiasm. Some of them had genuine reason to be worried. They were well aware of the danger of a loose tongue when a new faction came to power. They had been so sure that Perón was gone for good that some of them had waxed long and strenuously on the deficiencies of Perón and his lady and now expected to find promotion difficult in the coming years – if they survived. And Perón now looked as if he would survive anything thrown at him.

Even in the solidly built room with the windows closed the voice of the mass of supporters outside could be heard in ever increasing volume. 'Pe-rón! Pe-rón!'

Only Perón seemed unaware of the chanting as he shook hands and made polite conversation with his edgy brother officers. Colonel Mercante finally suggested that a council of war was called for and persuaded his friend to join Farrell, Avalos, Lima and several other officers in the President's office.

It suited Perón. The voices of his supporters could be better heard as they reverberated around the Plaza and bounced against the windows of the presidential office, shaking them in their frames. He declined the chair Farrell offered him and stood in front of the window overlooking the square, symbolically driving home the point of the masses at his back.

Farrell nodded to Avalos to go ahead and the general snatched an almost appealing look at the sullen Admiral Lima before coming to the point.

'*Coronel* Perón, we have asked you to come here today to explain what has happened. Unfortunately we were unable to contact you last week when certain sections of the community were demonstrating on the streets. The rioting became so bad that we had to agree to bringing you back to the city to answer certain questions about matters that were causing a good deal of worry. Our intention was not to arrest you but merely to put you in protective custody.'

Perón burst out laughing. 'Me? In protective custody? Thank you so much for your thoughtfulness, *mi General*.' He jerked his head towards the square. 'Perhaps I should afford you the same courtesy?'

Avalos' face went stiff but before he could continue Perón addressed himself to Farrell.

'I have been brought here because a situation was evoked that escalated until it became uncontrollable by anybody but me. Frequently I have told you that I had no ambition to become President. If you had kept faith with me I was willing to put the strength of my supporters behind you. Your actions against me in the last week leave me no alternative. For my own safety I must become President or flee the country to avoid the machinations of others jealous

202

of my support by the mass of underprivileged whom nobody else has tried to help.'

He paused and looked around the room finally coming back to the President. 'I am not vindictive, although God knows I have reason to be, so I will not walk out on that balcony and take control by universal demand. You all know that there is nothing stopping me doing this. If you will give me at least your tacit support I am willing to go to the country in a democratic election and let the people decide.'

He looked expectantly at the President. Farrell smiled and came forward with his hand outstretched.

'Perón – *che* – you know you have my support in whatever you do.'

The colonel accepted the hand of the President. He didn't feel any rancour towards his vacillating friend. It was Perón's decision that had put him in office and kept him there because Farrell had no strong opinions of his own. He could hardly be blamed if he was used in the same way by others.

Perón looked quizzically at Avalos. The general stepped forward and shook Perón's hand. Admiral Lima's struggle was harder. He was a man of honour. For a while he had harboured thoughts of becoming President and leading the country into a golden future. It was an idle dream. The Navy did not have the power that the Army enjoyed but Lima had hoped that the wide scope and realistic aims of his policies would convince the rival factions within the Military High Command that they would be able to serve under a naval president. To bow the knee to Perón would be a loss of prestige. He looked at Farrell and Avalos, now back in the fold, and at the other officers. He wanted time to think. But then it would be too late.

Confused, he shuffled forward and looked into Perón's amused eyes. He shook hands because he couldn't think of anything else to do. The chanting in the square below had become so loud that it was difficult to talk in the office.

Farrell gestured to the door. 'You had better show

yourself before they shout the building down.'

Perón nodded.

As the window opened and the sound crashed into the room Perón was unable to move. It was like a dream when everything had a startling clarity but was constantly shifting and avoiding close inspection. Farrell touched his arm and urged him forward. Ten minutes the applause of the two hundred thousand throats below thundered out unabated. Repeatedly Farrell tried to bring order so that he could make an announcement but he was shouted down. Only when the over-taxed throats could take no more did Farrell get his chance. With his mouth close to the microphone he announced in his dramatic style, the about-face of the government on the embarrassing arrest and release of one of its top executives. He called Juán Domingo Perón forward and clasped him to his chest in a manly *abrazo*. Choked with emotion he turned back to the microphone.

'People of Argentina! Here is the man you have all been waiting to see, the man we all love, the man who has conquered the hearts of all Argentinos: Juán Domingo Perón!'

Perón stood with head bowed as the thunderous ovation swept over him. At last he walked over to the microphone and held his muscular arms up calling for silence. As the cheering died away he began to speak in a low, emotion-packed voice to the eager, sweating workers, a vast sea of upturned heads drinking in every word.

'*Argentinos*! Workers of the *Patria*! Your reception today gives me new heart. Makes the blood sing in my veins. I have been ill and tired. Tired of the long battle to rid Argentina of the malaise that has affected our people. Tired of being told that the workers do not know what they want. That money would only turn you into drunken savages incapable of pushing your *patria* to the bright future I see on the horizon.

'Of course the rich must say this. They have built their full soft lives on the foundation of serfdom. They quote their illustrious fathers who came to this fruitful country,

204

and, by the sweat of their brows and the strength of their arm, built up a mighty trade with the rest of the world.

'But they are not their fathers!'

'They live in the big *estancias* of ten thousand hectares and store up the gold that floods into the banks for jaunts to the playgrounds of Europe and the United States. They sell out their birthright to faceless corporations in Wall Street and London. Argentina MUST, and WILL, belong to ALL *Argentinos*. The poor as well as the rich. The poor must receive a share in the vast wealth of our soil.'

Perón collected his thoughts while the crowd exploded with hysterical acclaim for his promises. Unhitching his sword from his belt he held it high above his head.

'ARGENTINOS!' He looked at the bare chests of the men in the crowd. 'DESCAMISADOS! My shirtless ones, I discard the honourable and sacred uniform of my country to don the civilian garb of the worker!'

His voice was strong and vibrant now, taking on the cadences of the popular folkloric storytellers loved by the Argentinians. 'I want to join you in your struggle. Here and now I say *Adios* to the institution which is the backbone of the country: the Army.'

He thrust the scabbarded sword at President Farrell standing beside him. When the applause subsided his arms went out to embrace the crowd.

'I give my first welcome to you as a fellow worker. This huge crowd demonstrates the vigour and vitality of our great nation. Together we cannot fail!'

He let emotion choke his voice again. 'As a simple citizen, mingling with you in the factories, the shops and the fields, I wish to press you to my heart.' With the suspicion of a sob he let his head drop to his chest and stood there, a humble heroic figure, as the crowd took up the chant. 'PERÓN – PE-RÓN POR PRESIDENTE!'

Sitting alone, crouched beside the radio in her Posadas apartment, Eva listened to Perón's speech with tears streaming down her face. Much as she would have liked to share the moment with her lover, prudence had told her to leave it to him alone. But she would not let him forget who had stood by him, who had turned the tide when all seemed lost.

It was one o'clock before Perón and Mercante came back to the apartment. Both were in high spirits and had drunk their success in champagne and whisky. Perón swept Eva up in his arms and whirled her in a wild dance around the room, finally toppling over the end of the sofa and falling into the cushions.

Happily Mercante watched the scene and then went across to the cabinet where the drinks were kept and poured three glasses of whisky. Perón and Eva were sitting up now, excitedly discussing the events of the day. Mercante handed them glasses. 'To the next President of Argentina: Juán Domingo Perón!' he toasted.

Eva shrieked with happiness and took a stiff drink. She hated the stuff but it was in a good cause. Perón bowed with mock formality and then held his glass up.

'To my great friends: Domingo Mercante and Evita Duarte.' Mercante waited until Perón had drunk and then said softly and seriously: 'de Perón!'

Perón froze and looked incredulously at his friend. Marriage to Eva had never occurred to him. It wasn't done. You didn't marry your mistress, however useful the union might be.

Eva was equally shocked. The thought of marriage to Perón was constantly with her but she knew the taboos of society and hadn't dared to voice her hopes. She looked angrily at Mercante. By bringing up the subject she was afraid he might have queered the pitch for any future manoeuvring. Mercante avoided Eva's eyes and looked at Perón.

The big man sat, serious faced, while he considered the new concept. Finally he looked up and burst out in a long hoot of laughter that ended in a fit of coughing.

Eva didn't move. She wanted to cry. It hurt enough that he didn't want to marry her but to have to bear his ridicule was too much. She struggled to rise to her feet. Perón grabbed her wrist and pulled her down on top of him. 'Of course. Señora Evita Duarte de Perón – and Juán Domingo Perón: the perfect couple! Me with the brains and you with the brawn. When do you want to be married, my little guerrilla? Name the day and we will have the biggest wedding this city has ever seen.'

Eva looked at him, not sure if he was teasing her. Perón gently pushed her off and stood up to face Mercante.

'*Bueno*, Matchmaker, arrange for the wedding.' He looked back at Eva. 'Will three days' time be too soon?'

Stupefied by the suddenness of Perón's decision Eva could only nod.

'*Bueno* – the twenty-first of October 1945 will be the day.' A frown furrowed his brow. 'Hold it a moment,' he said softly. Eva's heart sank. It had all been a cruel joke. 'We will have the civil ceremony then but we will keep it quiet for the time being. Until my formal nomination has been entered. Then we can have the church service with all the trimmings.' He looked questioningly at Eva. 'Okay, *mi vida* – you don't mind?'

Again she could only nod.

'And you, you romantic old fraud, can I count on you as best man?'

'Congratulations, Juán. You can count on me for anything.'

Perón looked at him and raised a quizzical eyebrow. 'How about the Vice Presidency?' he asked quietly.

Mercante bowed. 'Whatever pleases my President.' He put down his glass. 'Now I must go. I leave you to plan your wedding day while I get down to practicalities.'

He shook Perón warmly by the hand and then gave him an affectionate *abrazo*. Eva recovered from her daze and threw her arms around Mercante's neck and kissed him passionately, tears again flooding from her eyes. He gently extricated himself and turned her towards Perón.

'Look after each other,' he said sincerely and slipped out of the door while they kissed.

TWENTY-TWO

José Espejo bowed gravely forward, his hands clasped in an attitude of devotion, chest high. He stretched his lip across his teeth in a mechanical grin and held the uncomfortable pose while he examined it in the carefully angled mirror on the washstand. He wished his old friends in Rosario could see him now. Whenever he went back to see his mother they treated him like a traitor. Someone who was too soft for the comfortless life of a *gaucho*, a scavenger in the garbage heaps of the city.

Espejo straightened up and looked with satisfaction at the tight, dark blue suit he was wearing. That would demand respect. Once more he peered at his reflection and patted his thinning, grease-stiffened hair to make sure that the polished surface was unblemished. He gingerly picked up the heavy black Homburg, which he had coveted all his life but never been able to afford, and placed it cautiously over his sleek hair.

The cheap alarm clock on the mantelpiece in his little basement room told him it was time to leave. In the underground garage he made his way to the bulky Buick that had claimed four hours of his time earlier and, avoiding touching its gleaming paintwork, climbed in and drove it around to the lift that serviced the apartment block above.

Ten minutes passed. The sound of a car coming down the ramp from the street above attracted his attention. Colonel Perón's Dodge swung around one of the pillars and made a slow circuit of the garage before coming to a halt behind the Buick.

Espejo stood in the circle of light from the security lamps above the elevator door and watched as Lopez Rega prowled between the half dozen or so vehicles parked in the
208

immediate vicinity of the lift, checking them for unwelcomed guests. Satisfied he walked across to Espejo.

'*Bueno*. You're ready!' he stated with total lack of warmth or interest.

Espejo ducked his head in acknowledgement but knew better than to risk the embarrassment of offering to shake hands. Lopez Rega frightened him and made him feel like a schoolboy.

The sergeant picked up the phone at the side of the lift and dialled a number.

'*Coronel*? Lopez Rega. All clear.' He hung up and stood patiently in front of the lift door ignoring Espejo.

As the lift stopped he pulled back the outer door and stepped aside as a tall man, dressed in a military uniform with the insignia of colonel, and a pretty blonde woman, came out. They superficially resembled Perón and Eva and in the dark interior of the car would foil anything but the closest inspection. Lopez Rega ushered them to the second car, nodded curtly to Espejo and drove out of the garage. Silence settled down once more.

Espejo paced nervously up and down, occasionally stopping by the lift door to listen. He knew that the timing of the operation had been detailed with military precision so that the decoy car of Lopez Rega could be given ample time to lead any observers away from the area but the sick, nervous tension in his stomach couldn't be quieted by abstract practicalities.

At last the lift whined to a halt and Espejo eagerly tore the outer door open. Eva, a drab scarf pulled over her extravagant hair, stepped out. Her face looked tense and strained, the result of a sleepless night and the dragons of doubt that had tried to convince her that something would happen to spoil her day. Mercante followed her. He also looked solemn and his eyes behind his rimless spectacles were devoid of their usual humour.

Only Perón seemed unawed by the occasion. He winked at Espejo and clapped him heartily on the shoulder.

'Everything okay, José?' he boomed. His voice was

picked up in the echo chamber of the concrete walls and bounced around.

Espejo gave him a harassed affirmative smile and opened the car door. Mercante handed Eva in and then held the door while Perón followed. As they drove from the garage, Mercante, sitting in the front seat, looked carefully around.

As far as he could see their ruse had worked and the handful of reporters who seemed to camp out permanently under the lime trees of Calle Posadas had been drawn off on the false scent laid by the efficient sergeant. Once away from the immediate vicinity the three men in civilian clothes and the quietly dressed woman weren't likely to attract attention.

Perón reached out and covered Eva's cold agitated fingers, mindlessly picking at the white cotton gloves in her lap, with his strong warm hand. He gave her an encouraging smile.

'It will soon be over, *linda*. Give us a smile. It's a wedding we are supposed to be going to, not an execution.'

His sympathy prompted tears and as they flowed down her face she was glad that she had gone easy on the mascara that morning. Perón hooted with laughter and drew her to him.

'Come on. A registry office wedding's not that bad. And I solemnly promise that you can do it with flowers and confetti as soon as the nomination is confirmed.'

Eva nodded and wiped her eyes. 'I know, *mi vida*. I know,' she managed to force out. 'It's just that everything's so . . . so . . . perfect. So . . .' Again the tears came and choked her voice.

Perón kissed her gently on the forehead. 'I love you, *mi amor*,' he said quietly, the banter gone from his voice.

Eva sobbed and laid her head contentedly on his shoulder.

Juán, Eva's brother, met them outside the town hall at Junin, the town where Eva had grown up. He had already installed their mother and sister Elisa in the room that was going to be used for the ceremony. Eva's wedding was the greatest thing that had ever happened to the Duarte family and he lived in dread of some unforeseen incident that would threaten it. Already he was reaping the rewards of his sister's association with power and he wanted it to continue.

In the four days since Perón had so dramatically been brought from prison to the balcony of the Casa Rosada the mood of the country had changed and now it would be a foolish man indeed who doubted that Perón cracked the whip.

Only the mayor, who was going to perform the ceremony, was allowed into the room. Although he had been totally unaware of Eva's existence when she lived in the town, he now greeted her like an old friend. Eva eyed him coldly, the days when she felt compelled to fawn on minor officials buried in the past.

In the dusty little room, brightened only by a vase of fresh spring flowers and the bouquet that Eva felt obliged to carry for the occasion, the most dramatic partnership of the twentieth century was welded together in total obscurity.

The white telephone on the night table shrilled out urgently into the dark. Before it could ring a second time a hand clicked on the reading lamp and then picked up the receiver. A gaunt face topped by thinning, lank hair moved into the aura of light escaping the dark lamp shade.

'Yeah,' he said in a slow, dry drawl.

'Excuse me for waking you, sir,' the nightporter apologised, 'but it's an urgent call from the American Embassy in Buenos Aires. Shall I put it through?'

The man swung his pyjamaed legs out of the bed and, one-handed, put on his small, rimless spectacles. 'Yeah, sure,' he answered and waited expectantly while the telephone clicked and hummed as the connection was made. He heard someone on the other end.

'Spruille Braden here,' he announced himself.

A faraway voice came mechanically through the atmospherics. 'John S. Bamberg, Private Secretary to the Ambassador here, sir. He asked me to get in touch with you with the latest report on the election.'

Spruille Braden grunted. 'Hold it a second while I get a pen.' He found what he wanted in the drawer of the night table. 'Okay, John, go ahead.'

As the voice recited the state of Argentina the United States Under Secretary of State for Latin American Affairs made notes on his night pad.

'Colonel Juán Domingo Perón had a total majority of 1,527,231 votes against Tamborini's 1,207,155. This gives him 304 votes out of a possible 376, in the electoral college and puts him in the House of Representatives with a two-thirds majority. Voting was above eighty per cent. Observers say that the vote was honest and there has been no attempt to tamper with the polls.

'That's all the information I have at the moment but I'll see you get anything else of interest that comes in. Is that okay – Mr Under Secretary?' Bamberg concluded.

Spruille Braden dropped the pen wearily on the pad. 'Yeah, thanks John. Give my regards to the Ambassador and tell him I'll be on to him later. Goodbye.' He hung up and slumped back on the bed.

How could he have been so wrong? After all his years in politics how could he have provided the ammunition, unwittingly, that was to give the fascist Perón that last leg up to the presidency?

It was all timing of course. If he could have just stayed as Ambassador for a little longer he might have been able to do something. Staring at the ceiling he had to admit that it wasn't likely. Perón was a new breed of adventurer politician who was prepared to run huge risks to get what he wanted. And then, of course, there was the totally unexpected advent of his wife onto the political scene.

Spruille Braden had warned the Argentine government that Perón's espousing of the fascist cause, that had foundered in Europe, could only lead to international condemnation. Instead of sorting their own problems out they had flirted with disaster until it was too late.

What hurt the American was that it was the mishandling of his treatise on the death of liberty and the growing power of the Argentine police state that had been used to entice the undecided patriotic waverers to support Perón's bid. With the help of the US government he had prepared a damning indictment against the Perón-controlled administration in the form of a booklet entitled, somewhat pompously: 'Consultation among the American Republics with Respect to the Argentine Situation' but known as the 'Blue Book'.

It had laid out in detail the atrocities committed in Argentina and blamed Perón for the rapid rise in police brutality. Unfortunately the book had been late in arriving and then was sent to anti-Perónistas who were already aware of the facts.

Perón had labelled the United States as a hungry vulture poised to leap on a moribund Argentine economy and haul off the prize pieces for the USA. Spruille Braden's book gave him just the rallying point he needed. Few of his supporters had read the book but believed Perón when he told them that it was an attempt to meddle in the internal affairs of the Republic of Argentina. The anti-Americanism had filled the void created by the withdrawal of Perón's approval of Jew-baiting. The crowd needed an external effigy of hate and Uncle Sam fitted the bill.

The thought of his mishandling of the delicate Argentinian situation made the Under Secretary squirm. He turned out the light and tried to sleep but the thoughts still crowded in. He remembered the growing unrest in Buenos Aires before he left. The conviction that Perón must go that was the topic of every conversation at every dinner party or soirée in the capital.

That was the problem. His carefully tuned ears had listened to the wrong orchestra.

TWENTY-THREE

When the war in Europe ground to a halt fleeing Nazis were common in Buenos Aires. They arrived, checked in with one of the screening agents, made arrangements to pay the required *coima*, the bribes that were an unofficial tax on any deal done in the city, and then disappeared to the south or north in one of the expanding pseudo-Bavarian towns that had agreed to take them.

What they did or how they survived when they reached their destination didn't concern the Argentine police. At least not until the War Crimes Commission had published evidence that a large number of major war criminals, including Eichmann, Mengele and other top Nazi brass, were hiding out in Latin America. Even Adolf Hitler himself had been reported on the streets of Buenos Aires. Perón discussed the growth of the German conclaves with Lopez Rega who, it was decided, should make an investigation.

As the big Dodge bumped along the uneven road cut in the natural granite of the Andean foothills, Lopez Rega wondered what he was about to see. Beside him, looking cool and sophisticated in spite of the heat, Therese von Quast watched the wild countryside stretching away below her as they rounded an outcropping of rock and started to go downhill. Without warning Lopez Rega gave a surprised whistle and stopped the car.

Therese followed his gaze and blinked with amazement. She looked furtively at her companion but didn't speak. She had long learned that Daniel didn't like unsolicited comments.

He looked at her. 'What do you make of that? A bloody

Bavarian village in the Andes.'

He let off the hand-brake and drove slowly down the hill. In spite of the rustic appearance of the village he appreciated the care that had gone into making it practically assault-proof.

He studied the rock cliff guarding the rear of the village. It was too steep and uneven to make it anything but a hazardous descent for anyone trying to break in the back-door but had the disadvantage of being open to bombard-ment from above. No doubt that had been taken into consideration and an adequate deterrent had been installed as part of the defences. A machine gun nest perhaps.

He searched the open ground for confirmation of his guess but couldn't see anything suspiciously like a bunker. There seemed to be about fifty, steep-roofed houses with white plastered walls and glistening, heavily varnished clapboard upper storeys adorned with pretty, colourfully painted, shutters. On some of the buildings an artist had painted giant rural scenes from the homeland.

The houses were clustered around a high-towered church that made the perfect focal point for the beautiful scene. As Lopez Rega drove carefully into the narrow street he was disappointed not to see *Lederhosen* clad boys chasing pina-fored girls through the trees in a Kitsch idyll. There was a charming little general store with sparkling, small-paned windows and an air of timelessness. The few people on the street semed uninterested in the sudden appearance of the ugly Dodge to spoil their artfully planned beauty.

Lopez Rega stopped outside the general store and climbed out of the car. Through the window he could see someone watching. The tiny brass bell tinkled as he pushed open the door and went into the aromatic interior. Before he could speak a middle-aged man held out his hand.

'*Willkommen in Hildburghausen, mein lieber Herr Lopez Rega. Ich hoffe Sie hatten eine angenehme Reise? Mein Name ist Rudolf Keller.*'

Lopez Rega looked vague, not understanding a word of what was being said. He looked toward the car but before he could call in Therese as an interpreter, the German spoke in a thickly accented, but understandable Spanish.

'*Ach, perdoname*, Señor Lopez Rega. You do not speak German, of course. The President informed us of your visit to inspect our little village. My name is Rudolf Keller. I merely wanted to welcome you to Hildburghausen and express the hope that you had a good journey.' Lopez Rega nodded brusquely. 'But first would you mind going up the road a little way to the office of the *Bürgermeister*. He will be able to help you much better than I can.' He looked out of the window. 'Fräulein von Quast should stay here I think. My wife will be happy to entertain her until you return.'

Keller and Lopez Rega walked up the road to the office of the *Bürgermeister*, where they were met by a tall, distinguished man, well above average height and bearing his sixty odd years with military precision. He was wearing a light linen suit that somehow contrived to look like a uniform. He bowed politely in front of the Argentinian before shaking hands.

'Good day, Señor Lopez Rega,' he said in passable Spanish. 'I am the *Bürgermeister*, Johannes Gerber. I have made arrangements for you to stay in a special guesthouse we have for visitors. I'm afraid we do not have a hotel although we have a very good restaurant which you may use whenever you wish. Fräulein von Quast will join you here as soon as she has taken some refreshment with Frau Keller. In the meanwhile I suggest we have a beer in the garden and you can ask me any questions you like and, as far as I am able, I will answer you.'

Gerber waved his guest along the hall and they came out onto a terrace facing the mountains. The house was set at an angle to the steep rampart that so effectively defended the rear of the village. The view from the terrace was around the side and across to the open plains beyond. It was a magnificent setting but the ex-sergeant had seen mountains before and hardly spared it a glance.

He was more interested in a cave halfway up the escarpment. It seemed too symmetrical to be anything but man-made. His curiosity aroused, he searched for other signs of alteration to the natural rock of the mountain. He could see nothing obvious but he was interested to see that there were curiously featureless buildings that appeared to be actually recessed into the rock. He made up his mind to try and get a closer look if he could.

His host seemed not to notice his scrutiny of the mountain. As they settled in the rough pine chairs Gerber clapped his hands and a fresh-faced blonde came running out from a door further along the terrace. She was in her late teens, still weighed down by her puppy fat and a tendency to spots but good-natured with a ready smile.

'Señor Lopez Rega, I would like you to meet my daughter, Hannelore. Her Spanish isn't too good at the moment but it is improving. Unfortunately the *Jungvolk* still prefer to speak in their native tongue while they are together. We try to forbid it but I'm afraid they have no respect for us old fogeys.'

Gerber ordered beers and made idle conversation until his daughter brought the steins.

'*Prost* – or should I say *salud*?'

Lopez Rega shrugged indifferently. 'Whatever suits you best, *señor*.'

He was beginning to get edgy. Now that he was in the Nazi stronghold he wanted to find out what was going on and he didn't feel that sitting on a terrace drinking beer was the way to do it. He wiped the froth from his mouth with the back of his hand. '*Bueno. Gracias señor.* But now, if you please, I would like to talk with whoever is in charge. Is it you?' he said.

Gerber threw up his hands in pantomimed sorrow. 'Alas, no *señor*. Our leader has been unexpectedly called away. An emergency concerning one of our people, I understand. He asked me to present his abject apologies and assure you that he will be here to meet you himself in the morning. In the meanwhile, my home is yours. If there is anything I can help you with before he returns you have, of course, only to ask.'

Lopez Rega eyed him speculatively and wondered what

he was hiding. It might be coincidence that the boss was away or it might have some deeper significance. What it might be he couldn't even start to guess. Looking at the tall, patrician figure opposite it was hard to believe that he was a man already indicted among the most brutal and sadistic of Nazi criminals.

Lopez Rega looked around at the peaceful scene. 'You know, I thought there would be more people about. Of course, I don't know the exact figure but the impression I got was entirely wrong. How many have you got here? Two hundred – three maybe? The police are always talking in thousands.' He shook his head, apparently confused by the anomaly.

Gerber helped him out. 'There are a few more than you estimate, Señor Lopez Rega but not the thousands your police think. We have about fifty families here, that totals up to about one hundred and eighty, then we have the bachelors' quarters.' He pointed to the low buildings backing on to the mountain. 'Another fifty there. But then we are smaller than the settlement at Chubut. We send the older families and men there. It's more of a farming community than anything else. This way we are able to be reasonably self sufficient.

'So – there's another five – maybe six hundred there. Then there are four other camps. Mainly artisans. Say another four, five hundred. Some of our people have preferred to stay in the towns. We are still trying to complete the register of these but it shouldn't total more than a thousand.' He gave Lopez Rega an innocent smile. 'So you see. There is nowhere near the number that your excellent police force feared.'

Lopez Rega looked satisfied. 'The police are always exaggerating. It makes them look more efficient.' He frowned and looked around with a bewildered expression on his face. 'But what do you do up here in the mountains? It must be so different from what you are used to in Europe.'

Gerber's face went serious. 'You are right, *señor*. But our people need the change. Europe has gone mad. Our people
218

are sick and exhausted. For a decade we have firmly believed in our destiny as a nation. When that destiny was almost in our grasp we faltered. We took the wrong road. Most of us now agree that we should have pursued our former policy of peaceful intercourse with other countries. Showing them, by example, how to build a strong, interdependent economy. Now we need time to ponder on our mistakes and see if there is anything we can do to right the wrongs we have done in Europe.'

Lopez Rega didn't believe it for a second. 'And this is to help you forget?' he asked wryly.

The German smiled. 'Not to make us forget Germany. No! This is to make us remember Germany as it should be.' A gentle smile settled on his long face and he looked around the village.

Lopez Rega nodded understanding but thought *or to mislead inquisitive visitors!*

Before he could ask more questions, Therese and a fat, smiling woman of about fifty came out onto the porch. Gerber leaped up immediately and introduced himself. Therese looked happier and more relaxed than Lopez Rega had seen her for a long time. He put it down to ancestral memories of a homeland she had never seen.

He suddenly felt annoyed that the Germans so underestimated their hosts' intelligence that they thought they could fob them off with a chocolate-box imitation of a non-existent Germany.

'If you wouldn't mind directing us to our quarters, *señor*, we would like to shower and change our clothes,' he managed to say with a veneer of grace.

'Of course! Of course!' Gerber exclaimed, neither relieved nor worried that they wanted to be left on their own. 'Frau Keller will be pleased to show you to your quarters. If you need me I will be here.'

TWENTY-FOUR

Gerber informed Lopez Rega that the village leader had returned and was waiting to welcome him to their community. Rega noted how carefully Gerber avoided giving him a name and wondered just who had slipped through the net and was now perched in the mountain eyrie, hoping to avoid joining his compatriots on the hard wooden pew of Nüremberg.

Outside, standing patiently in the morning sun, a straw hat jauntily settled over its ears, a small dappled pony waited in the shafts of a gleaming governess cart. Gerber invited his guest up onto the driving seat and then took the reins and urged the dapple into a well-practised trot. Lopez Rega found himself losing his temper again. He liked to be in control. The continued condescension of the model denizens of this picture-postcard mountain retreat was beginning to unnerve him. He wished they had allowed him to bring Therese. His ignorance of the German language cut him off from the chance remark, or the hidden nuance.

As he had guessed, Gerber picked his way through the village in the direction of the bachelors' quarters. The governess cart wasn't the only traffic on the narrow streets. He saw several other carts and a few men riding on horseback but by far the greater number were pedestrians. It looked as if the whole population of the village were heading for the mountain. Surprised Lopez Rega looked at Gerber for an answer. The *Bürgermeister* merely smiled and cracked his whip.

As they cleared the village and headed up the slope the Argentinian noticed that there was a bigger clearance than he had thought between the last house and the buildings that were their destination. Instead of backing onto the village there was an open space of about half a kilometre. Gerber stopped outside one of the buildings and handed the reins to a man waiting there.

On closer inspection the bachelors' quarters differed from the houses in the village in their basic construction. Each hut was cast in reinforced concrete straight onto the rock. He also noticed that the majority of villagers entered through one of the other huts.

Lopez Rega seemed to be the only visitor to the middle one. The interior was flimsily partitioned off into cubicles, each with a single bed, a locker and a small straw mat on the painted concrete floor. It bore out the description 'bachelors' quarters' but destroyed any notion of happy-go-lucky youths frolicking in high spirits. The spartan nature of the accommodation spelled military discipline. Lopez Rega hadn't seen anything like it since he was a raw recruit at training camp.

Gerber led the way to a door at the far end and went through. A young man in civilian clothes leaped smartly to his feet clicking his heels with a resounding crack in the stark room. He reached around the corner of a door leading into the ablutions and pressed a hidden button. The wall in front of him shuddered and then moved smoothly aside. For the benefit of his guide Lopez Rega pretended he was startled by the opening door but by now he was prepared for anything. Even the thoughts of seeing a secret Nazi hideout cut deep into the rock. It either meant that they didn't intend that he should ever return to Buenos Aires or for some reason they wanted to impress him.

Stretching away in front of them, bending to the right, was a narrow corridor hewn out of the natural rock and strutted in places with thick columns of reinforced concrete. Fluorescent strip lighting added to the starkness of the passage.

Gerber led the way. The passage curved in a constant arc to the right. Most of the thick steel, airtight doors were on the left but the doors on the right were mostly interlocked double doors and the few people they passed seemed to issue from or disappear into the right hand side.

Lopez Rega had lost all sense of direction when they stopped outside one of the double-doors. A black-uniformed guard looked them over suspiciously and then pressed a buzzer and waited. The guard's uniform interested Lopez Rega. To his uneducated eye it looked like the real thing. So had all the other uniformed personnel they had passed in the corridor. He wondered if they had been specially imported – and how? A green bulb lit up above the door and the guard turned the handle and pushed the heavy door open. The ease with which he did it suggested precision engineering and hydraulic counterbalancing.

After the stark corridors of harshly lit rock the room came as a pleasant surprise. It was high and airy and warmly bathed in subtly concealed lighting augmented by table lamps. The cream walls were covered by book-cases and a heavy maroon curtain at the far end added to the warm friendly atmosphere. The floor was completely covered in a matching carpet. In the centre of the room two long, well upholstered leather settees faced each other either side of a low, marble-topped coffee-table. Across the corner, between the curtained wall and the right hand wall, was a functional wooden pedestal desk. It had been carefully placed so that the chair behind it was in a deep pool of darkness. Dominating the room on the left was a lifesize oil painting of Adolf Hitler.

A rich, faintly accented voice came from the darkness. 'Welcome, Señor Lopez Rega. I hope you are enjoying your stay.'

The Argentinian didn't bother to try and pierce the darkness but gave a slight bow in the direction of the dimly outlined figure he could see sitting there. The leader's caution was reassuring. It meant that Lopez Rega was expected to survive his trip into the maw of the cavern.

The voice dismissed Gerber brusquely and waved Lopez Rega to a seat. It recommended the iced tea already waiting on the table and declined Lopez Rega's artless suggestion that his host might join him. When his visitor had settled

222

down with his glass the man behind the desk spoke in a soft conversational tone.

'I expect you have been surprised by all this.'

Lopez Rega nodded.

'Good? I wanted your reaction. As you have no doubt guessed the quaint Bavarian village is for the casual visitor. I wanted to show you what is really going on here so you can report to President Perón that we are being completely open with him.' He paused. 'Your helpfulness in the past has, of course, been brought to my attention. I want personally to thank you for that. We are desperately in need of friends at the moment.'

Lopez Rega nodded sympathetically.

'But what I feel is more important is that our work here is explained to President Perón by someone who has his confidence and whose work he respects. That is why I was eager to meet you when your visit was suggested. I want to show you something.' A thick hand reached out of the darkness and pressed a switch on a control panel on the desk. The heavy curtains at the end of the room rolled aside. Underneath was a map of the world. On it were six large red pins, amongst a dozen or so different colours, marking the German encampments in Argentina.

'As you can see, our people are spread out in the less well populated areas of your country. This was arranged for us by President Perón. When we originally approached him it was thought that we would use these areas to provide resources of food for our armies in Europe.'

He let the curtains swing back into place and made a helpless gesture with his hands. 'It was not to be. We had to use the property we had bought for other purposes.'

The disembodied hand reached out again and Lopez Rega noticed that the nails on the white sausage-like fingers were bitten to the quick. At the press of a button the picture of Hitler moved upwards revealing an armoured glass observation window. It commanded a view of a cavernous workshop fitted for light engineering. There were about fifty workers in overalls industriously fashioning raw metal

223

into precision artefacts which were beyond the scope of Lopez Rega's experience.

The hidden man explained. 'As you know, Germany was well ahead of the rest of the world in rocket propulsion. Von Braun and most of our top men were snatched up by the Americans. But we have the benefit of their work and a great deal more. Here we are trying out techniques to overcome the problems of the weight-to-power ratio that is so vital to the size of the payload in rocketry. Heat is another difficulty so we are looking for a lightweight alloy with a high tolerance to heat.'

He laughed. 'I don't really understand anything but the principles. If you want to know the technical side I can get someone here to explain.'

Lopez Rega shook his head. 'I am like you, *señor*, untechnically minded.'

'I want you to realise the tremendous resources we can put at the command of the Argentine government. We admit that we made a debacle of our attempt to unify Europe into a strong federation capable of withstanding any future aggressive tendencies that either the USA or the USSR might cultivate. From what I understand of President Perón he has the same fears and looks for the same solution. A mutual defence pact between all the nations of Latin America.

'Geographically and ethnically the concept is unassailable. What is going to stop it from happening is that the other countries will never accept Perón as the head of the consortium or Argentina as the dominant country. What we can offer is the power to enforce his doctrine throughout Latin America. United under one leader the United States of South America will be the most powerful State in the world. The minerals, raw material and food resources, collectively are greater than those of Canada and the United States put together.

'We are willing to help Perón to achieve his aims if he will give us his promise to help us to overcome Europe. With our two similar governments spread out across the world we can make the USA and Russia do as they are told. But it's not just weapons we are offering. Our scientists here also came up with a highly effective nuclear reactor that will produce cheap energy on a scale never before envisaged. It will provide the source for a revolution in industrial economy and production.

'It will be the end of war, of strife, hunger and hatred. We can then beat our guns into ploughshares and move into the Golden Millennium promised by our Führer.' The voice stopped suddenly as if embarrassed by the outburst. In the silence that followed Lopez Rega had confirmation of the sound-proofing of the luxurious quarters. In spite of the factory complex that surrounded them there wasn't the slightest sound to permeate the heavy silence.

'*Bueno*. I think my President will be very interested in your proposition. He has been trying to consolidate the policy of the Latin American countries for just the reasons you suggest,' he said thoughtfully.

Lopez Rega had, in fact, been responsible for infiltrating Argentine agents into the other Latin-American countries to organise support for Perón's bid to emerge as President of the sub-continent. He looked pointedly in the direction of the map covered by the thick curtain.

'And the coloured pins. What are they for?'

'The red are the main bases such as this one. The rest are other bases working on different aspects of the same project. The Führer feels that –' He stopped short and carefully corrected himself. 'The Führer felt that it was necessary to diversify our project so that it would be more difficult for anybody, the USA for instance, to destroy what we are building. As we are largely self-sufficient we can keep rigid control over anyone entering our installations. Not all are as elaborate as this and most are guarded more obviously.'

The shadowy figure lapsed into silence.

Lopez Rega considered his position. It was obviously too big for him to offer any opinions on the likely outcome of the breathtaking possibilities opened up by his brief meeting. He had learned of a continuing Nazi ambition to

225

dominate not just Europe but South America as well.

The quiet voice broke his train of thought. 'Is there anything else I can show you or are there any more questions you would like answered?' it enquired helpfully.

Lopez Rega shook his head. His host read his thoughts.

'Well, I expect you want to get back to Buenos Aires and report to President Perón. Please, give him my respects and tell him I am at his command whenever he wishes to discuss our mutual interests further.'

The disembodied hand pressed a button on the desk.

In the dark immensity of the 'President's Room' Eva lay on her back in the wide, four-poster bed and stared at the ceiling. Occasionally, in the distance, she heard the strangled bleat of a car horn or the nervous chatter of a shunting train. In some inexplicable way the mundane sounds made her homesick.

Not for Junin and the rundown *pension* her mother had managed. It certainly wasn't for the soul-eroding dust of Los Toldos where she always felt they had to apologise for their existence. Her nostalgia was for a time rather than a place. A time when everything had been possible but nothing certain. When she could crow over a new acquaintance who was sure to give her the push she needed to break into the big time.

In her new world she seemed to be fighting constantly to retain her balance. Decisions had to be made instantly because to put them off or delegate was a sign of weakness that the *pirañas* that fed close to the President would seize in their sharp teeth and shake mercilessly.

She thought of the harsh words she had spoken out of insecurity during the day. Even the faithful Isabel was not safe from her tongue when she felt she was under attack. She thought of the man lying in bed beside her. He was so clever and his understanding on every subject was so all-encompassing she sometimes feared that their relationship couldn't last. That he would become tired of her stupidity and unnecessary seriousness. She turned carefully over onto her other side and stretched her tense body.

If only she had his ability to laugh at the absurdity of some of the things that happened instead of seizing anything by the throat and trying to force it to conform. Of course, he had his faults. And there was his weakness for young girls. She didn't feel any jealousy for his occasional flings. She was rather glad that he did go for the really young ones. They bored him so quickly.

Isabel had been a great help to her. The adoring girl filled the gap she felt in her relationship with Perón. He pampered her, bowed to her wishes, flattered her outrageously and was always ready to give her the floor in any company. But there was no tenderness. It was good she had Isabel. If only she could win over the wives of the officials and army officers as easily. They hated her and it hurt. It hurt so much that she overreacted and gave them more fuel for their malicious lies and rumours. Why couldn't they just accept her for what she was? The wife of their President. Why was it such a big thing that she came from a poor background and had to fight for anything she wanted?

Surely it wasn't too much for them to at least invite her for tea? Just one lousy cup of tea. She gritted her teeth and pressed her face into the pillow. They were going to be sorry. How she was going to make them sorry was a problem she was working on daily. At least she had the suffragette women out of her hair for the time being. Now they had been given the vote they were all busy running for cover in case they were thought to be unfeminine. Unfeminine? If you were a female how could you be unfeminine? Still it had given Perón three or four million supporters at a guess. Not that he was sold on the idea of female suffrage but he had seen the political sense in the voting strength it gave him. Added to the votes of the totally committed *descamisados* it made his position unassailable.

Los descamisados! She smiled into the darkness. What a weapon that name had proved to be. At first Perón had been sceptical. It was like calling his supporters 'tramps' or

227

'down and outs'. But the name had stuck and the 'shirtless ones' now proudly added their voices and political muscle indiscriminately to every project Perón undertook. If only the oligarchy could realise that Perón wasn't trying to degrade them but uplift the masses. They all pointed a finger and shouted 'communist' when really he was neither a communist nor a fascist.

Eva thought the *descamisados* understood. That was why she was always at such great pains to appear before them as beautifully and expensively dressed as she possibly could. They looked at her and imagined themselves in her position. The oligarchy didn't understand. They thought she merely did it for her own vanity.

'Pappi,' she called to the heavily breathing figure beside her.

Perón didn't answer.

'Pappi, are you asleep?' she spoke louder.

'Yes,' Perón answered shortly but turned over to face her. 'Why aren't you?'

'Pappi – why don't they like me?' she asked in a little girl voice.

'Who?'

'Señora Unzue de Alveár and her lot. You know they still haven't offered me the presidency of the *Sociedad de Beneficencia* yet. Every other president's wife has automatically been elected but they haven't even asked me around for coffee.' She paused and then continued with a sob. 'What have I done for them to hate me?' she asked.

Perón put his arm around her and reached for the cigarettes in a box beside the bed and lit one.

'Must you smoke in bed?' she complained.

Her husband ignored her and returned to her original question. 'They don't hate you. They are frightened of you. They have never seen such a tiger in the President's bed and are shocked by it. Don't run after them. Ignore them and they will come to you. Give their husbands a chance to get over the attack on their wallet the higher wages are making and you'll soon see. They can't afford to offend me in the
228

long run so they will make up to you so that you can say the right word in my ear.

'You haven't done so badly so far. They are not fools. They can see your brother Juán up there as my private secretary, your step-father at the Ministry of Communications, one of your sisters' husband in the Senate and the others handing out contracts and they will soon get the idea that I'm a pushover for anything you suggest. Now forget the bloody oligarchs and let me get some sleep.'

He kissed her lightly on the forehead, withdrew his arm from behind her head, turned over and settled down to sleep. Eva lay and thought over what he had said. She still wasn't convinced that all she had to do was sit around and everyone would come running.

'Pappi,' she said again.

Perón breathed heavily in exasperation. '*Si – mi vida*. What is it now?'

'You know that award, the "Cross of Isabel the Catholic" or whatever it's called that Franco wants to give you?' she asked.

'*Si*,' he answered, his curiosity aroused.

'Are you going to collect it?' she asked.

He shook his head in the darkness. 'No. I am not going to Spain to collect it. He's only after a trade deal and if the terms are right he can have that without pinning a medal on my jacket,' he said ungraciously. He lay waiting for Eva to volunteer the reason for her interest.

She didn't say anything so he had to ask: 'Why? What's that to do with your being loved by Señora Unzue de Alveár and her coven?'

'Can I go and get the award for you?' she wheedled.

Perón sat up in astonishment. 'You? What the hell for?'

Eva sat up beside him. 'Well – if I went to Madrid and then on to see the Pope in Rome and maybe the King in England they would have to be nice to me, wouldn't they?'

Perón threw himself back on the pillow and reached for another cigarette. 'You must be mad,' he said in a dazed voice.

TWENTY-FIVE

The spotlight picked up the join in the small curtain at the back of the stage. It came to rest on a grotesque head peering through the drapes. Big, revolving eyes, outlined by long blonde lashes looked disdainfully down over a furry nozzle split by exaggeratedly painted, cupid's bow lips. It brought a ripple of laughter from the audience. The spotlight expanded and the body followed the head onto the stage. A pantomime camel with two floppy humps covered by a lacy brassiere and gawky legs encased in black stockings held up by frilly garters.

It was the typical filler act that bridges time while the main artistes have a quick drink and change into their next costume. The pathetic performance limped to its climax. A roll of drums tried to summon bored attention. Feigning shyness the ungainly figure slowly came downstage to where a party of well-dressed patrons chatted, oblivious to what was going on until the spotlight flooded their area. Startled they looked up. Quickly the light focused on the exquisitely dressed blonde in the centre of the group – Eva Duarte de Perón.

The camel curtsied and Eva smiled wearily at the unwelcome intrusion on her conversation. Then, without warning, it turned to present its rear end to the spotlit celebrity. The tail shot upright and a hand thrust a gaudy bunch of artificial flowers at the stunned woman. There was a chord of music from the orchestra and the act came to an inglorious end. Eva sat staring in disbelief at the flowers that had been unceremoniously tossed onto her table. Around her the other revellers began to laugh, and the laughter spread like fire in a cornfield.

She still sat mesmerised by the flowers. Juán, her brother,

leaned across and patted her hand reassuringly. It broke the spell. Angrily she jumped to her feet, picked up her purse and without looking to left or right, swept through the restaurant towards the exit. Monsieur Gisard, the manager, had seen what had happened. It was one of those acts that could go either way. If the victim laughs all is well. But why try it on the notoriously fiery lady of Argentina? He saw Eva coming and tried to head her off but she was not to be diverted.

Trailing brother Juán, secretary Isabel, the Argentine Ambassador and their hosts the Minister for Supply and his wife, Eva stormed out of the door and waited on the pavement while the doorman got her car. Juán hovered beside her nervously while Isabel tried to calm her friend down. In the background the Frenchman was apologising to the Argentinian Ambassador but they were all ignoring the little manager who was close to tears as his reputation as a host lay in tatters.

Eva opened the car door and hurled herself inside without waiting for the chauffeur to get out of the cab.

'Ritz,' she barked at the driver and then slumped back in the corner, not wishing to discuss the matter with her companions. Once arrived at the destination, she blasted out of her seat, through the doors, and across the foyer to the lift. The few people standing around or sitting in the spacious hall looked with amazement. Eva, dressed in a beautiful white evening gown and trailing a silk cape, face set and ugly, storming across the foyer in the late evening was not a scene that the sophisticated Parisians expected. Eva stood impatiently while Juán nervously unlocked the door and held it open for her. She looked him in the eye.

'*Gracias*, my brave brother, for defending me so resolutely in front of that *mierda*. I don't know what I would do without you,' she said sarcastically. 'Now perhaps you could do something useful and get Perón on the telephone,' she demanded.

'Now?' Juán asked incautiously. It was four o'clock in the morning in Argentina.

'*Si, chico*, NOW!'

Juán glanced at Isabel and then went to do as his sister bid him. Followed by Isabel, Eva rushed into her bedroom. She tore off her wrap and threw it at the dressing-table, knocking over several bottles.

'Why?' she screamed. Bending down she pulled off her shoes and hurled them after her cape. 'Why? Why? Why? What have I ever done to those *hijos de gran putas* to treat me like this?'

Isabel tried to put a comforting arm around her but was savagely pushed away.

'It's those smiling bastards the Ambassador's always crawling up the arse of . . . Who the hell does he think he is? I'll bet that stupid little shit paid to have it done to me. He's probably on the telephone now telling his masters in Buenos Aires what a clever little dog he is. I'll show him. I'll show all those know-nothing bastards.'

Without warning the fight went out of her and she burst into tears and sank onto the bed. Instantly Isabel was at her side, cuddling and coaxing her in an effort to cheer her up.

'*Calmate, mi vida*. They didn't mean anything by it. They thought it was a joke. I'm sure nobody put them up to it.'

Furiously Eva struck out at her companion knocking her to the floor. 'You . . . you . . . *Puta*! You're on their side. How much do they pay you? How much? What do you have to tell them? All the little bits of tittle-tattle you can make up? Do you tell them about how I screw everyone who comes into the Casa Rosada? Is it you who makes up all those stories? Get out! Get out! You filthy little creep!'

Isabel just stood, close to tears. Before she could speak the door behind her opened and Juán Duarte poked his head nervously around the edge.

'The call will be through in ten minutes. I put it straight through.'

Eva guessed he had arranged to spend the night with one of the stable of willing young girls who appeared wherever he went. She was hurt and lonely and didn't want anyone to enjoy themselves that night.

232

'Don't go sneaking off. I want you to stay here the night. You can sleep on the sofa out there. After Perón I don't want any more calls. No apologies, no explanations. Nothing. Do you understand me?' she demanded.

'But . . .' Duarte began.

'NO but's! Just do as you're told, *comprehendes?*'

Sadly Juán nodded and closed the door. As Eva sank exhausted onto the bed again, Isabel gathered her into her arms. Soothingly she kissed her friend's forehead and gently stroked her hair.

'There, there, *querida*. Forget it. You're tired and upset. Do you have any pain?'

Dumbly Eva nodded.

Isabel hugged her closer. '*Mi vida*, you must see a doctor. You can't go on like this.' Eva shook her head slowly. 'Not now. I've too much to do. When we get back to Buenos Aires maybe. If the pain doesn't go away before then.' She pressed her hand into her abdomen and leaned for comfort against her adoring fan.

The urgent trill of the telephone made them both jump. Eva nodded, dismissing Isabel and picked up the handset.

'*Si* – Juán?' she asked.

'*Hóla, mi vida! Que pasa?*' her husband's long suffering voice came back clearly in spite of the seven thousand miles separating them. He was glad he had come home to sleep. It had been an effort to get out of little Annie's warm bed. 'Do you know what time it is?' he demanded.

'*Si* – Pappi. I'm sorry to wake you up,' she said putting on her little girl's voice. 'But I miss you so. I want to come home!'

'Home?' he asked, startled into wakefulness.

'I thought you were staying, for at least another couple of weeks?'

'I know, Pappi, but I've had enough. I want to come home,' she insisted.

'You can't just pack up and leave like that. I've had enough problems as it is. Everybody making insinuations about how much money we're spending. What about

233

England? And Switzerland? You know you HAVE to go to Switzerland?!'

'I don't want to go to England. They have only invited me to tea with the Prime Minister's wife. I haven't been invited to stay at Buckingham Palace as I wanted.'

Perón gave a short laugh. 'I told you that was out before you left. They have a Labour government in England now and they have no *gracia*. Go to England. You might be surprised at the reception you get there. They are starved of glamour after six years of war.' He tried to rouse some enthusiasm in Eva without success.

'I am not going!' Eva stubbornly refused to be coaxed.

Perón's voice became harder. '*Bueno*. It's up to you. The whole trip was your idea, if you remember. Nobody asked you to go. Anyway, you must go to Switzerland.'

'What for? I can't move without at least fifty people streaming along behind me. How am I going to shake that lot off?' She sounded desperate.

Perón saw he had to be careful. '*Bueno*. Okay. You can come home whenever you like but I really would like you to go to Zurich. It's important for us, *mi vida*. You don't have to go to the bank yourself. Give Juán a letter of mandate and let him go,' he said carefully. He hoped that the call wasn't being monitored.

'Okay, Pappi,' Eva agreed uncertainly. 'But then I come home.'

Perón heaved a sigh of relief. 'Of course, *mi vida*. Then you come home to Pappi. Now – is there anything else you want to tell me?'

Eva wanted to tell him about what had happened in the night club but was too uncertain of his response. It would be just like him to think it funny.

'No!' she said shortly.

'You all right?' Perón queried, surprised at her abruptness.

Eva pulled herself together with an effort, '*Si, si*. Just tired. I'd better let you get to sleep now. I will call you tomorrow. Goodnight, *mi amor*.' Without waiting for a

234

reply she hung up.

She stood cautiously, trying not to aggravate the burning pain she had been getting in her belly with increasing frequency and force over the last six months. She feared ulcers. The pain was worse when she became upset. The only person who knew was Isabel and she had been sworn to secrecy. Eva, who had been a sickly child, was terrified that now, when she needed to be healthy, she was going to revert to the weakness of her childhood. Panic made her strive even harder. She worked from 6.30 in the morning, not getting to bed most nights until at least two, in an effort to exorcise her fears. The pain was easing now. Talking to Perón had relaxed her tense muscles.

She called to Isabel and started to undress. Her friend helped her get ready for bed. As she tucked her in Eva reached up and pulled her head down so that she could give her a long kiss on the mouth.

'*Lo siento, Isabellita, corazón.* I didn't mean what I said,' she murmured.

Isabel took her hand and held it to her breast. 'I know, *querida*. Now just close your eyes and go to sleep. We will talk in the morning,' she said gently, tears of gratitude in her eyes.

Eva closed her eyes and snuggled down. Isabel turned out the light and tiptoed from the room. As she quietly closed the door Juán came up behind her.

'Is she asleep?' He tried to look into the room.

Isabel shook her head. 'Not yet.'

'*Mierda!*' Juán cursed and went and poured himself another drink. Isabel watched him. She felt sorry for him in an irritated way. She knew he was unhappy. To be suddenly thrust into the international limelight had been too much for him. He was a playboy who didn't know how to play. Gambling had been his first foray into his newly acquired life of money and leisure. In the end Eva had got tired of paying his gambling debts and insisted that he came to live in Buenos Aires, coercing Perón into taking him on as 'private secretary'. He still didn't have any work but he was in a position where Eva could keep an eye on him, and incidentally, on Perón.

Isabel looked at him now, as he sprawled on the brocade covered sofa, his feet on the delicately carved wooden arm. He had taken off his coat and let his braces dangle. His hair was sticking out untidily, stiffened into spikes by the liberal portions of brilliantine he plastered onto his thinning hair. Drink was beginning to bloat his already pudgy face and he had developed a nervous habit of screwing up his eyes. Only his neatly trimmed, Clark Gable moustache told of the hours he spent in the barber's reclining chair.

Isabel walked to the door. Her room was on the other side of Eva's. 'If you are thinking of sneaking out I would forget it. If your sister finds you gone there will be hell to pay. Get a good night's sleep for once. You could use it.'

Duarte looked annoyed. 'Good night's sleep? On here?' He kicked roughly at the arm of the sofa with his shoe.

'Goodnight, Juán. Don't leave her, huh?' Isabel coaxed as she shut the door.

Juán looked at the door and finished his drink. Frustrated in his intentions of spending the night with a French starlet he had been introduced to earlier in the day he considered the advisability of trying his hand with Isabel. To hell with any problems that might arise later. Everything was a problem – what matter if there was another. The whole tour had been a problem. From the moment Perón had made his theatrical speech sending Eva, the 'Heart of the Argentine' as a 'Rainbow' between the new continent and the old, she had been in a foul mood. Only Franco's rapturously stage-managed welcome had sweetened her temper. She enjoyed playing Madame Bountiful and handing out charity as if she were digging into her own pocket. And then she had become so carried away with her leading role that she had to go and throw her hand up in the Fascist salute.

In Europe! After the concentration camps. Juán shook his head in disbelief and poured himself another drink to soften his sense of melancholy. Although nobody had made any remark at the time, the world's press came out bold and self-righteous. It was this slip in diplomacy more than anything that had contributed to the noticeably cool reception she had received in Italy and France. Now the problem with Britain. Why couldn't Eva just go, smile and wave her hand a bit, pose for the pictures and then take herself off. Why did she insist on staying at Buckingham Palace as a personal guest of the King?

Duarte stared miserably into the bottom of his glass, maudlin tears not far away. And, of course, on top of everything else that stupid bloody comedian had to hand her a bunch of flowers out of the arse-end of a camel. He tried to settle on the uncomfortably contoured settee. It was no good. If he was going to sleep he was going to have to drink a lot more of her whisky. He got another stiff drink and sat back on the settee. Italy had been the worst. Eva had invited herself to see the Pope and then arrived twenty-five minutes late. *Il Papa*, not the most forgiving of men, had then kept her waiting in the reception room and, when they finally got together, gave her a rosary and some also-ran Papal order. And not even for her. To take home to Perón. Eva, naturally, put it all down to her aristocratic enemies, above all to Señora Unzue de Alveár. She had banked on the Pope giving her a Papal Marquisate that would force the snobbish old matriarchs to recognise her.

And why the hell did she care? That's what Juán couldn't make out. She had got more than she could ever have dreamed of. The President's wife, cheered wherever she went, a pipeline straight into the treasury. But it wasn't enough for Eva. And she thought she was so clever. Ordering people about. Making arrangements that others had to keep. If she was half as clever as she thought she wouldn't let Perón use her as much as he did. Obligingly she rushed about spouting whatever claptrap he had given and then went away satisfied that she had progressed the destiny of her leader. She didn't see the little smiles and the snide jokes that Perón entertained his intimates with.

Juán Duarte did. But he could do nothing. Perón treated him like a page-boy or ignored him altogether. Now Juán was drunk and almost incapable. He tried to concentrate on the pert little French girl he had promised to take out that night. Before Eva let her filthy temper get the better of her and made him stay at home. As if it was his fault.

There was a faint knock on the door. Stupidly he stared at it trying to think of the French word.

'*Entrez*,' he finally managed. Isabel came into the room carrying some blankets and a pillow. 'I thought you might like some blankets,' she explained.

Juán peered at her blearily. She wasn't bad really. Quite pretty if you liked the quiet, dowdy type.

'If you are going to share them with me . . .' he said with a leer.

She ignored him and put the pillow at the end of the settee.

'Are you going to tuck me in and kiss me goodnight?' he asked.

As she bent to cover him with the blanket he grabbed her and pulled her on top of him. She struggled to break his grasp. 'Stop it! Don't be foolish.'

He tried to put his hand up her skirt but she caught hold of his wrist and pulled herself away. The nightmare of her rape on the garbage behind her father's shop made her frantic. She gave a little scream and struck him a heavy blow across the face. He blinked but didn't let go. Before she could get away he rolled off the settee, pulling her to the floor. In spite of her struggles he ripped open the front of her dress and buried his face between her breasts.

'What the hell do you think you are doing!'

The hard icy tones of Eva's voice cut into Juán's alcohol fogged mind like a surgeon's scalpel.

He looked down at the half-clad, weeping girl beneath him and then turned fearfully to his sister. Eva stood in the bedroom doorway, her silk nightdress accentuating her figure, hair, soft and loose, falling around her shoulders in a feminine halo. But there was nothing feminine about the look on her face. It was hard and frozen.

Juán rose unsteadily, leaving Isabel drawn up in a protec-

238

tive foetal position. Eva walked slowly across the room. Juán was terrified. He had never seen her like this. Her eyes blazed, unwinking, unmoving. Her lips, usually so soft and sensual, were held in a straight line drawn back from her clenched teeth. Mesmerised, Juán watched her hand draw back and then lash forward with stunning force across his face. As he backed away he tasted blood from his teeth-gashed cheek. Eva stalked him, cursing and pushing. He sank onto the floor in the corner and snivelled into his hands.

'You stupid, cock-brained, shit-house. Just like the rest of them. I'll make you pay for this. You dirty rotten son of a bitch. You'll pay. My God – you'll pay!'

Exhausted she staggered back across the room and sat on the arm of the sofa looking down at Isabel. 'And you? What are you doing here? Haven't you got the sense you were born with? No wonder you get yourself raped. You ask for it. Now go to bed and we'll talk about it in the morning.'

Isabel got slowly to her feet and walked towards the door. As she passed her, Eva put a hand on her arm and kissed her gently on the cheek. 'Don't worry, *querida*. Get a good night's sleep.'

She watched the distraught girl close the door and then went and stood over her brother, still crouched in the corner. 'Listen to me. I have enough problems. I don't need you to add to them. Do what you like with the whores you pick up at nightclubs but stay away from Isabel. Now go to your room and sleep it off.'

Alone Eva stood for long minutes staring at the black door then suddenly gave a suppressed scream of frustration and picked up the porcelain-based table lamp and hurled it to destruction at the wall. Her sleep shattered she lay for the rest of the night worrying about the future and holding her stomach where the nagging pain persisted.

Isabel, quiet and subdued, poked her head quietly around the edge of the door just after 8.30. She hadn't been able to sleep either so had got up early rather than lie aching and restless in the soft, lonely bed. A number of times she had

239

been on the point of getting up and going to creep into Eva's bed, as she often did when she was low, but she wasn't sure of her reception. Eva might be blaming her for the scene with Juán. And who could blame her?

Isabel's cheeks flushed as she remembered the pulse of excitement she had felt as she knocked on the apartment door. If Juán hadn't been so drunk – who knows?

Eva was already awake and beckoned her in. 'You all right, *qerida*?' she asked bluntly.

Isabel nodded. '*Bueno*,' Eva dismissed the subject of the night by not referring to it again. 'I want to get out of here as soon as possible. Cancel all my engagements. Tell them I'm tired or anything you like. I don't want to speak to anyone. Not even the Ambassador.' She pushed back the covers and got out of bed. Isabel held out a white, frilly negligée which she slipped into and then went into the bathroom. Through the open door she continued to give instructions.

'Order my usual breakfast now, would you, *querida*? Get the driver to pick up the dresses I've bought and send them on to Buenos Aires. Then get on to the Embassy and arrange for cars to take us to Zurich. You got all that? Any problems?'

'No, Eva,' Isabel said hesitantly. 'Only . . . what about England? Aren't we going there?'

'No we're not. Tell the Ambassador to present my apologies and tell the King that he can stuff his tea with the Prime Minister's wife!'

TWENTY-SIX

Pinpoints of light behind and to the right of him were the only points of reference he had to orientate himself. If it wasn't for those and the thin nylon rope grazing his face he wouldn't have known which way was up. Carefully he tested the minute ledge his blindly questing toe had managed to find. He let his weight gradually rest on it before searching for a fingerhold.

Abe Rubel was a cautious man. That was one reason why the newly formed CIA had taken him on. His questing foot touched rock and he stopped and slid it as far each way as he could manage. It had to be what he was looking for. He pushed himself outward with his foot and let the forward swing take him onto the ledge. Now, inside the giant opening, he could feel the warm, oil-scented air tug like gently flowing water at his clothes and hair. Quickly he dropped to one knee and took the flat automatic from the pouch on his thigh. Only the steady rumble of the fans and the murmured vibration of the airvents disturbed the night.

Rubel took out a slim, pencil-beam torch and, carefully shielding the light with his body, examined the rock on which he perched. It had been chiselled out to a depth of about fifteen feet and then the back of the cave sealed off with a wire mesh, to discourage birds trying to nest in the ducting. The designer had discounted the possibility of anyone scaling down the side of the cliff in full view of the village.

On the right hand side there was a small, hinged gate in the grill used by the maintenance men for reaching the ledge when it became necessary to clean off the mesh. Rubel shone his torch around the edge but could see no evidence of wiring of any sort that might indicate an alarm. There wasn't even a lock on the door, just a simple bar-slide. He poked his head through the opening and risked using his torch. An iron ladder was bolted to the side of the ducting and disappeared into the black abyss below. Inside the cave the rumble in the ducting became a continuous roll of muted thunder so the intruder had no fear of being heard.

Steadily climbing downwards he tried to get a sense of his surroundings. From the way the sound echoed around him, he deduced, correctly, that the installation had been built on the inside of a natural cavern deep in the mountain, probably volcanic originally, and the ducting had been constructed inside one of the blow holes that had drained off the pressure and prevented the lava thrusting up through the top of the mountain. The luminous dial on his watch told him that he had been going down for five minutes when his feet hit a metal catwalk. From the increase in the level of sound he knew he was standing next to the extractor fans. This meant he could only be a few feet above the working area of the cave's interior. The fans were bound to be sited as near to their extraction points as possible to give maximum efficiency. Now he had to find a way inside.

Automatic in his right hand, torch in his left, he prowled catlike along the metal walkway. At the end was a pair of service doors. Slowly, a millimetre at a time, he prised the door away from the jamb and put his eye to the gap. The service hatch for the air-conditioning was about twenty feet above the floor of a well-equipped engineering shop in a rock chamber about a hundred feet long and fifty wide. It was obvious that whatever was being made below was something more ambitious than milking machines.

He ran a practised eye over the room for security. A jolt of disbelief almost made him wrench open the door in surprise. He had been so busy trying to discover what the engineers were fabricating below that he had not noticed the catwalk running along the wall directly opposite where he was standing. But it wasn't the catwalk that claimed his attention, it was the two men, leaning on the guardrail and watching the activities below with casual vigilance. They both wore the black, silver-trimmed uniform of the SS. It was like a nightmare.

Rubel forced himself to be calm, closed the door and went back the way he had come to explore the other direction. The ducting ran along at head-height but he was unable to get even the most fractional glimpse into whatever was on the other side of the wall. Another door, similar in design to the one at the other end of the passageway, opened out onto the same type of installation.

As he went to close the door he noticed something on the wall to the left. He eased the gap a little wider. Hanging on the wall, staring disdainfully over the heads of the workers below, was a giant picture of Adolf Hitler.

Abe Rubel had seen enough. Before the sun came up to silhouette the mountain and bathe the charming little Bavarian backdrop in warm light, Rubel was contacting his control in Brazil to pass on the details of his discovery.

The journey to Berne had been too short. Eva had done her best to heal the breach of embarrassment between her brother and her best friend but so far without success. Isabel was willing, for Eva's sake, to forget Juán's attack, but he remained sullen and withdrawn.

Isabel looked worried as Eva, unsmiling and terse, greeted the diplomatic party in the VIP lounge and then let them escort her out to the waiting cars. She was not at all her busy excited self. There was a small crowd, but instead of happy adoring workers that had turned out in their thousands to greet her in the other countries she had visited, they were quiet, motivated only by curiosity.

Juán had left straight from the airport for his appointment with the bankers in Zurich. It had been Eva's idea. She felt that the fewer people who could pinpoint Juán Duarte as her brother, the better. She didn't want her brother's activities known to anyone but herself. As they sped smoothly through the narrow streets of the canton small groups of people, mostly students, shouted hostile slogans and waved banners. Used to almost universal acclaim, and having the means to eliminate anything less in her homeland, Eva sank deeper into her depression.

Isabel saw Eva's clawing hand surreptitiously knead her stomach. She leaned across and patted her hand comfortingly but Eva pulled back with a cold, detached stare. As they approached the villa the crowd at the side of the road became thicker. Men banged on the speeding car with their hands or sticks. As they approached the tall, wrought-iron gates guarding the drive to the house, two men stepped from the crowd and hurled stones at the windscreen. There was a crack like a pistol shot and the glass crazed in a web of cracks.

Eva threw herself forward into Isabel's lap and screamed a cry of such abject terror that the girl's hair prickled. Protectively she threw her arms around Eva as the driver punched savagely at the opaque glass to clear his view. Too late he saw the hunched, black-clad figure of an old woman step off the pavement practically under the wheels. Even as he slammed on the brake he knew it was too late.

At the last moment the woman looked up, her toothless mouth opened in a silent scream as the heavy bumper struck her legs and threw her up onto the bonnet. Eva looked up to see the grotesque, broken body in a flapping black shroud, slide up to the frame of the shattered windscreen, hang there for a second, the wide, staring eyes fixed accusingly on Eva, before sliding off sideways and sprawling, a broken ragdoll, in the side of the road.

Hysterical screams went unheeded by the occupants of the car. Mentally stunned by the horrendous turn of events they could do nothing but sit and watch the driver accelerate through the gate and make for the front of the house. Behind them the duty police, detailed to guard the villa, swung shut the heavy gate before the crowd could recover and storm through seeking bloody revenge on the occupants of the car. Unheeded, half-starved, a burden to her family in life, the old woman had suddenly become a martyr, a symbol of Fascist oppression. Switzerland, after sitting out the war in neutrality, was perhaps absolving its

244

conscience by making Eva the scapegoat for her country's tacit indulgence of the Axis powers.

A doctor was called and Eva was put to bed and given a tranquilliser. All through the night Isabel sat by her friend's bed holding her hand and crooning a soothing dirge. At eight o'clock she allowed the nurse to persuade her to go to bed but extracted a promise to be called the moment Eva awoke.

Eva slept through until two in the afternoon. By this time Isabel was back, sitting attentively by the side of the bed holding her hand. She smiled and touched Isabel's cheek.

Isabel's relief was so great at seeing her awake at last that she burst into tears and had to be comforted by Eva. The President's wife was calmer now. She inquired after Juán and was relieved to find he had returned from Zürich. More tentatively she asked about the old woman. When she was told that the accident had been fatal she crossed herself.

In a firmer voice Eva told her secretary to get Juán Duarte. She ignored the suggestion that she should be examined by the doctor. She had more important things to do. When Juán arrived she dismissed Isabel and told him to give her a full report. He told her that he had opened the numbered bank account with the deposit of 250,000 dollars and put the bonds and jewellery in a deposit box in the vaults of the Schweizerische Bank Gesellschaft.

He gave her the key to the box and the number of the secret account. She insisted that he also had a copy. In the future he might have to operate her account for her.

Eva's return to Buenos Aires was a stupendous event. Supporters from all over the city had crowded the docks since early morning. Again and again they had sung their popular rallying song 'Muchachos Peronistas', 'Perón's Boys', and cheered anybody who looked as if they might have anything to do with the return of their goddess. By midday there were a quarter of a million workers turning the quay into a festival.

Perón had needed a show of solidarity to convince the

wealthy *porteños* that they couldn't hope to stand against him. Cipriano Reyes had put the word around that he wanted a full turnout and persuaded any reluctant employers that they would find it a lot easier to give the workers the day off with full pay than have to renegotiate pay claims.

As the ship came in sight the noise of their cheering reached out across the water. Eva went onto the bridge and watched as the crowded quay became more visible. She had been told on the radio telephone that there was a big reception committee but the wildly cheering throng, pressed into a solid, colourful mass on the docking jetty and hanging like animated puppets from cranes and hoardings all over the docks, surpassed her wildest dreams.

It hadn't been easy to dress for the occasion. Isabel had been brought close to tears as the pile of rejected furs and dresses had spilled from the bed onto the cabin floor and furniture. Finally she had chosen a simple silk dress by Balmain, her latest wild mink fur and a chic forage cap. The Christmas tree effect of her jewels hanging around her neck, sparkling on her constantly moving hands and jangling on her wrists, was for her *descamisados*.

Perón was waiting on the quay as the gangplank was run out and he sprinted up to the bridge, cheered on by the crowd, and picked the slight body of Eva up in his arms and whirled her around. As they kissed, a long, passionate kiss, the excited supporters roared their approval. Perón impetuously pulled Eva to the front of the bridge and presented her to the crowd.

As she raised her arms in welcome a chant started up. Eva was used to the sound of Perón's name roared in unison on the lips of his supporters and for a moment she couldn't understand what was happening. Warmth flooded through her body and threatened to reduce her to tears as the expression of love welled up from the crowd, a strong, rhythmic chant of adoration.

'E-VI-TA! E-VI-TA! E-VI-TA!'

TWENTY-SEVEN

President Truman sat at his desk in the Oval room of the White House and read through the report that had dropped on his blotter that morning. He didn't know quite what to make of it. South America was one of his smaller problems at that time. The growing uneasiness of some of his aides had been dismissed as over-active imagination in a dark world of famine, political intrigue and GI brides.

Truman pressed the button on the intercom and spoke into the receiver. 'Get me Spruille Braden. Tell him I would like to see him immediately if he is in the building.'

Laying the memo aside he turned his attention to the multitude of other problems that turn up on the US President's desk. Most of the memos were for information only but the ones that needed a reply he dictated in a rapid, ungrammatical style to his secretary.

The President kept Braden waiting a short time while he dealt with his mail and then the secretary ushered in the Secretary for Latin-American Affairs. Truman's nutty face split in a puckish grin and his eyes glinted with vitality behind his glasses. He wasn't a man to beat around the bush.

'Glad you could come, Spruille. Read your note on South America.' He picked up the piece of paper and glanced at it again. 'I'm not particularly worried about the Germans in Brazil or all the other places you mention. They had to go somewhere and as long as they keep out of our hair we can sleep easy.'

He tapped the memo and stared at Braden. 'This one's a shaker. This Abe Rubel, can he be trusted? You are sure he's not a nut seeing Nazi war criminals in every foreign accent?'

Spruille Braden shook his head. 'It's not just what Rubel

reported, sir. In fact, he only confirmed suspicions that we have had for some time. He could not identify what was being manufactured. We built up a picture of this from known facts and observation on various colonies that the Nazis have in other parts of the Argentine.'

Truman mulled over the implications. 'Why the Bomb, though? Couldn't they just be making conventional missiles?' he asked.

'It would be pointless. It's the Bomb all right.'

'And you have talked it over with our people and they agree with you?'

'Yes, Mr President. There seems to be no doubt that they have scientists as good as anybody in the States. They have only one problem. Fissionable material. Hiding out in the mountains working under cover it will be difficult for them to produce enough uranium.'

Truman smiled with relief. 'Then the answer's obvious. We make sure that they don't get any.'

Braden frowned. 'Normally that wouldn't be a problem. Trouble is that Perón has been slipping in some funny remarks in his speeches. Hinting at a new source of power and so on.'

'That sounds like he has found a coal mine. We know he has the oil. Probably more than us if he got himself organised to get it out of the ground. What makes you jump for nuclear energy?' Truman asked.

Braden got up and excitedly walked about the office. 'We know there is no coal in Argentina. Besides, it all fits.' He ticked off the points on his fingers. 'We know that the Nazis were pouring money into Argentina as early as 1936. Towards the end of the war they sent shiploads of heavy equipment secretly to Buenos Aires disguised as farm machinery. We got that from the few remaining records of the German central transport office. We also know that after Hitler ordered the cessation of their Atom Bomb project Bormann hustled most of the scientists out of the country. We looked for them but they had disappeared. Now we know they went to South America.'

248

He stopped and drew a deep breath before rushing on. 'We believe that the Nazis have offered Perón nuclear weaponry to hold us to ransom while the Germans try to retain control of Europe. As a side issue, and to produce the necessary uranium, they have promised Perón nuclear energy for domestic use.' Braden stopped and looked at his chief.

'Who do you think's heading up the organisation?' Truman asked.

Braden shook his head. 'We don't know. Various top Nazis have been suggested but there is no conclusive evidence to put any of them on the spot.'

Truman took off his glasses and cleaned them vigorously on a piece of chamois leather he kept tucked in his breast pocket. 'Bormann?'

Braden shook his head. 'No. Bormann's dead. We have absolutely no evidence that he got out of Berlin.' He spoke with more conviction than he felt.

Truman sat and stared at his fingers for a long time.

Tomas Bravo never forgot his arch-enemy Cipriano Reyes, the instigator of the horrific murder of his wife and children. Once a moderate man, Bravo had been a union official too, but on the day of his election as president of the Office Workers and Civil Servants Union, his family had been gunned down in cold blood. The example had been noted by the other officials. Bravo was cast out, and was now an isolated man, driven by revenge. He watched the power of Cipriano Reyes with the unions and plotted his downfall.

Whenever anything detrimental to the Peróns' quest for absolute power happened he told his handful of followers that Reyes was the architect. They whispered the union leader's name in receptive ears confident that it would reach the ubiquitous Secret Police that permeated every stratum of Argentine life.

Bravo was aware that Perón was preparing a *putsch*. The long honeymoon with his tough labour leaders was over. Suddenly they discovered that in accepting Perón's protection they had sold their unions into the political arms of the President.

Bravo stood now outside the Colon Theatre, crushed by the crowd of excited workers waiting to see the arrival of their President and his fairy princess. He was careful to stay well back in the crowd and show the same degree of excited anticipation. Always in the crowds were the faceless men ready to snatch off anyone who didn't show enough enthusiasm, to the notorious cellar in police headquarters.

There was a stir in the crowd and excited voices announced the arrival of the presidential car. Bravo saw hands pitch tiny folded pieces of paper into the clear path from the car to the theatre door. It had become a sort of unofficial lottery to throw requests written on small squares of paper into the path of Evita. The President's wife would pick up two or three of these and the lucky winners would be invited to the Secretariat of Labour and Welfare to put their case before *La Señora Presidenta*.

There was a gasp from the crowd and then everybody started thrusting back, trying to get away from the vicinity of their President. Perón stared, mesmerised, at the can lobbed from the crowd and coming to rest at his feet. Eva gave a terrified scream and tried to bury herself in Perón's chest.

Perón didn't know what to do. Too frightened of public opinion to turn and run he did the only thing he felt he could do in the circumstances. He bent down and picked up the home-made bomb, handed it to one of his aides and went into the theatre supporting the fainting weight of Eva under one arm. Instantly the crowd surged back, natural curiosity driving them into the danger area to catch a glimpse of the bomb that their President had so nonchalantly ignored. Bravo was satisfied. It didn't matter that the bomb had failed to explode.

Quickly, before the police could recover and throw a cordon around the area, he slipped out of the crowd and went to his car parked unobtrusively a block away and joined the heavy evening traffic on the Avenida Nueve de Julio. By the time the last chords of *Aida* had died away, the bomb-throwing student, picked up with hundreds of others, had confessed his complicity in the assassination attempt. And he named Cipriano Reyes as the arch-conspirator. He genuinely believed that the name fed to him by Bravo was the name of the man who had made the bomb, put it in his hands and pointed him in the right direction to throw it.

The Police Chief, Colonel Velazco, was waiting in the foyer when Perón and Eva left the theatre and joined them on the ride back to Olivos. Already at the residency was Lopez Rega. He had been brought up to date on developments and guessed it was going to be a long night.

Perón was relaxed and in a surprisingly good mood considering the close call he had received only a few hours earlier. Eva's mood was quieter and more strained. She still had trouble believing that anyone hated them enough to want to kill them.

Perón settled them all down in his recently decorated study and ordered a pot of coffee. '*Bueno, amigos!* It seems the gods, or the low standard of engineering in the universities, are with us. We can now unleash our righteous anger and clean out whatever nests house vipers. First Cipriano Reyes. Have you picked him up yet?'

Velazco shook his head. 'Not yet, *Presidente*. He was out when we called but there should not be any problems.'

'Good. Now who do you think was in it with him?' Perón asked innocently.

'The oligarchs!' Eva blurted out without hesitation.

Perón gave her a sad smile. 'Too broad a front, *mi vida*. They are easy targets for a guerrilla war but a frontal attack would amalgamate them with the Army and that could cause more problems than I want to face at this time.'

A servant arrived with the coffee. Eva took it from him and shooed him out unceremoniously.

Velazco coughed. 'The Communists. There are a lot of Russians in town at the moment and the union members are used to being warned against communist intervention,' he suggested.

Perón shook his head. 'No. Not the Russians. We need them as window dressing at the moment. They want to lend us money.' He looked at Lopez Rega. 'What's your suggestion?' he demanded.

Lopez Rega shrugged. 'Obviously this gives us the reason we wanted to move against the union leaders. That gives us a pretty free hand. Do we need anything more?' he asked.

Perón nodded his head furiously. 'Yes! We need an external instigator. We blame the Americans. Put it down to a dastardly plot by the conniving *Norte Americanos* who subverted our loyal friend Cipriano Reyes and, even now, are undermining our Labour movement by paying its leaders to disrupt our efforts to build the New Argentina.'

He turned to Eva. 'You can put that over. An emotional appeal to the masses to stand behind us in our sad ordeal. That will make them stand still while we get rid of the troublemakers in the unions and replace them with more trustworthy men. José, you work with Velazco. I want a clean sweep. Quickly! Don't give anyone a chance to talk.' He clapped his hands together. '*Bueno, muchachos.* To work?'

Lopez Rega worked unceasingly over the next three days, compiling lists, suggesting raids, consulting with Perón.

Not all their victims were caught napping. Many of them had already made their arrangements for hurried departure to the political exiles' haven across the Rio de la Plata. The jails were overflowing. Private houses and warehouses were taken over to accommodate the excess. Businessmen flew to their most distant estates and hid in the *pampa*. Evita fed Velazco names that she wanted to get even with for real or imagined slights.

It was a week before any sign of normality returned and by that time there was a new line-up of union leaders, all hand picked by the Peróns, and the Americans, after protesting strongly that they weren't involved in the assassination attempt, were trying to find some way of getting back in Perón's favour.

They were aware of the Russian interest in South

America and were now ready to turn a blind eye to any right-wing activity that was likely to run counter to any communist-inspired policy for the sub-continent. Perón was content. He had Eva firmly installed as the champion of the masses. The labour unions were run by his own men. He controlled radio and press. And now the USA were indicating an interest in filling his depleted coffers with dollars to keep him out of the hands of the Reds.

TWENTY-EIGHT

Eva's eyes opened. She felt the pain stabbing and crawling in her stomach. Sweat broke out of her pores and drenched her body. The sweat worried her more than the pain. It seemed too much sweat for so little pain. Carefully she slid out of bed and picked her way in the dark to the bathroom. Without switching on the light she found the painted wicker chair beside the bath and sank down into it.

Now the pain was back she had to face facts. There was something radically wrong with her. Always she had been troubled by the tendency to put on excess weight. Now she was losing weight steadily regardless of how much she ate. And her strength wasn't as dependable as it had been before. Now she had to drive herself to put in the punishing fourteen-hour day she had set as her target. There was still so much to do.

She thought of her achievements. The *Sociedad de Beneficencia* of Señora Unzue de Alveár had been disbanded, cut off at the roots on Eva's insistence that the subsidy the government paid to underwrite the charity, was terminated. Her own Eva Perón Foundation was getting into its stride building hospitals, clinics, rest homes and donating cash for research. It could now command millions of dollars annually and was rarely refused a donation from businesses and commercial enterprises wishing to function in the city.

Her mind turned to one of the factory owners who only the week before had refused to give her the contribution she had suggested. The Mu Mu Chocolate Company was one of the largest and best known sweet manufacturers in the country. When Eva had told the managing director that a donation to the fund would be appreciated he had refused.

A couple of days later food inspectors had called at the

factory. Rat-hairs had been found in the chocolate and the premises closed down by the Sanitation Department. Eva had made sure that journalists were on hand to record the event and the newspapers had been plastered with the story. Overnight Mu Mu Chocolate had crashed. Too late the owner hastily dispatched a cheque to the Foundation. But the damage had been done by the rat-hairs that the inspectors had so surprisingly discovered in one piece of chocolate. The destruction of one of Argentina's leading businesses didn't concern Eva. The publicity the closure had received would act as a spur to other companies and they wouldn't be so foolish as to deny her demands in future.

The pain in her stomach receded and Eva had a shower to wash away the sweat and then carefully made up her face. She had now abandoned the actress make-up she had affected in the past and used a pale base, mascara lightly applied to her long lashes and a less brilliant lipstick. Her hairstyle was also less exotic. She had forsaken the pompadour creations for a tight, close-to-the-head style swept back into a braided bun at the nape of her neck. Even her clothes had changed. Suits had replaced the extravagant dresses. Still tailored to perfection by the best couturiers in the world they underlined her acquired self image of the no-nonsense executive, working to bring about the economic revolution the Peronista government had promised.

As Eva dressed she thought about her appointment with the architect, Doctor Repetto, who was responsible for the construction of her pet project, the *Ciudad Infantil*, the Children's Town on the edge of the beautiful Palermo Park. For the first time she was going to see it complete. Since the project had begun she had worked closely with the committee which she had appointed to run it in her name but had kept away for the last month while the finishing touches had been made because she wanted to see the whole picture for the first time.

Today was the day. Excitement pushed away the worry about her health and she finished dressing and went to wake up Perón just as the maid arrived with the early morning

255

coffee and fruit that started their day.

Perón sat, morose and sleepy, propped against the padded headboard while Eva excitedly told him about the completion of the *Ciudad Infantil*. He had heard it all before but grunted diplomatically knowing that a lack of interest would provoke an attack that he was not at his best to withstand in the early morning. It was Eva's insistence that they started their day at 5.00 am. He would have preferred a more civilised time. At last Eva swept out and Juán sank down in the bed for a stolen half hour.

The black, official limousine waited outside the main entrance of the Secretariat of Labour and Welfare while Eva attended to a few important items and glanced through the intelligence reports of what had happened while she slept.

Isabel arrived ten minutes later and reminded her that her brother Juán was due back from Zurich on the afternoon flight. Colonel Mercante, now Governor of Buenos Aires Province, had sent an acceptance of Eva's invitation to speak at the Eva Perón Feminist Party rally and a deputation from the Railway Workers Union was coming to the Casa Rosada later in the day to present her with a gift of appreciation from the union members.

With nothing urgent to keep her at the office she told Isabel to drop whatever she was doing and come with her to see the *Ciudad Infantil*, completed and ready to receive its first inhabitant. Like two excited schoolgirls they rushed down to the waiting car and giggled away the fifteen minute drive to the Figueroa Alcorta site.

Eva stopped the car outside the gleaming white gate and then got out and walked forward to meet the collection of officials, alerted to their arrival, who stood in the courtyard in front of the newly completed building. Impatiently Eva walked along the line of men and women who were to manage the home for the children of the poor. She wanted to get away on her adventure. To see the result of her dreams to provide all the things she had been denied as the youngest child of an impoverished family living in the sticks.

Unable to wait any longer she pulled Dr Repetto towards the entrance. With her entourage walking in unaccustomed haste behind her she swept through the bright, clean dormitories with their pretty curtains and bedspreads. She opened the miniature chests of drawers and showed Isabel the dresses, shirts and underwear that had been donated by clothing manufacturers. Each wardrobe had rows of dresses or little suits. Everywhere dolls and toys filled ledges or lay on the beds waiting for the children who were to fill the home.

In each room, above the bed, was a cross flanked by a photograph of an avuncular President Perón and his beautiful wife. The large well-appointed kitchen and spacious day-rooms were swept through at a fast pace. Eva pushed open the all french windows leading out onto the immaculate lawn lined with cypress trees and divided by a sculptured fountain of two young, naked children looking rapturously into the benign face of a semi-nude woman, artfully draped in a shroud, that had obviously been modelled on the home's benefactress. Water sprayed over the figures in a lacy film taking the heat from the sun with its gentle gurgle and splash.

Eva let the beauty of the scene sweep over her. Repetto turned to say something but Eva silenced him with a raised finger. She didn't want to have the moment spoiled by words. Impulsively she took Isabel's hand and, like two children, they ran across the lawn and through the cypress arch to the open square beyond.

At least it had been an open space before. Now, even Eva, aware of what had been planned, gasped with amazement. Set out in the morning sun, like a Lilliputian village, half-scale buildings with red-tile roofs and crisp white walls, filled the area bounded by the cypress hedge. There were ten chalets, a town hall, steepled church, fire station, several shops of different kinds, a service station and a village pond.

It wasn't just a playground, it was meant to be lived in. Each chalet was fully furnished with scaled down furniture and the shops were stocked with goods. Even the service station had a number of toy cars in front of the pumps.

As Eva and Isabel stood, too overawed to go forward, the sound of an orchestra came from the direction of the far hedge playing the Argentine National Anthem, the orchestrated hymn to the *Pampa* taking on a sweetness and heartwarming quality in the still, warm air. The music stopped and Eva was about to urge Isabel forward when it started up again. This time it was the marching song that had become the Perón anthem, '*Muchachos Perónistas*'.

At a pre-arranged signal all the tiny doors in the village opened and white smocked children walked, solemnly singing, out onto the road. A woman in a nurse's uniform quickly organised them into a long marching line and the children, singing selfconsciously, filed past Evita. Tears coursed down her face as she watched and suddenly she could stand still no longer. Rushing across to the tots she hugged and kissed them, leaving lipstick smears on their soft cheeks.

She held two of them, a boy and a girl, by the hands and bent down so that their heads were on the same level. 'Come on, my babies, show Auntie Eva everything.' She tugged at the children, overcome by the excitement. 'Come on, show me everything,' she cooed at them.

The boy took control. Solemnly he led the way to the little house he had just left and stood politely at the door waiting for Eva to enter. She smiled and caressed his cheek. The doorway was to scale with the house and Eva had to bend to enter.

As she straightened up a searing pain exploded in her stomach. She drove both hands deep into the pain, trying to squeeze it out. She felt the pain reaching out for her brain. The tiny room pressed in on her. She tried to tell the little boy and girl not to be afraid but pain choked the words in her throat.

Another explosion of pain buckled her knees, she staggered towards the child-sized bed covered with dolls and soft toys. Behind her she heard Isabel's sharp anxious voice and tried to tell her not to worry. With her last strength she propelled her failing body at the bed and crashed down scattering dolls and pillows to the floor.

The pain receded but she didn't seem able to function. Far away she heard the sound of an ambulance and she was aware of being moved. Isabel was sitting next to her as they rushed through the streets to the Policlinica.

Perón left his meeting and raced across the town when he heard the news of her collapse. He arrived at the hospital only minutes after his wife and demanded to see her. Although only semi-conscious, Evita smiled up at his anxious face and patted his hand to tell him not to worry. He watched with tears in his eyes as she was wheeled away to the operating theatre.

The director of the hospital Dr Finochietto escorted Perón to his office and gave him a drink. While they waited for the doctor's report on Eva's condition Perón paced up and down the room refusing to be consoled.

The telephone rang. The director answered it and then smiled with relief. '*Bueno*. I will tell the President.'

Perón hung expectantly over him as he returned the handset to its cradle.

'Señora de Perón is suffering from appendicitis. It is nothing to worry about, a simple operation. May I suggest, your *Excelencia*, that I call you as soon as I have further news.'

'How long will the operation take?' Perón asked.

'We should know in an hour,' the director told him.

'*Bueno*. I'll wait,' Perón said.

Finochietto bowed acceptance. '*Si, Excelencia*. Please use this office. I will let you know what is happening.'

As he went to leave Perón stopped him. 'I want this kept secret. No statement to the press or anything. Say that I came here to see a friend and that I have left,' he ordered.

Relieved, the director again bowed and left.

Perón sat at the desk and lit a cigarette. The sudden collapse of his wife had shaken him but now he began to look at the probable side effects. The unions were still his main worry. Despite the changes in leadership there were too many agitators.

Now that they had a decent wage, holidays, sick pay and medical care they wanted more. He wanted them to have more but if he gave them all an increase now there could be no sweeteners for the election. And that was the most pressing need. Perón hadn't rejigged the constitution, making it possible for an incumbent president to run for a second six-year term, only to see it fail because the unions couldn't hold their hand for a few months.

It had been arranged that Eva was going to speak to the unions, urge them to unite behind him to guarantee his re-election. Eva had wanted something out of it of course – the vice-presidency!

Vice-presidency – Perón had to smile with admiration. His little mate couldn't be accused of lacking ambition. He knew that the Army would never stand for it. Still, he couldn't think of any reason why Eva should be discouraged at this early date. Let her get the *descamisados* behind her and then, if she had to stand down, it could be laid at the door of the Army.

Meanwhile something had to be done to hold everything steady until Eva was back on her feet again. He picked up the telephone and told Lopez Rega to get to the hospital as soon as possible. He lit another cigarette and turned his thoughts to Juán Duarte. The boy was getting to be a pest. If he could have put him to graze somewhere out of reach he would. But Duarte knew about the Zurich accounts. In fact he was the only one who did know the full details. Perón had to take Eva's brother on trust because he dared not get himself in a position where the accounts could be connected to him. Perón just prayed that the money the playboy skimmed off from the people wanting favours was enough to keep him happy.

There was a knock on the door and Lopez Rega came in.

'Thanks for coming, *che*,' Perón said in a friendly voice. 'We have a problem.'

Lopez Rega raised an eyebrow. 'Problem, *Excelencia?*'

'Yes – a problem, *señor*! My wife has been taken ill. Appendicitis. Nothing to worry about but it does create a difficulty.'

'In what way, *Presidente*?'

Perón rose and went across to the window which overlooked a pleasant lawn bordered by the wings of the hospital.

'The unions. Eva was to meet a deputation this afternoon. As you know they are getting restless. Want more money. Trouble with this new pack of sheep in wolves' clothing that we have put into the unions is that they have no balls. They let the members lead them by the nose. Not like your old buddy, Reyes. Still, we can't have everything. For the moment it is essential that the unions are kept quiet. As soon as Eva is on her feet she can do a bit of rabble-rousing but for the moment I don't want to hear a murmur.'

He turned to look at Lopez Rega. 'Can't you manage that?' he asked.

Before the ex-sergeant could answer there was a knock on the door and the director of the hospital returned. He had another man, dressed in the smock of a doctor, whom he introduced as Patocki, the consultant in charge of Eva's case. From their faces Perón knew there was going to be bad news. His mouth went dry.

He looked at Finochietto. 'Well?' he asked sharply.

The doctor looked doubtfully at Lopez Rega.

'Go ahead,' Perón gave him permission to speak in front of the other man.

'Well, *Excelencia*. There is a complication. The appendectomy has been successfully carried out but we have reason to believe there is an abnormality in the uterus. With your permission we would like to do a biopsy,' the doctor explained hesitantly.

'Cancer!' The word flared in Perón's mind. He sat down shakily. 'What does that mean? Is it cancer?' he asked.

The doctor shrugged. 'It's too early to say, *Excelencia*. If you would give permission we will make the test and give you the results in a day or two.'

Perón thought quickly. He desperately needed Eva. If there were complications that put her in hospital for a long stretch he might not be able to contain the unions. 'What happens then?' he asked.

Again Finochietto shrugged. 'I can't say until I know more. It might be something we could put right in a few days or if it should be something serious, it might take considerably longer.'

Perón cursed under his breath. The two medical men waited for his decision. He looked at Lopez Rega and wished he had asked him to leave earlier. Carefully controlling his feelings he looked at the hospital director.

'*Bueno*, doctor. You must, of course, make your tests. However I would be obliged if you made your report to me personally and did not let my wife know there are any complications. Will you do that?'

The doctor nodded. 'Of course, *Excelencia*. I shall let you have the report as soon as possible. In the meanwhile try not to worry. It may be something else completely. We just have to be careful.' He smiled his best bedside manner.

Perón got up and shook hands with both men. '*Gracias, señores*, for your help. I leave my wife in your capable hands. Is it possible to see her for a few moments?'

The director looked at Patocki for confirmation. 'Yes. I expect that will be all right, *Excelencia*. She is of course still under the influence of the anaesthetic but you can see her,' he said.

Perón smiled gratefully. '*Bueno*. Now – if you could just give me a few minutes alone with Señor Lopez Rega I will be ready.'

The medical men bowed and left.

Perón smashed his fist into the palm of his hand. '*Mierda*! What do you think, José?' he asked.

'I'm sure she'll be all right,' Lopez Rega said diplomatically.

'What?' Perón looked at him frowning. 'Oh – not that! What do you think about the unions. Can we get them to hold fire if Eva's in hospital for longer than two weeks?' he demanded.

Lopez Rega looked non-committal. 'Possibly. We will have to I suppose.'

Perón stood in front of him. 'Not now, Lopez Rega. Not now. Forget the flannel. What do you think *hombre*!' He demanded forcefully.

'It is going to be difficult. They were expecting some sort of assurance today. If they don't get it the members are going to push for strike action. I can hold them up for a while, but if we leave it too long the men with the mouths are going to flap them and it will be very hard to stop them. Especially as we need their support to start the campaign for the *señora's* vice presidency.' Lopez Rega gave his considered opinion cautiously.

Perón snorted. 'That's what I think. What about if I approach them myself?' he asked.

Lopez Rega raised his eyebrows. 'Of course they would listen, Don Juán, but then there is no room for you to manoeuvre. If the *señora* speaks to them she can then say that she is going to bring it to your attention. Then she can say that you have been told all the facts and you are looking into it. If you speak to them yourself they will expect instant decisions.'

Perón nodded his agreement. '*Bueno* José. You are right. Let us hope that the *señora* is up and about in a couple of weeks,' he said as light-heartedly as he could.

Perón turned to the door. 'See the union delegation this afternoon. Lay on the anxiety over Eva's health and tell them I am anxiously kneeling by her bedside pleading for divine intervention. So far nothing has got out about her collapse so make it sound as if it's nothing. Just a matter of overwork. I'll talk to you later. *Ciao*.'

Lopez Rega looked at the closed door for a long time after the President had left. It was time he began to cover himself in case events started to move against the Peróns. Lopez Rega remembered that Juán Duarte was returning that afternoon. Perhaps that would be a good place to start.

TWENTY-NINE

Perón followed the doctor along the wide, pungent corridors to the private section of the hospital.

Eva looked terrible. Her make-up had been cleaned off and her hair controlled under a linen cap. Perón had to force himself not to turn away as he saw the transparent plastic pipe up her nostril and the other strapped to her forearm. He disciplined himself to bend and kiss her cheek and her eyelids fluttered. Her unfocused eyes slid around the room. She didn't appear to notice Perón standing beside her.

'Pappi?' she called in a low, cracked voice.

Perón took her hand. '*Si, mi vida.* I'm here,' he reassured her.

'Pappi?' she repeated, still unaware of his presence.

He looked at the doctor who just shrugged to indicate that he doubted if she knew he was there. He watched as a soft smile washed over her ashen features. It moved him that even in her unconscious state she could think of him with such affection. It made him feel guilty.

He was fond of her. Probably felt more for her than he had for anyone in his life but he was aware that it wasn't total commitment. He didn't want anything to happen to her but didn't fool himself that he would be finished without her. She was an essential part of the set-up as it ran now. If he was going to have to go on without her he would have to change the construction. He had managed before she came along and would manage again.

He gave her arm a parting squeeze and let the doctor follow him out of the room.

'*Gracias*, Doctor. I know you will do your best. Now to practicalities. I will have to put a guard on the place. You will issue no statements regarding the *señora*'s health. This will be done from the Casa Rosada. You will not let anybody – anybody at all – go in to see her unless they have been cleared by me. You understand, this is vitally important. Meanwhile if you want to get in touch with me urgently you will be able to do so no matter where I am. I must be kept informed of any change in my wife's condition. Thank you once again for all you have done, Doctor, we will not forget you.'

Juán Duarte sat in his favourite corner of El Gato Loco, only a shout's distance from where Perón was entertaining some girls from the Buenos Aires High School, and worried.

He worried about his health, his position, his safety, his love life, his relationship with Perón, his money piling up in banks all over the world, his ability to keep on top – everything. He even worried briefly about his sister and the fact that Perón wouldn't give him permission to go and see her. But not very much.

'Señor Duarte. How nice to see you.'

He peered up in the dim light at the club owner. 'About time!' he thought. 'About time he showed some bloody respect. If I don't get some bloody respect he might find it hard to carry on in business.'

His thoughts calmed him a little. He had the power – what did he care about all these little people? They knew nothing. They didn't know what he knew. They didn't know that only a couple of days ago he had been in Switzerland with more money than they would ever see in their whole life. And he, Juán Duarte, was in charge of it. Whatever he wanted – he got!

'Hello, Luis, *que tal*?' he asked.

Luis raised his shoulders non-committally. 'Not bad, Señor Duarte, not bad. Is there anything I can get you?'

Before Duarte could reply the club owner appeared to notice a girl sitting, alone and detached, to his left.

'Señorita von Quast. Nice to see you,' Luis said. He looked around. 'Are you alone?'

Therese nodded, 'It looks like it. I was supposed to meet

265

my brother here. Have you seen him?' she asked.

Luis shook his head in a well-rehearsed 'sorry'. Lopez Rega had called him earlier and given him the script. 'No, I'm sorry, señorita. I expect he will be here at any minute,' he suggested.

Therese shook her head. 'No. It's just like him. Always making dates and then forgetting them. I go now. If he arrives, tell him I couldn't wait.'

Luis turned to Duarte.

'I'm sorry, Señor Duarte. Do you know Señorita von Quast?'

Duarte tried to push himself erect but had to be content with a half surge upwards and flopped back. 'Pleased to meet you, Señorita von Quast,' he said politely. 'Perhaps you would like to have a drink with me until your brother arrives.'

Therese looked doubtful and Luis rushed in to help out.

'*Si, si, señorita*. Please have a drink with me. I insist you are both my guests for the evening,' he told them. It didn't make any difference to him. Duarte had a habit of not paying his bill anyway. And Luis was confident that doing a favour for Lopez Rega was going to be profitable in the long run. If for no other reason than he had the power to make the Vice-Squad have a touch of selective blindness where El Gato Loco was concerned.

Therese suddenly appeared to come to a decision. '*Gracias*, Luis. Now I'm here – I might as well enjoy myself.' She slid along the seat towards Juán.

He was flustered. As a soap salesman, five years ago, he had always been considered a bit of a ladies' man. With certain women he had maintained, and even broadened, his reputation since he had become a part of the nepotic Perón regime. But cool, cultured women threw him and they made him feel coarse and ungainly.

Therese seemed perfectly relaxed. She listened, apparently absorbed, while Duarte told her about his trip to Europe and let slip his relationship with the President and Evita. She feigned surprise at the knowledge and asked questions about Evita whom she claimed to admire. When she finally decided that it was time to go Juán insisted on seeing her home.

At the door of her apartment building, Therese gave him a smile and said she would be happy to have dinner with him. He walked back to his car feeling ten feet tall. Therese was a complete contrast from the usual line of actresses and shop-girls looking for an introduction or a hand-out.

He slumped down in the seat and dropped off in a drunken doze. The driver looked at him in the mirror and sighed. It looked as if he would have to carry him to bed. He just hoped that the amateur roué wasn't going to be sick all over the car again.

As Duarte was making his way home Therese slammed the door of her flat and went into the lounge. Lopez Rega was sitting with his feet up on the sofa. She dropped her handbag on the table and bent down and kissed him.

'What a bloody bore that man is,' she said.

Lopez Rega didn't look up. His attention was on an array of photographs he was laying out on the floor beside him.

'I don't want a character analysis. That bloody bore might be useful some day. Just do as you are told. You made a further meeting with him?'

Cowed, Therese whispered, 'Yes.'

'Good.' He held up some of the photographs for her to see. 'Take a look at your boyfriend. He seems pretty agile for his weight and drunkenness.'

The pictures were all of Duarte making violent and gymnastic love to a variety of women. Lopez Rega had commissioned them in case they should come in useful but he knew that there was really no way he could use them. Threatening to publicise them would be a joke. Those papers Eva didn't own she controlled and, although she wouldn't allow them to be published, she was not likely to be shocked at the sight of her brother's profligacy. He only showed them to Therese because it amused him. The girl returned the pictures to him without comment and went into the bedroom.

Lopez Rega scooped them up and pushed them into a large envelope before placing them carefully in his suitcase. He was about to open the front door when Therese came out of the bathroom and saw he was gone.

'DANIEL?' she called, a sob in her voice.

'I'm off,' he called from the doorway. 'See you after you have been out with Duarte,' he told her in a matter of fact voice.

She ran down the passage to him. 'Daniel. Don't go. Please, stay for a little while.'

He looked at her, her superb body outlined against the light through her lace negligée and almost let himself be drawn back. The moment passed and he looked coldly at her. 'Go to bed. You've done a good job so don't spoil it.'

Perón sat beside Eva's bed holding her hand and bringing her up-to-date with what was going on. She looked better now. Before he had arrived she had carefully made up her face and had Julio, her hairdresser, style her hair into braids. She looked small and vulnerable in the crisp white sheets surrounded by flowers and presents from well-wishers, like a little girl on Christmas morning.

Perón's mind was only half-occupied by what he was saying. The doctor had asked him into his office when he arrived and told him the result of the biopsy. It had been positive. Cancerous cells had been discovered and it was imperative that Eva had an operation without delay.

What had shaken Perón was the doctor's insistence that it would be at least three months before Eva would be fit to resume her work. And then only very carefully. The doctor had made no bones about the fact that failure to operate immediately would mean that the disease would run wild and could prove uncontrollable in a very short space of time.

Perón knew he had to tell Eva. Too many people in the hospital must be aware of her condition for him to ignore the doctor's advice and not tell her. On the understanding that Eva would be on her feet shortly, he had planned a rally with the union leaders to take place in ten days' time. If they now had to cancel, Perón shuddered to think what might be the consequences.

'What's the matter, Pappi?' he heard Eva ask and pulled himself together. It was obvious what he had to do. He had to convince Eva to ignore the doctor's advice. If she did it and he appeared to be trying to convince her that she should go ahead with the operation nobody could point a finger at him in the future. Anyway, doctors were always over-cautious, they had to be. Once Eva had shown herself to the unions she could have the operation and everything would be all right.

He gave her a diffident smile. 'It's nothing, baby. The doctors are worried that's all,' he said enigmatically.

Eva frowned. 'What about? The operation was successful wasn't it?'

Perón nodded. '*Si, mi vida,* but . . . they did a test while you were out. They say there is a problem.'

'A problem?' Eva sounded worried.

Perón gave her a weak smile and broke it to her carefully. 'Yes. Something to do with your uterus. They want to keep you in for observation and, maybe, well . . .'

'How long?' Eva demanded.

Perón splayed his hands doubtfully. '*Quien sabe!* It may be for months.'

'Impossible!' Eva snapped. 'What about the rally? What about the vice-presidential nomination?'

'I expect we will manage somehow,' Perón said uncertainly.

Eva looked at him without speaking for a while. She was scared. So scared she didn't want to pursue what her husband hinted at. Besides, there were more powerful considerations.

Eva spoke quickly to dispel her fears. 'What do you mean – you'll manage. You know very well without me the unions aren't going to listen. If you have to meet their demands now you are going to alienate the generals. Once we have the nomination we can rely on the *descamisados* to look after our interests. We go ahead with the rally. After that we will see.'

Perón covered his relief. '*Pero mi vida*. Your health comes first. What does it matter if we lose the election as long as you are all right?' he protested.

Eva impulsively caught his hand and pressed it to her lips. His concern made her weep. 'Nothing must stop us, *querido*. Only you can save our people. Only you care enough. Once we get back we can do all the things we planned. We can show the world what you can do if you are allowed. My life is nothing if your work goes on! It is a sacrifice I am willing to make a million times as long as I am sure of your love.' Sobbing, she pulled Perón to her.

Surprised, he found the tears rolling down his face and mingling with hers . . . He put his arms around her.

'*Mi vida*. Is it worth it? Perhaps the doctors are right. You should have the operation.' He spoke with sincerity suddenly ashamed of his manipulation of his wife.

She pushed him back and forced a smile through her tears. 'Pappi. Thank you. Thank you for loving me,' she fought the tears. 'I'll be all right. You'll see. Once I get the nomination nobody will be able to stop us.' She pulled him back to her again. 'Don't worry Pappi. It'll be all right. Now you had better go. I want to get some sleep so that I'll be strong enough to get out of this bloody place.'

She suddenly wanted to be alone. Alone to face the terrifying thought of her illness and the possible outcome of letting it grow. Perón gave her a long, lingering kiss and walked out with tears in his eyes.

THIRTY

On the order 'Eyes Right!' the young officer cadets in their
trim, buttoned to the neck tunics and their cut-down shako
caps, snapped their heads with military precision towards
the group of officers and the lone woman on the dais.

President Perón, in his general's uniform, stood, a tall,
powerful looking man, an inspiration to the troops, taking
the salute. Eva stood a pace behind his right shoulder but
slightly in front of the staff officers attending the passing-
out parade of the new generation of leaders.

As the troops marched from the parade ground Eva
slipped her arm through Perón's and climbed carefully
down from the platform. She had lost a lot of weight in
hospital and her nose appeared to thrust aggressively,
hawklike, from her gaunt face. Perón had tried to discourage her from coming with him but she had insisted that
she needed the exposure. She had been too long away. After
two weeks she needed to reassure her followers that they
still had a leader.

He knew that her presence was going to infuriate the
other officers who considered all parades in general and this
one in particular, sacrosanct. To violate the parade ground
with the presence of a woman was therefore sacrilege.

Lunch was served in the huge refectory used as the
officers' mess. When the meal was over Eva excused herself
and left the room. Instantly General Avalos sprang into
action. He stood before Perón.

'*Señor Presidente*. Could you do me the honour of
accompanying me to the trophy room. There are a number
of important issues I would like to discuss in private with
you,' he stated trenchantly.

Perón tapped the ash off his cigar and got langorously to

his feet. 'But of course, my dear Avalos. I am always happy to discuss any urgent business with you.'

'Look Perón . . .' he began but faltered to a halt as the President gave him an imperious state. '*Presidente*,' he began again more formally. 'I represent a group of officers who wish to complain about the presence of the *señora* on the dais for the passing parade this morning. As you know, this parade has special significance for all those present and we feel that the presence of an outsider cannot be tolerated.'

He paused to see how Perón was taking it.

Perón seemed unruffled. 'Really, General Avalos? If you had told me you had such strong objections before I would have considered what you said. As it is I fear it is too late to make any difference.'

'*Presidente*. There is something else we must talk about. This rally tomorrow. My informants tell me that the unions intend to ask your wife to run as vice president in the election. Is this true?' Avalos asked.

Perón looked at him and feigned surprise. 'True? How do I know! If the unions wish to nominate my wife that is their business surely.'

Avalos shook his head vigorously. 'No, *mi Presidente*. It is our business. The trade unions do not run this country. They are very strong and can prove an obstacle not easily overcome. For this reason I hesitate lining the Army up against them.' Avalos drew himself up and raised his voice. 'Therefore I have been asked by my fellow officers to get your assurance that you will discourage your wife from seeking election. If she does, ill-advisedly, continue on her course for power, the Army will be forced to intercede.'

'Forced to mutiny,' Perón corrected. 'Your threat is one of mutiny – nothing else. However as you have raised the subject perhaps you could tell me what your "fellow officers'" position is on my nomination for *Presidente*? There is no constitutional reason why I should not run for a second term. It was not my intention to do so but the unions have threatened to strike if I retire so I am forced, for the sake of the country, to continue. Do I have your

272

support or must I rely only on the loyalty of the workers?' Perón demanded.

Avalos glanced nervously at the door. Obviously he had not expected to be cornered on the subject of his support for Perón. Not that the Army were intending to drop Perón. They would if they could. They had little affection for the populist Perónista Party. But they had no strong candidate that could unite them.

'Of course, *Presidente*, if our present problem can be resolved, if you can promise us that your wife does not intend to run for official office, then you can count on the support of the Army,' Avalos affirmed.

'Very well, General Avalos. You force me to accede to your request. I will guarantee that my wife does not run for office. There, does that satisfy you?'

Avalos looked uncomfortable. '*Si, mi General*. And the rally tomorrow? That will be cancelled?' he asked.

Slowly Perón shook his head. 'No. That must go ahead. If that is cancelled the unions will get out of hand.' Perón bit his lip and looked concerned. 'As you know the *señora* isn't well. I don't want her to be upset unnecessarily. She will be at the rally but I will see that she does not accept the nomination.'

Perón saw the look of doubt cross Avalos' face and laughed. 'Don't worry, General, you have my word. Now, shall we finish the whisky or is there anything else you wish to demand?' he asked sarcastically. Without waiting for a reply he strolled back into the dining room.

The tall windows looking out on the Avenida Nueve de Julio were open. Around the room, conservatively dressed in double-breasted suits and slicked-back hair, favoured politicians joked and gossiped with smartly uniformed, moustachioed officers.

It was a well rehearsed routine. Those at the moment in favour were asked along to a cocktail party and then, when the clamour from the crowd outside reached the right decibel level, they would follow Perón and Evita onto the platform and applaud the long rhetorical speeches their leaders gave.

Tonight there was a slight variation. Usually Perón and his wife spent the hour or so before the balcony scene chatting to their guests. Tonight only the President made the rounds. Eva was resting in one of the small siderooms with Isabel in attendance.

Through the heavily curtained windows she could hear the crowd in the wide avenue. The eager, friendly crowd that wanted to lift her up to the pinnacle of her ambition.

Eva was happy that Perón had gone along with her plans. With two million voices rooting for Evita to take on the mantle of vice president it was going to be difficult for the 'Moustachioed Pedros' of the Army to deny her the honour.

As the giant, floodlit pictures of Eva had gone up around the City her confidence flooded back.

Eva smiled at Isabel. '*Bueno, querida,* time to put the show on the road.'

She stood by the door and delved down into the reserves of dynamic energy that had sustained her for so long. She forced vitality into her eyes and mentally rehearsed the firmness of her tread as she crossed the room beyond the door. Satisfied, she nodded to Isabel and bustled into the party, joking and scolding as she made her way towards Perón. He broke off his conversation and welcomed her with a smile.

'Ah, *bueno, mi vida.* You are ready? I think it is time to go out and speak to the people,' he suggested.

Eva agreed eagerly, her whole body craving for the applause she needed, but she wanted to make sure her appearance had the right impact.

'Yes – I'm ready. Now, you have got it arranged? We must not make it look as if I am too eager.' Eva whispered instructions to Perón who smiled broadly and agreed.

He put his glass down and turned to his guests. 'Gentlemen, shall we show ourselves?' he asked.

Joking and laughing they followed Perón out of the room. They walked along the covered walkway, leading to

274

the platform, and looked down onto the sea of faces in the street below. Instantly the crowd exploded into rapturous applause. Paper confetti sprayed into the air from thousands of waving hands and drifted, a delicate, swirling snow, over the upturned faces.

Perón gave a quick look towards the corner of the podium where a technician crouched beside the distribution board that fed the loudspeakers which hung in profusion along the wide street. The man saw the President look his way and nodded. When the applause began to die away Perón stepped forward and raised his arms in his familiar gesture of greeting. A chant started in the crowd and was soon picked up in all corners of the square.

'*La chaqueta! Quite la chaqueta!* – Take your jacket off!' the *descamisados* roared.

He pretended not to understand in a well-rehearsed routine. Louder the demand thundered up from the Plaza like a savage litany. Perón pretended to understand for the first time. Slowly he took off his jacket and held it above his head before tossing it disdainfully over his shoulder. It hit one of the naval officers in the face but nobody noticed. All eyes were on Perón as he unbuttoned his sleeves and rolled them up above the elbow. Again he held his arms above his head. Roars of delight rolled up to the platform, engulfing him.

Inside the building Eva smiled to herself. The sound swelling in the throats in the crowd had a galvanising effect on her depleted nerves. Again she felt her power return as the chorus continued. 'EVI-TA! EVI-TA! EVI-TA!'

Perón turned to one of the generals behind him. 'Get the *señora*,' he ordered.

The soldier hesitated.

'Get the *señora*!' Perón commanded imperiously. The general saluted and left.

Eva was waiting for him just inside the door and allowed him to lead her out to the platform. Even louder than before the welcome crashed out and continued unabated for three minutes. Finally Espejo, now head of the powerful CGT, a long way from his humble origins as a janitor, and master of ceremonies for the occasion, managed to make himself heard.

'Señora – EVITA – I have been asked – NO – ordered, by your loyal *descamisados* to plead with you to accept the heavy burden of running, with our gracious leader, for the presidency. With you and your husband at the helm we are confident of success in our fight to make our *patria* the envy of the world.'

While the applause confirmed his invitation Espejo took Eva's hand and led her to the microphone. Everything was going to plan. Now all she had to do was display a becoming hesitation and then let her objections be swept aside by the mob. She spoke. '*Descamisados mios*! I thank you from a full heart for the honour you do me. But I am but a humble woman. It is Perón who is the light. I am but a frail sparrow and he a condor. He is the light and I but a follower. I, like every true Perónista, would lay down my life for Perón because without him I am nothing. You ask me to join him in his glorious crusade. I say that his crusade is my life, that his ultimate victory is my salvation. Nothing must come between my *descamisados* and my beloved husband, Juán Domingo Perón!

'It is for this reason I hesitate to accede to your wonderful vote of confidence. Perón has many enemies who plot his downfall constantly. Certain elements in the Army, jealous of his success, the rich oligarchs who hate him for becoming the defender of the poor and the weak. Foreign powers ceaselessly try to infiltrate our institutes through the press and commercial interests. They think that money can dim the eyes of the people to Perón's light. These enemies are constantly trying to harm our President. For this reason I hesitate.

'I would rather cast off these baubles with which Perón has seen fit to adorn my worthless body, and live in the meanest pigsty in the most inhospitable corner of the land, than give Perón's enemies the chance of attacking him through me.'

Perón, standing slightly behind her caught the eye of the

technician in the corner and nodded imperceptibly. As Eva continued a banshee howl assaulted the ears of the crowd below. The electronic shriek faded and was replaced by a deep, vibrant hum. Disconcerted Eva looked towards the technician. He appeared to be desperately trying to correct the fault. Like patrons in the cinema when the film breaks the men in the crowd below began to shout and whistle.

Eva tried to continue but it was useless. By the time her voice could be heard again she had lost her impetus. Savagely she whispered to Perón: 'What the hell is happening?'

'*Nada, mi vida*. A technical problem. It's okay now. Go ahead,' he told her.

Eva shook her head, close to tears. 'Not now! I've lost them. Tell them I will give my decision in four hours. Say anything you like.'

With the last murderous look at the technician in the corner she stormed back into the building. But she wasn't looking for sympathy. As they tried to follow her she slammed the door viciously in their faces. Isabel's gentle approach was countered with a tirade of gutter Spanish.

In her frustration she wrecked the little room before falling exhausted onto the chaise-longue and bursting into bitter tears. When Perón finally came to her she was quieter. He sat on the chaise-longue and took her tenderly in his arms.

'They don't want me, Pappi,' she sobbed into his neck.

'Who?' he jerked out in surprise. Perón assumed that his wife thought that she had been the victim of a chance electrical fault. 'Who don't want you, *mi vida*?'

'The Army!' Eva said, her voice now under control.

Perón looked at her strangely. Her eyes were bright and her white face glistened with sweat. It frightened him. Half an hour earlier she had almost been her old cocksure self. Now she was revealing an almost divine insight into what was going on and had accepted defeat. He hugged her closer to him but she pushed him aside and got slowly and painfully to her feet.

'I know there has been a lot of opposition to my vice-presidency.' She looked at him and gave a strained smile. 'You wouldn't know. They hide it from you. But it exists. I know that in the last few days the Army have been trying to cancel the rally. They couldn't do it and I thought I could fight them. But I can't. I'm too weak.'

Perón tried to protest but she silenced him.

'It's the tiredness I can't fight. If you are to win the election you need all your energy. You won't be able to carry a passenger. I'll help where I can.' She paused and her voice broke as she continued.

'Forget the vice-presidency, give Mercante or someone the honour. We have to concentrate on securing the presidency. My informants tell me that some of the officers are trying to force a revolution. We must be ready.'

Perón stood up and lit a cigarette. He didn't know what to say. His wife's blind faith and loyalty touched him. He should have known that Eva was aware of the feelings running against her. It was her stock-in-trade – her ability to gather information. Perón dismissed her fear of revolution. She didn't know about the deal he had done with Avalos and he hoped she never would. He went back to her.

'You're tired now, *querida*. Why don't you have a sleep? Later you will see everything in a more optimistic light.'

Eva looked him in the eyes and shook her head. 'No. I can feel it. I'm finished. The doctors told me about the cancer. They didn't tell you because they probably thought you would worry too much. They said I must have an operation. Every day I don't makes it worse. We have to move quickly before it gets too bad. Buy off the generals. Tell them I will not stand for office. That will give us time.'

Perón looked at her puzzled. 'But . . . aren't you going to have the operation?'

Eva smiled. 'Of course, *mi vida*. But not yet. It will wait. That's one of the advantages of cancer, it won't go away by itself.' Eva's joke sounded flat even in her own ears.

Perón tried to protest but she cut him short.

'Enough, *mi vida*. Take me home. I'll feel better tomorrow.'

278

THIRTY-ONE

It was 28 September 1951. Things had gone well for Perón that day. An Army *coup* against him had failed. There had been fighting, but the *descamisados* had rallied to his support. His success was hardly surprising, since the attempted coup had, in fact, been engineered by Perón himself in conjunction with his co-conspirator Avalos. It would enable them to destroy certain factions in the armed forces hostile to them both.

As he hurried to his ailing wife, he hoped the news of the day's events wouldn't have drained away too much of her dwindling strength. With the rapid deterioration in Eva's health Perón had arranged for the election to be brought forward four months. But he was still worried that she might not last so long. Eva could hardly get from her bed and for much of the time she had to be kept sedated. Isabel Ernest rushed to meet him. He grabbed her by the shoulders and looked at her tear-wet face. For a moment he feared the worst.

'What is it Isabel?'

Isabel pulled herself together. 'It's Señora Evita, Don Juán. She insists on making a broadcast to the country. I'm afraid it will be too much for her. You should see her, Don Juán. She's so weak and every movement is agony but she insists on making the speech. The technicians are setting up the equipment in her room now. Please, stop her, Don Juán. Please!'

Perón helped the sobbing woman to a chair and then ran up the stairs two at a time. Eva was sitting up in her bed, a frail, skeletal memory of her former self. Determination had brightened her eyes and strengthened her hand and Perón could hear the tones of her faded power as she gave instructions to the radio crew fixing up the microphone and wiring the amplifier.

Perón went across and kissed his wife gently on the mouth. He hid the distaste the smell of her drug-laden breath caused.

'*Bueno, mi vida*. What do you think you are up to? I thought you were supposed to be resting,' he demanded with mock seriousness. 'Instead I come home to find your bedroom full of men.'

Eva smiled at him. 'I have to broadcast to my people. To tell them not to follow anyone but you, Pappi. Without me they feel lost. They lose their bridge to you.'

Perón patted her hand and addressed himself to the radio technicians. '*Bueno, amigos*. Would you leave us for a moment. I want to talk to my wife alone.'

He waited until the door shut and then sat on the bed beside Eva. 'Forget the Army and their little pranks. It's all been sorted out now. What we have to sort out now is you.'

Eva looked surprised. 'Me?'

'Yes.' Perón asserted forcefully. 'You! You've been putting off the issue for too long. Dr Zawarski refuses to go on treating you unless you co-operate.' He put his arm around her thin shoulders and drew her to him. 'For me, baby. You must get well for me.' Perón spoke softly and sincerely.

Eva reached up and stroked his face. '*Mi pappi*. If that's what you want I'll do it – only . . .' her voice trailed away.

Perón looked at her sharply. 'Only what?'

Eva gave him the shadow of her old confident smile. 'Only – not until after the 17th of October. I must be there on the great anniversary of the people calling you to lead them. You know I must.'

There were still two weeks to go before the Loyalty Day rally. Two weeks was a long time in Eva's condition. But Perón had to admit to himself that her presence, obviously desperately sick, would have an electrifying effect on his supporters.

'We'll see what Dr Zawarski has to say about that,' he told her.

Eva nodded agreement. She could handle the doctor. 'And . . .' she said provocatively.

'And . . .?' Perón repeated suspiciously.

'I want to make a broadcast now,' Eva rushed the words out as one.

Perón grinned and stood up in mock anger. 'Very well. I know when I can't win. I'll be back with Dr Zawarski at eight o'clock. Don't forget what you promised me.' He bent and kissed her once more on the cheek. 'And don't go causing any more revolutions on the radio. One's enough for today.'

He opened the door and called the technicians back in and then went to the bedroom he had been using for himself during Eva's illness. He undressed and stood under the shower and let the soothing water cascade over his body.

He felt good. For some indefinable reason he felt as if all his problems had vanished. Even his ulcers and his acne agreed and had temporarily withdrawn. He peered at his face in the steamed-up mirror. The scars were still there but there was no evidence of fresh activity. Refreshed he lit a cigarette and stretched out on the bed. Expansively he blew smoke at the ceiling. A bonus of having separate bedrooms was that he didn't get nagged about smoking.

He picked up the telephone and told Isabel to get Dr Zawarski for him and to let him know when Eva's broadcast was on the air. Zawarski wanted to bring in a consultant immediately but Perón forbade it. He told her that until she was sure of her facts she must keep her mouth firmly buttoned.

She promised to be there at eight o'clock to make the examination and take whatever samples were necessary and then to report back to Perón for further instructions when she had the facts.

Perón put the receiver down and drifted into a doze. The telephone woke him with a start. Isabel told him that Eva's broadcast was about to start. Perón switched on and lit another cigarette.

Down the corridor Eva sat, propped up with pillows, in

front of a suspended microphone. Only her producer was in the room and he had agreed to leave as soon as she started to speak. He listened intently on the earphones while the announcer at Radio El Mundo made the introductory remarks and then pointed his finger at Eva to give her the go-ahead and tiptoed from the room.

Eva concentrated her last energy into keeping her voice low and vibrant. Tears formed in her eyes and ran steadily down her cheeks as she spoke. She had not fooled herself. Her insistence on not being examined by the doctors was because she was aware of the inevitability of the outcome.

'Comrades, my beloved Shirtless Ones, I have insisted that I was given the chance to thank you for the way you have supported the *Presidente* today in his hour of need. The infamies of his enemies will not escape their just rewards. But it is to you, to my people, to the true *compadres*, that I speak in love and the knowledge that you will continue to support Perón, until your death, because he deserves it. To all of you I give you a great embrace from my heart. For me there is nothing in the world but the love of Perón and the love of my *descamisados*.'

Her voice sank away in exhaustion and as the producer cut away to the studio she collapsed back into the pillows on the borders of consciousness. Perón heard the weakness in her voice and hurried to her room but Isabel was there before him. He didn't wait to be told. He raced back to his room and again telephoned Dr Zawarski.

Within twenty minutes she arrived and anxiously Perón accompanied her to the sick room. Isabel was there, sitting on a chair next to the bed of her sick friend. Eva looked unconscious and Perón moved to the other side of the bed and took her limp hand.

Eva's eyes opened, she tried to smile as she looked at her husband and then her attention was attracted by a movement of the doctor at the end of the bed. Her grip on Perón's hand tightened and she pulled him near.

'Remember – not until after the 17th of October?' she whispered.

282

He nodded understanding but she gripped even tighter. 'Promise me, Pappi. Promise me!' she begged.

He looked into her poor, tortured eyes and had to struggle to keep his voice steady. 'I promise, *mi vida*,' he pledged.

With Eva in hospital seriously ill, Loyalty Day preparations went ahead. Eva's sickness became a point of honour, with her supporters trying to outdo each other in their exhibitions of loyalty.

Rumours ran rife in the cafés and streets. Perón's cancellation of his country-wide, whistle-stop tour provoked the story that Eva hovered at death's door and he had to be constantly on hand. Less kind gossips said that it was all a publicity stunt to get public sympathy.

The truth of the matter was that Dr Zawarski's examination had revealed what she had expected. Eva's uterus was badly infected with cancer. The nine months delay since the Policlinica had reported their suspicions had allowed the growth to spread to an alarming extent. It was imperative that she had an operation immediately. Even then the prognosis was not good.

Eva was adamant. She had waited that long, she could wait another couple of weeks. Zawarski appealed to Perón to convince his wife of the urgency of her case. He was already feeling guilty that he had encouraged her to delay the operation in the first place. In desperation he pleaded hard and long to convince his wife that he needed her and that she would die without immediate medical care. It was useless. Eva had already faced the fact of her death.

Fatalistically she realised that she had to pay for her success. Although she had never been particularly religious she believed that her fate had already been sealed. God had heard her often demanded plea to be allowed success. She had even offered the bargain herself. In return for success she didn't mind how short her life was. In fact to die while she was still young and pretty appealed to her. To be old, raddled and lonely wasn't her style. The thoughts of her

283

achievements supported her.

Even the pain she could take philosophically. It was the punishment for the evil acts she had performed. Pain and her approaching death drove her to find a spiritual reason and that reason was Perón. Since they met Eva had lived in awe of the charming, intelligent leader. In spite of the fact that she often bullied and argued against him she sincerely believed that he had a divine mission.

The identification, never far from her lips, solidified. Perón was a latter-day Christ come back to earth to lead the chosen people to the promised land. Having accepted her death, she bore the pain of martyrdom with determination. Only one goal filled her fevered mind. She must survive until Perón took up the presidency for the second term. Then she could rest in the knowledge that her divine role had been fulfilled.

Eva had one more positive contribution to make. She had to be at the Loyalty Day rally to tell the *descamisados* once again what they must do. They were like children and like children they were easily led astray and forgot. Each day was a test.

She couldn't eat or sleep. Daily blood transfusions had no effect. Only Eva's intensely alive eyes flaring up from the white skin stretched drily over her jutting cheekbones spoke of the Herculean struggle she was putting up.

At last the day came. Perón tried to get her to stay in bed and listen to the celebrations on the radio. She wouldn't hear him out. Like an electrical condenser she had lain quietly building up the energy for the last surge of power that she would need. It was too precious to waste on abortive arguments with those around her.

Isabel carefully dressed her in a warm, red costume and wrapped her furs around her in the wheelchair she grudgingly used when she found she was too weak to stand. Her concentration was such that she didn't notice her journey to the Casa Rosada or the people who came forward to greet her. Eva's whole being concentrated on those few square metres of tiled balustrading where so many times she had

284

stood and spoken to the people and rallied them to the 'Cause'!

Already lined up on the balcony were the faithful who had come along on her wild ride to success, Espejo, Freire, Campora, Apold, Aloe, Father Benitez, even Colonel Mercante was there. Recently they hadn't been seeing eye to eye but now she looked at her old friend affectionately and remembered the afternoon in the Posadas flat when he had jogged Perón's elbow and suggested that he married Eva.

She pulled her mind back to the job in hand. She was terrified that if she let extraneous thoughts enter she might not have the strength to regain control. José Espejo was talking. Eva couldn't see the massed *descamisados* below but she didn't have to. She could feel their presence like a clean, untainted part of herself.

The little ex-janitor carefully placed the Laurels of Grateful Distinction, First Class, an award from the CGT around her neck. Then Perón got up and made a long speech.

Eva looked at him and urged him under her breath to get it over with so that she could tell her people what they must know. There was a roar of applause and she could hear the chanting start up in the crowd below.

'EVI-TA! EVI-TA! EVI-TA!'

Perón came towards the seated figure, in his hands was a gem-studded award made specially for the occasion.

'Come on! Come on!' Eva begged silently.

The President fixed the glittering decoration on her breast. The Grand Perónista Medal, Extraordinary Class, in recognition of her selflessness in renouncing her candidacy for vice president. For a moment she clung to him, weeping softly. Gently he disentangled himself and turned back to address the people waiting below.

Eva checked the tears. The drain of energy was a price she couldn't afford to pay. Again she silently begged Perón to save the eulogy for the funeral and let her have her moment with her people.

She heard him say her name and then call for complete

285

silence so that Eva wouldn't have to overtax herself to make her voice heard.

Her powerful husband bent down and practically lifted her to her feet and then stood behind her grasping her around the waist to give her support. As she came to the front of the balcony, she heard a gasp from those nearest as they saw her emaciated face and body enveloped in the voluminous furs. She dismissed her personal worries and addressed the hordes of supporters silently waiting for her to speak.

'My beloved shirtless ones, this is a day of great emotion for me. With all my soul I have desired to be with you and with Perón on this glorious day of the Shirtless Ones. I could never miss this appointment that I have with the people on each October 17th. I assure you that nothing and no one could have prevented me from coming, because I have a sacred debt to Perón and to you, to the workers and the boys of the CGT, and it does not matter to me if in paying it I must forfeit my life.

'I had to come and I came to thank Perón and the CGT and the Shirtless Ones and my people. To Perón, who has just honoured me with the highest distinction that can be given a *Perónista*, I shall never finish paying my debt, not until I give my life in gratitude for the kindness he has always shown me. Nothing that I have, nothing that I am, nothing that I think, is mine; it is Perón's. I will not tell the usual lie and say that I have not deserved this; yes, I deserve it, my General. I deserve it for one thing only that is worth all the gold in the world.

'I deserve it because all I have done is for love of this country. What I have done is of no value; my renunciation of the vice presidency is of no value; what I am and what I have is of no value. I have only one thing of value and that is my heart. It burns in my soul, aches in my flesh, stings in my veins; it is love for the people and Perón. And I give thanks to you, my General, who have taught me to know you and love you. If the people asked for my life I would give it singing, because the happiness of one *descamisado* is worth more than my life.

286

'I had to come to give thanks to the CGT for the Laurels with which they have decorated me. For me they are the dearest momento of the Argentine workers. I had to come to thank the workers and the CGT who dedicated this glorious day to a humble woman. I had to come to tell you, as I told the President, that it is necessary to keep an alert watch on all sides in our struggle. The danger is not past. The enemies of the people, of Perón and of the *patria*, do not sleep. It is necessary that each Argentine worker keeps on the look-out and that he should not sleep, for the enemies work in the shadow of treason and sometimes they hide behind a smile or an outstretched hand.

'I had to come to thank all my beloved *descamisados* from every corner of the *patria* because on September 28th you knew how to risk your lives for Perón. I was sure that you would know, as you have known before, how to act as a trench for Perón. The enemies of Perón and of the *patria* have known for a long time that Perón and Eva Perón are ready to die for the people. Now they know that the people are ready to die for Perón.

'I just ask one thing of you today, *compañeros*, that we all swear publicly to defend Perón and to fight for him and we will shout our oath aloud for the space of a minute so that the sound of it may reach the furthest corners of the world.

'I thank you, *compañeros* for your prayers for my health. I thank you from my heart. I hope that God hears the humble people of my *patria* so that I may soon return to the battle and continue fighting with Perón for you and with you for Perón until death.

'I have wanted and I want nothing for myself. My glory is and always will be the shield of Perón and the banner of my people, and even if I leave shreds of my life on the wayside I know that you will gather them up in my name and carry them like a flag to victory.

'I know that God is with us because he is with the humble and despises the pride of the oligarchs, and so the victory will be ours. Sooner or later we will reach it, cost what it may and fall who must.

My Shirtless Ones, I would like to say many things to you but the doctors have told me I must not talk. I leave you my heart and I tell you I am sure, as it is my wish, that I shall soon be in the fight again, with more strength and more love, to fight for this country that I love so much, as I love Perón. I am sure that I will soon be with you, but if because of my health I cannot, help Perón, be loyal to Perón as you have been until now, because this is to be loyal to the *patria* and to yourselves. And all those Shirtless Ones of the interior, I embrace them very close to my heart and I hope that they realise how much I love them.'

As her voice faded away to a whisper a clamorous ovation swelled out from the crowd. As it died away the voices took up the more formal beat of a chanted slogan that Eva had just given them.

'*Mi vida por Perón! Mi vida por Perón!* My life for Perón!'

But Eva could not hear them. Her carefully stored dynamism exhausted, she collapsed and had to be put to bed in one of the rooms of the living quarters in the Casa Rosada – too weak even to be taken back to Olivos.

THIRTY-TWO

Dr Pack, an American expert on cancer and the man that Dr Zawarski had gone to for confirmation of her fears of Señora Perón's condition, flew into Buenos Aires in secret.

Eva's fear of doctors was even more intense when the doctor was a foreigner so his presence was kept from her. In one of the specially fitted-out vans that Perón sometimes used to go about the city unseen he was whisked away to the Policlinica and hidden away until the time came for the operation.

Ostensibly Dr Finochietto was to do the operation with Dr Jorge Albertelli, a top gynaecologist and Dr Roque Izzo, director of the medical school of Buenos Aires in attendance.

In reality it was Dr Pack who did the actual surgery. As soon as Eva was under the anaesthetic Pack was brought in. The operation took five hours.

Outside the operating theatre Perón paced nervously up and down smoking endless cigarettes. The acne on his face erupted so violently that a dermatologist was called in from one of the other wards to try and bring him some relief.

Dr Pack carefully cut away all the affected tissue he could see. He was worried about his patient's ability to withstand the shock. He looked at her wasted body and shook his head. Why had they not called him in before while she still had the strength to fight for her life?

The clock of destiny ticked away in Eva's brain.

On the morning of the election she once more dug into her limited reserves. A special ballot box was brought to her bedside so that she could cast her vote. Isabel had to help her but she insisted on sitting up and briefly talking to journalists and photographers. Eva had hoped to broadcast to the nation but this time the doctors prevailed and instead a prerecorded message made before the operation was put out. While others around her assured her that she was recovering and would soon take her place with Perón she was not fooled.

When the result of the ballot was announced she again forced herself out onto the balcony to greet their supporters. She was so weak that Perón had literally to hold her up. Now that victory was his the feeling of guilt returned. He blamed himself for not insisting that she should be operated on a year earlier when something could have been done to save her.

When they were together they spoke of the things they were going to do but Perón realised that it was more of a reminder of tasks still to do than a discussion of their mutual future. In spite of the intensive care lavished on her and the steady procession of specialists trekking past her bed Eva's decline continued. Only one objective remained.

Somehow she must keep her failing body functioning for eight months until Perón's official inauguration for his second term of office.

In a drugged haze she whiled away the days in her frilly boudoir among the dolls and fripperies she had never had as a child. As she gazed out of the open window and watched the trees stirring restlessly in the wind from the *pampa* she liked to relive again the precious moments of her short life. But it was only her life since she met Perón that she lingered on. Eva's mother and sisters were frequent visitors at her bedside but she hardly acknowledged them. Juán Duarte, when he came, she ignored. Only Perón brought any real response. When he returned in the evening he could come and sit by her bed and tell her what had happened during the day.

Sometimes, if she were feeling stronger, it would ignite a spark of her old spirit and she would give Perón instructions. But mostly she just lay, holding the big hand enclosing hers and, gazing into Perón's long friendly face, remembering the time they had met at the tennis match or recalling their conversation in the secluded corner of Luna Park. As if in respect to the dying woman the tumultuous political scene marked time.

The *estancieros* still fretted that they were being bankrupted, the *porteño* dowagers still spoke scurrilously of the little *resentida* – the resentful one; and in the Senate the shackled politicians of the opposition parties still riled petulantly at the shameless excesses of the *Perónista* Party. But they were kept muted by the obvious agony of Eva's *descamisados*. Although the newspapers carried very little information on her state of health her followers knew that they were losing her. In their grief they would have torn anyone apart who dared to intrude on their leader's last days. Even the Army kept silent.

A few days before the inauguration ceremony Perón awarded Eva the highest decoration that Argentina can bestow: the Grand Collar of the Order of San Martin, made from 785 diamonds, emeralds and rubies, bridged by 3,800 gold and platinum elements. The main pendant consisted of a diamond and emerald rosette, containing an image of Argentina's liberator against a background of sixteen rays of gold and platinum.

It insured that no last-minute interference by Army or Senate could deny the people the final tribute of a state funeral.

The award seemed temporarily to revitalise Eva. All those months of agony were swept aside. She made Isabel, who never left her side, tell her about the arrangements. Her hairdresser Julio was called in to do her a special style. Irma the maid paraded the contents of her numerous wardrobes for her to select from. She watched, bright-eyed while Isabel placed the contents of her jewellery boxes on the counterpane in front of her. Occasionally Eva would finger a particular piece and think of some happy event in her past that was connected with it.

On the morning of the Inauguration Isabel, Irma and her nurse helped her to dress in the outfit she had selected. Helen

291

Zawarski called and gave her an injection of narcotics that would help to get Eva through the ordeal ahead and deaden the pain.

Eva hated having to go in a wheelchair but even her Olympian self-discipline couldn't put the wasted muscle back on her legs and back.

As she sat beside Perón on the balcony and watched him acknowledge the crowd, heard their voices lift up in the anthem she had taught them, 'My life for Perón!' she felt the fear and pain washed away. In a drug-induced dream she saw her husband formally accept the sash of State for the second time. She seemed to float as he bent down to embrace her in his strong arms.

Somehow she found the strength to force life into her wasted muscles. The acclaim of the crowd washed over her.

'EVI-TA! EVI-TA! EVI-TA!'

Again and again the mighty sound reverberated around the confining walls of the Plaza. The sound never left her.

Five days later, her work completed, she died peacefully in her favourite room at the Olivos residency.

THIRTY-THREE

Juán Duarte was flying home, sick with fear. He called the stewardess and ordered another whisky. He tried not to think about Eva's funeral, of a whole nation in mourning, of the shock he had when he saw the results of the work Dr Ara, the embalmer, had done on his sister's body.

He tried to think about Therese von Quast, how after an uncertain start their affair had blossomed. Well, maybe not blossomed but at least she had become more sociable. But the dark thoughts kept crowding in. Above all, that of the insane thing he had just done. Of course it wasn't his fault. Without the protection of his sister he was totally at Perón's mercy. And Perón despised him.

When the president had called him to his office a few days after Eva's death and told him that he wanted details of all the accounts held by Eva outside the country, Duarte had felt the cold current of defeat lap his heart. In spite of being so close to the source of power he had not been able to tap any of the energy at the root. He was a moth fluttering on the rim of an active volcano.

Perón had believed Duarte when his weak-willed brother-in-law had told him that he would have to go to Europe to get all the information the President needed. Duarte secretly scuttled off to Zurich and Berne, with Perón's approval, to gather together the fortune amassed there and put it into one account that would be easily accessible to Perón. Instead Duarte had cached them in another depository of which only he had knowledge.

Instinctively he knew that this was his only protection. Perón would have to think twice if Duarte held the keys to his clandestine fortune. Knowing Perón's power didn't help. Duarte also knew the power of Perón's secret police and didn't kid himself that he would be able to withstand the sort of torture he had witnessed in the special rooms under police headquarters. When he thought about it he wanted to be sick.

By the time the DC3 touched down on the tarmac at Ezeiza Airport Duarte had drunk himself into semi-consciousness. He walked unsteadily through the airport concourse to his waiting car. The chauffeur drove rapidly along the narrow, arrow-straight highway back to the city.

It wasn't until the more erratic speed imposed by the capital's suicidal traffic called his attentions to his surroundings that he realised that they were not heading for his apartment.

'*Donde vas?*' he asked.

'Casa Rosada, *señor,*' the chauffeur answered matter-of-factly.

Juán slumped back in the seat and took another swig at the remains of a bottle of whisky.

Perón kept him kicking his heels outside his office for a couple of hours before buzzing and telling him to come in. His head throbbing and his stomach cold and shifting, he tried to put on a front as he walked across the wide expanse of carpet to the President's desk at the far end of the room. Perón looked him over shrewdly. He saw the sheen of sweat on his brother-in-law's unnaturally pallid face and the scarlet, crazed veins in his eyes.

'*Bueno, che,*' Perón said softly. 'How did it go?'

Dumbly Duarte nodded. He still hadn't made up his mind what he was going to say.

'You have transferred the funds?' Perón inquired.

Again Duarte nodded.

Perón held out his hand, '*Bueno.* Give me the key.'

Duarte hesitated. It was essential that Perón was aware of what he had done. It was the only way he could be sure that he wouldn't get rid of him out of hand. But his nerve failed. Quickly he fumbled open his briefcase and took out a leather key pouch. In it were two safe keys. Duarte had taken the precaution of opening a second deposit box with a few bits and pieces of inexpensive jewellery in it as a blind that would give him a little time to consider the best way to handle the situation.

Perón took the keys. He slipped them into his pocket without a second glance.

'*Gracias* Juán,' he said, dismissing him. 'Go home and get some sleep. You look awful.'

Amazed that he had got off so easily Duarte hastily backed from the room and went to his apartment where he spent the rest of the evening drinking and trying to telephone the elusive Therese von Quast.

Perón sat on the wide, cushioned windowsill in the room that had been his wife's during the last days of her illness and watched the scene at the pool below. He was unshaven and his usually immaculately combed hair hung in untidy strings across his ears and forehead. Even the white terry-towelling robe he wore looked dishevelled and grubby.

By his side was a large cut-glass ashtray filled to over-flowing with twisted butts. Perón took the cigarette out of his mouth to take a long draught from the half-filled tumbler of whisky and made a silent toast to the unsuspecting party below.

The sounds of the splashing water and girlish laughter were interrupted by a knock on the bedroom door.

Perón frowned. 'Who is it?' he asked testily.

'Mercante,' came the reply.

Perón looked puzzled. Relations hadn't been too cordial with his old friend for some time. 'Come in,' he called.

Domingo Mercante closed the door quietly and looked around the room. Nothing had been changed since Eva had been carried out after Dr Ara had completed the preliminaries of the long embalming process which was to make her body incorruptible.

Perón effected not to notice him but stared out of the window.

'Hello, *che*. Good to see you,' Mercante said, holding out the olive branch.

Perón turned towards his old partner. '*Ciao, amigo*. Have you come for the peep-show?' he asked jokingly.

'Peep-show?' Mercante queried.

Perón waved his cigarette towards the scene below the window. 'My own private Grecian Idyll. What do you think of it?'

Mercante joined him and looked out. Below was the blue-tiled swimming pool surrounded by a ranch-style fence. On the grass surrounds were a number of sun-loungers and umbrella-shaded tables.

The Governor of Buenos Aires blinked with astonishment. About twenty young girls, aged between thirteen and seventeen, were sprawled around on the loungers and the tiled surrounds of the pool watching others splashing and diving into the clear water. And they were all completely naked.

'What the hell is that?' he blurted out.

'That – *viejo* – is pussy. Fine, young, unadulterated pussy!' Perón assured him with a proprietorial smile of smug satisfaction.

'But where do they come from?' Mercante wanted to know. His question went unanswered. A young girl with long black *Indio* hair and lovely pert features was climbing up on to the diving board at the end of the pool and Perón was giving her his full attention. He had been attracted to the girl from the start and had made some inquiries. She was not quite fourteen, the youngest daughter of a retired junior civil-servant. She was bright and intelligent with a maturity beyond her years.

Nelly Rivas was already aware of the President's interest in her and encouraged it. As she got to the end of the diving board she stretched up onto her toes and ran her hands down her well-rounded figure. The other girls laughed but it wasn't for their benefit that she put on the show. Of all the girls there she was the only one to realise that Perón was watching from the observation point which he thought was a secret.

As Nelly dived into the water Perón returned his attention to his visitor. 'What were you saying?' he asked.

Mercante shrugged. 'Forget it. I know where they come from. It's one of the reasons I'm here.'

Perón looked at him steadily before emptying his glass and going to pour another. He offered Mercante a drink but he declined.

'Go on!' Perón told him.

'There's a lot of unrest about the way things are going. We seem to be slipping back instead of going forward,' Mercante began.

Perón blew a noisy raspberry. '*Dios mio*. Not the bloody Army again,' he said with exaggerated boredom.

'No – not the Army,' Mercante agreed quietly.

Perón stopped on his way back to his vantage point and turned back. 'Not the Army? Who then – the unions?' he asked slowly.

Again Mercante disagreed. 'No – not the unions either,' he told Perón enigmatically.

Perón exploded. 'Well, who the bloody hell else is there?' he shouted.

'The church!' Mercante stated flatly.

Perón forgot the sights below for a moment and came back towards him. 'The church? You're joking!'

The Governor shook his head. 'No joke. You know yourself they haven't accepted the legalisation of prostitution nor your insistence that divorce be recognised. Now that *Perónista* propaganda has to be included in religious instruction they are united. Even Cardinal Copello is talking out against you,' he warned Perón.

The President savagely ground out his cigarette butt and lit another. 'Okay – so they don't like a couple of laws I've passed. So what's new?' Perón asked facetiously.

Mercante looked him squarely in the eye. 'What is new is that they have been instructed from the Vatican to resist any inroads that civil government is making into the ecclesiastical domain. They want you to stop the bill to do away with religious instruction in the schools –'

Perón cut in on him. 'What do you mean?' he asked

297

tersely. 'Who do you think gave them their religious freedom. Before me they had no freedom. Now the smarmy bastards want to dictate to me, do they?'

Mercante ignored the outburst. 'They are serious. They demand that they are allowed to counsel their followers according to their conscience and unimpeded by the State.'

Perón laughed and went back to the window. 'And what do they reckon they can do about it?' he asked.

'Excommunication!' Mercante let the word hang between them.

For a moment Perón was quiet. He wasn't deeply religious but had paid lip-service long enough to fear the eternal damnation threatened by the church. He took another mouthful of whisky and let it warm his defiance.

'Excommunication?' He began to laugh drunkenly. 'Is that the best they can do? Tell Copello to come to see me. I'll introduce him to some of my little friends out there. I'm sure that would interest him more than a religious dialectic.' He gave an ugly laugh and returned to the window.

He was disappointed to see that the girls had left. Perón was suddenly annoyed at the intrusion that had robbed him of his eagerly awaited voyeurism. He looked at Mercante coldly.

'Is there anything else that can't wait?'

Mercante started to say something, but Perón cut him short. 'Save it for some other time. Now, if you don't mind, I have better things to do.'

His friend looked at him in anger but instead of arguing turned and left the room without a word. Sarcastically Perón held the whisky glass up in a mock toast.

Perón went through to the bathroom and took a shower. He wrapped a towel around his spreading waist and picked out what he should wear for the day. Since the death of Eva his routine had become more elastic – might even, uncharitably, be considered non-existent. He no longer arrived at his office at the crack of dawn, preferring to lie in bed or sit by the pool until the early afternoon whenever possible. Most of the time he now lived in the splendid apartment on

298

the Calle Vicente Lopez that Eva had bought a few years earlier. Part of the residency in Olivos had been turned over to the Buenos Aires High School for Girls as a recreation centre.

Perón retained a suite of rooms there and would drop in two or three times a week to talk to the girls or hand out prizes. Politically it was a good move and originally this had been his only conscious consideration. Now, as he became more uncertain about his future he found the attraction of the children more compelling.

'The only privileged in Argentina are the children,' Eva had often claimed. Looking at their clean-limbed, active bodies and eager, fun-filled faces Perón wanted to claim some of that privilege for himself.

As he struggled into his trousers there was a knock on the door. Surprised he slipped on his shirt and opened it. Standing outside the door, her long black hair gathered back into a chignon and wearing the white smock of a student was Nelida Rivas. Perón stared stupidly at her for a number of seconds. She gave him an open smile and curtsied.

'*Perdoname, Excelencia.* We are about to have our lunch and we wondered if you would do us the honour of joining us.'

Her offer was so unexpected Perón didn't know what to say. 'Don't you know this part of the house is out of bounds?' he asked roughly.

Nelly wrinkled her nose and pretended fear. 'Sorry, *Excelencia.* What will happen to me?' she asked.

He laughed thickly, excited in spite of himself by her presence. 'I expect I'll have to whack your bottom with a thick stick,' he told her, unable to avoid the eroticism of the situation.

Nelly giggled. 'Well – will you?'

Startled Perón blurted out, 'What?'

Round-eyed the girl looked at him innocently. 'Have lunch with us, of course,' she demanded.

Perón didn't know if he should invite her in. He decided against it on such short acquaintance. From experience he knew that young girls could be unpredictable and cause problems. 'Who else will be there?' he asked cautiously.

'Only the other girls,' Nelly informed him.

He nodded. '*Bueno*. I'll get my coat.'

Nelly caught hold of his hand and pulled him impatiently. 'Don't worry about your coat. We are eating in the garden and if you don't hurry it will be all gone.'

Protesting comically he let himself be dragged along by the exuberant teenager.

A light lunch had been set out by the girls in the *asado* area. When Nelly arrived with the shirtsleeved Perón in tow they all rushed across and swarmed around him. Nelly took control. She pushed a way through the girls and sat him at the head of the table.

'There you are, *Excelencia*,' she said and then stopped. 'What do we call you?' she asked thoughtfully. 'It sounds so silly saying *Excelencia* all the time.'

Nodding, Perón agreed. 'You can call me "*Pócho*"!' he told them. It was the name his mother had used.

When Lopez Rega arrived an hour later he was amazed at the spectacle he found on the back lawn. Perón, bare to the waist and blindfolded, stomped carefully around, arms outstretched in an attempt to catch the group of girls teasing him by flicking at his torso with napkins. Lopez Rega stood in the shade of a tall cypress and watched as Perón caught one of the girls but let her slip away.

'*Pócho* can't catch us!' the rest chanted.

Nelly Rivas waited until Perón was nearly on her then pretended to slip as she darted away. Her struggles, even to the distant Lopez Rega, seemed more an effort to excite her captor than to get away. Perón bent down to kiss the warm mouth of his captive and was surprised at the eagerness of the response. Intrigued he slid up the blindfold and found Nelly's black eyes staring suggestively into his own. Momentarily he was overcome but then he gave an uncertain laugh and watched as Nelly slipped away to join her friends.

Lopez Rega was worried. Since Eva's death he had

watched as Perón became daily more despotic and unpredictable. When Eva had been alive Lopez Rega had not appreciated the control she had exerted on the President's private life. She also probably gave him the confidence he lacked to deal with the problems that multiplied daily.

The ex-Sergeant was no fool. Through his web of spies spread throughout the country he knew more about the rumblings underground than anyone. And he had no illusions.

Perón had lost his way. The patriotic, intelligent and ambitious officer had been replaced by a selfish, unpredictable despot. He reacted irrationally to pressures that a few years earlier he would have turned easily to his advantage. Lopez Rega had only to think of the carnage that Perón's hysterical outburst after the bombings in the Plaza the other day had unleashed to realise how dangerous he had become.

Lopez Rega spent many hours communing with his spirit-guide, the Archangel Gabriel, trying to decide what he should do without resolving the situation. It all came back to his deep involvement with Perón. If he had wanted out he should have planned for it years ago.

Now, as Lopez Rega walked across the grass towards him, Perón detached himself from the girls and came to meet him.

'Gracias a Dios . . .' he gasped. 'Give me a *palito*, *che*, these kids are going to kill me.'

Lopez Rega didn't smoke himself but he always carried a packet of the President's favourite brand for emergencies. Perón breathed in a grateful lungful of smoke and let it trickle out through his nose.

'*Gracias*, José. What are you doing here?' he asked, his mind preoccupied with watching the girls, and particularly Nelly Rivas, as they scampered about clearing the table of the remains of the lunch.

Lopez Rega pushed the knowledge of the President's quickening interest in young children to the back of his mind. It was just another aspect of Perón's increasing unreliability. A folly that could blow up in their faces and cause an unexpected crisis that he would be unable to talk himself out of easily.

'You told me to meet you at the office. As you didn't turn up I decided I must have made a mistake and came out here.'

Perón thought for a moment. 'Yes. I remember,' he said thoughtfully. 'I want you to go to Europe.'

It was Lopez Rega's turn to look surprised. 'Europe?' he repeated.

Perón nodded. 'Yes. I've had a curious anonymous letter sent to me. It said that Juán Duarte is double-crossing me. Whoever it was writing the letter knew enough about my affairs to convince me that Duarte has been talking out of place. That being the case I want to make sure. It seems he gave an actress called Maliza Zini a piece of Eva's jewellery. An expensive piece. I have some valuables I want depositing in Zürich. If Duarte is lining his own nest I want to know. I'll give you the pass and key. You go and check up. If there is anything amiss I want to know.'

Lopez Rega nodded understanding. It suited him fine. He knew about the millions pouring into Zürich but had never been directly involved before. Once he knew the secret of the vaults he would have a practically unstoppable hand.

Before he passed beyond the corner of the house Lopez Rega looked back. Perón, with the squealing Nelly Rivas mounted on his back, was charging around the garden in a boisterous race. Lopez Rega shook his head. If he didn't move fast he was likely to get washed away in the dam-burst that threatened the dilettante *Presidente*.

THIRTY-FOUR

Allen Dulles, director of the powerful CIA took the seat opposite the new master of the White House, Dwight Eisenhower.

It was the first time he had been able to get the President to discuss the problem of Argentina's essay into the nuclear game and he wanted to be sure of his reaction to what he was about to suggest.

Eisenhower smoothed down the flag draped behind his desk and gave a well-tried smile. 'Well, Allen. I've read your communiqué and I've assessed the problems. Now! What we want is a plan to flush the Germans out without creating an international stink. Not from the Germans, of course. They will be forced to keep their security guard up whatever happens. But President Perón isn't going to stand still for an invasion of his territory. He screams Yankee imperialism every time a bottle of Coca Cola crosses his border. So what do you intend to do?'

Dulles watched while Eisenhower carefully lined up the pencils, blotter, telephone and odds and ends on his desk into military order. He wanted the President's undivided attention. How he reacted to the CIA's plan would indicate their future strategy on other operations.

'We feel that we have to get access to the factory and destroy their equipment. We have considered every other possibility including assassinating the scientists responsible but feel that anything less than total destruction will be counter-productive.' Dulles quirked his mouth in a nervous smile and blinked his pale-lashed eyes earnestly.

Eisenhower nodded understanding and reformed the bric-à-brac on his desk into fighting formation. 'What is your plan of campaign?'

'We have a contact close to Perón. Given the right incentive we feel that a deal could be negotiated with him. This guy has a considerable undercover army but is totally dependent on Perón. When his boss falls it's his end too – and he can be under no illusions about it. Nobody thinks Perón can survive too long. Our contact will want a way out. We suggest that we offer him safe passage when the shit hits the fan in exchange for using his men to destroy the German installation. That way we can't be accused of interference in the internal affairs of the government. What happens to our contact afterwards depends on circumstances.'

The President rose, his lean jaw jutting aggressively, and stood next to the Stars and Stripes. 'Go ahead, Allen. You, of course, realise that this operation is to be kept under strict security. Officially I am to know nothing of what is going on.'

Lopez Rega waited in the small security office until the guard and the vaults manager had left, then locked the door. He looked with satisfaction at the two strong boxes, side by side, on the table in front of him. He checked the key and then inserted it into the lock of the first box. The precision machined lever slid back soundlessly and he hinged the lid open. His eyes tightened and he turned his attention to the other box.

He picked up the white canvas bag lying in one of the trays and emptied it into the bottom of the box. A small pile of industrial diamonds winked mischievously in the bright neon light. He threw the bag on top of them contemptuously and went back to the first box. In a lined compartment were a few bearer bonds and about five thousand dollars.

Lopez Rega sat on the high stool at the table side and stared at the piggy-bank haul where he had expected to find the contents of Aladdin's cave. He knew what had happened. Now he had to figure out what he must do about it. Whether he should tell Perón and let him deal with the matter or whether he should take Duarte to task himself.

Lopez Rega knew what he wanted. He wanted control of the money. Just control. It was still Perón's and he had no intention of trying to steal it. But control it he must! That meant that he must find out where it was hidden and only one person knew that.

Lopez Rega emptied the contents of his briefcase into the strong boxes. It was the best place to keep it. He knew where it was and when the time came he could easily pick it up.

Once back at Buenos Aires airport, after the dreary journey across the Atlantic, he got one of the customs officials on his payroll to smuggle him out so that his arrival in the capital wouldn't be noted and automatically signalled to Perón. He had taken care of the passenger list with an alias which would escape scrutiny unless someone should dig around to see who had paid for the ticket and there was no reason why anyone should do that.

Instead of calling the motor pool for a car he took a taxi and directed it to Therese's apartment. She had just finished eating a meal she had cooked herself when Lopez Rega knocked on the door. She had intended to have an early night and had bathed and put on her nightdress in anticipation. She hesitated before opening the door.

'*Quien es?*' she asked cautiously.

'Daniel. Open up.' The voice sent a thrill of excitement through her. Her gradual addiction to drugs and her perversion for the pain that Lopez Rega readily inflicted had deadened her will.

She still functioned normally and only close observation could have detected the signs of her moral disintegration. Signs too subtle for the drunken Juán Duarte to read. He still followed her around like a lost lamb, bleating his undying love and pleading for the warmth of her understanding. She let him bleed his heart out. It was what her Daniel wanted so she did it.

Therese flung the door wide and risked Lopez Rega's displeasure by throwing her arms around his neck in an eager embrace. He didn't appear to mind so she pulled him

305

eagerly through the door. Lopez Rega kissed her on the mouth and then disentangled himself.

'Get me a coffee, will you *querida*?' he said. Therese rushed happily into the kitchen to get it for him. She hardly liked to leave him for a second when he was in a good mood. They were so rare and lasted for such a short time that she begrudged the time spent away from him. He allowed her to sit on the floor beside him with her head on his knee while he drank his coffee. She was frightened of breaking the spell so didn't speak. Lopez Rega stroked her hair.

'Have you seen Duarte recently?' he asked her.

Therese started guiltily. She tried to avoid the unwelcome attentions of the President's brother-in-law as much as possible. Earlier that evening he had telephoned to ask her to dinner. 'Not for some time,' she said honestly.

Lopez Rega said nothing and Therese rushed into the pause. 'He rang this evening but I didn't feel like going out.' She glanced at Daniel to see how he was taking it.

He slid his hand down her neck and fondled her breasts. She stretched herself luxuriously, swept away on an orgasmic tide by his touch. His voice pulled her back.

'*Perdóname*, Daniel. What did you say?' she asked.

'Ring Duarte and tell him you want to come over right away,' he repeated.

Shocked Therese pushed herself upright and looked at him. 'Now?' she asked unbelievingly.

Lopez Rega took his hand from the front of her dressing gown and stood up. 'Yes. Now!' He picked up the telephone. 'What's his number?' he asked and dialled when she told him.

As he heard the telephone at the other end answered he handed the receiver to her. 'Tell him you want to see him. Right now,' he instructed her.

She took the telephone obediently. '*Hóla Juán*?' she said. 'Therese. I want to come over to see you.' She listened and shook her head. 'No. Not here. I will come to you.'

Again she listened. 'I just want to see you Juán. I'll be there in about fifteen minutes.'

Duarte put the handset down unbelievingly. In all the months he had known her she had never suggested coming back to his flat.

Some hours later Lopez Rega stood out of the line of sight of the opening door and nodded for Therese to go ahead. She pulled herself together and pressed the bell. Before she could take her finger off the button the door opened and Juán Duarte stood in front of her, eager and smiling.

'*Hóla, Juancito,*' she said in her low provocative voice that drove all other considerations out of his head. She held out her hand and he bowed to kiss it. Before he could straighten up Lopez Rega moved forward and walked into the apartment.

Duarte spun round. 'Hey, what do you want?' he demanded in surprise.

Lopez Rega nodded to the door. 'Shut it. I want a few words with you.'

Duarte couldn't grasp the turn of events. Instead of shutting the door he went after Lopez Rega and gripped his forearm. 'Get out of here. I've got nothing to say to you. The President will hear about this,' he shouted indignantly.

Lopez Rega looked down at the hand on his sleeve and then slowly up into the puffy face of Duarte. The cold, blank eyes washed the resistance out of the man who dared to lay a hand on him.

Fear hit Duarte like a physical blow. He had never felt so alone. It was the first time he had fully realised the dangers of the shark-infested waters of the Casa Rosada without his sister and the President to guard him against his own folly.

He dropped his hand hastily from his visitor's arm. 'I was just going to bed but if it's something important . . .' His voice trailed away ingratiatingly.

'It is,' Lopez Rega assured him tersely.

Duarte shut the door and suddenly remembered Therese standing there watching the scene. He felt foolish. He drew himself up and cleared his throat. '*Bueno.* I don't think you know Señorita Therese von Quast,' Duarte said with as much assurance as he could muster.

'Señor Lopez Rega – Señorita von Quast. Señor Lopez Rega works –'

Lopez Rega cut him off and walked into the sitting room. 'We know each other. Señorita von Quast came with me.' He turned to observe Duarte as he broke the news.

Juán wasn't having a good time. Drink had slowed up his thinking process and Lopez Rega watched while he laboriously plodded his way from point to point. Before Duarte could ask more questions Lopez Rega took one of the upright chairs from the wall and placed it in the centre of the room.

'Sit down, Señor Duarte,' he told his host politely.

The ex-soap salesman looked from the chair to Lopez Rega and to Therese and back to the chair. He opened his mouth to try and say something but his unwelcome guest killed his attempt at conversation.

'Sit down,' he snapped again, a ring of undeniable authority in his voice.

Duarte did as he was told. Lopez Rega looked at the silent Therese and indicated to her to sit in one of the chairs by a small occasional table. She sat down and elegantly crossed her legs, took out a cigarette and lit it. In spite of the threat to his safety Duarte watched her every move, his eyes lingering on the slim, silk covered legs.

Lopez Rega said nothing but stood patiently in front of Duarte until he had looked his fill.

'I do not intend to waste time,' he said clearly and succinctly when he was sure he had Duarte's attention. 'I have just returned from Zurich where your brother-in-law sent me to check up on the deposit boxes you had obtained for him there.' He noticed with satisfaction the terrified look in Duarte's eyes. 'I don't have to tell you what I found. Now! I want the key to the real boxes containing the deposits your sister and the President have made and I want them now.'

Duarte opened his mouth to speak but was cut off by Lopez Rega. 'I warn you. All I want is the whereabouts of the money you have misappropriated. No explanations, no excuses.' Lopez Rega's voice, flat and menacing, sent chills through Duarte's blood. But the keys were his protection, he reassured himself. While he had those safe nothing could happen to him. He sat up straight in the chair and tried to outstare the hard eyes in front of him.

'I don't know what you are talking about. You must have gone to the wrong place. President Perón has the keys and he is satisfied with what I have done.'

Lopez Rega unbuttoned his coat and reached round to the back of his waist and pulled out a heavy, long-bladed knife with a silver filigree handle. It was the *facon* of the *gaucho*. An all-purpose knife always honed to perfection. Lopez Rega held the knife casually in front of Duarte's eyes.

'You are sure you don't want to co-operate,' he enquired in a reasonable tone.

Suddenly the ex-soldier swung the blade and crashed it down across Therese's hand, resting, cigarette between the fingers, on the occasional table beside her. As if internally animated the three middle fingers seemed to jump away from the hand, cigarette still in place, and fall with a soft plop to the floor. Therese looked at Lopez Rega and then down at her ruined hand. The blood had begun to pump, thick and red, from the stumps of her fingers. Unbelievingly she held her hand to her face. Blood splayed down the front of her white suit in great spreading stains.

She opened her mouth to scream but no sound came. Duarte hadn't moved. It was like a nightmare. He watched as Therese threw back her head. He watched the white flesh of her beautiful neck and knew what was coming. Duarte tried to shout a warning, to throw himself between the girl and her torturer but the terrible events had robbed him of all will-power.

Almost caressingly Lopez Rega brought up his scarlet-stained knife and slashed expertly across the offered flesh. One word Therese managed before blood rushed in through the gaping wound in her windpipe to suffocate her.

'Daniel,' she whispered.

A word of love and release.

The two men watched immobile as she took a faltering step and crashed down to the carpet in a welter of blood. Duarte buried his face in his hands. Lopez Rega reached into his pocket and took out a pistol. He pulled out the clip and laid the gun on the coffee table near where Duarte was sitting. He bent down beside Therese's blood-covered body and pulled her further onto the carpet so that the spreading stain would be absorbed by the material. Then he forced Duarte's hands from his eyes and made him look at the mutilated body.

'Listen to me, Señor Duarte. I was very fond of Señorita von Quast. You, I don't like at all. It would be quite easy for me to arrange for you to be accused of her murder. I'm going to telephone for a couple of my men. They are both regular plain-clothes police officers. If I tell them to get rid of the body that is the last you will hear of it. But, *che,* if by the time they arrive you haven't given me the keys and details of the deposit boxes, they will arrest you and I shall personally see that you don't survive the police cellars to die in prison.'

Lopez Rega gave him a few seconds to let the threat sink in and then walked across to the telephone and dialled a number. He stood with his back towards Duarte.

Duarte's eye was caught by the automatic Lopez Rega had placed on the coffee table. Without stopping to think of the miracle that had materialised the weapon, he grabbed it up and pointed it at his tormentor's back.

'Put the telephone down,' he ordered in a thin, unnatural voice.

Obligingly Lopez Rega dropped the handset back on the rest and turned round. Duarte waved the gun menacingly.

'Why did you have to kill her?' he asked, a sob in his voice. Lopez Rega shrugged and started to walk forward.

'Stand back!' Duarte screamed at him and then squeezed the trigger as Lopez Rega kept coming. He was still frantically squeezing the trigger when Lopez Rega took hold of the barrel, wrenched the gun out of his hand and whipped the butt of the gun across the terrified man's face, knocking him back into the chair. He walked behind Duarte and, carefully avoiding touching the handle of the gun, silently slid the full clip back into place. With a handkerchief wrapped carefully around the butt to preserve the finger-prints he put the automatic in his side pocket and kept his hand on it as he faced Duarte. He grasped the snivelling man's hair and roughly slammed his head against the wooden seat back.

'You still think it's worth it, *mierda*?' Lopez Rega asked him in a conventional tone. He forced Duarte's head towards the horrifying corpse of Therese. 'Do you still think it's worth it?' he repeated.

A low desperate scream filled Duarte's throat. He wren-ched himself away from his tormentor and opened a lacquered Chinese cabinet. Lopez Rega kept the gun in his pocket trained unerringly on Duarte's stomach as Duarte wrenched one of the drawers completely out of the cabinet and turned it over. Taped to the bottom were two vault keys and a bank identity card. Without a word he hurled the drawer across the room at Lopez Rega and fell to the floor sobbing.

The ex-sergeant bent down and detached the keys and card and examined them closely. 'It's a pity you didn't do that in the first place, it would have saved a lot of trouble,' he told him with mild understatement. He led the quaking ex-soap salesman back to the high-backed chair and sat him down facing the remains of his loved one.

'Don't worry, Juán. I'll look after you,' he said sooth-ingly as he quietly took the pistol wrapped in the handker-chief from his pocket. He picked up a cushion and covered the automatic with it to deaden the sound.

Holding the gun about a yard from the weeping man he pulled the trigger. Feathers from the exploding pillow sprayed around the room settling on the still figure of the killer and drifting onto his victims.

THIRTY-FIVE

Domingo Mercante waited until he saw Alfonso de Benedetti coming through the door before he switched off the
engine and stepped from the car. The capital was becoming
a place of sudden death and disappearance. Who planned
and executed the coups, left wing, right wing or just old-
fashioned villains needn't really matter – the result was the
same.

Public figures now had to walk carefully, knowing that
there were forces lurking in the shadows ready to take
advantage of the first wrong move. Invitations to meet at
isolated *estancias*, alone, were best treated with caution,
regardless of who originated the meeting or for what
purpose.

Mercante had hesitated to accept as soon as he saw the
reason. Although he no longer shared Perón's trust he shied
against the idea of actively going against his old friend. And
a meeting between General Lonardi, now the accepted head
of the rebel officers, Cardinal Copello, Primate of Argentina and de Benedetti, one of the few wealthy landowners
who had once been an avowed *Perónista* but was now a
member of a semi-secret oligarch organisation called the
Gorillas, could only mean a move to unseat the President.

Mercante was in a cleft stick. He was fully aware of
Perón's growing unreliability. The activities of Olivos,
which he had seen first hand, had become an open scandal.
Perón was openly living with Nelly Rivas although he made
a half-hearted attempt to pass her off as his niece
occasionally.

De Benedetti opened the meeting. 'Thank you for coming, gentlemen. I think we all know why we are here. We
are all representatives of some faction of the community
312

that deplores what is being done in the name of the *patria*. I therefore suggest that we listen to what His Eminence Cardinal Copello has to say and then we try to thrash out a course of action.' He smiled at Copello. 'Your Eminence,' he prompted.

Copello clasped his hands beatifically in front of him and looked at his fellow conspirators. 'His Holiness the Pope has informed me that, should the laws proposed in the Senate regarding the legalisation of prostitution and divorce be implemented, he will declare excommunication on the government of Argentina.' He delivered his bombshell without emphasis and waited to see the reaction.

De Benedetti was obviously shocked. A strong Roman Catholic ancestry had imbued him with a fear of the ultimate punishment the Church could render. Lonardi also blanched at the thought.

Only Mercante appeared unmoved. Practically he thought that Perón was unlikely to get into a blue funk because an old man in Rome told him he wasn't going to heaven.

Copello continued, 'My informant tells me that Perón is determined to force his divorce and prostitution bills through the Senate. When this is done we must be ready to strike. Perón has turned his supporters against the clergy. The common people are feeling confident now. Blasphemously they are close to deifying both Perón and his late wife. Indeed, the Pope has recently been approached by the unions to canonise Señora de Perón as *Santa Evita*.' He paused for effect.

'I don't think that it will be possible to completely mobilise mob opinion against the President. What I suggest is that we try and panic him into leaving.'

He again looked around at the other men. They nodded understanding. The cardinal went into some detail of how he saw the Putsch developing. Lonardi promised Army support that he wasn't really qualified to give and de Benedetti gave an assurance that the *estancieros* would rise as a man when the call came. He didn't qualify it by adding 'if

313

they aren't in Paris or London at the time' but he knew it to be a major problem.

They looked expectantly at Mercante. He was at a loss what to say. He finally agreed that he would take whatever steps would ensure peace on the streets in the aftermath of revolution although he couldn't begin to think how that could be done. As he drove back along the long unmetalled roads to the city he wondered how many other groups were gathering for the kill. With the tiger skulking in his lair, bored by politics and intrigue, abandoned to the pursuit of sensuality, the jackals could have their day. If they didn't tear each other to pieces in the resulting *mêlée*.

Abe Rubel waited until he heard the scrape of the key in the lock before going into action. In one swift movement he stepped forward and jammed the barrel of the pistol into the man's ear.

'Don't move, *amigo*!' Rubel hissed in accented Spanish.

Lopez Rega froze.

Rubel kept his little Derringer in his captive's ear until they were inside and the light had been turned on. Then he prodded Lopez Rega to a chair and stood back. 'I'm working for the American government. Your name was given me as a possible helper in an operation we are planning in Hildburghausen.' He watched Lopez Rega relax as he learned whose prisoner he was so Rubel put the gun away and sat opposite him.

'My orders are to get inside and destroy the installation,' Rubel told him bluntly and watched the expressionless eyes to see how Lopez Rega took the news. He got nothing from them.

'Why come to me?'

Rubel smiled. 'You are well known, *amigo*. We want to do a deal. Your days are numbered here too, like Perón's. We think we can help each other.'

Shaking his head slowly Lopez Rega leaned towards him. 'If I did a deal it wouldn't be for money.'

Rubel's eyebrows rose. 'Not for money, *che*. For patriot-

314

ism then?' he asked sarcastically.

'*Si.* Call it patriotism,' Lopez Rega agreed.

The American took a folded map out of his breast pocket and smoothed it out on the table. He pointed to the Chilean border. 'I have two hundred men hiding out here. They will come in over the mountain when I give the word. I want to get inside and set charges and be out before the Germans know what hit them.'

The Argentinian nodded understanding. 'So you get two hundred men with hand weapons across the border. How do you reckon to get inside? Have you seen the place?'

Rubel nodded and told him about his previous trip down the mountain and in through the air vent.

'In that case you know that it is impossible to approach the entrance without being seen from the village,' Lopez Rega said. 'You'll need more men if you intend to try an open assault.'

'That's where you come in,' Rubel told him. 'Can you put another two hundred men in the field? Maybe with anti-tank guns with armour-piercing shells to penetrate the front of the building.' He took another map from his tunic and laid it out on the table. It was a plan of the village and mountains. He pointed to a building on the edge of the town.

'I kept the place under observation for a while and that looks like being some sort of pillbox to me. Probably others but I couldn't get close enough to see. What we can rely on is that they will have a pretty watertight plan of defence worked out. We have to surprise them.'

'How do you do that?' Lopez Rega asked.

Rubel jabbed his finger at the outline of the mountain. 'There's an air vent here. I went down there before. I figure a couple of us go in from the top and drop a few grenades down there. After the ventilator has been wrecked we drop some gas cannisters. That should smoke them out into the arms of our men around the front. My demolition men will move in with gas masks using the ventilation shaft and set the charges and return the way they came. We are interested

315

in destroying the plant. Once that is done we clear out. How does that grab you?' Rubel asked the soldier.

Perón heard that the rebellion was about to start as he arrived at the Casa Rosada. He spent a few minutes with his staff getting a full report on what the rebels intended to do then evacuated the Casa Rosada for the safety of the Army Ministry.

It was a drab, chilling day, the end of an Argentine winter. Heavy mist covered the capital like fine rain and the streets were bare and slimy. Perón reclined on a camp-bed smoking cigarettes and joking with his staff as the flight of bombers swept low over the Plaza. Bombs rained down on the Casa Rosada and the surrounding buildings killing many innocent civilians. In the cellar, talk died as the vibration of the continuous bomb explosions swayed the naked light bulb hanging from the ceiling and made dust filter from between the cracks in the bricks.

The opening attack killed several hundred people and many more were injured. As the planes flew back to their bases the naval shore battery, situated behind the Casa Rosada, opened fire. By this time Perón's loyalists, already in position for the counter offensive, attacked the naval installation with gun-carriers, tanks and armoured trucks.

Perón's troops soon gained control but a second wave of bombers caused more deaths although they were not allowed the easy passage they had had on their first run. Ack-ack guns had been included in the inventory of weapons to guard the government building and those kept the raiders at bay.

Most casualties were amongst the civilians, fooled by the lull in hostilities, who had crowded into the Plaza to finger the bullet holes in the stonework of the buildings and collect bomb fragments as souvenirs. Caught in the open they had nowhere to hide when the planes opened their bomb-doors and hastily jettisoned their load before clawing away from the probing ack-ack guns.

Perón was more cautious. He had no intention of getting

caught in the open and stayed in his shelter until nightfall in spite of the obvious fact that the revolution against his regime had once again failed.

He kept abreast of developments as reports came in. The fiasco amused him. When he had been told of the plan, relayed faithfully to him by spies in the enemy camp, he had felt a moment of fear. The plan was good. If the strike had been swifter, denying him the chance to get his intelligence service into operation, and the weather had been kinder the rebels could have won. The mist had saved Perón.

As darkness closed in on the shattered Plaza de Mayo hiding the heaps of earth and the stains of blood, the white flag was run up to the masthead at the Naval Ministry and troops moved in to round up the rebels who had not escaped across the water while they had a chance.

Perón led his people back to the Casa Rosada and made arrangements to talk to the nation on the radio. As he looked around his shattered office he tried to feel trium-phant. The revolution had failed. It had confirmed his self-esteem as the most able manipulator in the land. But it also confirmed that he was the prime target. If only he had remained the faceless arch-intriguer he had been before Eva had persuaded him to set his sights on the presidency.

Perón signed deeply and went out onto the balcony followed by an impressive array of uniforms that had rushed to his side to pledge loyalty when they saw the revolution attempt fail. The floodlights came on and the loudspeakers hummed as Perón took up his familiar place in front of the microphone.

Below him a thousand or so of his most ardent supporters had gathered waiting for him to tell them how to avenge the insult. The number was rapidly increasing as supporters converged from all parts of the city. Rain had started to fall heavily and drifted across the lights like dirty lace curtains. Not the best time to whip up fervent displays of loyalty.

Perón held up his hands to still the fragmented cheering that had greeted his appearance. He pitched his voice low as he spoke. A sad, disappointed man who couldn't understand why he had been so mistreated.

'*Compañeros!* Thank you for coming to me on this terrible night to help me mourn the innocent dead. The women and children who want nothing more than to be left in peace to live out a decent hard-working life. The families who have this day been shattered by the cynical indiscriminate bombing of our city streets. And who is to blame? Is it the Army who have for so long been the bastion of the people – NO! Who is it then who is so base, so callous that they can exhort our Navy and our Airforce to rain death on our people?' He paused and appeared to listen to the clamour of voices answering his question.

'That's right, my friends, it is Rome that decrees that our people should die. They want Argentina to bow to orders from Italy.' He let his voice die away and his head sink on his chest. Abruptly his mood changed.

'Who are these people that they dictate to us? There is not a country in the world more God-fearing, more obedient to the lawful claims of the church than Argentina. But we do not intend to bow to a church that has become so rich, that it listens to the voice of Wall Street rather than the voice of God. Think! When was the last time a priest helped you get a rise in salary? Think! When did a priest deny the pleasures of the table of the oligarchs to sit in your humble homes and eat good Argentinian food. Christ threw the usurers out of the temple. It is our turn to pledge our faith in Christ by continuing his work.'

He finished his exhortation on a rising note. As the excited agreement crashed out from the crowd he knew he had done his work well.

Perón lowered his voice. 'I leave it to your own consciences. Are we to be ruled by the Vatican or ourselves?' he asked with quiet sincerity and without another word walked back into his office.

His entourage filed in behind him and stood silently around the room. Perón took a cigarette from his big onyx box, a present from the CGT, and looked them over.

Their bland, unfamiliar faces made him feel lonely. He
318

thought back to the old days, the exciting days that he had spent in that office. When the faces of his subordinates meant something. Faces that had character, Espejo, Avalos, Mercante, occasionally men from the streets like Reyes. And, of course, Evita to stir them all up with excitement and demands. Wheedling and scheming or raving like a fish-wife she was worth a hundred career politicians.

'Thank you, gentlemen,' he said simply, 'for your support.'

The swift reaction of parts of the armed forces to the Vatican's excommunication proclamation and the near success of their coup forced Lopez Rega to accelerate his plans. He told Perón he had business in Mendoza and made arrangements to meet Rubel there. They got down to business immediately.

'When can you be ready to move?' he asked the CIA man.

'Man, we have been sitting on our butts for months. When do you suggest?' Rubel asked him.

'I think now is the time,' Lopez Rega told him. 'The Army is in turmoil. Half the officers got caught up in last week's fireworks and had to flee. It's left great gaps in the chain of command. There should be no military around for hundreds of miles if you move now.' He considered for a moment. 'You have made the arrangements?'

Rubel grinned. 'Sure have. As soon as you give the word there will be a Paraguayan gunboat sitting in Buenos Aires harbour to take you and the President out. Our people have arranged temporary asylum in Paraguay.'

'Temporary? Why temporary?'

'What do you expect? We can't go laying it on the line without tipping your hand. If we demand permanent asylum it means that everyone has to be informed and word will get out that Perón is going AWOL. This way we get an agreement with an official who owes us a favour and that gets us over the first hurdle. While the Paraguayan government are arguing about what they intend to do with you, you can work out your own salvation.'

It was less than Lopez Rega had hoped for but he had to agree. '*Bueno*. Now, can you be ready in three days' time?' he asked.

Rubel confirmed that he would have his men in position and wait for Lopez Rega to show. The Argentinian would bring the bulkier artillery and provide transport for Rubel's men to make a rapid withdrawal to the frontier after the raid. Lopez Rega returned to Buenos Aires and Rubel headed back to his hideout on the Chilean side of the Andes.

THIRTY-SIX

Among the thousands of government opponents seized in the periodic police swoops and round-ups Tomas Bravo lay in the cold hut of the concentration camp and longed for death. He had lost count of time. Every day, for hours on end, he had been tortured. Sometimes they made him stand for what seemed like eternity, burning him with cigarettes until he staggered back to his feet if he fell down. He wanted so much to die but long experience had taught his persecutors when to stop. In desperation he told them everything they wanted to know. It didn't make any difference.

His body broken, practically unable to move, he had lain on the filthy floor of his cell and waited on the borders of unconsciousness for his captors to return and continue the torment.

Then they didn't come.

In his semi-conscious state Bravo didn't notice at first. The food still came, thrown on the floor beside him to eat like a dog. On the second day he pushed himself up against the wall and applied his pain-racked brain to the enormous task of trying to remember how long it had been since his persecutors had last been there. It was too much for him and he passed out.

Later he had felt himself picked up and carried out. In the security of his rambling mind he felt happy. They were going to kill him, to release him from the agony of his broken, unset bones and suppurating cuts. He fainted as he was dumped in the back of a van and only recovered when he felt a cool cloth placed on his forehead.

The face looking down at him was full of anxiety. Bravo wanted to thank him but didn't have the strength. Through all Bravo's pain and fever the man who slept in the bunk

above him tenderly cared for him. He took out the loose
shattered teeth that made it impossible for Bravo even to
attempt to eat the coarse food. His broken fingers were
gently splinted and the raw tips, where the nails had been
torn from the roots, cleaned and bandaged.

Bravo waited eagerly for his return whenever he went out
to work on the jobs to which prisoners were daily allocated.
A few of the other prisoners occasionally came to see him
but he didn't have the strength to acknowledge them. He
was dying and he was glad.

Alone, during the day, he let his mind return to the time
when he had been young and full of hope. He thought about
his wife and their two children. Since their death he had not
thought about religion but now he began to hope that there
was a life after death. The hope became a conviction. Now
the wish to die became stronger. In his mind he could see his
wife and children waiting for him. He came out of his dream
to see the strong, compassionate face of his friend looking
down at him. He didn't even know his name.

'What is your name?' he whispered.

The man couldn't hear him. He bent closer with his ear to
Bravo's lips. Bravo tried to concentrate but he was feeling
tired. Warmth spread through his body and the pain died
away. He wanted to tell his friend. He looked into the face
above him and smiled as it faded away. The man sat and
looked at Bravo's vacant staring eyes and then gently closed
them.

The man on the bunk behind him looked across. 'He's
dead?'

The man nodded.

'What was he trying to say?' the man on the bunk asked.

Cipriano Reyes stood up and looked down at the man
whose life he had destroyed. 'I don't know, couldn't hear.
Anyway, the poor bastard's gone now. He's lucky.'

The frigate lay at anchor as close into the headland on the
north extremity of Bahia Blanca as it could get. Admiral
Isaac Rojas stood on the bridge and watched anxiously as his

322

distinguished guests were piped aboard in style.

First aboard was Cardinal Copello. Rojas was grateful to see that the churchman had made the concession to secrecy of wearing a plain dark suit instead of his distracting cardinal vestments. The idle thought crossed Rojas' mind that Copello would probably be shot for a spy if he was caught out of uniform but he didn't have time to pursue it as General Lonardi stepped aboard.

There were three other men but Rojas didn't retain their names in his anxiety to get the party below out of the range of possible binoculars from the shore. Safely installed in the wardroom he relaxed and ordered drinks for the company as they sat down and made themselves comfortable around the oblong table.

Lonardi spoke first. 'We would like to thank you, Admiral Rojas, for making your ship available to us for this important meeting. You know Cardinal Copello, of course. This is General Domingo Molina from Mendoza.'

The short, thickset man at his side jerked his head forward in acknowledgement. Lonardi indicated the two men on the other side of Copello. 'General Juán José Uranga of Curuzu Cuatia and General Bengoa from Puerto Belgrano.'

Having performed the introductions Lonardi handed over to Copello. Even in a civilian suit the primate managed to appear clerical.

'Gentlemen. We are gathered here on a most important mission. As you know, the Vatican are deeply concerned with the way Argentina is being run by the present administration and feel that they must support any leader who can assure them that individual freedom to worship in the Roman Catholic faith will be restored.'

He leaned back and looked across to Lonardi. 'General Lonardi will fill in the details,' the cardinal said, washing his hands of the mechanics of the conspiracy.

Lonardi sat up straight and putting on a thick pair of horn-rimmed spectacles he read the notes he had made before leaving home that morning.

323

'Well, gentlemen. We have asked you to come to this meeting today because it is in all our interests to overthrow the present regime. Previously we had tried to organise a revolt purely in Buenos Aires, then taking it to the provinces as a *fait-accompli*. It was not a success. What we want to do this time is start a revolution simultaneously in various parts of the country. The reason that Perón has been able to survive so far is that he is able to call up his union-led workers to stifle any opposition by sheer weight of numbers. To succeed the Army would have to fire on civilians and that doesn't endear them to the masses.'

He consulted his notes and then carried on, looking at the men one by one as he spoke. 'General Molina, can you promise to raise the garrison at Mendoza?'

Molina nodded. Uranga promised the Curuzu Cuatia Army base and Admiral Rojas pledged ample naval support. Lonardi and Copello exchanged relieved glances.

Lonardi turned to Bengoa. 'I want you to take over the police force. You are the only man we have with any practical experience of running the civil force and it would be too big a job for an inexperienced officer.'

'I shall be happy to take over the police force,' Bengoa reassured him.

Lonardi marshalled his papers together and took off his glasses. '*Bueno*. We will meet again to sort out the details. Are there any questions?'

Bengoa tapped the table in front of him with his finger to call attention. 'Two questions. When do you anticipate going into action and what about Cordoba and Rosario?'

Lonari pulled his lower lip reflectively. 'Date? That can't be set yet. We must prepare properly this time. But we aim at a month to six weeks – two months at the outside. Too long and Perón will get wind. Rosario and Cordoba? We haven't decided who to ask to join us from Rosario, perhaps some of you have ideas. I will command Cordoba. When the time comes I will co-ordinate operations from there until such time as we are sure that we can take over the city without opposition.'

'And Perón?' Admiral Rojas asked quickly.

Lonardi again glanced at Copello before answering. 'If Perón goes without causing too much trouble we will not try to stop him. If he fights, however, he will be arrested and interned until we can see what the best course of action is.'

The men around the table nodded in agreement. Traditionally the overthrown president was allowed to escape to offset any problems arising among his supporters from an assassination or imprisonment.

'And who takes over?' General Molina asked without beating around the bush.

Copello got in quickly. 'Initially we will form a *junta* representing the three Armed Forces. When we have settled the country down we can then decide what to do. As soon as possible I would like to see a democratically elected government but that is outside my sphere of influence, of course,' he finished modestly.

Lonardo again looked around for questions and Bengoa again spoke up.

'What about the Airforce? Can we bank on their support?' he asked.

Lonardi fiddled with his glasses case. 'It's a problem. The Airforce rarely like to take a stand. We know a number of officers who might be persuaded to join us but they will want an assurance that their interests will be looked after. Unlike the Army and the Navy they are vulnerable. The last couple of times they have tried to join in they have returned to their bases to find that the Army has knocked out the runways. They will want assurance that this doesn't happen again. It's something we must think about.'

Bengoa nodded. 'The problem with the Airforce is that they are so elitist they can't bear the thought of not being on the winning side.'

The rest of the men laughed and the meeting broke up. Admiral Rojas stood on the bridge of the frigate and watched the tender make for the shore. On the foredeck he could see the able-seamen preparing to weigh anchor. He wished they would hurry. He was committed to the revolution but he had a deep psychological need to get out to sea and enjoy the clean, well-ordered life of the Navy before leaving it behind to claw a way through the murky political scene.

In the dark Abe Rubel retraced his course of months earlier. But this time he wasn't alone and didn't have to worry about the security of the rope at the top of the cliff. So far everything had gone according to plan.

Lopez Rega had turned up at the rendezvous with his men and the promised artillery equipment. As soon as it got dark they had moved in, Lopez Rega staying with the troops lined up on the other side of the village whose task it was to bombard the entrance to the underground factory and clear a way for the infantry moving in on foot.

Rubel had taken a dozen men to the cliff top with him in addition to the four demolition men. They had with them a pair of bazookas, a machine gun and half a dozen Bren-guns as well as .303 Lee Enfield rifles and a sten gun for each of the men who would act as guards when the demolition experts were setting their charges. The weapons had been chosen carefully so that in the event of a setback to their plans there would not be an obvious connection with the USA.

The American was hoping that Lopez Rega with the artillery and a couple of hundred men fighting in the streets would prove a big enough diversion to keep the villagers occupied while he went about his side of the operation.

Rubel's foot touched the ledge and he pushed off to get the momentum to swing inside the opening. Free of the rope he jerked it twice to signal the next man down and then left him to help the others while he found the little hatch at the side of the ventilation shaft and unlocked it. Soon sixteen men were waiting on the wide ledge for his instructions. He silently pointed out the steel mesh guarding the outlet of the ventilation ducting and waited patiently while they cut through it.

All the men were from a specially trained commando force and Rubel had absolute faith in their ability. They had rehearsed exactly what they were to do and while the explosives experts prepared their charges Rubel pointed out the small door leading below.

One of the demolition men touched his arm to tell him that the charges were ready.

Rubel's earlier reconnoitre had not been sufficiently detailed to be able to say whether there were any safety grills internally in the trunking of the air conditioners so a small charge was fed down on a rope. Tensely the men watched as the rope disappeared into the darkness without stopping. There was no second grill.

Quickly and efficiently the dark figures crouched beside the wide opening lowering a bigger charge down the chute. When it reached bottom they tied off the rope and connected the two bare wire ends of the detonator to the hand generator and signalled. Rubel checked that the cannisters of tear-gas were ready to drop once the air conditioner had been destroyed, ordered gas masks to be put on and gave the signal to detonate the explosives.

There was a tremor through the rock under their feet and a blast of air. The demolition men dropped the cannisters of gas down the shaft. Rubel led the way down the iron ladder fixed to the side of the ducting praying that the Germans would be confused long enough to give him and his men time at least to reach the catwalk.

The sound of the explosion, magnified and condensed by the solid rock of the mountain, reached the Nazi leader in his reinforced concrete command post. He didn't hesitate. His thumb flicked up the guarding flap on the red emergency button at the side of his desk and his finger stabbed down. Instantly all doors leading to the corridors and outside locked into place. Quickly he raised the top of his desk to reveal the control panel that gave him a status report on the security of the factory.

All the check lights were out showing that none of the doors had been breached. He briefly considered a rock fall but pushed the thought aside. What he had heard had not sounded like falling rock. It had been an explosion. He looked quickly at the indicator for the factories and laboratories – nothing.

His massive forefinger flicked down the master switch on the tannoy system. 'Control here. Report status by numbers.'

As the workshops, warehouses and offices checked in as trouble-free he began to frown. Something was wrong. The rocket shop was just reporting in when he heard a gasp.

'What is it?' he asked.

'I don't know,' the voice rasped and began to cough.

'What's happening. Report. Do you hear me? What's happening!' He heard a long shuddering breath.

'Gas! I think there is gas leaking in through the ventilators. Open the doors. We will die . . .'

The Nazi leader ignored the plea to open the doors and disconnected. 'Gas!' he said aloud.

Quickly he rushed around the room shutting the ventilators. He didn't waste his time trying to guess who the attackers were.

Another explosion shook the floor. The alarm was sounding all over the underground installation but nothing could be done until he opened the doors. It was a calculated risk.

He put the second explosion down to the intruders blasting a way through to the factories. He could sit there, in the gradually decaying air, while the raiders blasted their way through, door by door, or he could open the doors and let his stormtroopers fight it out.

His mind was made up by the sound of distant thuds as Lopez Rega's artillery opened up on the main entrance. He swept his hand across the board opening the internal doors. He left the door to the outside closed. Then he sat placidly in his chair and listened to the sounds of the pitched battle relayed to him over the tannoy system as the black-clad stormtroopers fought the group of commandos dedicated to destroying the workshops and all the equipment.

He heard the explosions as the demolition workers blew up specific parts of the factory. The Nazi leader waited no longer. He went across to the drape-covered map-wall that he had shown Lopez Rega earlier, and slid aside a secret panel leading to a bolthole that he had had specially cut into the rock when the office was being made. It was this sort of forethought that had made him prepare his South American haven while the rest of the Nazi hierarchy were still indulging in misty-eyed prognosis of the Thousand Year Reich.

The tunnel went into a natural flue that led to an outlet on the lower slopes of the mountain on the opposite side from the village. Before he left he went to a locked box, opened it, and pressed one more button. Then, at a smart pace he walked through the tunnels and was in the car he kept hidden away for such an eventuality before he heard the rumble of the delayed explosion he had just detonated. Lopez Rega felt it too. He had halted the barrage of shots that were thudding uselessly into the mountain on the other side of the village. Whoever had designed the fortress had not intended it to be easily subdued by cannon.

Below him he could still hear sporadic fighting in the village as his marauders did their work. He scanned the base of the cliffs with his binoculars. Rubel had told him that he would signal before he blew up the inside of the cavern in case Lopez Rega's men had already got in. It would give them a chance to withdraw before the explosion. No signal had been given so Lopez Rega suspected that something had gone wrong. Whatever it was it would have to wait for morning. Lopez Rega didn't intend to start rushing around in the dark.

As the first rays of sunlight touched his face Lopez Rega's eyes opened. He looked quickly around. Nothing had changed. Except that the firing in the village had died away. Cautiously he eased himself forward so that he could see what was happening.

Nothing.

He examined the houses more closely through his binoculars. There was a body sprawled across the terrace where he had sipped beer with the *Bürgermeister*. Some of the pristine white walls of the houses had disfiguring punctures in the plaster but that was about all.

Lopez Rega examined the mountain top. He thought he could make out the lines of the camouflaged machine gun but he wasn't sure. A movement away to his left caught his eye and he saw a man, in the brown, combat suit of Rubel's men, making his way up towards the artillery post. The man fell down beside him.

'There's trouble inside the mountain, *señor*,' he spoke Spanish with a heavy American accent. 'There was an explosion about an hour after Rubel went in. I don't think it was anything to do with him. It looks like someone dynamited the workshops.'

The man stopped and waited for Lopez Rega to comment.

'What about going back down the air shaft?' Lopez Rega suggested.

The man shook his head. 'Whatever caused the explosion took most of the ladder away with the ducting. We can go down on ropes if you like?'

Lopez Rega spread his hands. 'You can do what you want, *amigo*. My part in the operation is over. Your people asked for help getting in and some artillery to keep the village closed down while you went in.' He stood up and dusted himself down. 'I've kept my side of the bargain. I can keep the police out of the way until this evening. All the wires were cut to Buenos Aires so I doubt if the Germans were able to alert anybody. If they had a radio there is nothing I can do about it.'

Carefully keeping below the rim of rock he walked over to the men on the gun. '*Bueno, muchachos. Adelante!*' he shouted.

As he turned to go the American shoved his pistol into Lopez Rega's chest. 'You're not going to walk out on us like this. Some of our men may be injured in there. We have to try to get them out. There are only four of us. Once you go the villagers will tear us apart.'

Lopez Rega disdainfully brushed aside the pistol. 'It's

330

your problem now, *che*. I'll leave my men in the village until twelve o'clock. That gives you six hours. I suggest you move quickly. Either clear out while the going is good or climb down the ventilation shaft and see what you can do. Remember! In the afternoon the police will be here and in six hours my men will be withdrawing. Me, I'm going back to Buenos Aires right now.'

He walked over to his second-in-command and then went off to get the jeep he had left hidden in some trees about a mile away.

The American looked after him with hatred in his eyes. He would like to have used his gun but didn't fancy his chances of survival at the hands of the tough crew Lopez Rega had left behind. He turned back to the mountain to try and find out what had happened inside.

Lopez Rega was well on his way to Buenos Aires when the Americans began their descent into the depth of the mountain on ropes tied to the steel ladder above the point where the trunking had been shattered by the explosion. The carnage they found below was unbelievable. They walked among the dead, the dying and the injured unable to help.

They found Rubel with his head crushed to a pulp lying across the body of a black-uniformed SS guard. The air inside was foul. The teargas had faded to nothing more than an irritant but the falling rock had started electrical fires and the burning rubber and plastic gave off noxious fumes that contaminated the air even further.

The rescuers spent some time trying to open the main doors but they had been jammed by the explosions and would need dynamite to shift. That would probably cause an even greater rock fall. Realistically they decided that there was nothing to be done. They spread out and searched where they could, administering the *coup de grâce* to the dying, and then left. At least their mission had been successful, whatever the cost. The devastation below was so complete that it would take years to clear up and then the Germans would have to find the workers to carry on where the dead had left off. To the statisticians of the White House it would look an outstanding success.

Only seventeen Americans killed.

THIRTY-SEVEN

The afternoon watch was nearly over. In the signals room of the Casa Rosada Corporal Vicente Caracól was looking forward to a night on the town. Traffic had been slack all day – unusually so – and the time had dragged by.

Idly he spun the radio dials and listened to snatches of conversation and morse but none interested him. As he flipped through a number of prearranged frequencies he frowned. He checked he was on the right waveband and then slowly monitored the frequencies again. Caracól could find nothing there. He sat back in the chair and thought about it. There was a sheaf of papers on a clipboard giving any changes in procedure and other up-to-date information. He leafed through it slowly. Nothing there to explain the blank on the Cordoba frequency.

He tried Rosario – only the heavy throb of the carrier wave. More alert now he checked through the main official frequencies. Almost all were silent and did not respond to his signal. Caracól dialled Lieutenant Carman in the next room.

'*Teniente* Carman? *Señor*, I think there is something wrong. I cannot raise Cordoba, Rosario and most of the other set frequencies.'

'*Bueno*, Corporal. You have double-checked everything? There is no mistake?' the lieutenant asked.

'No, *Señor*,' Caracól assured him.

'When did you last check?' Carman wanted to know.

'Fifteen minutes to the hour, *Teniente*. It was all right then but on the hour there was nothing,' Caracól told him.

'Very good, Corporal. Listen out on all frequencies. I will be there in a few moments.' Lieutenant Carman replaced the receiver and quickly phoned through to Lopez Rega.

'Señor Lopez Rega? *Teniente* Carman here. You asked me to report anything unusual. I don't know if there is anything in it but it seems that our Category A frequencies went off the air at six o'clock and we can't raise them now.'

Lopez Rega didn't need to know more. 'I'll be along right away.'

Lopez Rega and Carman hurried into the signals room. Corporal Caracól spun the dials to the Cordoba station and stopped, surprised, to hear a voice speaking. It was just his luck, he thought, now he had started a panic everything was all right.

'. . . heads of the Argentina Revolutionary Force under the leadership of General Eduardo Lonardi. We appeal to all citizens to help by staying off the streets while the Army . . .'

Lopez Rega cut in on the announcement. 'Try San Juán,' he ordered.

The corporal made the adjustments.

'. . . to save the country from the excesses of the present regime which has brought the nation to bankruptcy . . .'

'Try Rosario.'

As the corporal tuned in around the country the picture emerged. The revolutionaries had concentrated on taking over the main garrisons and towns outside Buenos Aires. It was a clever move. It meant that Perón couldn't mobilise his *descamisados* to discourage the insurgents.

Lopez Rega cut in on the announcement. 'Try San Juán,' he ordered. had to move fast. Back in his office he dialled the pre-arranged number and gave the message to his Buenos Aires contact that would bring the promised Paraguayan gunboat into the harbour before daybreak.

He reckoned that would be time enough. Whatever Lonardi did in the provinces he still had to take over the capital. And that was going to be difficult. Difficult enough to hold him up for at least a day. That was all the time Lopez Rega needed. He went down to the car park and took one of the battered but powerful Dodge sedans that would go

334

unnoticed and made his way across the suddenly deserted city to Olivos.

As he rounded the corner at the side of the house he braked violently to a halt in surprise. Around the swimming pool coloured lights were strung out over a number of long tables covered with white cloths and laid out for dinner. Half a dozen white-coated servants fussed around the tables making minute adjustments to cutlery or plumping up a serviette.

Behind the tables on the edge of the trees, an *asado* fire trailed ladders of fiery sparks up into the deepening dusk as cooks dressed in traditional *gaucho* costume prepared to roast meat and fish over the open fire. Lopez Rega stared in astonishment. Somehow he had expected to see sand-bags and gun emplacements being prepared around the house. He couldn't believe that the President had not been told of the crisis.

He got out of the car and nodded to the soldier on guard outside the back door and went through to the kitchen. From the state of turmoil it looked like it was going to be a big party. Lopez Rega gave up and went through into the house. Silence! He mounted the stairs and knocked on the door of Perón's room and waited.

No reply.

He listened. He could hear the sound of splashing water so assumed that Perón was taking a bath. Lopez Rega rapped again, this time louder. A voice called out something unintelligible. Lopez Rega hadn't time for niceties. He took it as an invitation to enter.

On the bed were a pair of *bombachas*, the baggy *gaucho* pants, a shirt, a wide silver-adorned belt and a black hat. Lying next to the outfit were a chequered cotton dress and a black woollen shawl.

He walked across to the bathroom and pushed the half-open door wide. Perón and Nelly Rivas were sitting at either end of the wide pink bath that Eva had installed. Neither was aware of his presence and continued to splash each other. Perón suddenly caught the girl and tried to pull

335

her to him but she squealed with laughter and fought him off. Nelly suddenly stopped as she saw Lopez Rega reflected in the mirrors surrounding the bath. Her face became sullen and she slumped down into the water. Lopez Rega frightened her. Perón followed her eyes. His face flushed red with anger.

'What the hell do you think you are doing here, Rega?'

The ex-sergeant bent down and picked up a terry-towelling robe from the chair and held it out to Perón. 'I have to speak with you urgently, *Excelencia.*' Lopez Rega spoke respectfully but there was no mistaking the authority in his voice.

Perón looked at him hard but made no comment. He winked at Nelly and gave her a reassuring smile before getting out of the bath and leading the unwelcome visitor into the bedroom. He swung round to face Lopez Rega, a mixture of anger and impatience in his face.

'*Bueno, Sargento,* what is so important?'

Lopez Rega carefully shut the bathroom door before replying. 'Have you heard the news? Lonardi has taken over in Cordoba and announced a provisional government,' he told Perón.

The President raised his hands at his side and let them drop in bewilderment. 'Of course I have heard the news. So? Half a dozen officers playing games in the Provinces is hardly likely to make me lose sleep.'

Nelly came into the room, a towel draped around her. Her black hair piled on top of her head and her red, pouting lips made her look very attractive. Perón put his arm around her and drew her close. Lopez Rega shook his head. He turned and walked from the room.

If Perón was not going to do anything to protect himself it was down to Lopez Rega to see that their mutual interests were safe. Already there were scattered groups on the streets carrying banners and marching, a little hesitantly, towards the Plaza de Mayo. Lopez Rega ignored them and went to one of the flats he owned in Las Heras, close by the headquarters of the Eva Perón Foundation, and dialled a number on the telephone. When he heard a voice at the other end he dispensed with preliminaries.

'Thirty minutes. Van and five men. Rendezvous 4,' he said brusquely and only waited to hear the instruction repeated before dropping the handset back onto the cradle.

In the bedroom he took from the wardrobe a Thompson sub-machine gun and deftly checked it. From his shoulder holster he took the Luger he now carried and checked the functioning of that as well. Satisfied with his weapons he turned his attention to his clothes. Quickly he took off his jacket and tie and pulled on a turtleneck sweater. Bending down he unlaced his shoes and changed them for a pair of rubber-soled combat boots.

He made sure his holster was in place and tested to see that the gun was not inhibited. He completed his outfit with a khaki army jacket from his wardrobe and picked up his sub-machine gun and slipped it into a canvas bag. Instead of taking the lift to the ground floor he climbed the stairs to the roof and walked along to the next apartment house.

From his Army jacket he took a key and opened the firedoor and entered. The entrance to the next apartment block opened out onto one of the side streets. Before stepping out he stayed in the shadows and watched for movement.

Nothing stirred.

A car was waiting at the end of the block and he got in. Instantly it pulled away from the kerb and circled the block. He carefully watched the rear. Satisfied that no one was following he told the driver to go ahead. He picked his way through the early evening traffic, taking the most circuitous route he could devise and then, as the rendezvous time came up, accelerated and arrived at the back of the CGT head-quarters just as a small van, with the name of a radio repair shop on the side, pulled in ahead. The driver looked at Lopez Rega for instructions and he signalled for him to sit tight while he got out and approached the van.

Two men sat in the front and there were another four in the back. Like the driver of the car behind they were policemen in the pay of Lopez Rega, but unlike him they were in civilian clothes. The ex-sergeant banged on the back of the van and the four men jumped out followed more slowly by the two in the front. Silently they followed Lopez Rega across to a small door in the back of the building and waited. The uniformed policemen went to the big, double doors at the front and banged loudly. When the nightwatchman came to see who was there the policemen kept him in conversation while Lopez Rega and the others quietly opened the back door and filed through.

Once inside Lopez Rega led them up the stairs to the old committee room which had been converted into a shrine. Standing on a raised bier in the centre of the room, amidst a display of flags, porcelain saints and photographs, was a metal coffin with a glass face plate.

In the flickering light of the eternal candles at each corner of the coffin Lopez Rega looked down on the peaceful face of Eva Perón. At a word the six men gripped the handles on the sides of the sarcophagus and picked it up. Strong as they were they had difficulty in carrying it. Once again Lopez Rega led the way. While the men struggled to the van he locked the door and sidled around so that he could signal the 'all clear' to the policeman at the front.

The other men had got the coffin aboard by the time Lopez Rega got there. He took a thick envelope out of the inside pocket of his jacket and gave it to one of the men. As he climbed in the van and started the engine he saw them disappear into the night. Careful not to attract attention Lopez Rega drove the van across town to a warehouse and went through the open doors.

THIRTY-EIGHT

Lopez Rega flagged a yellow and black cab and directed it to Olivos. The mob was thickening in the Plaza. At the moment it was the anti-Perónistas who dominated. The *descamisados* were hardly to be seen. Lopez Rega hoped they would stay that way and not do anything heroic that might make Perón decide to stay and fight it out.

He arrived to find the party in full swing. Nelly was decked out in jewels that sparkled and flashed in the light from the fire and the coloured bulbs. The jewellery had been Eva's but it pleased Perón to shower it on his young mistress. Perón was in his shirtsleeves and perspiring freely with the exertion of dancing and the large quantity of wine and meat he had consumed.

When he saw Lopez Rega he called him across and insisted that he had some food. Picking sparingly at the piece of meat brought by one of the *gauchos* he watched the scene around him. There were about twenty men, practically all unknown to him but he guessed they were young Army officers, and twenty-five to thirty girls. Really girls. He doubted if their average age was fifteen.

Perón picked Nelly up and pitched her into the water and then followed. His guests followed suit and within seconds the pool was full of squealing girls and drunken men trying to get their clothes off. Lopez Rega envied them their stupidity. When the axe fell they would never even realise that they could have done anything to ward it off. They would just moan about their 'bad luck' and nurse their headaches.

Perón climbed out of the pool, bare to the waist, carrying Nelly Rivas who somehow had contrived to lose everything but the diamond necklace around her neck and a gold bangle on her wrist. The President looked down at the naked body in his arms and without a word to anyone turned and headed for the house. Several other revellers had the same idea and soon there was only a handful left, mostly girls, around the pool.

Lopez Rega shrugged his shoulders and made himself a *maté*. Carrying the little kettle he made his way into the house and finally managed to find an armchair, not already occupied by a squirming couple, and settled down.

Later he dropped off to sleep and when he woke up the sun was shining and all the guests had disappeared. He found a telephone and got through to the Casa Rosada. It had been a quiet night. Several inflammatory speeches had been made by different generals in league with Lonardi. The Navy now seemed fully committed to the uprising although the Airforce was divided in its loyalty. Buenos Aires was still secure with the Army carrying out its functions of protecting the President and the government in the approved manner.

Lopez Rega glanced at his watch as he put the telephone down. 7.30 am. Even he didn't care to wake the President yet. He went into the kitchen and got one of the maids to make him some breakfast. At ten o'clock he went into the kitchen and brewed some coffee and made his way to the President's room once more. He wasn't looking for trouble so he had put an extra cup on the tray for Nelly. His knock went unanswered so he opened the door and went in.

Perón was lying on his back, his mouth open and his hair an untidy mess about his face. Nelly lay in the crook of his arm, a pretty child sleeping peacefully. Lopez Rega put the tray on the table and gently shook Perón awake. The President looked blearily around and swallowed several times to ease his wine-dried throat. When he finally recognised his visitor he gently extricated his arm from Nelly's recumbent figure and pushed himself up in bed and took the cup of coffee Lopez Rega offered.

Perón went to the bathroom and came back wearing a robe beckoning for Lopez Rega to follow him quietly from the room so as not to disturb the sleeping girl. In the passage he let Lopez Rega give him a cigarette and then led the way, coughing, to his library on the ground floor.

Perón sat behind the desk and calmed his abrasive vocal cords with a draught of water. 'Come on then, José. Get it off your chest,' he said in mock boredom.

Lopez Rega didn't smile. '*Excelencia*. I think it is time to get out of the country,' Lopez Rega started as gently as possible. 'Most of the garrisons are in the hands of the rebels. The Navy is even now standing off shore and half the Airforce has defected. And I can't guarantee the police will stay loyal for long.'

Perón laughed. He felt more relaxed than he had done for years. Even his acne had subsided since he had got over the traumas of Eva's head-on conflict with everyone who said anything about the administration. 'Come on, José. Without control of Buenos Aires they have got exactly nothing. And they won't get Buenos Aires!'

Lopez Rega shook his head in disagreement. 'This revolt is different. They have planned it in detail. Now they have secured the provinces there is somewhere for the dissidents to run. Every rebel in the country will be on their way to join Lonardi by now. Once they are ready they will call out the Army around the capital and that will be that.'

'Bullshit,' Perón exploded. 'The Army is loyal.'

'I'm sorry, *Excelencia*. I can't agree. There are officers sitting in the Campo de Mayo at this moment waiting for the call. We must get out of the country before it comes.' Lopez Rega looked quickly around as if to surprise secret onlookers. 'There is a ship in the harbour from Paraguay. They have agreed to take you to Azuncion whenever you are ready. I think we should go while there is still time.' Lopez Rega's voice was persuasive but there was a hard look in his eyes.

'*Bueno*. I will promise you something. If I can't sort it out in forty-eight hours, we go. Now hang on while I change and then we will go down town.' Perón flicked his cigarette through the window and left.

Lopez Rega went out to the car and waited. His annoyance was hidden behind his calm, wooden features.

General Perón was wearing his uniform when he joined Lopez Rega in the car but he had covered it with a light raincoat and wore a brown trilby drawn well down over his eyes. He wasn't taking chances that demonstrators would recognise him.

There were signs of arson on the way back to town, mainly directed at ministry establishments. Some of the statues that had proliferated along the roadsides during the last decade, of Perón and Evita, had been either broken or vandalised in some way. That disturbed Perón.

By the time he reached the Casa Rosada he was angry. Standing in his office he told his aide to make contact with the rebels. After a couple of hours, he managed to get in touch with General Molina who had established a base just outside the city.

'Molina, you know what happens to officers who mutiny – they get shot. I suggest you give up these wild games you are playing and come into the capital to talk. I'm willing to listen if you call off your revolt now – right now. If you are not prepared to do that no quarter will be given.' He glared across the room at Lopez Rega half reclining on the Empire chaise-longue.

'General Perón!' Molina's tinny voice in Perón's ear said, polite but firm. 'I think it is you who would do well to surrender. We have a warship less than two miles out from the shore with guns trained on the Casa Rosada. If I give instructions they will open fire.'

'You wouldn't dare!' Perón snarled. 'My *descamisados* would tear you to pieces if you shelled the city.'

Molina gave an unpleasant laugh. 'Your *descamisados*, my friend, have got no-one to fight at the moment and we do not intend to move on the city until you have agreed to resign. If we do not have your resignation in our hands by four o'clock this afternoon we will bomb Mar del Plata and after that La Plata. It's up to you, General.'

Perón hurled the telephone to the ground and walked up

and down the room, his hands clasped tightly in front of him. He turned to Lopez Rega. 'Get me any of the top Labour leaders you can find in a hurry. I want plans for Buenos Aires agreed so that if the Army do decide to move against us we are ready.'

Resignedly Lopez Rega got to his feet and walked to the door.

Perón stopped him. 'What's wrong? We have been in worse shape before and got out of it. Why so defeatist now?' he asked.

Lopez Rega turned and looked as if he was about to explain his position but thought better of it and snapped, '*Es nada*. I'll see what I can do, *señor*.' He turned and left.

Perón stared at the closed door, a worried look on his face. He dismissed Lopez Rega from his thoughts and buzzed for his aide. When the major appeared Perón relaxed and forced himself to speak in a calm friendly voice.

'*Bueno*, Major. Give me a quick run-down of the situation as you see it at the moment.' He glanced towards the shuttered window leading out onto the balcony above the Plaza. Chanting and an occasional burst of cheering could be heard. But Perón was aware that it wasn't for him.

'Start with what is going on outside.'

The major quickly pulled his thoughts together. He still hadn't made up his mind which side he was on. 'There is a small crowd outside. They seem to consist mainly of white-collar workers urged on by the owners of the factories. Earlier some of the CGT men tried to form a counter-demonstration but they weren't out in sufficient numbers at the time to have any effect.'

The absence of Perón's *descamisados* was what worried the major. If he was to stay with the President he wanted to see some sign of strength. 'The Army is loyal and on stand-by. In the capital, at least. As far as we can ascertain from the radio most of the main provincial towns are under rebel Army rule,' the major continued.

Perón raised an inquisitive eyebrow. 'What towns are loyal?' he asked.

343

The major looked uneasy. 'Other than Buenos Aires, La Plata, and Mar del Plata all the big centres have gone with the revolutionaries, your Excellency.'

Perón's face hardened. 'Very well. Get me Colonel Olivera and anyone else that you can contact in the next hour,' he ordered briskly.

The major didn't move. '*Perdón, mi Presidente*. But *Coronel* Olivera and most of the other staff officers have returned to barracks.'

'Who's here then?'

'I'll see,' the major assured him as he backed from the room. He knew he was the highest ranking officer in the building but he didn't feel obliged to feed the cornered President that piece of news himself. Anyway, now that he could see that so far Perón had not thought of a cogent plan to stay in power the major had to look after himself. From now on the highest rank in the seat of government, discounting Perón, would be the radio lieutenant. The major picked up his hat, loosened his pistol in its holster and cautiously followed Lopez Rega from the building.

Ten minutes later when Perón finally went to look for some assistance, after repeatedly trying to get through on the intercom, he found the building deserted except for the lieutenant, isolated in his security-fortified radio room, and the guards. And he was under no illusions how long the guards would remain at their posts after they realised that the officers had flown.

Perón went back to his office and quickly threw the few bits and pieces that remained in the office into a small valise. He was emptying out the wall-safe when there was a tap on the door. Before answering he took a firm hold on the pistol in the safe.

'*Adelante*,' he said over his shoulder and watched as the door slowly opened and the lieutenant apologetically poked his head through the gap.

'*Perdón, Excelencia*, but the major is not here and I have – important news,' he said.

Perón relaxed and continued filling his valise. 'What is it,' he asked shortly.

The lieutenant gave him a piece of paper. He preferred not to have to tell him the bad news.

MAR DEL PLATA OIL REFINERY SHELLED BY NAVAL GUNS. CASUALTIES NOT YET CONFIRMED, FEARED MANY DEAD.

It was signed by a colonel of the infantry at the moment on manoeuvres just outside Mar del Plata at Lagos de los Papas.

Perón cursed and threw the paper on the floor. 'Get back to the radio and let me know what develops,' he told the lieutenant although he didn't have much hope that the boy would stay when he realised that his superior officers had all deserted.

A burst of cheering penetrated the shutters and thick curtains. He looked at the windows speculatively. Perón tried to convince himself that he should go onto the balcony and win over the angry crowd below. He thought of Eva. She would have rushed out into the storm and bullied and bribed her way out of the crisis. He poured himself a strong whisky and felt his face. Like scarlet mushrooms the eczema, fertilised by fear, stretched the flesh of his cheeks and neck.

The balcony drew him like a moth to a flame. The ghost of Eva seemed to beckon him on. To tell him that he must face the angry mob calling for his blood. He pulled back the curtains. Before he could open the glass doors the telephone rang behind him. Perón shook himself out of his trance and snatched up the handset.

'*Hóla*,' he said grateful for the chance to talk to someone.

'I would like to talk to General Perón,' a prim voice whispered in his ear.

'Who is it?' Perón asked.

'I am calling on behalf of General Lonardi, Provisional President of the Republic of Argentina. He would like to speak to General Perón,' the voice informed him.

'*This* is the President of the Republic of Argentina speaking. Put *General* Lonardi on immediately.' There was a click and another voice spoke.

Perón cut in immediately. 'What is the meaning of this? Do you realise that falsely calling yourself the President is punished by death?'

'I am aware of my responsibilities, General,' a dry, slightly humorous voice informed him. 'But I wanted to speak to you about your responsibilities. As you probably know we have shelled the oil refinery at Mar del Plata. If you do not announce your resignation by 10.00 am tomorrow we will do the same with La Plata. After that Buenos Aires.'

Perón's strong hand closed on the telephone threatening to snap it. 'You murderous bastard!' he shouted.

'We want your resignation by 10.00 tomorrow morning or we fire on La Plata and Buenos Aires. Good day, General.'

Lonardi hung up.

Perón stood and stared at the dead telephone in his hand. A voice spoke from behind and he spun around, his heart thumping with sudden fear. It was Lopez Rega.

'Nobody is willing to come, *señor*. They insist that they will rally behind you but not tonight.'

'What the hell does that mean, not tonight? It's tonight we need them,' Perón shouted.

Lopez Rega turned his hands up expressively. 'They want to wait and see what happens first,' he said simply. The noise outside the window was getting louder and uglier all the time. 'We have to get away, NOW!' He picked up Perón's valise. 'If we don't get out of here soon they will come in and get you. Most of the Guard have already gone. The rest won't be far behind.'

Unceremoniously Lopez Rega took Perón's arm and hustled him to the door. Perón looked back at the window leading out onto the balcony and made a futile gesture but Lopez Rega kept him moving.

In the car park below the ex-chauffeur put his bags in the back of his nondescript van fitted out with armchairs and drove out of the guarded gates. Perón sat quietly in the back staring ahead.

Lopez Rega was relieved to see that there was still a guard on the gate leading into the Olivos residency. As he helped the suddenly old man from the back of the van he came to a decision. He would let Perón get a good night's sleep in the security of the well-guarded residency and then insist that they left first thing in the morning for the gunboat.

THIRTY-NINE

As Lopez Rega drove back along the river road towards Olivos the wind buffeted his car and sent fountains of spray drifting across the road. The guard was still on the gate but the ex-soldier sensed a current of unease among the men. There was nothing he could do about it. Anyway they had served their purpose.

He went into the kitchen and told one of the maids to prepare some coffee and then sat and reviewed his arrangements once more. Everything seemed taken care of. Now all he needed was the President and they would be on their way. He took the coffee from the maid and went up to Perón's bedroom. He knocked and getting no answer, went in. The bed had been slept in but was now empty. Lopez Rega tossed the tray onto the bed and sprinted to the bathroom door smashing it back against the wall.

Empty!

He didn't need to consider the next move. There was only one place that Perón would go. Lopez Rega vaulted down the stairs and ran for the van.

Without knocking Lopez Rega went to the President's office. Perón had the telephone to his ear and said an occasional defeated '*Hóla!*' into the mouthpiece hoping that a miracle would happen and someone would speak to him. He watched Lopez Rega approach and stand opposite him. Perón's smile was not reassuring. Out of the corner of his eye Lopez Rega saw the door through to the reception open. Without hesitation he dropped to his knee and the pistol from his shoulder holster seemed to leap into his hand. Just in time he stopped himself pulling the trigger.

Nelly Rivas, wearing one of Eva's sable coats, walked

through the door with a jug of coffee in one hand and a couple of cups in the other. She watched in amazement as Lopez Rega got to his feet and clicked on the safety catch on his Luger.

'What is she doing here?' he breathed out through clenched teeth.

Perón ignored the question and shook the telephone as if to see if it was working properly. Lopez Rega reached out and gently took the handset from him and returned it to the rest.

'It's no good, *mi General*,' he said softly. 'They have won.'

Perón looked at him and was about to comment when Nelly put the cups on the table and started to pour the coffee. He took a cup with a smile. She didn't offer to get Lopez Rega a cup. '*Señor*. We must get away while there is still time. There is a Paraguayan ship in the harbour and they have agreed to take us to safety.' Lopez Rega leaned across the desk so that his face was only inches from the general's. 'But we must go now! If we leave it any longer we will be caught.'

Perón gave him a crafty look. 'Just how much are they paying you to get me out before I raise my *descamisados*? Very clever. But they forget who they are dealing with. I know more about revolutions than any man on earth and I tell you they haven't got a chance.' He flopped back, a smug look on his face. 'So tell that to whoever is paying you, *Sargento*,' he said viciously.

Lopez Rega pushed himself upright, and looked towards Nelly Rivas. 'Get her out of here, General. We have to talk.' He spoke in a conversational tone but there was no mistaking the menace in his voice.

Perón looked annoyed. 'I give the orders here, *Sargento*,' he warned.

Lopez Rega walked towards the girl. She looked at his face and began to cry. 'Don't let him hurt me, *Pócho*. I'll go. Please, don't hurt me.' She turned and ran out of the door she had entered by.

Before Perón could speak Lopez Rega turned back to him and spoke quietly and respectfully. '*Señor*. I had hoped to convince you to go without having to resort to force,' he began. He hurried on as he saw a slow smile spread over the big man's face as he thought of Lopez Rega trying to manhandle him. 'You remember you sent me to Europe to check on the deposits there?'

Perón nodded.

'Duarte cheated you. The key he gave you had unlocked nothing of any importance. I managed to persuade him to tell me what he had done with the rest. Only I know where to get at it,' Lopez Rega said.

'You killed Duarte?'

'*Si*!'

'Why are you still hanging around then, *Sargento*? Shouldn't you be on a flight to Zurich by now?'

Lopez Rega spoke quickly. 'I want you to come with me. The money is yours. I am only looking after it in case you decide to do something foolish. Like fighting a lost battle,' he said.

Perón was amused. 'Such loyalty. Or is it that you know you are a marked man if you try to get away with all the loot by yourself?' He stood up. 'Never mind. We can talk about that later. But I don't intend to run. They know they can't unseat me in the capital – that's why they have played games out in the provinces. They wouldn't dare to shell the city. When I am back in power you lose, José.'

He sounded almost happy to be engaged in a minor piece of intrigue.

'And the *señora*'s body?' Lopez Rega asked quietly.

Perón looked at him, not sure that he had heard right. 'What about the *señora*'s body?' he asked.

'I have it,' Lopez Rega told him bluntly.

Perón still couldn't grasp what he was being told. 'You have it? Why?'

'Because I think we need it. With the *señora*'s body we can be sure that the spirit of the *descamisados* stays with us. If the Military take it and bury it or get rid of it in some way, the magic will be gone.'

'But where is it?'

'Safe.'

Perón got up from the desk and walked towards the french windows leading out onto the balcony. 'Well, it seems you are calling the tune, *Sargento*. What do we do now?'

Lopez Rega nodded Perón back into his seat. 'We wait. If Lonardi does what he promised there will be so much confusion here shortly that no-one will notice us when we slip away. The weather is so bad the Navy are not going to be able to lay down a barrage with any accuracy. You can go on the radio from Paraguay and say that you left so as not to cause the revolutionaries to fire on civilians. It will make you a martyr.'

Perón saw the sense of that so he relaxed and mentally started composing his speech.

The morning dragged by. Nelly came back and took her place on Perón's lap. Lopez Rega sat on one of the upright chairs, wide awake and primed to react.

Perón had just dozed off when the first salvo landed. It overshot the Casa Rosada and ploughed into the city. Instantly Lopez Rega was on his feet.

'Come on. Let's go.' He raced across to the door and opened it. Nobody was about. He signalled to the fleeing President, and Perón, holding Nelly's hand, followed him across the room.

Lopez Rega barred the way. 'She can't come.' Another shell crashed into the buildings flanking the Plaza. Lopez Rega punched her hard in the face and she skidded across the polished floor in an untidy heap. Perón hesitated for a moment. Then he hurried away with Lopez Rega to the back entrance guarded by the police sergeant and his men.

The rain was a curtain of water quickly flooding the courtyard to a depth of four inches. The wall on the opposite side was only dimly discernible. As Perón peered uncomfortably at the rain Lopez Rega tapped his arm and handed him the valise he was carrying. He motioned for Perón to follow.

The two men hurried across the wide Avenida Colon and then took a small, cobbled alley, skirted on either side by wired-off wasteland, and came out near the depressing array of green painted, corrugated iron sheds that were used by the customs service. The deep pools of water on the rough open ground appeared to boil in the savage downpour. The cold and the fast pace set by Lopez Rega was having a debilitating effect on the older man but there was nowhere to rest so they splashed on through the ankle-deep water. The landscape was alien and deserted although it was scarcely past midday.

At the rear of the customs shed was the dock gate. Lopez Rega spoke urgently to the two policemen on guard. One of them addressed Perón.

'Good luck, *mi Presidente*,' he said sincerely.

Perón rallied to the occasion. He looked anything but the charismatic leader of the Casa Rosada balcony. His black hair was plastered down on his face and his suit sagged with the weight of water it had absorbed. He pulled himself erect and conjured up one of his famous smiles.

'*Gracias, amigo*. When I return I will not forget your assistance.' He would have liked to say more but Lopez Rega tugged insistently at his arm and indicated that the guards couldn't turn a blind eye indefinitely.

Once inside the gate Lopez Rega led the way obliquely across the docks. He didn't want to chance keeping to the roads and running into anyone less interested in being accommodating than the police had proved to be. As they picked their way carefully across the railway lines and around the trucks in the goods yards Perón caught a glimpse of a sudden movement on the periphery of his vision. Lopez Rega pushed Perón's valise into his hands and took out his Luger. He waved the gun to indicate he should take the lead and at an increased speed they trotted towards the jetty where the safety of the Paraguayan gunboat waited. They were running between two lines of cattle trucks when a

352

figure loomed in front of Perón.

Terrified, he slid to a halt. In a lightning flash he could see the dark features and black hair of the man blocking his path. He wore a shapeless, sodden suit and an open-neck shirt. He made no menacing move but in the split second of lightning as Perón faced him, Lopez Rega acted. Like a striking cobra his hand came over Perón's shoulder, and at point-blank range fired into the man's eye.

His head disintegrated in a welter of blood as his body jerked backwards and fell between two carriages. Perón stood stupefied, stunned by the suddenness of death in front of him.

Lopez Rega pushed him in the back and hurled him forward. They were nearing the jetty now. Through the trucks they could see the lights of the waiting ship. And Lopez Rega had seen something else.

Closing in on them were a number of silent rain-drabbed figures whose intention seemed to be to cut them off. Perón had seen them too and redoubled his efforts to get to the ship. The figures were close behind them as they burst from the shelter of the sidings and dashed across the open dockside. The sudden movement attracted the attention of the pair of marine guards at the bottom of the gangway and their weapons came up into the firing position.

Perón started to slow as he saw the guns barring his way but was forced onwards by Lopez Rega. 'Don't shoot, President Perón. *Presidente* Perón,' Lopez Rega shouted to the guards and the President saw their guns swing away to cover the pursuers who he could hear splashing through the puddles close behind.

An officer appeared at the top of the gangway and as he bounded down, pistol drawn, shouted an order at the marines. They ran forward to cover the fugitives and then backed up as they passed.

Perón was exhausted. It was a long time since he had been the leading Army athlete. As he reached the end of the gangway he staggered and would have fallen if the officer of the watch hadn't put a supporting arm around him. As he sagged against the safety rail, the valise, on which he had retained a tight grip throughout their mad flight across the docks, hit the metal barrier and jerked out of his hand. He watched it fall between the dock and the ship and splash into the water, settle and then sink.

Wearily he pushed himself erect and looked back the way they had come. Beyond the trucks lining the side of the jetty he could see nothing for the pounding, drifting downpour. Standing cowering against the side of the boxcars for protection Perón could see a number of grey figures. He would have liked to know who they were but he didn't make the effort to find out.

Perón allowed the officer of the watch to help him up the gangplank but as he reached the top he saw that his arrival had attracted the attention of the crew and a reception committee was forming at the top. He shrugged off his helper and quickly brushed his wet hair into place as best he could with his hands. He straightened his tie and stoked up his smile and stepped onto the deck like a monarch about to confer a knighthood on a victorious admiral.

He clasped the captain's hand warmly and allowed him to introduce his ship's officers before being escorted below to the warmth of the wardroom.

Lopez Rega stood on deck in the shelter of one of the lifeboats and watched him go. As the crew deftly discarded the gangway and let go the hawsers attached to the dock bollards he watched the men who had pursued them through the docks. They were still huddled against the box-cars.

The engine throbbed and gradually the gap between the ship and the dock widened as the bow swung out. The screws thrashed and slid the hull through the fomenting water. Grey figures detached themselves from the blending background and came to stand by the abandoned gangplank, silent stelae with blank, indistinguishable faces. They reminded Lopez Rega of the stone effigies of Easter Island, effigies with undoubted magical properties. As the rain obscured them from view he counted them: seven! A good number.

354

As the ship picked up speed and the land disappeared into the consuming gloom, Lopez Rega thrust his gun back into the shoulder holster and followed the fallen President below.

JUAN DOMINGO PERÓN

1960 Perón settles in Spain with the blessing of General Franco.

1960–72 Perón controls Peronista party from Madrid. One third of the Argentine nation are Peronistas.

1964 Perón tries to return to Argentina, is kidnapped in Brazil and sent back to Spain.

1966 Third wife 'Isabel' Maria Estella Martinez de Perón announces his return to Argentina.
President Lanusse allows Perón candidacy.

1973 Elections. Perón forced to hand over presidency to Hector Campora for residence problems.
September, re-run of elections, Campora forced to resign. Perón wins with 61% majority, with his wife Isabel Martinez de Perón as Vice-President.

1974 1 July, Perón dies of a heart attack in Buenos Aires and is succeeded by his widow, 'Isabel' Maria Estella Martinez de Perón.